"I don't know why she's doing this, but Darcy would never hurt those kids."

"She already has," Peter snapped. "She kidnapped them. Don't you remember how that felt?"

He sighed, not wanting to tell Alanna about his own past, but wondering if that was the best way to reach her.

"I do remember. I still have nightmares about it sometimes. I know you don't understand how I can—" she took an audible breath "—love them."

"I do understand that." Or at least, he understood that she thought what she felt was love, instead of a complicated mix of fear and dependency multiplied over fourteen years. "Stockholm syndrome is real. It's—"

Her snort of disbelief cut him off. She looked offended. "I got a psychology degree after I left Alaska. I understand why you think that's what's happening here, but don't forget—I'm the one who turned them in. They both went to jail because I left that note. My... Julian died because of me."

TRACKING
A FUGITIVE

ELIZABETH HEITER
& NICOLE HELM

Previously published as *Alaska Mountain Rescue*
and *Hunting a Killer*

Special thanks and acknowledgment are given to Nicole Helm for her contribution to the Tactical Crime Division: Traverse City miniseries.

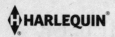

HARLEQUIN®

ISBN-13: 978-1-335-47377-6

Tracking a Fugitive

Copyright © 2022 by Harlequin Enterprises ULC

Alaska Mountain Rescue
First published in 2020. This edition published in 2022.
Copyright © 2020 by Elizabeth Heiter

Hunting a Killer
First published in 2021. This edition published in 2022.
Copyright © 2021 by Harlequin Enterprises ULC

PLEASE RECYCLE
THIS PRODUCT IS RECYCLABLE

Recycling programs for this product may not exist in your area.

For questions and comments about the quality of this book, please contact us at CustomerService@Harlequin.com.

Harlequin Enterprises ULC
22 Adelaide St. West, 41st Floor
Toronto, Ontario M5H 4E3, Canada
www.Harlequin.com

Printed in U.S.A.

CONTENTS

Elizabeth Heiter likes her suspense to feature strong heroines, chilling villains, psychological twists and a little romance. Her research has taken her into the minds of serial killers, through murder investigations and onto the FBI Academy's shooting range. Elizabeth graduated from the University of Michigan with a degree in English literature. She's a member of International Thriller Writers and Romance Writers of America. Visit Elizabeth at elizabethheiter.com.

Books by Elizabeth Heiter

Harlequin Intrigue

A K-9 Alaska Novel

K-9 Defense
Alaska Mountain Rescue
K-9 Cold Case
K-9 Hideout

The Lawmen: Bullets and Brawn

Bodyguard with a Badge
Police Protector
Secret Agent Surrender

The Lawmen

Disarming Detective
Seduced by the Sniper
SWAT Secret Admirer

Visit the Author Profile page
at Harlequin.com for more titles.

ALASKA MOUNTAIN RESCUE

Elizabeth Heiter

This book is for my new brother and sister,
Farris and Lamia,
who have made the word *in-law* sound amazing.

Acknowledgments

Writing a book is often just me, my parrot and my computer. But the process of bringing a book to life takes many! My deepest thanks to my editor, Denise Zaza; my agent, Kevan Lyon; and everyone behind the scenes at Harlequin who helped get *Alaska Mountain Rescue* to readers. A special thanks to my family and friends, who are always my biggest cheerleaders: Andrew Gulli, Chris Heiter, Kathryn Merhar, Alan Merhar, Caroline Heiter, Kristen Kobet and Robbie Terman. And a special thanks to my writer pals, who met me virtually or in person to get all the words: Heather Novak, Dana Nussio, Tyler Anne Snell and Janie Crouch.

Chapter 1

The whispers started the moment she stepped into town.

"It's *her*. The kidnapped girl. The one from five years ago."

"The one who almost got her real sister killed?"

Alanna tried to ignore the sidelong glances from the two women peering at her from the open door of the grocery store. In a place like Desparre, Alaska, the stares and chatter were likely to bring more people.

Alanna hunched her shoulders, trying to disappear into her heavy coat as she picked up her pace. Still, she felt their accusatory gazes bore into her. The pace of her breathing picked up, sweat breaking out all over her body. This was the side effect of sending the "parents" who'd raised her for fourteen years to jail and then returning to another state, to a family she'd tried so hard to remember but didn't quite fit into anymore. The side effect of spending too long dodging reporters desperate to be the one to break her silence and get the inside story of her abduction.

The voices faded as the women disappeared back into the grocery store, one of a handful of buildings that lined Desparre's small downtown area. It looked so tiny compared to the suburb on the outskirts of Chicago where she'd returned after living in the remote wilderness of Alaska with the family who'd kidnapped her.

Even after being gone for five long years, in many ways, Alaska still felt like home.

Alanna took a deep breath of the crisp, cool air and closed her eyes, letting the familiar sounds and smells and sights calm her. At her side, her St. Bernard, Chance, recognized her method for coping with anxiety and scooted up against her, then promptly sat.

A minute later, the sound of Chance's low, sustained growl made her eyes pop back open.

The St. Bernard was definitely a gentle giant, more likely to thump his tail and wait for a belly rub than go after anyone. But his size and his warning growl never failed to make people who were a little too aggressive back up fast.

In the past, Chance had used that growl on a handful of particularly determined reporters who'd stuck with her for years, following her around and ambushing her at the most unexpected times, seeking a candid photo or a sound bite. Because no matter how much time passed, she was still one of *those* women. A name that had made national headlines. A story she could never outgrow. Today, Chance was using his growl on the police officer who'd somehow managed to get close while her eyes were shut.

His startling blue eyes darted to her dog, then back to her. "Miss, do you need hel—"

The words trailed off as those blue eyes widened slightly. In a face made up of sharp angles and pale skin, his eyes were especially compelling. His tone was less friendly, more suspicious as he said, "Alanna Altier?"

"Morgan," she corrected. The name of her birth family, instead of the family who'd raised her for most of her childhood. After five years, the name Morgan was finally starting to feel less foreign on her lips.

"Morgan," he repeated. His gaze swept the space behind her, as if the woman who'd raised her—who'd helped kidnap her and four other children over the span of eighteen years and then escaped from police custody five days ago—would suddenly appear.

Anxiety started to swell again and Chance scooted even closer, his warm fur pressing against her leg, his big head nuzzling her.

Absently petting him, Alanna kept her eyes on the officer. She didn't recognize him. Not that she would—the Altiers had kept her and her "siblings" far from prying eyes, especially law enforcement eyes. She'd been to town before, but more often she'd stayed home, spending most of her days inside the house she'd helped build. Or in the dozen acres surrounding it that the Altiers owned, a buffer from them and the rest of the world. At times, it had felt like an oasis. At others, it had seemed more like a cage.

The officer's narrowed eyes locked on hers again, unsettling in their singular focus. "I thought you'd moved back to Chicago, with your real family."

It was somewhere between a statement and a question and Alanna tried not to fixate on the word *real*.

She loved the Morgans, the parents who'd enveloped her in hugs the moment she'd stepped back through their door, who'd kept all her belongings from when she had disappeared from their lives at five years old. The big brother, who'd stared at her with huge, teary eyes before breaking into a shaky smile and whispering, "I can't believe it. You're finally home." The older sister, who'd traveled across the country on the slimmest of leads, who'd almost died trying to save her.

"I did," Alanna finally answered. "But—"

"But Darcy Altier is back to her old tricks. And you think…what? She's coming back here?"

Darcy Altier. The woman she'd called "Mom" for fourteen years. Alanna had always known she'd been kidnapped, remembered with startling clarity the moment when Julian Altier had yanked her out of her yard in Illinois and into his car. But Darcy and Julian had never harmed her. They'd treated her like their own child, held her when she cried, smiled with her in happy times. They'd loved her. Despite everything else, she knew that.

Over those fourteen years, she'd grown to love them, too. She'd also grown to love the other children the Altiers had kidnapped, her "siblings." She missed all of them with an ache that was hard to explain to anyone, least of all the family who'd waited and searched for her all those years.

"Well?" the officer pressed, shifting so his right side was angled toward her. The side where a gun was holstered at his hip.

Her anxiety ratcheted up again and Chance stood up, stepping slightly forward. Protecting her, the way he'd done since the moment she'd brought him home. He'd been a tiny, emaciated puppy then, who had somehow managed to survive in cruel conditions until he was taken away and eventually ended up in her care. Now, though small for a St. Bernard, he outweighed her by twenty pounds.

Alanna put her hand on his back, pressed down slightly. Telling him to stay put.

"I don't know," Alanna answered, her gaze darting to the police station behind him. She *was* here for Darcy, because from the instant she'd seen the news report about her "mother's" escape, she'd known it deep down. Nowhere had felt like home to any of them the way Alaska had. But she wasn't about to say that to an officer who'd stared at her with barely veiled suspicion since the moment he'd realized who she was.

Seeming to recognize her discomfort, the officer took a step backward. But he still held the odd angle and she couldn't stop staring at that weapon.

"I think we got off on the wrong foot," he said, the words sounding strangled. "I'm Peter Robak."

Robak. The name floated around in her mind, vaguely familiar, and Alanna tried to place it. Before she could, he was speaking again.

"Why are you back in Desparre, Alanna?"

"I…" She was on a fool's quest. One that would have horrified her family back in Chicago if she'd told them about it in person, instead of in the note she had left. One that had definitely frustrated her boss, when she'd called to let him know she was taking time off in the middle of the work week and wasn't sure when she'd be back.

But who else knew Darcy Altier like she did? It was one thing that Darcy had escaped police custody. Alanna knew the woman belonged in jail, but that didn't mean she liked the idea of the person who'd helped raise her being behind bars. If it had simply been an escape, Alanna would have stayed in Chicago. But when a child had gone missing...

Straightening her shoulders, Alanna told him, "I was actually on my way to the police station."

Peter eyed her with distrust for another minute, then stepped slightly aside. He swept his hand forward, gesturing for her to lead the way.

She felt him close behind her for every step of the short walk into the police station. Opening the door, she led Chance inside with her, not caring how the officers would feel about that. Technically, he was a service dog.

Inside the station, a wall of warm air hit her, reminding Alanna of just how cold it was outside. In her years living here, she'd gotten used to it and when she'd made the trip back, she'd packed appropriately. Yanking the hat off her head and unwinding her scarf, she looked around.

It was a tiny station, with a counter up front and an officer who glanced up, then returned to his paperwork when he saw Peter.

Peter said, "Alanna Alt... Morgan is here. Is the Chief around?" And suddenly the officer looked a lot more interested.

"Hang on a sec," he replied, giving her one last look before he disappeared behind a door marked Police Only.

Alanna planted her feet in a wider stance, tipping her chin up. A trick she'd taught herself to help her feel more confident, more in control. Chance's familiar form pressing against her leg didn't hurt, either.

From a back room, the police chief appeared, leaving the door to the bullpen open behind her. She was young for her position, but strode through the door with a genuine confidence Alanna envied. With the chief's dark hair pulled back into a bun and her expression somehow serious and friendly at the same time, Alanna could see her both putting victims at ease and scaring criminals.

The chief nodded once at Peter, then held out a hand. "How can I help you, Alanna?"

The officer who'd been sitting behind the counter settled back in his seat, this time ignoring his paperwork, unabashedly interested. Another officer stared at them through the open doorway, curiosity on his face. Alanna tried to shut them all out and just focus on the chief. Focus on the reason she'd come all this way, back to a place she thought she'd never see again.

"I…" Clearing her throat, Alanna said, "I'm sure you are already aware that Darcy Altier escaped from custody when she was allowed to go to my fa… Julian Altier's funeral. And that a child went missing a few miles from where she escaped and she's a suspect in the case."

It was a bold, dangerous move, something Alanna had never felt Darcy was capable of. At least, not until the moment Darcy had picked up a shotgun and fired at Alanna's sister, Kensie, who'd flown to Alaska to try to save her.

Shutting that memory out, Alanna continued, "I think she might come back to Desparre. I want to help you find Darcy." She wanted to help them bring her in safely.

The chief smiled, the expression half pitying and half amused, and Alanna felt her cheeks flush deep red.

The woman reached out and put a hand on Alanna's

upper arm. She squeezed gently, as if Alanna was the sheltered, scared nineteen-year-old from five years ago. Back then, officers from a neighboring town had taken her away from the only family she'd known for four-teen years and brought her to the hospital, where her biological sister waited.

Now Alanna was twenty-four, in the process of get-ting her master's degree and catching up on all the things she hadn't really known she'd missed while she was hidden away in Alaska. But she suddenly felt nine-teen again when the chief said, "We appreciate that, but I think we've got it handled."

The chief continued with words of sympathy about the man who'd kidnapped her, who'd been a father to her for so many years. The man who'd been buried five days ago, whose service Alanna had longed to attend, but hadn't, knowing how it would hurt the family who'd missed her since she was five.

Alanna barely heard the words. Instead, she heard the snicker from the officer behind the counter.

Humiliated, Alanna spun back in the direction she'd entered.

The officer who'd brought her into the station—Peter Robak, who she remembered suddenly as someone she'd seen on TV a few years ago, a war reporter who'd al-most died covering a hostage release—stood in her way.

He stepped slightly aside as she pushed past him, back into the frigid Alaskan air with Chance at her side, like always. She hurried across the unpaved street to-ward the truck she'd rented when her plane set down at the closest airport, which was still hours away. Then she stopped, spun back around, and looked up and down the small street. Despite the fact that it was still only midday, it was empty now.

Her St. Bernard stared up at her with his soft brown eyes. Then his head pivoted at the sound of a hawk's call overhead. Chance wasn't used to the vast emptiness of Desparre compared to the suburb outside busy Chicago where they lived.

Right now, there was only a light sprinkling of snow on the Desparre streets. But that could change at any time. Winter came here early, hard and fast. Sometimes, it got hit with enough snow to make leaving Desparre impossible until spring came.

When Chance's gaze returned to hers, there was a question there, as if he was asking, *What are we doing here?*

Being in the police station had made coming back here feel like a big mistake. But somewhere nearby, Darcy and a small child were hiding. Alanna was sure of it. And that child—like some of the "siblings" she'd grown up with—was young enough not to remember his family if they didn't find him in time.

For fourteen years, Alanna had been afraid to speak up, afraid to try to get help. At first, that fear had been because she hadn't known how her abductors would respond. Would they hurt her? Would they kill her? Later, it had been because, despite everything, she loved the Altiers and the four kids she'd called brothers and sisters. She'd become afraid of what would happen to all of them if she tried to sneak away and told anyone the truth.

For the past five years, she'd felt guilty about all of it. Seeing the pain she'd caused her biological parents and siblings Kensie and Flynn, wondering if some of the other kids wouldn't have been kidnapped if she'd spoken up sooner.

She couldn't change the past. But she could change the future.

This time, she wasn't staying silent. She wasn't going home and she wasn't staying out of this investigation, whether the police wanted her help or not.

"We're going to do this," she told Chance. "We're going to find them."

"She's got a lot of nerve, showing up here," Peter muttered to no one in particular.

As usual, his partner, Tate Emory, heard him. "I don't know. I feel bad for her. Imagine what she's been through. It can't have been easy to write that note and turn in the only family she'd known since she was five years old."

Peter shifted and scowled at his partner, who'd strode over to stand beside him, moving silently. Or maybe Peter just hadn't heard him, since Tate had come up on Peter's left side. The side where his hearing was mostly gone.

Being new to the force, new to policing in general, hadn't been a smooth transition for Peter. Most of the officers here still stared at him like the rookie he was. Worse, he knew plenty of them hadn't wanted him accepted onto the force in the first place because of his hearing disability. Some of them were still trying to push him out.

He'd never felt that from Tate. His partner had only been on the force for five years, just long enough to have been present for Alanna's dramatic rescue.

It had all started with a simple note, left between

some money at a general store on the outskirts of Desparre. The note had been as straightforward as it was confusing, since at the time there'd been no indication Alanna was even alive, let alone that her kidnappers had taken other children. *My name is Alanna Morgan, from Chicago. I'm still alive. I'm not the only one.*

The FBI had done a quick investigation and called the note a hoax, yet another dead end in a more than decade-old cold case. But Alanna's sister had believed it, had traveled over three thousand five hundred miles across the country in search of a sister she'd only known for five short years. The rescue had been sensational, making national news and putting the sleepy town of Desparre in a spotlight it desperately wanted to avoid. Now that spotlight might be returning.

Back then, Peter had been overseas, doing something he thought he'd stick with until it was time to retire. The scandal of the kidnapping had caught his attention only because he grew up in Luna, the little town next to Desparre where Alanna had finally been reunited with the sister who'd come to Alaska to find her.

Peter stared at the closed door Alanna had disappeared through, trying not to picture the embarrassment in her eyes. Yeah, he felt sorry for what she'd gone through, but five years had passed. Enough time to create a new life for herself with her real family, people who must have gone through hell thinking she was lost to them forever. She should have been home with them now, not out looking for a kidnapper. Because no matter what she said, he didn't quite believe she was here to put Darcy Altier back behind bars.

Alanna Morgan might have started out as a victim, but now she could choose her path in life. And every nuance in her voice, the flickers of emotion he'd seen in her eyes, told him she was choosing all wrong. She was here for Darcy Altier, all right, but not to get her arrested. To help her hide.

"Why do you think she believes Darcy returned to Desparre?" Tate asked.

Peter shrugged, his gaze still fixed on that closed door. It was a good question. Darcy Altier had been granted furlough to bury her husband, who'd been killed in jail. She'd managed to slip free of her guards and run, but that had been in Oregon, back near the prison. A smart woman would head as far from the site of her original crimes as possible. So why did Alanna think that Darcy was here? Why was *Alanna* here?

"They've been in contact." Peter spoke his thoughts out loud. It was the only logical explanation.

"Seriously?" Tate scoffed. "Alanna's the one who turned her in. You really think Darcy would reach out to her after that?"

Peter turned to look at his partner. Tate was a couple of inches taller than Peter's five-foot-ten-inch frame, his skin and hair a couple of shades darker. From the moment they'd met, Peter had felt a strange kinship with Tate, a sense that both of them had known hardship they didn't speak of, that both of them had a restless desire to move past it.

"This woman raised her since she was five years old," Peter insisted. "Alanna spent most of her childhood with her. I bet she barely remembered her real family. How much do *you* remember from before you were five?"

Tate shrugged. "Enough. Obviously Alanna remembered them or she wouldn't have left a note for them to find her."

"Sure, but then she continued to hide with the people who kidnapped her."

"That's a little harsh. She was nineteen. How much freedom do you think they gave her? You, of all people, should understand—"

Peter let out a humorless laugh. "Understand what? The lengths people will go to in order to protect someone who hurt them?"

That was something he definitely understood. He'd gotten an up-close look at the unnatural attachment a hostage could develop for their captor. That experience had destroyed his career as a war reporter—had destroyed much of the hearing in his left ear, too. There was no chance of recovering his hearing, no surgery or hearing aid that could improve it.

Peter had no doubt that Alanna had a similar unhealthy attachment, that she was suffering from serious delusions about the woman who'd stolen her away from her family. It made her motives questionable. Worse, it made her dangerous.

Tate was shaking his head, but Peter kept going. "You're right. I do understand. Ultimately, it doesn't matter if Alanna has spoken to Darcy or she just knows her well enough to predict her movements. If Darcy is crazy enough to actually come back here, Alanna is the key."

Speaking the words aloud made anticipation swell in his chest and his gaze dart back to the closed door. Alanna *was* the key—and not just to locating a fugitive and solving a kidnapping, but to Desparre's reputation as a quiet, safe place to be left alone. And to Peter's future on the Desparre police force.

"Uh-oh," Tate said. "I know *that* look."

"Alanna is going to lead us to Darcy Altier and the missing kid." He headed for the door, gesturing for his partner to follow. "We're not letting Alanna out of our sight until she does."

Chapter 2

Alanna stared through dense woods at the house where she'd grown up. She'd helped build it on this mountain-top, dragging wood alongside her "siblings" and helping her "parents" lift the framework into place. All those months of hard labor, of watching the house slowly take shape. When it was finally finished, she'd been proud of her home.

Now it looked derelict and empty, snow covering the driveway that no one had bothered to shovel. Likely no one wanted to buy a house built by a pair of kidnappers, once home to five stolen kids.

Once upon a time, she'd stared at it with happiness and love. Now, there was bitterness, too, with the memory of her "mother" and "older brother" firing weapons at Kensie as she risked her life to bring Alanna home.

Alanna swallowed hard as she stepped out of the

truck she'd parked at the end of the gravel driveway. Chance bounded out after her, quick despite his size, loving the heavy snowfall in Alaska. He stuck close to her, a faithful companion who needed no leash.

She'd come here straight from the police station, not even bothering to check in to her hotel yet. Now, she wondered if she should have taken a break, given herself a chance to emotionally acclimate to being back here.

Her attention snagged on broken bits of scattered wood. The sign with her "family's" name and a No Trespassing warning had been smashed to pieces.

She bent down and picked up the largest piece, a splintered slab of wood that read Altier. She ran her gloved fingertips over the hand-carved lettering, remembering when Darcy had made it. The urge to take it with her was strong, but what if her family in Chicago saw it? They'd be hurt and full of questions she didn't know how to answer any better now than she had five years ago, despite the degree in psychology she'd earned since coming home. So, instead, she set it carefully back on the snow, tucked her hands in her pockets and strode toward the house. Chance walked beside her, comfortable in the frigid weather that made Chicago seem mild.

It would be foolish for Darcy to come here. But she and Julian had spent so many years running from state to state, never staying long in one place, afraid to draw any attention. In this remote patch of Alaskan wilderness, they'd finally felt like they weren't being chased. They'd been willing to put down roots, trusted that the children they'd raised wouldn't turn them in for kidnapping them from families they either barely remembered or, in the case of Alanna's youngest "siblings," didn't remember at all.

Walking around the edge of the house, her feet sank into deeper snow that dampened her pants just below the knees, where her boots ended. She peered through each of the windows on the ground floor. Nothing. No sign that anyone was inside, no sign that anyone had been here in a long time.

The furniture they'd picked out or built had been moved around—chairs knocked over, drawers hanging open with the contents spilled. All the things she and her "family" had left behind, had never been able to come back to claim. Alanna rubbed the bare finger where she used to wear a worn ruby ring, an Altier family heirloom that was the only thing she'd taken with her back to Chicago. She'd stopped wearing it when she'd noticed her parents and siblings constantly eyeing it, though they'd never actually come out and asked what it meant to her.

Focusing on the house again, Alanna leaned closer, peering through the windows into the living room, looking for any sign that Darcy had been here recently. The dirt on the wooden floors had faded to a light gray with no new tracks in the dust. It was clearly old, from when a slew of police officers had traipsed through, looking for her "family" five years ago. Back then, they'd already fled, but not far enough, not fast enough. The police had caught up to them.

Alanna squeezed her eyes closed against the memory of a circle of officers training weapons on her "parents" and screaming at them to get down. Of watching Julian and Darcy be flattened to the ground in deep snow, officers' knees pressing hard into their backs as they were cuffed. Of her youngest "siblings" crying and clinging to her. Of her older "brother" scowling, the tension in his body telling her he might do something stupid.

Chance nudged his big head against her thigh, hard enough to almost make her stumble. Her eyes opened, a laugh breaking free despite the pain in her heart. "I know, boy. You don't understand what we're doing here." She sighed, stroking her gloved hand over his soft head. "I used to live here." Her attention drifted to the dense woods behind the house, the steep slope of a mountain that dropped off suddenly. Protection from fears she hadn't totally understood as a child. "I used to be happy here."

The rumble of an engine nearby made Chance's head swivel. Alanna peered around the edge of the house, toward the street. This part of Desparre wasn't on many maps. Houses were set apart by miles, far from the road and hard to find if you didn't know where you were going. They were up higher in the mountains, in an area more prone to avalanches and deeper snow. Even locals didn't often come this way without a reason.

Her heart rate picked up as she squinted at the street for any sign of life beyond the thick trees. Could it be Darcy? If it was, how would she react to Alanna's presence?

Five years ago, Alanna's older "brother" Johnny had started talking about wanting to get married. It had put an ache in Alanna's heart with the realization that she'd never have any memories with the family she'd tried for fourteen years to remember. Not unless she acted.

So, she had. When Julian had taken her into some stores on the outskirts of town, she'd slipped a note into the stack of bills they'd used to pay. She'd been so afraid

Julian would notice. She hadn't been afraid he'd hurt her—she'd stopped fearing that long ago. But she *had* been scared of how he'd react if he found it.

Yes, he'd kidnapped her. There was no way to spin that; it was just wrong. But he'd loved her. He and Darcy had raised her; they'd homeschooled her in every subject so well that when she'd returned and taken her GED, it had been ridiculously easy. She'd sailed through college, too. But it hadn't just been academics. They'd taught her to be self-reliant in the dangerous wilderness, taught her skills that Kensie and Flynn still shook their heads at with awe. They'd raised her with love and, as the years went by, she couldn't stop herself from loving them, too.

Back then, she had been so focused on seeing her birth family again. She hadn't let herself consider the possible consequences for the people who'd raised her, or for the kids she'd called brothers and sisters, who she still missed desperately. She knew if she'd paused to think about all of that, she never would have done it.

The sound of the vehicle reached her ears again, this time the slow grind of tires over snow that hadn't been packed down yet. Was it Darcy, noticing the unfamiliar truck in the driveway, afraid to approach?

Alanna stepped out from behind the house, hurrying toward the street with Chance bounding after her. He loved the snow, thought it was a game, but she was too anxious to pay much attention. Would Darcy stop if she saw Alanna now? Or would she speed away?

When Alanna reached the street, a dark SUV backed quickly out of view. It was too quickly to decipher who was in the vehicle, but there were two people in the front seat. One thing Alanna knew for sure: it wasn't a child in the passenger seat. It looked like there were two men in the car.

Pinpricks of awareness swept across her arms. The Altiers had built this home in as secluded a spot as they could find. But that seclusion worked both ways. Right now, it meant no one would hear her cry for help.

Back in Chicago, the news stories had called her a hero, had highlighted how it all ended, with her leaving a note for her family to find her. But in Alaska, it was different. In Desparre, she wasn't the girl who'd helped five kids go home to families who missed them. She was the girl who'd put their sleepy, intentionally below-the-radar town on a national stage. She was the girl who'd been hiding in the woods for years, never reaching out for help. Because while the locals might have a live-and-let-live attitude about someone else's business, they also protected their own. If she'd asked, they'd all said, they would have helped her.

In all the years she'd lived in Desparre, she'd never asked. It was pretty clear some of them hated her for it.

"Chance, come on." She tapped her thigh twice, then ran for her truck, the dog close on her heels.

They hopped into the vehicle and then Alanna was speeding in the other direction, away from the strange SUV, away from the downtown. Deeper into the mountains.

"We scared her off." Tate stated the obvious as Alanna and her St. Bernard jumped into their truck and took off at a speed that would normally get them pulled over.

Silently, Peter cursed himself for getting too anxious, getting too close. But he'd been intrigued by the house deep in the wilderness where five kids had been hidden away for years. Like a lot of Alaska, Desparre was known for being a place where people could get lost. Most people were here for legitimate reasons—wanting to run from some tragedy in their life, wanting to recharge in Alaska's wild beauty or even wanting to hide from someone who meant them harm. But Alaska sometimes attracted people for the wrong kind of reasons, too... People like the Altiers.

The house wasn't what he'd been expecting. It was pretty, a log cabin set back in the woods at the crest of a mountain. The isolated location was particularly creepy, though, as he considered the dangerous drop he knew was right behind the house and the dense woods where a family could hide with shotguns. That last part had actually happened when Alanna's real sister had come searching for her and almost died in the process.

When police and the FBI had gone through the house after the Altiers had been arrested, they'd found a stash of forged documents. They'd also found years' worth of family pictures. According to police gossip, the earliest pictures showed obviously distraught kids, but as time went by, that changed. The pictures started to show what looked like a happy family. The most disturbing thing of all, according to one of the Desparre police department's veterans, was how much they'd all looked like a real family. Apparently the Altiers had grabbed kids who looked like they were related. The veteran had confided in Peter that what haunted him most was that if Alanna hadn't left the note, no one would ever look at the seven people living in this house and think for a second they weren't a legitimate family.

To Peter, the scariest part was how that lie still

seemed lodged in the mind of the person who had been the least brainwashed, the one who'd ultimately turned the kidnappers in.

Still, rumor had it that the Altiers had learned from their mistakes—when two of the kids they'd kidnapped couldn't forget their real families, they had started abducting younger children. It appeared that Darcy was sticking to that pattern, because police believed she'd grabbed a three-year-old boy not long after she'd escaped custody.

"Let's see where Alanna is headed next," Peter muttered. He was normally good at stakeouts, at making sure no one spotted him or his vehicle in a town full of naturally suspicious residents. It was a skill he'd learned as a reporter, when he'd sometimes go on scouting missions with soldiers. When he'd needed to keep up and keep quiet. But apparently the Altiers had taught Alanna to be hypervigilant and wary of strangers, and to run at the first indication someone might have noticed her.

It was ironic, really, that she still lived by that credo. After being plucked out of her front yard by a stranger as a kid, she should have been hypervigilant in a totally different way. Crowds should have been a source of comfort—more people to notice if something went wrong. Instead, she was still following what she'd been taught by the couple who'd kidnapped her and hidden her away from the world.

All of those things told Peter where her allegiance still lay. It was obvious to him that when it came to a choice between helping bring Darcy in—the line she'd given the police—and helping her escape, she'd choose the latter. Most likely, she'd do it regardless of the cost to others.

His hand was halfway to his left ear before he realized and yanked it back down.

"We need to be objective here," Tate said, somehow sensing what Peter was thinking.

Peter hadn't told Tate about his experiences overseas, but his last assignment as a war reporter was something few people in and around his hometown had missed. It had made national papers—along with a picture of him, blood dripping from his head, a cloud of dust covering his entire body and a stunned look on his face. The cameraman who'd caught the shot had done so seconds before the horrific aftermath of what Peter had just seen, what he'd just experienced. Only later would Peter realize most of the hearing in his left ear was never going to return.

"What we need to do is keep her in our sight," Peter grumbled, following the tire tracks in the loose snow. This far on the outskirts of Desparre, the roads saw minimal traffic. People who lived out this way all had snowmobiles for days when the snow got too deep for driving.

"It didn't look like anyone had been at the Altier house in a long time," Tate continued, unperturbed or indifferent that Peter was annoyed. "Don't you think if Darcy and Alanna had been in touch, Alanna would have known where to go? It seems like she's guessing as much as we are."

"Well, maybe they haven't been in touch. Or maybe they have and all Alanna knows is that Darcy is coming back to Desparre."

"If Alanna really wanted to help Darcy, why would she stop by the police station and offer us her help? Until she did that, no one was looking for Darcy here."

Peter let up on the gas slightly as Tate's words sank in. The search for the kidnapped boy—and escaped felon Darcy Altier—was making national news, but the search itself was centralized in Oregon. If anyone in law enforcement had reason to think Darcy was coming here, no one at their station seemed to know it.

Peter frowned and pressed down on the gas pedal again, hoping he was still following the right tire tracks but not willing to get within visual distance of Alanna's vehicle. Not willing to risk scaring her off again. She might have left five years ago, but when it came to the most remote part of Desparre, she definitely knew it better than he did.

"Where's she going?" Tate asked, his quiet tone suggesting he was talking to himself more than Peter.

"No idea," Peter answered anyway. "A second meetup point maybe?"

Tate shook his head and Peter could sense he was rolling his eyes. "I know Desparre isn't exactly a hotbed of crime and no one is likely to be missing us right now, but I seriously doubt Alanna Morgan came all this way, knocked on the police's door and gave us a heads-up she thinks Darcy is here, then headed right to her."

"Maybe not," Peter conceded. "But she's obviously searching for Darcy. And no one in Desparre knows her better."

"Okay," Tate agreed. "It still seems unlikely that Darcy would run back to Desparre, but if she *is* here, Alanna has a better shot at finding her than any of us."

"Glad you're seeing it my way," Peter said with a grin as he wound around another steep bend, taking them farther up the mountain. He cranked up the heater, feeling the temperature dropping as they climbed.

"If Alanna actually does find Darcy, she might need our help," Tate said.

"Why's that?"

"She's the reason Darcy Altier spent the last five years in prison. She's the reason Julian Altier died in prison."

"I don't think we can pin all of that on Alanna." Despite his suspicions about her motives now, she wasn't responsible for their actions or what had happened to them. It must have taken enormous fortitude to eventually turn them in. He had to give her that.

"I'm talking about Darcy's perspective, Peter. Alanna might think the woman who raised her will be happy to see her and will hand over this kid, but honestly? I think she's just as likely to take a shot at Alanna like she did at her sister five years ago."

Peter frowned, the idea of Alanna Morgan facing down a shotgun making him push the gas pedal harder. But when he rounded another bend, the road ended. A big wooden sign half-buried in snow announced it a dead end.

He hit the brakes hard and the SUV skidded to a stop, the four-wheel drive groaning. He glanced around, searching for a trail that snaked off somewhere, but saw nothing. "Where did she go?"

Tate shook his head, a hint of a smile on his lips. "I think she's a lot savvier than we gave her credit for. We lost her."

Chapter 3

"Hey, Chief, have you talked to Colter Hayes lately?" Peter asked as he strode back into the police station's bullpen the next day, Tate on his heels.

Chief Hernandez frowned back at him, disapproval in the lines between her eyebrows.

Peter had met Keara Hernandez when he had applied for the police officer position but knew little about her. In a town where people respected others' right to privacy, she hadn't shared much of her background with her officers. All Peter knew was that she'd come from somewhere in the Lower 48, where she'd been a detective. The move to the remote town of Desparre was a chance for a promotion, sure, but they didn't see much crime here. Undoubtedly, she was running from something—like so many of their civilians—but Peter had found her to be a fair boss. Her one shortcoming was her tendency to cut off ideas she didn't like, shutting them down fast.

He could see it coming before she opened her mouth, so he preempted her with another question. "When's the last time Colter was in Desparre with Alanna's sister?"

Colter Hayes was a Desparre transplant, a soldier who'd seen his entire unit die and decided to spend the rest of his life in the solitude of Desparre. Then he'd met Kensie Morgan and eventually followed her back to Chicago. But first, he'd helped Kensie track down Alanna—and in the process, uncovered the Altiers' kidnapping scheme.

The chief crossed her arms over her chest, turning to face him from where she'd been standing in front of the station's overworked coffeepot. "I've had some contact with him. He hasn't been back in about a year now. His wife is pregnant. Actually..." Chief Hernandez's eyes lifted upward, then she nodded. "No, by now, they've had the baby. I'm guessing they're pretty busy back in Chicago."

"Because—"

She cut him off with a single dismissive word, spoken with authority. "No, Peter."

Despite the fact that she was only six years older than his twenty-nine years, she said his name the way his mom had when he got in trouble as a boy. It made him feel like a kid and he scowled. He might have way more experience as a reporter than a police officer, but he knew how to follow a lead. And Alanna Morgan was a lead.

"Alanna Morgan was a *victim*," Chief Hernandez said. "It's sad that she can't let go of her past, but it's not our problem. I've talked to the federal agents handling the investigation back in Oregon and there's no reason to suspect Darcy Altier came this way."

"Is there a reason to suspect she went anywhere else?"

Chief Hernandez gave him an exasperated sigh, her gaze darting once to Tate, who stayed silent, then back to Peter. "What is this fixation with the Altiers? I didn't assign you to look into this. Alanna is on a mission for herself, Peter. She probably feels guilty for everything that happened, even if it wasn't her fault. She wants to help, but she's out here guessing. It's our job to make sure she's safe while she's here. But she's not a lead worth following. Leave her alone."

"What if she's right?"

"I already—"

"Alanna didn't fly all this way for nothing. Sure, maybe she does feel guilty, but if she thought Darcy was still in Oregon, wouldn't she go there?"

"Peter, this woman isn't law enforcement. She doesn't have any insight into this case that we don't."

"She does have insight into Darcy Altier that we don't," Tate contributed.

Peter glanced at his partner, who was leaning against the wall, looking unruffled by the argument with the chief. But Tate didn't feel as strongly about Alanna being a lead. He definitely didn't have as much to prove as Peter.

Giving him a quick nod of thanks for the support, Peter turned back to the chief. "Maybe Darcy Altier isn't here. But maybe she's on her way. I've read through the case information and Desparre is the only place the couple stayed for more than a year. Darcy got comfortable here. If anywhere is home to her, it's our town."

Chief Hernandez's forehead creased and her eyes narrowed, like she was thinking over his argument. Then she shook her head. "Whatever we don't know about the Altiers' motivations or mindsets, we can say this—those kids felt loved. The Altiers raised them like they were really their own children. That couple created a makeshift family for themselves. She and her husband got away with it for eighteen years, from the time they kidnapped that first boy until they were caught. They're not stupid. They know their house was searched and ultimately seized. She's not coming back here, Peter. And I won't waste your time—or Tate's time—following Alanna Morgan around."

"This isn't five years ago, Chief," Peter insisted. He thought of Alanna racing to the street to get a look at his SUV back at the Altier cabin. The expectation on her face, the hope that had shifted into wariness as he'd reversed at high speed.

Alanna believed the woman she'd called mom for fourteen years was returning to Desparre. That meant Peter believed it, too.

"That image of a happy family was all an illusion," Peter reminded her. "I'm not saying they didn't love those kids, in their own messed-up way. But Darcy and Julian made Desparre their hideout. In the end, this place destroyed them. Darcy spent five years in jail. Her husband died there. She watched all her 'kids' being taken away. This time around, do you really think she'd repeat those mistakes?"

The chief's arms dropped from where they'd been crossed over her chest for most of the conversation. Reluctant interest sparked in her eyes. "Wouldn't coming back to Desparre be a mistake, then?"

"That assumes she's thinking straight. She could be operating on pure emotion. Wanting what she had, where she had it. Or wanting something else, something stronger. Maybe this time, her goal isn't to steal herself a new family."

"Except she's already started one, with that little three-year-old boy in Oregon," Tate argued. But even he had pushed away from the wall and stepped closer, looking more interested in the conversation.

"Maybe the plan isn't to start a new family with this little boy. After all, where's the rest of Darcy's 'family'? Dead. Or back with their real families. Maybe this time, she's out to prove something."

"What?" Chief Hernandez asked, but the question was less hostile now.

"That she can outwit us all. Maybe Alanna's right, in a way. Maybe Darcy is coming back here to get revenge on us. The town that gave her up."

Chief Hernandez's lips twisted upward in the corners, but she was nodding slowly. "Except it wasn't really Desparre who turned Darcy in. It was Alanna."

"Exactly," Peter said. "Which means if Alanna isn't in on Darcy's escape, she might be a target."

Tate stepped a little closer. "So, you think we need to keep following her, to keep her safe?" he asked, probably assuming this was Peter's roundabout way to keep chasing that lead.

"Sure," Peter said. "That's one reason to keep following her."

"What's the other?" Chief Hernandez asked, eyes narrowing like she already knew the answer.

"She's our bait to catch a kidnapper."

* * *

"Alanna?" The high-pitched voice gained volume and then a hand gripped Alanna's arm hard. "Alanna Morgan?"

Reluctantly, Alanna turned to face the woman with long blond hair and perfect makeup who'd stopped her as she and Chance stepped out of their truck in the parking lot of Jasper's General Store. The store where Alanna had left her fateful note five years ago.

"I thought it was you," the woman said, her voice too cheery, her eyes too bright. Her breath swirled between them in the cold, doing nothing to obscure the raw ambition in her gaze.

No doubt about it. She might not have a microphone or a camera crew, but she was a reporter.

Alanna had been here for twenty-four hours and already a reporter had found her.

From the way Chance let out a low rumble—not quite a growl, but not friendly—when she reached her hand toward Alanna, he knew it, too.

The woman withdrew her hand quickly, her too-huge smile slipping just a bit, and Alanna felt herself being transported back five years.

The flight home had seemed to take forever. She'd been heading to a suburb outside of Chicago, to a home she'd never seen because her parents had long since moved out of the place where she'd been kidnapped in the front yard. Clutching Kensie's hand too hard on the turbulent flight, having never been on an airplane before. Nerves churning her stomach as she prepared to greet parents and a brother she hadn't seen in fourteen long years.

The drive from the airport to her parents' house, where she'd soon be living, had gone by in a blur but the moments afterward were the ones Alanna would never forget. She'd expected her parents and brother, had known their extended family was waiting to give them a private reunion first. They didn't want to overwhelm her, they said.

But she hadn't expected the reporters. The news vans had made it nearly impossible for their driver to pull up to the house. The bursts of light from camera flashes going off all around her had made it hard to see. The reporters and their crews had pushed in on her from all sides, making her feel claustrophobic. Their questions screamed at her from all directions. *What's it like being home after all these years? Do you remember your real family? Did the Altiers hurt you? Why did you leave that note? Why didn't you come forward sooner?*

Trying to shake off the memories, Alanna leveled the woman with a hard stare and pulled her arm free. "No comment."

Five years ago, Kensie had snapped those words at the reporters, pulled Alanna protectively into the crook of her arm and propelled her forward into the respective quiet of the house. Inside, Alanna had immediately been folded into hugs by her parents, while her teary-eyed older brother stared at her in wonder.

Of course she'd known they would have changed in fourteen years. Just as she'd changed from a curly-haired five-year-old into a young woman.

Still, it had been a shock to see the streaks of gray in her mother's dark hair, the worry lines on her father's forehead and at the corners of his eyes. The scents of her father's aftershave and her mother's perfume had swirled around her, subtle but still making her eyes water—she was used to the outdoorsy scents of the Altiers when they hugged her. Her parents had looked older than their years. Alanna had been struck with the guilt of realizing it was probably from having their youngest child ripped out of their lives, from the years of searching and always coming up empty.

Then there was Flynn, standing stock-still, his lips trembling as his tears started to spill at the corners of his eyes. It had been hard to reconcile the twenty-three-year-old man staring at her with the nine-year-old brother she remembered. He'd been thinner than she'd expected and there was something desperate in his gaze she realized only later had come from years of bad decisions and addictions he'd fought hard to break. He had started when he was a teenager, feeling neglected by parents who'd been constantly looking for the daughter they'd lost, forgetting the two children they still had left.

All of it, ultimately leading back to her. To all the small moments over the years that were chances she might have had to reach out sooner, but hadn't taken. There hadn't been a lot, but she'd definitely had opportunities. In the beginning, she'd been far too afraid to take them. As she grew up, as she grew to love the family she lived with, she'd been scared of what it would mean for all of them.

In the early years with the Altiers, she used to squeeze her eyes closed tight and hold the images of her family in her mind, desperate not to lose them. As she'd grown, those images had blurred around the edges. Memories had faded, leaving behind only vague images and the feeling of having once been loved by a totally different family. With fourteen years between them missing, the homecoming she'd expected to be joyous had been happy but awkward. At that moment, the idea of rebuilding a life she barely remembered with a family she'd only known as a young child had seemed overwhelming.

"Are you sure?"

The reporter's voice cut through her memories and Alanna realized she'd frozen in the parking lot while the woman stared at her quizzically.

As Alanna's gaze refocused, the woman rushed on, "No one's ever really told your side of the story. What it was like to say goodbye to four kids you'd considered your brothers and sisters. What it was like to go home to a family you hadn't seen since you were five. I can do that for you."

Alanna's gut clenched at the reporter's insight, but she shook her head and turned away, rushing for the store with Chance keeping pace. She didn't take a full breath again until she was inside with the door closed behind her.

Here, at least, things looked the same. She'd been inside Jasper's General Store only a few times over the years they'd lived in Desparre. The Altiers had feared someone would recognize her, even years later and so many thousands of miles from where she'd been kidnapped. But as time went on, she'd eventually been given more freedom.

Trailing her hands over the rusting metal shelves filled with household staples, Alanna walked slowly toward the counter where an old man sat. The owner, Jasper. The man Julian had asked her to hand over the money to for their groceries. The man who'd unknowingly taken the note within her stack of cash.

He stood as she approached, recognition in his deep brown eyes. His gaze flicked once to Chance, walking happily along beside her, then returned to her. "Alanna Morgan."

"Hi." She stuffed her gloved hands into the pockets in her coat. "I was wondering—you knew my... Julian Altier once. Did you know Darcy?"

Jasper had a reputation for being cranky and unapproachable, and as he came around the counter, his pace was slow but determined. But when he stopped in front of her, there was compassion in his gaze and sadness in his voice. "I didn't really know either of them. I'd only seen Julian a few times over the years. I'm sorry I never noticed anything wrong. I wasn't even sure how that note got into my stack of cash."

Alanna shook her head, squeezed the hand he'd reached toward her. "It's not your fault. Even when I handed over the money and the note, I didn't act like anything was wrong." In some ways, nothing had been wrong. In others, everything had been.

"So you wouldn't recognize Darcy if she came through here?"

His eyes narrowed, making more lines crease his weather-worn skin. "I'd recognize her now, of course, with all the media coverage. But back then? I don't know. She might have come through here with Julian before, once or twice over the years. Hard to say."

"But not recently?" Alanna pressed, trying not to get discouraged.

"No way. People around here would know her now. We'd turn her in."

He said it like it was exactly what Alanna would want to hear, but her shoulders dropped. Maybe the police were right. The people in Desparre felt betrayed by Julian and Darcy, were angry with all the negative attention the couple had brought them. If there was any place Darcy would be recognized quickly, it was an insular town that promised anonymity but recognized and distrusted anyone who didn't live here.

"Thanks," Alanna said, her voice coming out in a squeak. She saw Jasper's lips twist in sympathy as she spun toward the door.

"Come on, Chance," she said as her St. Bernard lagged slightly behind, probably wondering what they were doing.

She'd been a fool to come here, to think she could make a difference. A fool to think that Darcy would return to the place that had once made her most happy, instead of doing what she'd been truly doing all along: running.

Alanna had been a fool to risk the bonds she'd spent five years rebuilding with her family to chase after her kidnapper.

Shame and anger filled her as she pushed the door open a little too hard, almost slamming into someone.

The "sorry" died on her lips as the person on the other side caught the door and flung it the rest of the way open.

Then he was filling the doorway with his scowl, the gaze of his too-blue eyes drilling into her. Peter Robak. The cop who thought she was in cahoots with Darcy.

Only after she'd slipped away from the SUV following her yesterday—making a quick turn onto a wide path not meant as a road—had she realized who was chasing her. Not a threat like she'd imagined, a pair of men who'd spotted a woman all by herself in an isolated area. But police officers who thought she was little better than a criminal.

"You can stop following me around now," she snapped at him, taking an aggressive step forward despite knowing it was a bad idea to get inside a cop's personal space. But the fear she'd felt yesterday shifted into fury now. The shame and guilt and frustration felt better channeling outward than inward. "I'm finished here, okay? You can leave me alone."

From the corner of her eye, she saw Peter's partner—the other man in the SUV yesterday. Surprise was on his face, his hand dropping away from his weapon as if he'd reached for it when he saw someone rush toward Peter, then changed his mind when he saw it was just her. Just a foolish woman chasing a past that was better left alone.

"You're leaving?" he asked.

But it was Peter's words that drew all of her attention: "You were right."

Dread dropped into her stomach. "Right about what?" Was Darcy here after all? Had someone spotted her?

People here were often armed, ready to protect their own when help could be far away. The residents understood that Desparre usually attracted people who just wanted solitude, but that it could also attract those trying to escape something they'd done, something that had the law chasing them. Had one of those people seen Darcy and taken aim? Had the police arrested her? "What happened?"

Peter frowned at her, studying her like he was trying to unravel all of her secrets, all of the years she had spent happily living with a pair of kidnappers, then turning them in one day. "Darcy's not in Desparre. Not yet. But I think she's on her way."

"What? Why?"

A slight smile twisted one side of his lips, but there was nothing happy about it. "We know she's headed in this direction from Oregon."

"Why?" Alanna pressed, every second she stood there waiting to understand adding to her anxiety, making her stomach churn and her breathing turn shallow.

Chance let out a low whine and nudged her with his nose.

She put a hand on his head, stroking his fur to assure him she was okay, even if it wasn't true.

"She was spotted in Canada today. They didn't catch her, but now this has become an international chase, Alanna."

Alanna sensed Peter's partner stepping closer, as if he planned to intervene in whatever Peter was going to say next, but she couldn't take her gaze off Peter.

He stared back at her, his uncompromising expression only cracking as he said, "Darcy kidnapped another kid today."

Chapter 4

"What's Darcy's endgame?"

Peter's words were angry and suddenly he was the one getting into her personal space.

Alanna backed up a step and Chance pushed his way between her and the police officer, using his size and St. Bernard strength as a warning.

"Chance," Alanna said, tugging his collar just enough to let him know he should back up, too. But her mind was still trying to get a grip on the words Peter had spoken a moment ago.

Darcy was partway between where she'd escaped custody and Desparre. Now she had two kidnapped kids with her instead of one.

"It makes no sense."

She didn't realize she'd spoken the words out loud until Peter asked, "What? How many kids does this woman have to kidnap before you see her as a threat, as a criminal?"

Anger made her heat up underneath her winter gear and she could feel the flush rising to her cheeks.

"Peter," his partner said, his voice quiet but firm. "Go easy."

Then he stuck a hand toward her. "I'm Officer Tate Emory. I was in the police station yesterday when you came in to offer your help. We'd like to take you up on that."

He was the officer she'd noticed watching her exchange with the chief from the bullpen yesterday. Her eyes narrowed as she looked from him to Peter. "Why? Because now you know I can lose you when you follow me around?"

Tate's lips twitched, like he was holding back amusement.

Peter took a step closer. "Because it's the right thing to do." His tone was less raw anger now, more accusatory, as if daring her to say she *wouldn't* help the police.

The police had scoffed at her offer before. Then they had two officers follow her around like she was a criminal. And now?

She wasn't sure how Darcy would feel seeing her again. But she figured the woman was way more likely to let her get close if she was alone than if she had a pair of police officers trailing her every move. Especially police officers Alanna didn't trust.

Peter might say helping them was the right thing to do, but how could she believe they'd do what was right when the time came? Would they trust her to talk Darcy into turning herself in, into turning over the kids she'd kidnapped, rather than run or fight? She doubted it.

"I think you ought to leave her alone."

The voice came from behind her. When Alanna glanced over her shoulder, she saw Jasper scowling at the cops, his arms crossed over his chest.

She gave him a thankful, shaky smile before Tate drew her attention again.

"Look, we should have been up front with you," he said, giving Peter a glare that clearly said *go easy*. "We didn't have any reason to believe Darcy was coming here before. Now we do. And you have insight into the places she knows in and around Desparre. You have insight into her as a person. You can help us bring those kids home to their families."

She stared back at him, at the guileless look on his face, and saw something else there. Not the distrust Peter broadcasted whenever he spoke to her, but pity.

Averting her gaze, she felt a familiar discomfort well up. The feel of too many eyes on her, all evaluating, all judging. Not just reporters, but also all the people who read or watched their stories. To this day, she still got mail from some of them, letters of encouragement or morbid curiosity or misplaced anger.

She was sick of all of it.

Forcing her gaze back up, she told both officers, "I was wrong. I don't think I can help you. But if I find anything, I'll let you know."

She wasn't sure if the last words were a lie or not.

"Alanna—"

Peter stepped closer still, despite Chance angled protectively in front of her.

Chance let out another low warning growl, but Peter only glanced at him, seemingly unconcerned. Apparently he recognized that the St. Bernard wouldn't hurt anyone unless they were a real threat to her.

"This isn't like Darcy," Alanna admitted, the words breaking free before she'd even realized she thought them.

It was true. The Altiers had gone years between grabbing kids. Abducting two within a few days, while on the run from the law, was reckless.

Was Darcy trying to create a brand-new, ready-made family? Did she want to re-create what she'd had with Alanna and her "siblings"? Had she simply snapped from the grief of her husband's death, after years being locked away, after losing the kids she'd raised?

It was possible. And yet, something didn't seem right. It didn't seem like Darcy at all.

"Are we sure she's the one who took those kids?" Alanna looked from Peter to Tate, trying to read the truth in their eyes because she wasn't sure she'd hear it from their lips.

The pity intensified on Tate's face, in the way his lips crumpled, in the tilt of his head.

Peter just looked exasperated. "What do you think? That someone else is following her—an escaped fugitive—and they just happen to be doing what she did for eighteen years? Really?"

"No," Alanna said softly, because it sounded ridiculous. Obviously it was Darcy. But if she was acting this out of character, even if Alanna could find her, would she be able to get through to her? Would she be able to change anything? Or was coming here a total waste of time?

The door to their old home had been left unlocked. It opened with a hard shove, groaning in a way that told

Alanna no one had been through in a long time. She slipped underneath the faded yellow tape that had probably once read Do Not Cross but had become illegible over five Alaskan winters.

Her heart began to pound as she stepped over the threshold and a thousand memories hit her at once. Darcy and Julian sitting side by side, holding hands on the blue couch Darcy had upholstered herself. Alanna's older "brother" Johnny staring at the chessboard in the corner, contemplating his next move in a long-running game with Julian. Her younger "siblings" Sydney and Drew sitting cross-legged on the floor, teaching their youngest "sister" Valerie to make a pair of snowshoes.

After Darcy and Julian had been arrested, Johnny had stared at her with disbelief and confusion. In all the years since, he'd refused to speak to her. Five years of Alanna's letters had been returned unopened. Yet at least once a year, Alanna still tried.

Sydney, three years younger than Alanna and the "sibling" she'd always felt closest to, had tried to keep in touch. In the beginning, she and Alanna had spoken on the phone almost nightly. Slowly, though, the frequency of those calls had decreased, until now Alanna only heard from her every few weeks.

Alanna stomped her feet on the heavy rug still lining the entryway as Chance pushed his way in beside her, knocking free one end of the police tape. The broken tape immediately blew outward, dancing in the wind. Alanna shut the door behind it, closing out the frigid wind and falling snow.

Beside her, Chance did a full-body shake, sending melted snow everywhere. Then he walked into the main room as if he'd been there a hundred times and settled in front of the dark fireplace. It was as if he knew this place had once been her home and he felt at home here, too.

She followed more slowly, each step farther into the house feeling as if she was stepping backward in time. As she ran her hand over the soft, worn blanket on the corner of the sofa, she could picture Drew and Valerie curled underneath it, one on each end of the couch, their toes meeting in the middle.

She'd tried to keep in touch with them, too, but their parents had cut off all contact when they'd gone home. Drew would turn eighteen next year, which meant Alanna could try again. But Valerie was only eleven. By the time she was an adult, how much of her time with Alanna would she remember? Valerie had been six when the Altier "family" had been broken apart—only a year older than Alanna when she'd been kidnapped. Had her memories of Alanna already blurred around the edges, the same way Alanna's had of the Morgans over the years?

The "siblings" she'd spent the majority of her childhood with were now scattered across the country, no two in the same state. Her video chats with Sydney were the closest she'd come to seeing any of them since that day when police had stopped their car and screamed at her "parents" to get out.

Alanna blinked back tears that suddenly flooded her vision. She wasn't here to wallow in regrets or wonder if she'd made the right choice five years ago. She was here for clues.

It had been two days since Darcy was spotted in northern Canada, since she'd grabbed another young child, this time a two-year-old girl. According to news reports, there had been no confirmed sightings of her since.

Two days ago, after talking to Peter and Tate, Alanna had been ready to head home. Yesterday, she'd even packed her small suitcase and looked for flights. She'd finally picked up one of the calls from her sister Kensie, promising she'd be heading home on Saturday. Instead, today, she'd texted Kensie that she was staying a little longer. She might not be able to talk Darcy down as she'd planned, but she could still help. If anyone could find Darcy now, it was Alanna.

The problem was, if Darcy was speeding back to Alaska, kidnapping more kids along the way, it meant five years in prison had definitely changed her. But not in the way Alanna had expected.

Throughout her childhood, Alanna had always seen Darcy as the "parent" who was the dreamer. Easily distracted, always lost in her own thoughts, she had a million ideas but rarely the initiative to see them all through. It was Julian who took her ideas and made them reality.

All through the house were examples of the way her "parents" had fit together, worked together. The fireplace, for instance, with its border of colorful tiles, had started as an idea Darcy had sketched out to resemble the aurora borealis at night. But it was Julian who'd purchased those tiles, taught all of them to affix them to the fireplace. Darcy had envisioned the extra room toward the back of the house as a place to homeschool and Julian had found schoolbooks for all of them. Then, of course, there were the kidnappings.

Alanna hugged her arms around herself, cold despite

being out of the wind and snow. But the heat was off in the house, her breath making cloud puffs in the air.

One of the clearest memories she had—the memory that still woke her in the middle of the night—was that moment when Julian had reached out from his car and yanked her inside. Darcy had been at the wheel, speeding away dangerously as Alanna yelped in surprise and fright, squirming to look out the rear window. She had watched Kensie get smaller in the distance, even as her sister ran after their vehicle, screaming for help.

When Alanna was taken, the Altiers had already had Johnny for four years. Even then, Johnny had barely remembered his birth family and he'd already adjusted to living with the Altiers. The four of them had moved constantly in those early years, never staying in one place too long.

Alanna had only been five years old then, totally reliant on three people she didn't trust. Peter was probably right that being so dependent on them from such a young age had helped forge a deeper connection. Slowly, Alanna's fear and hatred had shifted. Her "parents" and "brother" had worn her down with love and caring. As guilty as she'd felt about it, she'd started to care for them, too.

By the time they'd grabbed Sydney, Alanna hadn't forgotten the Morgans. But she'd felt like she had a new family.

That was when she'd learned how the kidnappings worked. Darcy and Julian always talked about wanting a big family, but apparently Darcy couldn't get pregnant. Every few years, Darcy would see a kid—one who looked like an Altier—and felt as if the child was already hers. Then Julian would make it a reality.

Darcy doing the kidnappings without Julian seemed so counter to the way her "mother" worked. Alanna had come here thinking she could talk some sense into her, make her realize her actions were emotional and unethical. But abducting *two* kids, in such a short span of time? It meant Darcy was different now, that she was taking on both hers and Julian's past parental roles. It meant she wasn't the person Alanna remembered.

When Alanna was a child, she'd always been able to talk Darcy into things to make her happy. One more story at bedtime. A warmer pair of boots so she could spend more time playing in the snow. A later bedtime so she could stay up reading or playing games with her "siblings." But now? With everything that had changed while Darcy was in jail? Would Alanna be able to interrupt Darcy's plan?

Shutting out the memories along with worries of what would happen if she *did* find Darcy, Alanna took a deep breath and looked around the room. Chance had gotten up without her noticing and was standing next to her, staring up at her with those dark brown eyes. A string of drool in the corner of his droopy mouth nearly stretched to the wooden floor and made Alanna smile.

She stroked his soft fur, then said, "Let's get to work."

His head swiveled, as if taking in the small front room and asking, *Doing what?*

"We're looking for somewhere else Darcy could hide," Alanna told him.

He tilted his head at her, making the drool break free, and Alanna laughed. It loosened the tension in her chest, was the impetus she needed to get moving.

Five years ago, when Kensie had shown up at their

house searching for her, Darcy and Julian had bundled all the kids quickly into the car and fled. Alanna had initially thought they were going back to what they'd done years ago, skipping from state to state, hiding. Then she'd learned Julian had a specific hiding place in mind and it was nearby. They'd never made it, though, because the police had caught up to them. As far as Alanna knew, other property owned by the Altiers—in their name or some other name—had never been uncovered. But that didn't mean it didn't exist.

If Darcy was returning to Desparre, it was unlikely she'd come back to the cabin. That was too dangerous. But some other hiding spot her husband had scoped out years ago that police and the FBI had never uncovered? That seemed reasonable.

Alanna didn't know where it was. But there had to be a clue in this cabin. She walked from room to room slowly, her gaze lighting on every object, all the pieces of their lives that had been left behind. She picked up old books, looked through cupboards now littered with rodent droppings and then retraced her steps, trying to see it all anew.

Two hours later, she held a small piece of paper in her hand. She'd found it taped to the inside cover of one of Darcy's old drawing books. If the police had found it five years ago, apparently they hadn't thought anything of the random symbols. But they meant something to Alanna: a goofy code she and her "siblings" had created one particularly frigid winter when they'd all been stuck inside for two weeks. Darcy had encouraged them, laughing as they'd constructed what they thought was a tightly encrypted cipher. Translated, the symbols in Darcy's book were a series of latitudes and longitudes. Coordinates.

Alanna stared at the list, five places she knew in her gut were hiding spots. Then she looked over at Chance. "Let's start at the top."

Chance must have felt the mix of excitement and anxiety in her words because he got to his feet quickly and chased her to the door. When she flung it open, her excitement transitioned immediately to dread.

The snow that had been falling slowly for the past few hours had picked up intensity, racing faster for the ground, piling on top of the foot and a half's worth that had already come down over the past two days. Alanna squinted at the gray sky, then at the truck she'd rented. It was built for off-roading in the Alaskan terrain. But there was no rental vehicle hardy enough for the furious climate Desparre could spawn.

In November, conditions could turn dangerous fast. Alanna checked the weather app on her phone, which indicated that the snow was supposed to stop before the top of the hour, only a few minutes away. As if she'd willed it, when she looked back up, the speed of the falling snow had decreased, the snowflakes seeming to shrink in size.

"I think we can do it," she told Chance, glancing again at the paper in her hand. According to her navigation app, the first location was less than half an hour's drive. And she'd spent years in the unpredictable Desparre weather, understood how to take care of herself in it.

Chance bolted out the door, bounding in circles in the fresh snow before coming to a stop by the back door of the truck. He glanced back at her, as if to say, *What are you waiting for?*

She hurried after him, slower in the heavy snow, and opened the truck door for him.

Chance leaped into the back seat, bringing snow with him and making Alanna wish she'd brought more towels.

She ran to the front, turning the heat up to high as soon as she was inside. Tucking the paper into the inside pocket of her coat, she eased the truck carefully out of the driveway, happy to see that the snowfall was slowing even more.

Still, the roads near the cabin were unpaved. The town didn't bother to clear them and the people who lived out this way all had snowmobiles for when winter got too tough for even their all-weather vehicles. So, Alanna drove slowly and carefully, following in other tire tracks where she could. She headed farther away from Desparre, but down the mountain this time, on roads that wound around massive old trees.

It was the route they'd been on five years ago, when the police had caught up to them.

Snow shot out from beneath the tires, fluffy stuff that would have been perfect for building snowmen. Luckily, there was no ice underneath it. On one side of her, the mountain continued upward; on the other was the cliff edge.

She gripped the wheel tightly, slightly less confident after five years of living near Chicago, with their milder winters, snow removal services, far-reaching cell towers and easy access to help. She glanced in her rearview mirror at Chance, lying across the back seat, but his head up, watching out the window. He met her gaze in the mirror, trusting, and she wondered if she was making a mistake.

But when she glanced at her navigation app, she realized she'd driven farther than she'd expected. The snow had stopped falling from the sky, but every once and a while, a big hunk of it slid off a tree branch, startling her as it plopped onto the windshield. She was close now. Her heart rate picked up in anticipation of finding the hideout Julian had probably built, at the possibility of finding Darcy there now.

Then she rounded a corner and swore as she stomped on the brake. The truck swerved slightly in the snow and Alanna clutched the wheel harder, angling away from the steep drop to her right.

Ahead of her, the road was blocked. A pile of snow higher than the front of her truck covered the entire road to the edge of the mountain. She couldn't tell how far it went, but as she leaned forward and glanced up through her windshield, she could tell why it had fallen. Avalanche.

"Guess we'll have to move on to the next spot," she told Chance, but just as quickly, she decided to put that plan on hold. Where there'd been one avalanche, there could be another. Best to get away from the mountain and hope the snow melted.

She backed the truck up slowly, carefully as she got ready to round the bend again backward, since there was no room to turn around. But the tires slid on her anyway, and she overcorrected, more afraid of the drop-off than bumping the other side of the mountain. Except when her rear bumper hit the rock, the truck also slid into a rut. When she hit the gas again, the wheels spun, but the truck wouldn't go anywhere.

Cursing, Alanna pulled her hood over her head and hopped out of the truck to grab the shovel from the back. As soon as she stepped outside, a fierce shiver rushed through her body at the force of the wind. And as she opened the back door, Chance leaped out.

"No!" She made a grab for his collar even as he spun back toward her, but a noise overhead made her look up. A rumbling like thunder, but far too close. An avalanche.

Years of living in Alaska rushed back to her, as she stared at the mountaintop, instantly seeing the path of the snow. It would probably miss her if she backed away fast enough. But it was definitely going to take her truck. And Chance, standing too close to it…

She grabbed for him just as the wall of snow rushed downward, sweeping him up with it. Then her arms closed around him, just under his front legs. She clung tight, even as the snow slammed into her, hard and fast, shoving them both toward the edge of the mountain.

Chapter 5

Alanna Morgan knew something.

Peter had been following her around half the day. Unlike when he'd last followed her around with Tate three days ago, he was alone today. Saturday was his day off. Unfortunately, that meant he was in his personal vehicle instead of the police SUV. Although his truck could handle the Desparre winters, his police vehicle was equipped for anything. As Alanna headed farther away from Desparre, taking dangerous back roads down the mountain like she'd driven them a million times, Peter's knuckles went white gripping his steering wheel.

He'd grown up on the other side of the mountain, in an area almost as prone to crazy weather as Desparre. But the town of Luna—where his parents and older siblings lived still—was much flatter. They occasionally got nasty avalanches off this side of the mountain, but being at a lower altitude usually meant slightly fewer dangers. It definitely meant easier driving.

Since joining the Desparre police department last year, he'd been up on this mountain a few times, usually doing welfare checks. He'd driven it in far worse weather than this, but he'd never done it while chasing after a former victim, potential new accomplice or possible target. He'd never done it while trailing someone who seemed to know too well how to lose a tail.

Right now, she had good reason to try to lose him. Judging by the excitement on her face when she'd finally left the Altiers' cabin, she'd found something inside it. And the chances that she hadn't spotted him seemed low. So, when she rounded another corner and he heard snow crunching hard, as if she'd slammed the brakes, he eased off the side of the road and waited.

When her truck door slammed, he cursed and wedged his door open against the side of the mountain so he could climb awkwardly out of his vehicle. Better she stride over here, furious and ready for an argument than hide somewhere again while he drove past, clueless. But then she yelled "No!" and almost immediately—as if she'd been yelling at the mountain and it didn't want to listen—an ominous crash and boom signaled an oncoming avalanche.

His heart gave a quick, painful thud and then he was running toward her, rounding the corner before he could fully think it through.

Snow rushed downward from far above, a furious waterfall of white, slowing slightly along the road before it tumbled over the other side. There was a groan of metal over the rush of snow, only the top of Alanna's truck visible as it flipped sideways, then disappeared over the edge of the mountain.

Dread, anger and grief hit him unexpectedly hard. But he didn't have time to linger on it, because there she was, outside the vehicle, just a flash of her red coat in the flurry of snow.

He darted toward her and his left boot slid on the spilling snow, almost taking him down, sucking him under. He looked up quickly and saw that the avalanche was slowing, the end in sight way above him. But that flash of red was too close to the edge.

Fear threatened to freeze him in place, but he gritted his teeth and changed his angle, moving toward the edge of the mountain, toward a big old tree withstanding the onslaught of snow. Wrapping an arm and a leg around it, Peter reached out with his free hand, blindly now, since that flash of red had been overrun by snow.

Somehow, he grabbed her—or at least he hoped it was her. Cursing the thick gloves that made it hard to get a good grip, he clung to the edge of material. Then the snow yanked him forward, the pull hard and unrelenting, tearing at the socket in his shoulder.

The momentum ripped him around the front of the tree and the right side of his body burned with the contact. He clung to his quarry tighter, squeezing his left hand as tightly as he could, praying the coat wouldn't rip right out of his hand and take Alanna with it.

The snow shifted, taking a slight turn over the edge of the mountain, probably catching on the trees there. It pushed him back toward the big tree, easing the screaming pain in his shoulder and letting him get a better grip.

Suddenly, there she was, rising up on the curve of snow. First came her bright red coat, then a swash of long, dark, wet hair. Then her face, both too starkly pale and too bright red in places as she gasped for air.

"Your hand," he croaked, his voice lost beneath the still-thundering snow. He prayed she'd hear him, grab his arm and pull herself toward him.

If she replied, he couldn't hear it with his bad ear facing her. Instead, she tried to angle her body toward him in the snow and he saw both her arms wrapped underneath the front legs of her enormous dog. The St. Bernard was scrabbling for purchase with his huge paws and was actually managing to get a little traction, moving them both closer to Peter.

But then the last rush of snow swooped down and both of them disappeared underneath it.

Peter took a huge breath and squeezed his eyes shut as the snow claimed him, too.

She was suffocating.

The world around her finally stopped moving, but where had she landed? Had she tumbled over the edge of the mountain and managed to get wedged between some trees? Or was she still on the edge of the road, where one wrong move would send her flying over it?

She tried to move her fingers and felt Chance squirm in her arms. Tears pricked her eyes with the relief that he was still with her, still alive. But when she opened her eyes, there was only darkness. And cold like she'd never experienced.

The avalanche had buried them both. But how deeply?

She shifted along with Chance, not moving her arms from around his belly, not wanting him to go too far. Hoping there was a pocket of air, she finally had to open her mouth and gulp in a breath. There was a pocket, but it felt too little for both her and Chance, especially as her lungs demanded more, more, more.

Keeping one hand locked around Chance, she thrust the other upward, hoping to encounter fresh air. But there was only more snow. Was she really reaching up? Or had she been spun around so she thought down was up?

Don't panic, she reminded herself as her heart started thudding faster. She thrust her arm the other way, and this time she felt hard ground. At least, she thought so. Which meant escape was above her. But was it through a few feet of loosely packed snow, just above where her fingers could reach, or twelve feet deep and pressing down hard? Would movement help her get to safety or shift the weight of the snow so it crushed them both?

Her collapsible snow shovel was in her truck, which was probably buried under the snow with her. By the time she'd heard the telltale *whomp* of snow breaking free that signaled an oncoming avalanche, it had been too late. She should have known better; she never should have been out here in this weather. And now Chance, who'd suffered so much as a tiny puppy, who'd been her constant, loyal companion for the past two years, would probably die with her.

Stop it, she commanded herself. She needed to find a way out for both of them. For Peter, too?

Had she imagined seeing him at the edge of the avalanche in those brief moments when the snow had shifted and let her suck in a desperate lungful of air before it pulled her under again? Had she imagined his hand reaching out, yanking her backward, even as the avalanche tried to throw her forward, over the edge of the mountain? She reached behind her, felt a hand clutching her coat and her heart gave a hard thump.

He'd tried to save her. He didn't even like her, but he'd tried to save her life. Had it cost him his own?

The fingers locked in her coat weren't moving. She tried to scoot toward him, tried to urge Chance to come with her. She moved slowly, terrified of triggering more snow that might crush them, not sure how close they were to the edge of the mountain.

But as she slid toward Peter, Chance broke free from her grasp. She fumbled for him, her hands grasping nothing but snow, feeling clumsy in the cold.

"Chance!" As she gasped his name, she sucked in snow and more fell, closing the gap between her and her dog. She stretched her arms farther, but couldn't find him.

Panic took hold, squeezing her lungs tight as she turned her head and spit out the snow, trying to get more air. She found another pocket of it, but it felt stuffy, like it was already emptying of oxygen, and she tried to take shallow breaths. Reaching behind her, she tugged lightly on Peter's arm and he moved. But she couldn't tell if it was just gravity or if he was okay.

"Chance!" she tried again, even as she heard him moving away from her. Was he headed toward the edge of the mountain? She was too turned around to tell. Even if he managed to get free of the snow, would he fall over the edge?

Holding in a sob—for her dog, for herself, for Peter— Alanna shifted again, sliding closer to Peter. She tried calling for Chance again, but she couldn't hear him anymore. She yelled louder, even as she wondered if she was doing the right thing. Maybe Chance could get free of the snow and save himself, at least.

Now, she had to try to do the same for her and Peter. As she scooted backward toward him through the heavy snow, his hand moved again, this time sliding down to grab her arm. Relief made more tears fill her eyes, but she blinked them back fast, not wanting them to freeze on her face.

She wasn't shivering so much anymore. Either she was adjusting to the cold or—more likely—she was starting to face hypothermia.

"We have to get out of here," she told Peter, even as the tiny pocket of air in front of her collapsed and more snow crashed down on her.

The weight felt crushing, the sudden lack of oxygen making her panic. She swung her arms out, trying to find a new pocket of air.

Then something scratched against her leg, a frantic pawing that got faster as she instinctively jerked away. Chance! He was trying to save her.

He was behind her now. Did that mean he'd somehow dug free of the avalanche? Alanna moved her legs, trying to help him free her. She grabbed Peter's hand as Chance suddenly took her ankle in his mouth and tugged.

She slid backward about a foot, snow crushing her even more, making her lungs and chest hurt. Then Chance's paws were up near her head and the snow in front of her face suddenly broke away, giving her precious air as the weight on her eased. She scooted toward him, trying to pull Peter with her, but Chance had already turned away from her.

He had started digging frantically beside her and

soon Peter's torso and head emerged from the snow. Peter dropped her hand, somehow pulling himself forward, and then he and Chance were digging her the rest of the way out, dragging her free of the snow.

Struggling to her knees, Alanna threw shaky arms around Chance's back as she stared at the huge pile of snow. It was as tall as a house in the middle. Somehow, she, Peter and Chance had been at the edge of the avalanche, where it wasn't as high, where it hadn't smashed down hard enough to crush their bones or suffocate them. Her truck was gone, either buried under it or tossed over the side of the mountain, crashed somewhere below.

But she was alive. Chance was alive. And Peter was alive. That was all that mattered.

She stumbled to her feet and the bitter wind sliced through her wet clothes. Her teeth started chattering as Peter grabbed her hand.

"Come on. My truck's around the corner. We have to warm up."

As she stumbled after him, Chance at her side, Alanna realized his truck was far enough away that he could have avoided the avalanche altogether. He'd run toward it to save her, even though he didn't like her, even though he seemed to think she might be in cahoots with a kidnapper.

He didn't trust her. She didn't trust him, either. But he'd risked his life for her, which meant he was a good person. They might not agree on how to go about it, but they had the same ultimate goal: to save the kids Darcy had kidnapped.

They rounded the bend and Peter held open the door

to his truck, waiting for her and Chance, his face a bright, unnatural red from the cold.

She slowed and he urged, "Come on, Alanna. Hurry."

"I want to work together," she blurted.

"What?"

It didn't matter what they thought of each other. She'd figure out a way to convince Peter that he needed to bring Darcy in carefully, peacefully. He had resources she didn't, like access to whatever the Desparre police learned from other law enforcement. But she had resources he needed, too, and an insight into Darcy's mindset that he'd never figure out without her.

They'd be stronger together.

"Let's work together to find Darcy and save those kids."

He stared at her a minute, something pensive in his brilliant blue eyes, then he nodded. "Deal. Now get in the truck."

Chapter 6

It was amazing they'd lived through the avalanche.

He wasn't sure he could handle another minute out in this cold. Instead of running around to the driver's side and trying to wedge the door open so close to the upward slant of the mountain, Peter clambered into his truck behind Alanna and Chance. His limbs were clumsy from the cold. He slammed the door shut behind him, pressing awkwardly against the dog until Chance leaped into the back to get out of the way. Then, Alanna scooted into the driver's seat, giving him a little space.

He'd left the truck running with the heat blasting, but he could barely feel it now. He turned it up all the way, then yanked off his sopping wet gloves. He reached up to take off his hat and discovered it was gone. His short hair was iced over and when he ran his hand through it, ice and water flew across the seat. Thrusting his hands in front of the heater, he glanced at Alanna, who'd slumped against the seat and closed her eyes.

"Come on," he told her and started unzipping her thick coat, which was definitely made for an Alaskan winter but not for getting buried in an avalanche. His fingers felt too big, swollen beyond their normal size and clumsy. But at least he could feel them, the stinging pain assuring him the nerves still worked.

"What are you doing?" she demanded, but the question had no heat. Her eyes opened, then drifted closed again.

"We've got to get out of these wet clothes," he muttered, running his tongue over his lip, which was way past chapped and split open as he spoke. "Come on," he said again, and this time, Chance pitched in.

The St. Bernard pressed his big head through the space between the seats and grabbed Alanna's sleeve with his mouth, tugging on it until she opened her eyes again.

She turned toward him sluggishly. "You okay, Chance?"

"He saved us," Peter said, giving the dog a quick pat on the head. "I guess he knows St. Bernards are snow rescue dogs."

Chance let go of Alanna's coat long enough to give a brief bark, which made Peter laugh and startled Alanna, finally seeming to focus her.

"It's so cold," she said, trying to tug the zipper back up on her coat.

"Nope." Peter ignored the squelch of his own uncomfortable, freezing clothes as he shifted to get closer to her. He yanked her gloves off and tossed them on the floor behind them, then awkwardly pulled off her coat.

At least she could feel the cold. Her hands were bright red, which was definitely better than being unnaturally white, but they both needed to warm up fast.

Grunting at the uncomfortable angle and his aching body, he leaned over her and unlaced her boots, tugging them off her feet. Then came her thick socks. Her toes were too white and he rubbed them for a minute, then shoved her feet underneath the floor heaters.

When he came back up, she was shivering. A good sign.

"Get the rest of your clothes off," he said, slipping out of his own coat and dumping it on the floor behind him, careful not to drop it on Chance.

"Sorry, buddy," he said, leaning over the dog as he grabbed the stack of blankets he always kept in the vehicle in case of an emergency. Getting stalled out in Desparre could mean death if you weren't prepared.

He set most of the stack between him and Alanna, then tossed one over Chance, rubbing down the dog's back to dry some of the dampness.

Realizing Alanna was just staring at him, he yanked off his sweater and snapped, "Hurry up."

She flushed, a different shade of red flooding along her cheeks and neck, and quickly averted her gaze.

She was only five years younger than him, but he suddenly felt much older. He'd been inside war zones for years, lost most of the hearing in one ear and experienced huge change to his professional and personal life as a result. And her?

He realized he was still staring at her as she tried to cover herself with one of the blankets and shimmy out of her soaking jeans at the same time, so he turned the other way. Then he yanked off his boots and socks, sighing as the blast of heat hit his bare toes.

She'd been kidnapped at five years old and, if news reports could be believed, she'd lived a pretty sheltered life with the Altiers. What had her life been like since she'd returned home to Chicago? Had her real family smothered her, too, afraid to let her out of their sight again? Had she ever ventured out on her own before this?

Resisting the urge to glance at her again, he yanked off the rest of his clothes, shivering as the hot air hit his wet skin. There wasn't much space in the passenger seat, but he managed to get the itchy wool blanket wrapped all the way around him. Then he closed his eyes and let the warmth inside the truck seep into him.

Alanna was on his bad ear's side, but in the close confines of the truck, it didn't matter. All too easily, he could hear her moving around, presumably still in the process of undressing. He squeezed his eyes more tightly shut, suddenly picturing the paleness of her skin, the long, lean legs that had been encased in jeans earlier. Things he had no business imagining.

When the noise finally stopped, he asked tightly, "You covered?"

"Yes."

He opened his eyes, trying not to actually glance at her. But he couldn't help himself.

She was wrapped tightly in the dark wool blanket, covered up to her chin with her drenched hair draped over the front of the blanket and sticking to the seat behind her. Her cheeks were still a patchy red, but it was the bright red of standing outside in Alaska too long, not from embarrassment or shyness.

"You okay?" he asked, staring into her deep brown eyes. It suddenly hit him how beautiful she was.

He hadn't noticed it before, not really. He'd been far too busy trying to figure out how she'd gone from kidnap victim to accomplice, enabler and defender of criminals.

But she wasn't out here, risking her life, just for Darcy. She was here for those kids, too, kids she probably identified with because she'd once been in exactly their position. She had to be.

One of her hands slipped free from the mounds of wool and squeezed his arm. "Thank you for coming after me."

"It's lucky I happened to be following you around." As soon as the words were out of his mouth, he regretted them, but she laughed.

"Yeah, I guess so."

"Did you mean what you said earlier? About working together to find those kids?"

Tiny lines appeared between her graceful eyebrows. "Of course."

He leaned closer to her, glancing at the gas gauge, and relaxed when he saw that they still had plenty in the tank. They could sit here and warm up a little bit longer. Then again...

He leaned over her, angling so he was looking upward out the window. Being parked around the bend from where the avalanche had hit was a safer spot. The mountain above didn't come down at quite the same sharp angle. It was less prone to avalanches. Still, if the snow above was unstable, he didn't want to sit here and discover he was wrong.

Alanna had squeezed against the back of her seat and

he could practically feel her holding her breath until he sat back and put some distance between them.

"We should probably move."

She twisted in her seat, giving him a glance of bare shoulder as she smiled at Chance, who'd shaken free of the blanket and lay down on the back seat, looking far more relaxed than he should have after digging them out of an avalanche.

"You okay, Chance?"

Her dog lifted his big head, strained forward and licked her cheek.

"Guess so," she said, laughing as she turned forward again. She squirmed inside the blanket until she had it wrapped around her more like a towel, her arms and shoulders bare. Then she twisted and tucked it around her knees and gripped the wheel. "I'm not running around the truck to change seats and I think climbing over each other will be a disaster. So, how about I drive?"

He blinked back at her, suddenly conjuring an image of the two of them tangled together, wool blankets awkwardly between them and nothing else. "You drive and I'll direct. Let's go to my house and figure out a plan."

She stared at him a long minute, the air suddenly tense between them, until finally she gave a short nod and shifted the truck into Drive. She made a careful turn and they headed back up the mountain, past the Altiers' old home, and then downward again, back to Desparre's downtown.

With every mile, he snuck glances at her, her hands tense on the wheel, her hair slowly drying and curling slightly against the wool blanket. She seemed more serious in profile, older somehow, and Peter wondered which Alanna was the real one.

The woman who'd held tight to her dog, even at the risk of being tossed over the edge of the mountain by the avalanche? Who'd offered to help the police catch someone she obviously still cared about? Who'd blushed when he stripped his sweater off, even when she should have been more concerned about her own physical well-being?

Or was she the person who'd defended the couple who'd kidnapped her? Still the child who'd been molded by two kidnappers, who'd had her emotions manipulated for so long that her loyalty would always lie in the wrong place?

By keeping her close, he could keep her safe. But would he just be putting himself back in the same position he had two years ago, risking his own safety for someone who was beyond saving?

Alanna Morgan looked good in his house, looked good in his clothes.

Peter scowled at the ridiculous thought as he handed her a steaming cup of coffee and settled on the chair across from her, Chance on the floor between them. He'd started a fire as soon as they'd walked through the door. Now it was blazing, almost too hot, but it felt good after being buried in the snow. He took a long sip of his coffee, making a mental note to grab their clothes from his truck soon and toss them all in the dryer. The sooner she was back in her own clothes, the better it would be for his focus.

He still had his suspicions about Alanna, still wondered how much he could trust her, but now sympathy was mixed in with those other emotions. She had to be carrying so many conflicting feelings about her past, about Darcy, about her future. He knew that territory well, and he wanted to reassure her that she could make it through just as he had done.

The drive to his house had been quiet. All of Alanna's attention had been on navigating the Alaskan roads and she'd handled them better than most of the locals. It reminded him of something else he'd heard through the rumor mill: the Altiers had taught the kids they'd kidnapped all kinds of survival skills. He knew she could lose a tail better than most police officers. Still, when it came to searching for Darcy, she'd acted with emotion rather than intellect. Both he and Alanna should have known those back mountain roads could be dangerous, and still, they'd persisted.

Was it a mistake to bring her here? A mistake to let her get too close? Because even though she might help him find Darcy and those kids, Alanna was still a threat, too. Maybe not intentionally, but when it came right down to it, who would she choose to help? Those kids and a police officer she'd just met, or a woman who'd raised her for most of her life?

Right now she was glancing around his home with open curiosity. It was cozy in a definably Alaskan way, with big windows that showcased the wilderness outside, exposed wooden beams and huge, open living spaces. She took in the long row of black-and-white photographs on one wall. They were images from his time overseas, mostly inside war zones. Images his family always complained about when they came over, images they'd pushed him to take down as his nieces and nephews started asking about them. Images he still kept up so he'd never forget. There was only one photo he'd never hung, one that had appeared in newspapers across the country. He touched his bad ear, scowled when he realized what he was doing and refocused on Alanna.

She frowned slightly at the photos, then turned her gaze out the window as he studied her.

Five years ago, he'd been too caught up in his own life to pay a lot of attention to a group of kids, ages six to twenty-three, rescued from kidnappers so near his hometown. But when he'd first come home, feeling totally adrift and with no idea what he'd do with the rest of his life, he'd read a lot about the story. He'd scoffed at statements made by the victims saying they'd been loved and well-treated. But admittedly, he'd been biased by his own experiences. He still was.

"Tell me about life with the Altiers."

She shifted to face him, her suspicion of his motives all over her face. Still, she answered softly, earnestly, "I don't know why she's doing this, but Darcy would never hurt those kids."

"She already has," Peter snapped, regretting the words as he spoke them but unable to call them back. "She kidnapped them. Don't you remember how that felt?" Way to get beyond his own biases. "I'm sorry." He sighed, not wanting to tell her about his own past but wondering if that was the best way to reach her.

Before he could, she set down her coffee and leaned toward him. Chance's head popped up, glancing between them, obviously sensing the tension. "I do remember. I still have nightmares about it sometimes. I know you don't understand how I can—" she took an audible breath, then stared him straight in the eyes as she finished "—love them."

"I do understand that." Or at least, he understood that she *thought* what she felt was love, instead of a complicated mix of fear and dependency, multiplied over fourteen years. "The attachment you can develop for someone who holds you against your will is real. It can be necessary for survival and then it gets ingrained. It's—"

Her snort of disbelief cut him off. She looked offended when she replied, "I got a psychology degree after I left Alaska. I understand why you think that's what's happening here, but don't forget—I'm the one who turned them in. They both went to jail because I left that note. My… Julian *died* because of me."

Peter frowned, scooting to the edge of his seat, wanting to reach for her hand across the coffee table and assure her that none of it was her fault. But he'd done that once before in his life as a war reporter, and it was amazing he'd come out of that situation with only lost hearing.

She squeezed her eyes briefly shut, then continued, "I know what they did was wrong. I think *they* know what they did was wrong. But I lived almost my whole childhood with that family. They were the ones who held me when I cried, who made me laugh with their silly jokes, who cheered for me when I accomplished something. The only thing they ever did to hurt me was take me from my family."

"Isn't that enough?" Peter asked, straining to keep his voice neutral.

"That's how my family feels," Alanna said, her hands clasping together so tightly that her knuckles went white. "But how much do you remember from before you were five? If you'd gone to live with someone else for most of your childhood, how many memories would you have of your family before that?"

Probably sensing her distress, Chance stood and went to her, plopping his big head in her lap and making a brief smile spread across her lips. It faded as soon as Peter spoke.

"You're telling me you hardly remembered your family?" He tried to imagine that, being ripped from his family as a kindergartener by two people who then called themselves his parents, who treated him well and raised him with love. An ache twisted in his heart at the idea. Worse, he could suddenly picture it, could understand why she'd grown to love them and probably forgot more and more of life with her real family as the years went on.

"I remembered enough," Alanna answered, her voice softer now, as if she knew she was getting through to him. "But sometimes, love is irrational. And sometimes years of good actions start to outweigh one bad one, no matter how terrible that moment was."

"And still, you turned them in. Why?" What had changed after fourteen years to make her write that note?

"I didn't want to go the rest of my life without ever knowing the parents I vaguely remembered, the sister and brother I'd had."

Something passed over her face, a wave of sadness that told him she'd sacrificed a lot to fulfill that wish. More than just the loss of two people who'd acted like her parents most of her childhood, but also four other kids she'd loved as siblings. Four other kids who, from all accounts, had also felt loved in that household. Who probably missed Alanna as much as she missed them.

"Have you seen Darcy and Julian since they went to jail?"

She stiffened, straightened in a way that made his internal lie detector go off.

"No."

"But you've talked to them?" he guessed.

"No."

Was she lying? He couldn't tell. But if she wasn't... "Alanna, you need to be careful. I know Darcy and Julian loved you once. But you did turn them in. You said what Darcy's doing now makes no sense. Maybe she changed in prison."

He frowned, knowing that in terms of the investigation, it was a mistake to say any more, but he needed her to recognize the threat against her, to keep herself safe, too. She'd agreed to work with him, but theirs was a tentative truce, at best. She didn't trust him any more than he trusted her, even if he was beginning to sympathize with her. Even if he was starting to like her as a person.

That was a mistake, too, but one he couldn't seem to help. These days, it was his job to risk his life to protect others, even if they put him in danger.

He touched his bad ear again, watched her gaze narrow as she followed his movement.

"Darcy would never hurt me," Alanna said, but her voice lacked confidence.

"You can't know that," Peter insisted. "So, let's make a deal. You want to work together to find those kids? I'm in. But I'm law enforcement, so you're going to let me keep you safe. No more going off on your own to search for her. We stick together from here on out. Deal?"

She looked ready to argue, but after a long moment, she simply nodded.

"Now, where were you going today?"

"I think I have some ideas about where Darcy might go. Julian had backup hiding spots."

Anger flooded through him at the realization that she'd kept this to herself. She'd been gunning for one of those hiding spots and if he hadn't been following her, that information would have been lost. Those kids might have been lost. Maybe for fourteen long years, like she had been. Maybe longer.

This time, he held his anger inside and asked, "Where are these hiding spots?"

Panic rushed over her face and she leaped to her feet, making Chance jump up, too. The pair of them ran to his garage, and Alanna yanked open the back door of his truck, climbing inside as he caught up to them.

When Chance tried to climb in with her, Alanna put up a hand. "Stay, Chance."

The St. Bernard promptly sat, but he looked back at Peter as if to say, *Can't I go, too?*

"We're not going anywhere, Chance," Peter told him as Alanna climbed back out, unzipping an interior pocket of her bright red coat.

The coat was still sopping wet and so was the small piece of paper she pulled out of the pocket.

She unfolded it with infinite care, then swore as she looked back up at him, dismay in her eyes. "It's gone."

"What's gone?"

"The list of locations I found at the house. All the places Darcy might be hiding."

Chapter 7

"I can't believe it's gone," Alanna said, staring at the little scrap of paper. She hadn't been able to toss it in the trash, even after putting it under a blow-dryer confirmed that all the pencil marks were lost.

Peter sat next to her, taking the smaller spot on the couch to her left instead of the bigger space to her right. "You read the list, right? Maybe if you think about it, you can recall some of the places?"

The heat from his body warmed her still-cold legs and she tried not to fixate on his closeness. It was just residual embarrassment from stripping out of her clothes in his car. Even covered by a blanket, it had been awkward. She'd had to use a lot of willpower not to glance his way as he'd stripped off his clothes—thank goodness he'd eventually wrapped a blanket around himself.

The memory made her hyperaware of the shocking

blue of his eyes, the sharp lines of his face and the lean power of his build. He wasn't traditionally handsome, but there was something compelling about him. Maybe it was part of what had made him a good war reporter, the ability to project such intensity that it made it hard to look away.

"Alanna?" Peter pressed.

"I read the list. But it was coordinates, latitude and longitude, and it was in code."

"Code? Are you serious?"

"A silly code. My sis—the other kids and I made it up one winter when we had a bad storm and we were stuck inside. It was just a game, but we left codes for each other all over the house for a week." She shrugged at the interest in his gaze, remembering how much fun they'd had running around the house to find coded clues like a scavenger hunt. "My par—the Altiers got in on the game, too. I'd forgotten all about it until I saw this list."

"It sounds like a good time."

His tone was hesitant, speculative, and Alanna held in a sigh. Reporters—at least reporters actively chasing a story—got right to the point. But once anyone else would realize her history, they'd just pick at the edges. They'd ask sideways questions, looking for insight and pretending to understand, before they announced, "But these people *kidnapped* you." As if she didn't know.

Usually, for Alanna, that was the beginning of the end. It was too awkward to try to convince people that she'd been loved, that she'd loved in return. More awkward still to feel like she had to justify it. It was easier to break ties, keep to herself.

When she'd gone back to Chicago, she'd ventured outside her comfort zone with school and volunteer work. But after an initial burst of interest by anyone with the remotest connection to the Morgans, she'd found herself becoming more and more isolated socially. Kensie and Colter, Alanna's new brother-in-law, had decided something had to be done. Alanna had connected with Colter's dog, Rebel, a former Marine Combat Tracker Dog who had been as good for Alanna's anxiety as Colter's PTSD. So they'd found her a dog of her own, rescuing Chance to give to her.

She smiled at the St. Bernard who'd been so little two years ago, a victim of such cruelty that the vets weren't even sure he would survive. Now, still small for his breed, he was a total gentle giant. And he'd definitely rescued her as much as she'd rescued him.

At her smile, Chance pushed his way between the couch and the coffee table to drop his head in her lap. She stroked his head as she told Peter, "Drew and Valerie, the youngest kids, didn't remember their real families at all. They had no idea they were kidnapped. And we—Johnny, Sydney, and I—didn't tell them because they were so young and because honestly, we hardly remembered our own families. How do you break that to someone? Especially when they're happy?"

"Sydney was the one who remembered her family best, right? She was a few years younger than you?"

Alanna eyed him. "You've done your research."

He flinched, actually looking a little ashamed. "I read up on it when I came back home—to what used to be my home—two years ago. I lived on the other side of the mountain, in Luna, where you were reunited with your sister. When you showed up in Desparre this week..."

"You read through all the news reports again?"

He nodded, not quite meeting her gaze.

The coverage in Desparre hadn't been the most flattering, especially after time went on and reporters looked for a new angle to keep the story alive. They'd all seen her as that new angle. She might have turned the Altiers in, but the real story was how she *hadn't* spoken up for fourteen years.

"No wonder you acted like you already knew and disliked me as soon as you heard my name."

The Morgans had tried to keep the negative coverage from her at first. She'd been getting her GED and applying to college then, trying to get out into the world and reenter her life from fourteen years earlier. But she hadn't been able to stop herself from seeking out the news coverage on herself and the rest of the "family" she'd left behind.

"Hey." Peter's voice was soft, his eyebrows lowered as he put his hand over her free one.

She froze, her other hand stalling in Chance's fur, as his long fingers threaded through hers. The unexpected contact made her skin tingle.

"I didn't dislike you as soon as I knew who you were. I just—"

"Distrusted me?"

"Yes."

She hadn't expected him to admit it. Even though she'd already known it was true, the quiet word seemed to leave a physical mark on her chest. She slid her hand free and glanced away, hoping he hadn't seen that he'd hurt her.

She looked back just as quickly, tired of having to explain herself, tired of being judged by what people read in newspapers about her past instead of by who she was or her actions now. "Everyone thinks they would have gotten help right away, that they would have spent all those years hating the people who'd raised them. But if you haven't lived it—"

"I'm not judging you."

"No?"

Chance lifted his head from her lap at her sarcastic tone.

"Do you know why my fa… Julian was killed in jail?"

Peter frowned, gave a brief shake of his head.

"He was protecting a twenty-year-old kid who was being preyed on sexually. The predator stabbed Julian in the chest sixteen times for it." She choked on the last words, imagining the man who'd raised her being cornered, brutally attacked and dying on a filthy prison floor.

Peter reached for her and his intent to pull her into a hug was as clear as the confusion in his eyes. He was struggling to reconcile his idea of a child kidnapper with a man who'd risk his life to protect someone he barely knew.

She blocked his hug with a hand to his chest, resisting the urge to fist her hand into his sweatshirt and yank him toward her. To accept his hug along with the friendship he offered. Friendship she still couldn't tell was real or fake.

Standing, she swallowed back the tears that threatened every time she thought about the report the prison had issued. "I think I should go."

He stood, too, but slowly, caution in his expression. "I'm sorry. You're right. I have no idea what your life was like. All I know about the Altiers is what I've read in the papers or a law enforcement bulletin. I know better than anyone how those things can spin a story. But I spent years in war zones and I also know this— no one is one hundred percent good or bad. Everyone lives in gray areas, making right decisions one day and wrong ones the next. Sometimes the way we think of people is based on what side of the line the majority of those decisions lie. Sometimes, it's based on a single, dramatic incident."

His hand twitched upward, the way she'd seen it do before, and she had a sudden realization. He had his own single, dramatic incident. "What happened?"

He stared at her a long moment, not even pretending to misunderstand, before he nodded and sank back onto the couch.

Chance moved his head to Peter's leg, offering his quiet support in a way Alanna had seen him do hundreds of times at the nonprofit where she worked. From the very beginning, when she'd had him certified as a therapy dog so she could bring him to work with her, he'd had a sense of who needed him most.

"I was a war reporter," Peter said, and she nodded, having seen his bylines a time or two. Mostly, she remembered his name from an incident a few years ago, with a picture that had made national headlines: Peter, less fit than he was now, wearing a helmet and covered in sand and blood, one hand to his ear and an expression of horror and disbelief etched on his face.

"You were covering some kind of hostage release," she said, realizing that must have been the incident.

"It was supposed to be smooth and simple. I'd been in far more dangerous situations. The military had brought the ransom money. We were just tagging along—my camera guy and me—to catch the exchange. The hostage-takers hadn't covered their faces—they didn't think they could be identified or they didn't care. The CIA sent one of their officers to make the exchange. She was supposed to walk halfway and leave the money. Then the hostage would walk to us and the hostage-takers would pick up the money and leave. Well, they did take the money and leave."

Peter's hand went halfway to his left ear, then he set it on Chance's head instead, slowly petting the big dog.

"The hostage had been captive for almost six months. She'd watched the other two people who'd been kidnapped with her get killed. We thought she'd be running toward us. But the closer she got, I could see…"

He trailed off, his brows furrowed and his gaze on the wall of photographs across the room.

"What?" Alanna prompted softly.

"I've been to a few hostage exchanges before, where they're expected to go smoothly and our country wants a little good press. Sometimes, the hostages look terrified that something is going to go wrong at any second and they'll be yanked back into the hell they'd been living. Other times, they're crying with relief that it's finally over. And occasionally, they seem like they're not even aware of what's happening. Not this hostage. She was…calm, focused. Stoic, even."

His hand stalled on Chance's head and Alanna set her hand carefully on top of his, offering silent support the way he had for her. The same way she might at work with a survivor or a family member she'd gotten to know over months of visits.

He met her gaze briefly, a hint of a smile twitching on the edge of his lips. Then he looked back at his photos. "I was standing closest when the explosion went off."

Even though she'd seen the photos, had known he'd been close to an explosion, she still gasped at the idea of him being nearest to a bomb. Her fingers clenched reflexively over his. Chance's head tipped up, his attention bouncing to her, then back to Peter.

Alanna tried to remember the details of the article she'd read two years ago, but all she could recall were the details of the photo. Of Peter's face, dripping with blood. Back then, it had been a horrible sight, but now, knowing Peter made every detail more painful. She felt an ache in her chest thinking about what he'd experienced. "What happened? The hostage-takers threw a bomb during the rescue?"

He gave a humorless laugh, his gaze focused on her once more, all his intensity and cynicism directed at her. "They didn't throw anything. It was strapped to the hostage. She set it off herself when she got close to us."

Tension bloomed between them as she stared back at him. Suddenly, it all made sense. His instant distrust of her, his insistence that she must be working with Darcy. He thought she was just like the hostage who'd almost killed him: willing to do whatever it took to help someone she should have wanted behind bars, at the expense of anyone else. As that realization dawned, Peter said softly, "I quit my job after that. I'd wanted to be a reporter my whole life, but after that moment, I never wanted to go into another war zone. I sat around for a good six months, then saw a job posting for a police officer. This hostage almost destroyed that dream, too. The police have strict fitness and health requirements, and with the extent of my hearing loss… They only took me because they were desperate for officers."

His hand went up again, and this time, he did touch his left ear. "I lost most of the hearing in this ear in the explosion."

Alanna's heart gave a sudden, painful ache. He thought she was the same as that woman who, in the face of rescue, had destroyed herself and tried to take out everyone around her in the process. No wonder Peter didn't trust her.

He was never going to trust her.

Alanna was silent in the passenger seat as Peter drove her and Chance in his truck the long way around the base of the mountain the next day. They were headed for Luna. Five years ago, Luna police had stopped the Altiers and arrested them. They'd loaded her and her "siblings" into a police car and driven them to the Luna hospital to be checked out. It was the last place she'd seen any of the people she'd called family for most of her childhood.

Last night, Peter had asked if she wanted to go there, to get checked out at the hospital after being trapped in that avalanche. But she had no desire to go back to that hospital, to those memories. And besides still feeling cold and being exhausted, she'd been okay. The worst of it was calling her rental company to let them know what had happened to their truck.

The fastest way to get to Luna was actually to drive up into the mountain and then back down. But after the avalanche yesterday, that wasn't happening. So, she and Peter had spent an awkward hour and a half in his truck. They had at least another hour to go before they made it to the far side of town, where Alanna thought one of Julian's hideouts might be.

She'd spent a long time last night trying to decode the old cipher she and her "siblings" had created, without much luck. But in the morning, she'd had an epiphany about one of them. Hopefully, she was right, because she'd convinced Peter to trust her and come along without notifying his department.

There was a new tension between them since he'd admitted what had happened to him. The uncomfortable silence was worse than sleeping in Peter's guest bedroom, hearing him move around one room over. Smelling like his soap and shampoo, and knowing he hadn't insisted she stay at his place because of the roads, like he'd claimed. The truth was, he didn't trust her not to go off on her own, even though she'd promised she wouldn't.

She squeezed her hands tightly together and said, "Maybe that woman didn't blow herself up. Maybe the explosive had a remote detonator."

"No," Peter replied, not even sounding surprised to hear the suggestion after an hour and a half of near-silence. "There was an investigation. She set it off herself."

"Well, you don't know what they told her. Maybe she felt like she had no choice. Maybe they threatened to kill her family if she didn't do it. I've heard that more than once from victims of violent crime. The person who did it threatens someone they love if they ever talk. After the things they've suffered, the victim believes it. This could be a more extreme version."

"Maybe," Peter agreed. He glanced her way, looking intrigued, and she realized that he didn't know what she did for a living.

"I work for a nonprofit back home." Calling anywhere *home* besides Desparre still felt strange, especially now that she was back in Alaska, but it was true. Chicago had become her home now.

The thought wiggled around in her brain, bittersweet. Maybe she was truly starting to let go of the people she'd loved most of her life.

Her parents, Kensie, Colter and Flynn had all worked hard to bring her into their lives, to show her how much they loved her. There was still so much missing, so many memories with them she'd never be able to have, but she'd never stopped loving them, either.

Shaking off her musings for another time, Alanna said, "The nonprofit works with victims of violent crime."

"You're a therapist?" He sounded surprised.

"No. It's not that kind of place. We do have support groups, and I've gotten Chance certified as a therapy dog so he can come and sit with people. But we also help people navigate the legal system, act as an intermediary with police when necessary and help them transition back to their regular life. Technically, my job is as a case manager, so I help identify what people need when they first come to us."

"Why did you choose violent crime?"

She darted a glance at him, expecting to see suspicion on his face. When most people heard about her past and her career choice, they assumed she'd been harmed during her years with the Altiers, despite her insistence otherwise.

"I guess I just…" She sighed, wishing it was something she knew how to put in words. "When I came home, I got a lot of attention. All these people I didn't know wanted to help me. They meant well, even if it made me anxious to have them come up to me and ask for details, looking like they just wanted a good story. But in some ways, it was a good thing. The fact that we were all found after so many years inspired a pair of ex-cops who lived near me to start a cold case club. They've solved a dozen cases since then."

Peter nodded, his gaze catching hers briefly before he looked back out the front windshield. The road had been cleared yesterday, but had a new dusting of snow from the morning. "You're doing it out of guilt."

She frowned. "Not guilt—"

"I don't mean it in a bad way. Just—I get it. You feel like these other people who had it worse than you should be getting the attention, the resources, you did."

"Sort of." She fidgeted in her seat, uncomfortable sharing this but somehow feeling he'd empathize. No one else had understood it quite so well. "I also understand how confusing it is to try to fit back into your normal life. I don't identify with the way most of these people have been harmed. But I understand some of it. My case got a lot of press, so most of them recognize my name. They tell me it makes them feel more connected to me, because I've personally experienced some of it. And I like helping people."

"You're a good person."

There was such honesty in his voice, mixed with just a hint of surprise, that Alanna wasn't sure what to say. Her "thanks" was delayed and too quiet.

Peter shrugged, giving her a little grin that sent a

flutter of awareness through her. "Don't thank me. That's all on you."

She felt herself grin in response and the tension that had filled the truck since they'd sat together at his breakfast table this morning finally eased. Even Chance seemed to feel it, scooting forward and shoving his head through the space between the seats.

Alanna stroked his silky fur as she stared at Peter's profile. She had a sudden vision of the first moment he'd approached her four days ago, the way he'd angled his body, making his weapon more visible. But his right side wasn't just where he kept his gun; it was also the side with his good ear. He'd done it so he could hear her better, not to intimidate her.

Maybe there were other things she was misinterpreting, too. Yes, he'd admitted he hadn't trusted her when he'd met her. But he'd let her stay in his house. He'd called in to work this morning and she'd overheard him telling someone he was running a lead today and would be late for his Sunday shift. He hadn't mentioned her involvement.

It was the deal they'd struck. She'd share the location she thought she'd figured out from the ruined list and they'd check it out, just the two of them.

So far, he was keeping up his end of the bargain. She had her doubts that he would continue to do so if they actually found Darcy, but this seemed to be the best way forward.

She'd insisted on secrecy because she'd feared if police showed up, it would escalate everything and Darcy might do something stupid. Alanna's gut clenched at the memory of Darcy and Johnny shooting at Kensie five years ago. If the police were there this time, they would see the kidnapper lifting a weapon as a legitimate reason to open fire in return. Her concern had been that Darcy would end up getting herself killed.

But suddenly, she was struck with a totally different worry.

If it was just her and Darcy, Alanna wanted to believe she could talk some sense into the woman who'd raised her since she was five years old. She wanted to believe that if Peter's presence threatened Darcy, Alanna standing in front of him would keep him safe. But was that realistic?

Or was she fooling herself?

As Peter met her gaze again, giving her a quick, genuine smile, she tried to smile back.

He was prickly, and she still wasn't totally sure where she stood with him. But he was smart and capable and he'd run to save her when he could have just as easily stepped back and saved himself from that avalanche. From the moment he'd wrapped his fingers in her coat and held on even as the snow threatened to send them both over a mountain, she'd started to care about him. Probably more than she should.

If she was wrong about Darcy, was she risking Peter's life by bringing him with her?

Chapter 8

Peter stared at Alanna across the tiny wooden table in the overcrowded coffee shop in downtown Luna. She was back in the jeans and light purple sweater she'd been wearing yesterday, but he couldn't stop picturing her the way she'd looked last night in his too-large sweatpants and long-sleeved T-shirt.

She flushed at his stare, redirecting her gaze to the steaming cup of coffee in her hands. At her side, Chance sat patiently, his size making him look like her protector.

The coffee shop had been here since he was a teenager and he'd spent hours in front of the fireplace over the years. Playing board games from the stack the owners always kept on hand or reading a book from the shelves on the far wall. With a first date or a long-term girlfriend. With family or a group of friends. Or, in those first six months after coming home, feeling adrift and unsure of what the rest of his life held, by himself.

They were less than twenty minutes from the location Alanna thought she'd identified from the Altiers' coded list. Peter had told her he wanted to stop here to take a break from driving, to rest a little before a possible confrontation with Darcy. The truth was, he needed to give his fellow officers a chance to catch up.

He'd called in to the station that morning, giving the story he and Alanna had agreed upon: he was running a long-shot lead and would let them know how it panned out. She'd been just around the corner, listening in, not realizing he could see her reflection in the mirror across the hall.

When she'd slipped back down the hall, he'd quickly texted Tate with the real story. He felt guilty about it— and Tate had also reminded him that technically, the Desparre police department had no jurisdiction here. But he trusted his partner. He didn't know the Luna officers. He had no idea what Darcy would do if she was cornered, but he wanted to make sure Alanna was safe.

Still, he didn't like betraying her trust.

A few days ago, that wouldn't have mattered to him. He would have considered it a necessary lie for the possibility of rescuing those kids. Now, after the things she'd shared about her life with the Altiers, he understood why her loyalty was conflicted. For the first time in two years, he even sympathized with the woman who'd killed herself—and almost killed him—when she'd been on the verge of being rescued.

He'd always pitied her. But there'd been too much anger for more than that. Peter had always assumed the hostage had been brainwashed, that she'd hit that detonator to protect the terrorists who had taken her. Maybe he'd been wrong. Maybe she'd done it to protect her family, because after nearly six months of being terrorized, she could see no other option.

"What are you thinking?" Alanna asked.

When he blinked and refocused, he realized she was staring at him with an expression that said too many emotions had been obvious on his face.

"You're nothing like I expected," he blurted. From all the headlines, all the newspaper stories, he'd expected a conflicted, confused woman who'd grown up isolated and brainwashed, who'd come to Desparre for her own agenda.

A hesitant smile turned up her lips, warmed her deep brown eyes. "I assume that's a good thing?"

He was attracted to her. The realization slammed into him with an intensity that made him slump back in his chair. It wasn't just her long, silky hair, those plump lips or the secrets in the depths of her eyes. He'd seen too much as a reporter, on both sides of the camera, to really care about that anymore. It was the integrity of her character, the way she tried to do right by everyone, whether they deserved it or not. It was the way she'd clung to Chance in that avalanche, even when letting him go might have been safer for her. It was the way she challenged Peter at every turn, made him rethink his assumptions about everything.

"What?" she asked, sounding concerned as she leaned toward him, put her hand over his.

"Peter!"

What terrible timing. Peter slowly swiveled in his chair to find his parents standing behind him, both holding takeout cups of coffee. His father was looking at

Alanna curiously. His mother was smiling at him in a way that told him she'd totally misunderstood what was happening.

"Mom, Dad." He stood, hugged them both and then gestured to Alanna, who was also standing. "This is Alanna."

When Chance gave a short bark, attracting attention from nearby customers, Peter laughed and added, "And this big guy is Chance."

The St. Bernard wagged his tail at the introduction and Peter's mom scratched his ears as his dad shook Alanna's hand.

"Do you live in Luna, Alanna?" his mom asked, giving him a quick grin she probably thought was subtle.

He wanted to laugh and roll his eyes at the same time. Getting him to move back to Luna was a dream she was unwilling to give up on, even now that he'd lived and worked in Desparre for a year.

"Actually, I live in Chicago."

His mom's brow furrowed, then she breathed, "You're Alanna Morgan, aren't you?" Before Alanna could answer, she looked at Peter with concern in her eyes. "This isn't another story, is it?"

"No, Mom." He shook his head at Alanna for emphasis, but she didn't seem worried by the question, just uncomfortable that his mom had recognized her.

His mom seemed to realize it, too, because she smiled again and said, "Well, we're just off to a movie. You two have a nice time."

"Come by for dinner soon," his dad said as they headed for the door.

"They're nice," Alanna said.

"They're still upset I've moved to Desparre. They

thought when I finally gave up being a reporter, I'd come home to Luna like my brothers and sister."

She leaned toward him. "You've got siblings?"

Peter glanced at the front of the shop and saw his mom grinning back at him before she slipped out the door. He realized that she might have incorrectly thought this was a date, but in some ways, it felt like one.

"Three," he replied, shifting his full attention back to Alanna, suddenly wishing they could both shake free of their past baggage, of their reasons for being here together right now. Wishing it was really a date. But he could pretend it was, if only for a few minutes, to buy time. "Two older brothers and one older sister. They've all got kids and they all live in Luna. My parents keep hoping I'll follow their lead."

Alanna smiled, sipping her coffee. "That's nice."

He shrugged. "It's a nice idea." But he'd always been restless, always wanted to get out and see the world, do something that got his blood moving, that made a difference. For five years, he'd done it as a reporter. Since he'd returned to Alaska, he'd discovered that being a police officer filled that need. He'd never been able to understand how the rest of his family didn't have the same restlessness.

"You wouldn't ever move back to Luna?"

"Probably not. Don't get me wrong—I love my family. But it's not like there are tons of opportunities in Luna. They're lucky I got the police officer spot nearby."

"Well, it's close until Desparre gets a particularly bad snow and you can't get over here for months," she said, reminding him that she knew Desparre at least as well as he did.

"When I was a reporter, sometimes they wouldn't see me for six months at a time."

"It's got to be hard for them. First, you're in war zones and now you're a police officer, potentially under fire at any given moment." She looked a little queasy at the idea.

"My grandparents moved here from Czechoslovakia—back when that's what it was called. During the Czech uprising in 1968, when the Soviets sent in half a million tanks and troops, they fled. At first, they thought they'd stick around, be part of the protests. But they didn't like living among so many tanks, the constant unspoken threat of violence. Ultimately they decided they had to get out—about three hundred thousand people there felt the same way. My grandparents said they came here because they just wanted to be left alone. I grew up hearing their stories and the stories they'd been told by *their* parents about what their country was like at the time of the Nazi invasion."

Alanna nodded slowly, probably thrown by his change of topic. "I don't blame them for wanting to live peacefully, quietly, after all of that."

"Yeah, I guess," Peter said. His parents had wanted the same thing and so did his siblings. "But I always felt like it was in my blood to get out there and witness conflict. To record it for history and, hopefully, help prevent us from repeating it." He shrugged, suddenly embarrassed by how naive he sounded.

She reached across the table and put her hand on his. "I understand that, too."

She understood because in her own way, she'd chosen a similar path. They were both in professions to help others.

He smiled back at her, realizing how natural it felt to be sitting in this coffee shop with her, their hands stacked together. If this *had* been a date, if she was someone he'd met who lived in Desparre or Luna, he'd already be planning to ask her out again.

His smile faded. If she was right, if they found Darcy hiding in Luna, it would all be over. Alanna would return home and he'd never see her again.

From the moment they'd set foot in Alaska, Darcy and Julian had loved the mountains. So Alanna wasn't surprised when Peter slowed the truck near the location she'd identified and it was at the base of the mountain they'd driven on last night.

When they'd settled in Desparre, Darcy and Julian had built their home at the edge of the mountaintop, with the natural protection of a steep slope at their back. Here, apparently, they'd done the same thing in reverse. Only this time, there was just Darcy.

The cabin was much smaller than the one in Desparre. It looked like a single-room shack and if anyone drove close enough to see it through the trees, it seemed deserted.

Alanna's shoulders dropped as she peered through the windshield. "What if I'm wrong?" There had been four other locations on that list, but although she'd tried to recall the other symbols and decode them, nothing she'd worked out in the little notebook Peter had given her made sense yet. She wasn't sure it ever would.

Peter's hands were resting lightly on the wheel, but there was an excitement in his gaze that told her how much he loved chasing leads. "What's the likelihood that there'd be a cabin at the exact longitude and latitude you decoded?"

He was right about that. Like a lot of Alaska, the towns of Desparre and Luna were more open land than homes or businesses. Her discouragement turned to anxiety. "Maybe I should go up to the door alone. If she's there, I might be able to talk her into giving herself up."

"We agreed we'd go together," Peter replied, then turned into the driveway.

"If she's here, you're going to scare her o—"

The words died on her lips as the cabin's front door opened and Darcy stepped halfway through the threshold, backlit by a light inside that had been blocked by the heavy curtains on the windows.

Shock jolted through Alanna. She'd come all the way to Alaska to find Darcy, but after five years, on some level, she'd never expected to see her again. All the letters Darcy and Julian had sent from prison had gone unanswered, mostly because Alanna knew how much it would hurt her biological parents for her to respond, how badly they needed her to make a clean break. She couldn't bring herself to cut off her "siblings," so she'd made the choice to cut off Darcy and Julian. Every letter had been returned, unopened.

All these years later, it still physically hurt to wonder what Darcy and Julian had written her. Had they been letters of remorse, letters of love? Or had their love turned to hate over the note she had written and left in Jasper's General Store in an attempt to go home to the Morgans?

Darcy had been sentenced to sixty-two years in prison without the possibility of parole. Julian had gotten sixty-three years, and if he hadn't been killed in prison, he would still have died there. Since the moment she'd chosen not to communicate with them, Alanna had hardened herself to the idea of never seeing Darcy or Julian again. In so many ways, it had felt like the right thing to do, the only thing she *could* do. A penance she had to make for fourteen years of silence.

The Darcy in front of her was thinner, her hair almost entirely gray and lackluster. Her once stick-straight posture was now slumped, defeated. Every day she'd spent in prison seemed to show in the new lines on her face.

Alanna couldn't take her gaze off Darcy as she climbed out of Peter's truck and took a step up the driveway. Behind her, she heard Chance leap over the seat and out the door.

Across the thirty feet separating them, Darcy's eyes seemed to widen comically, then her gaze darted right. Toward Peter. Her eyes narrowed, her lips twisting into an angry scowl. When she stepped fully outside, there was a pistol tucked into her belt at her hip and a shotgun clutched in her hand.

It was a nightmare right out of her memory. Five years seemed to disappear, and instead of Peter beside her, it was Kensie, who had found her after so many years lost. She could see Darcy lifting that shotgun and firing at the truck where Kensie and Colter sat. Alanna heard the echoes of her own screams from back then in her ears as she threw her hands wide and ran toward Darcy.

This time, although Darcy's gaze kept darting toward Peter—and then toward the street, like she expected backup to come flying in, sirens blaring, at any second—she never lifted her gun. Instead, as Alanna got closer, slowing to a walk until she stood still a few feet away, Darcy shook her head and whispered, "*Why?*"

Up close, the lines on Darcy's face were even more pronounced, the dark circles under her eyes more hollow. Anger lurked just underneath the hurt that flashed in her eyes. The pain and betrayal she felt were as obvious in her voice as the tears she was trying to blink back. "*Why?*" she demanded again, this time almost a scream.

Chance stepped up beside Alanna and she reached for him fast, put a steadying hand on his head to assure him he wasn't in danger.

Darcy's gaze shifted to Chance and her lips shifted into a strange semblance of a smile, an echo of what it had once been. Too quickly, it dropped away. "When you were little, you always wanted a dog." She looked back at Alanna, blinking rapidly. "Guess you got everything you wanted."

Then somehow Peter was beside her, his hand gripping her arm too hard, keeping her in place. His other hand was on the butt of his weapon. "We just want the kids. That's it. You hand them over and we walk away."

Darcy did little more than smirk at Peter's offer, her hand shifting on the shotgun with an ease that told Alanna she might look older and weaker, but Darcy still had an unexpected strength. Then her gaze was back on Alanna.

"Who is this? Why is he here?"

"He's my friend, Peter," Alanna said, glad that it was common in Alaska for people to carry weapons. It didn't immediately mark him as law enforcement. "He drove me out here."

"How did you find me?"

"This is where we were headed five years ago, isn't it?" Alanna asked instead of answering.

Darcy's slight nod, as if she couldn't stop herself from responding, was enough to tell Alanna it was true.

Her own anger flared up, the unfairness of it all, the blame she felt from all directions no matter what choices she made. "And then what was the plan? To keep running, go back to what we did when I was little?"

"We wouldn't have needed to do that if you hadn't left that note. We were good to you. We *loved* you." Darcy shook her head, as if she still didn't understand it.

Alanna's gut clenched at Darcy's use of the past tense, but as much as it hurt, this moment wasn't about her. It was about those two kids who had to be in the cabin behind Darcy, probably terrified and confused like Alanna had been in those early days with the Altiers.

"There was another family out there who loved me, too." On some level, Darcy had to know what she'd done was wrong. Didn't she? "How do you think it felt, knowing I'd never get to see them again?"

Something flashed in Darcy's eyes, some mix of guilt and sorrow that was gone so fast Alanna wondered if she'd imagined it. Then Darcy's attention veered left, into the woods at the base of the mountain. Was that where she'd hidden her vehicle? Was she thinking about making a run for it?

"Please," Alanna whispered. "It's not too late to do the right thing."

A spasm of emotion passed over Darcy's face and for a moment, Alanna thought she'd gotten through to her. Then Darcy swung the shotgun up, past Alanna and Peter, high over the woods to her left.

Alanna's hand darted out to grab Peter, to prevent him from pulling his own weapon. What was Darcy doing? Trying to scare them? Had she lost her mind when she'd lost her "kids"?

The *boom boom boom* of the shotgun firing repeatedly echoed, followed by a louder, heavier rumble that made Alanna's heart seem to drop to her stomach. She recognized that sound, had felt the weight of the snow burying her only yesterday.

Her gaze traveled up the side of the mountain, to the weak spot where Darcy had aimed, an overhang of snow that was now rushing downward. It was far enough away that it was unlikely to reach them, so Peter's scream to *watch out* startled her, made her jump.

Then, suddenly, everything around her was noise and motion.

Peter raced toward the oncoming snow, Chance at his heels, as shapes emerged from behind the trees, people trying to escape the avalanche. People who shouldn't have been there at all. People who weren't moving fast enough.

Darcy's gaze lingered on Alanna for a drawn-out moment, then she darted the other way, back into the cabin, slamming the door behind her.

Alanna glanced toward Peter and Chance and the police officers who'd been hiding in the woods, who were being overrun by the snow. Then she glanced back at the cabin, where Darcy was hiding with two young children.

And she made her choice.

Chapter 9

For the second time in two days, Peter was running toward an avalanche.

He'd lived in Alaska for most of his life and managed to never get caught up in one before this past week. Like most people who lived this far north, he had a healthy respect for the power of nature but he'd always taken precautions, so he'd never feared it. The way his heart was thundering in his chest now, that had changed.

This time, he wasn't in any real danger of being buried in it. The snow had already stopped falling from above and the rush through the woods was slowing. That was both good and bad. The trees acting as a natural blockade for some of the snow meant it wouldn't spill over to the cabin, where he assumed those kids were being held. But it also meant more of it was piled higher in the exact location he'd last spotted his fellow officers. Including his partner.

"Tate!" he yelled. Now that the thundering of snow was quieting, his voice echoed along the mountain base, taunting him with the lack of response.

He slowed to a stop before he reached the snow, realizing he should have run to his truck instead to grab the collapsible snow shovel most people who lived in these parts always carried. He spun back even as Chance raced past him, right into the snow.

His call for Alanna to grab his shovel died on his lips. He scanned the area around the cabin. But there were only woods and an empty driveway. She must have followed Darcy inside.

Pain clamped in his chest as he glanced back to the snow, where Chance was frantically digging, then over to the silent cabin. He ran back the way he'd come, heading for his truck and shovel.

He had to pray that Alanna was right and Darcy wouldn't hurt her. He had to pray that Alanna would be able to talk Darcy into handing over the kids without hurting anyone.

There was no mistaking that the woman still loved Alanna like a daughter. It was equally obvious that she felt deeply betrayed and probably blamed Alanna for the years she'd spent in jail, maybe even for her husband's death. Peter could imagine things going shockingly well, that he might turn back and see Alanna ushering out two relieved kids and a sobbing Darcy. Or he might hear a series of shotgun blasts and then Darcy fleeing for safety alone.

Right now he had to trust that Alanna was right. That the love Darcy still felt for her was stronger than the hate. That the education in psychology Alanna had earned and her experience working with vulnerable people would have taught her how to navigate such a volatile situation. One thing he did know: Darcy hadn't fired that shotgun at him before because Alanna had called him her friend. If he burst through that cabin door as an officer, Darcy would shoot.

Alanna had a chance. But his teammates didn't. No way could Chance dig all of them out alone before someone suffocated.

Peter holstered his gun, grabbing his shovel and dialing his phone as he ran. "Chief," he huffed when Chief Hernandez answered, "I need help out here fast. Avalanche." He didn't wait for her response, just tucked his phone back in his pocket and started digging beside Chance.

The big dog had already uncovered the legs of an officer who was facedown. "Good boy, Chance," said Peter. The dog gave a quick bark, then left Peter to finish digging the man out. He bounded a few feet over and started digging again, his big paws sending snow flying, his strong nose right on target as another pair of boots appeared.

"Come on," Peter muttered, trading the shovel for his thinly gloved hands as he got close to the man's face. The fact that he hadn't moved the whole time Peter and Chance had been digging him out was a bad sign, but as Peter swept snow off the back of his head, he suddenly groaned and rolled partway over.

Charlie Quinn was a longtime member of the force, someone Peter had overheard more than once complaining about working with "the pity-hire who can't hear." But when Peter had asked for backup, he'd shown up without complaint.

"You okay?" Peter asked, helping him to a sitting position.

Charlie put a shaky hand to his head, nodding.

"More help is coming," Peter told him, leaving him there so he could go dig out the next officer Chance had found.

As soon as Peter got there, Chance gave him an encouraging *woof* and was off again, sniffing his way to a new spot.

"You're amazing," Peter breathed as he paused a second to watch the St. Bernard. Then he looked back at the partly uncovered officer in front of him and went to work. His hands, arms, and even his face stung as he shoveled snow aside and the cold seeped into him. Finally, he shoved enough snow away to identify the officer.

This wasn't Tate either, but Nate Dreymond. He was the second-newest officer on the force, a twenty-year-old who'd been hired six months before Peter. He was already moving around, flailing and trying to get free of the snow.

"I've got you," Peter said, dropping the shovel and pushing a heavy pile of snow off the young officer, who broke free of the rest covering him so fast and hard that he knocked Peter over.

Nate was gasping, tears and snot mixed with the snow he was raking off his face with bare fingers so pale Peter knew he couldn't feel them.

"Be careful," Peter said, pulling Nate's hands free to reveal he'd scraped up his own face. "Go over there." He pointed toward Charlie. "Help get him into my truck. The heat is on."

As Nate stumbled that way, unsteady on his feet,

Peter warned, "There might still be an armed fugitive in the cabin."

Nate didn't show any sign of hearing him, but Charlie looked up sharply, his hand already on the butt of his pistol. He nodded confidently at Peter, pushing to his feet with a grunt. Then the two of them were leaning on each other and moving toward the truck.

Peter spun away from them again, trudging after Chance, the snow up way past the top of his boots now. He was soaked almost to his hips, the cold making him shiver violently. Ignoring it, he took over from Chance's latest dig and the dog was off again, toward an area of snow that was moving, someone clearly fighting to get free.

Yet again, the man Peter finished digging out wasn't Tate. It was Lorenzo Riera, another veteran. As soon as he was freed enough from the snow to speak, he demanded, "Rook?" It was his nickname for Nate, who was his partner.

"He's okay," Peter assured him, glancing over at where Chance was digging away, praying his own partner was under there. How many officers had come to back him up today? How many were hurt right now because of a decision he'd made?

"Peter!"

Peter glanced back as a police SUV screeched to a halt at the edge of the woods, windows down and Chief Hernandez steering one-handed as she leaned partway out the window. The fact that she'd gotten here so fast meant she must have already been out somewhere on the edges of Desparre on a call.

"Status!" she demanded.

"We've got three dug out," Peter called back. "Not

sure how many more officers were out here. Presumably Darcy Altier is still in the cabin, armed, with the kids and now Alanna."

The chief was scowling as she slammed the SUV door shut. She had her weapon out of the holster before the door was closed and she nodded at the two officers who stepped out of the back of the vehicle, both in bulletproof vests and helmets.

"Luna police are sending backup. The state police sniper and hostage negotiator are both on another call. We're going to have to breach."

"No!" Peter took two steps toward her, then glanced back at Chance, still digging.

The big dog looked over at him once, let out a long howl, then went back to work.

"Just wait," Peter begged Chief Hernandez. "Give Alanna a chance."

As he pivoted toward Chance and whoever was still buried in the snow, Lorenzo stumbled over next to him to help.

"It's just Tate left. That must be him."

Peter fell to his knees next to Chance, not even bothering to run back for the shovel he'd dropped. He started digging with his hands, shoving snow away from Tate, who'd been moving before but wasn't any longer.

When an arm fell free, Peter tugged on it, trying to pull Tate out of the snow. His head appeared and while Lorenzo and Chance continued to dig around the rest of him, Peter cleared snow off his face.

Tate looked abnormally pale and his lips had a bluish tinge, but when Peter leaned close to listen for his breathing, Tate gasped in a large breath. Lorenzo cleared a big chunk of snow off his back and Peter helped pull Tate to his feet.

"We should have stayed on the road instead of hiding in the woods," Tate choked out, which made Lorenzo let out a relieved laugh.

Peter threw his arms around his friend, hugging him tight. Then he dropped to his knees and hugged Chance. "Good boy," he whispered, and got a big, slobbery kiss on the cheek in return.

Standing, he told Tate, "Now we need to get Alanna out of that cabin safely."

The look on his partner's face—one of dread and sorrow—made him spin to face the cabin.

Sam Jennings and Max Becker—the two officers who'd arrived in vests with the chief—were breaching the front door of the cabin, sending it right off the hinges with a powerful blow from a battering ram.

Peter's "*wait!*" was lost beneath the *boom* of the flash-bang tossed through the threshold. As white light exploded behind the curtained windows, the two officers rushed inside.

Even though he knew it was too late, Peter started running. His heart pounded harder than it had for his first raid. Every freezing-cold intake of breath seemed to seize his lungs.

A flash-bang was disorienting—basically a stun grenade that rendered your eyes and ears useless. When used on civilians, they dropped their weapons to cover their eyes or ears. By the time they figured out what was happening, they were being shoved to the ground by tactical officers.

But the Desparre police force rarely used them, and they didn't have a tactical unit. All they had were regular officers who received special tactical and weapons training each month in case an emergency unraveled too quickly to wait for state police or the FBI. Five years in war zones had taught Peter that sometimes it didn't matter what weapons or tactics were used. With a determined-enough opponent, impossible odds suddenly became possible.

He didn't know a lot about Darcy Altier beyond what he'd read and what Alanna had told him. But he'd witnessed her state of mind. She was volatile, desperate, prone to big swings of emotion. And right now she had three hostages who might be between her and the officers who'd rushed inside blind.

Chief Hernandez was moving, arms spread wide, to block him from rushing into the house. Peter paused, unsure whether to race around her or run right through her.

Then Sam and Max emerged from the cabin, looking grim and shaking their heads.

Peter choked on the sudden emotion that rushed up his throat, then he was pushing the chief aside and running into the cabin.

He waved his hands around to clear the smoke, expecting to see all of them—Alanna, Darcy and the two kids—dead on the floor. But there was nothing but an abandoned shotgun on the floor.

He glanced around, wondering if he'd missed another room, but there were no doors except the open one leading out the back. Darcy and the kids were gone.

So was Alanna.

Chapter 10

"Follow their footsteps," Chief Hernandez ordered, already out in front with her weapon raised.

Peter hurried up beside her, insisting, "We need to be careful. We have to assume Darcy is holding the kids. She dropped the shotgun, but she still has a pistol. Alanna is probably trying to talk her down."

Chief Hernandez gave him a look full of disappointment and disbelief, then motioned for Sam and Max to catch up.

They were tracking two fresh sets of footsteps that led away from the back door of the cabin, with stride distances that indicated the people who made them had been running. The tracks led through the woods in the opposite direction of where the officers had been buried under snow. Back in the direction of downtown Luna. But before that, they would hit a road that might take them toward Desparre or farther north into even more remote parts of the state.

There'd been no vehicle in the driveway, no garage. Had Darcy hidden it at the edge of the woods, near the road, so the cabin would look deserted? That was logical.

Peter put on a burst of speed, panting with exertion that would make his gun hand shake if he caught up to Darcy and she swung her pistol his way. He passed Chief Hernandez, Sam and Max, ignoring his boss's curse and shout to wait. If they hadn't already left, if Alanna was with them, Peter wanted to reach them first.

Darting around trees, Peter's gaze shifted back and forth from the footsteps in the snow to the area in front of him, hoping he wouldn't misjudge a step, run right into a tree and knock himself out. He slowed as the road became visible and then skidded to a stop at its edge, where the footsteps ended and deep tire indents marked the spot where a vehicle had once sat.

They were gone.

A big chunk of snow fell off a tree overhead onto his head, sliding down his face and inside the back of his coat. He wiped it away just as the chief caught up to him.

"This was a total disaster." Holstering her weapon, Chief Hernandez got in his face—not an easy task, since she was a good four inches shorter.

Still, Peter straightened and clamped his jaw shut. He knew better than to piss off the chief—at least any more than he already had.

"When I tell you to wait, you *wait*." She poked a finger at his chest, fury in her gaze. "You're *my* responsibility, Robak. We're not a big police force, but we're a team. If you want to be part of it, you need to act like it."

She strode past him, heading down the road back toward the cabin. Sam and Max followed her. Sam gave him an apologetic glance; Max ignored him entirely.

Peter's shoulders slumped and a shiver racked his body as the cold and exhaustion hit. His jeans and gloves were completely soaked through and the snow that had dripped down the back of his coat was uncomfortable. He looked once more down the road, then followed his fellow officers.

Had Alanna *chosen* to get in that vehicle with Darcy? Or had she been forced inside?

He frowned as he glanced at the ground in front of him. Was that an extra set of footprints he was seeing? Had someone else come back this way? Had Alanna chased Darcy, been unable to catch her before she took off in her vehicle, then returned to the cabin?

He hurried to catch up to Chief Hernandez Sam, and Max, noticed them frowning at the extra footprints, too. The chief even had her weapon out again.

The walk back to the cabin didn't take long—it was a straight line compared to the curved, roundabout route through the woods. But the frigid wind picked up and made him shiver harder, made it seem much farther than it really was. When they finally arrived, Tate was shivering by the road. Chance stood next to him, pressed up against his side as if trying to warm him.

"Did Alanna come back this way?" Peter asked. "And why are you out here? Why didn't you warm up in my truck?" Peter glanced around, realized it wasn't there and asked, "Did some of the officers take it back? Is everyone okay?" Was Alanna okay? Where was she?

"Everyone's fine," Tate said, his teeth actually chattering. "But it's not us who took the truck."

"What do you mean?"

"Apparently, while you were still digging me out and the chief was busy watching the front of the cabin, Alanna ran back from the road and took it."

Peter frowned, realizing that Darcy had been gone long before they'd tried to track her through the woods. That meant Alanna had been climbing into his truck instead of running into the snow to help him pull out Tate.

Tate shivered harder, wrapping his arms around himself. "Nate and Charlie said she was alone. I guess they thought it was okay, since she'd been on your side the last time they saw her."

"She's still on my side," Peter said, although suddenly, he wasn't sure.

Chief Hernandez shook her head and holstered her weapon, heading past them toward her vehicle. Sam and Max followed.

Peter just continued to stare at his partner, trying to understand. Why would Alanna come back here but not wait for him? Why would she take his truck but not explain herself to any of the officers?

At least she was okay. She wasn't a hostage. She wasn't dead.

But if she'd taken his truck, she was trying to chase Darcy down alone.

"We need to catch up to her," he told Tate. "She could be in trouble."

"Right now, we all need to warm up and change or we won't be good for anything." Tate stroked Chance's head with hands that shook. "Since Alanna took off, maybe we can make Chance here our K-9 representative."

Tate had been trying to convince the chief they needed a K-9 unit for as long as Peter had known him. The chief had always countered that the department barely had enough money to pay for officers and their training, let alone add dogs to the mix. Maybe today would change her mind.

Chance looked up at Tate, then over at Peter, as if asking where Alanna was.

"We'll find her, boy," Peter told him.

"Robak! Emory! Get over here," the chief called from inside her SUV. The rest of the officers were already crammed inside. "I'm driving you to the spot the other vehicles were hidden before this unsuccessful raid."

Peter felt himself jerk at the term *raid*. The plan had been for the other officers to be backup, in case things went south. Not for them to jump into action from the outset. Hadn't it?

He glanced sideways at Tate, wondering if anyone else had noticed the slipup. Or if his partner would look guilty for hiding the true nature of their "help." But Tate was just striding toward the SUV, looking miserable.

Still, his fellow officers had hidden in the woods. They'd obviously waited while Peter and Alanna tried to talk Darcy down. Maybe a raid had been a last resort if the negotiation soured. Or maybe they would have run straight in if it had been clear they could get to the kids safely.

"No one who was in the avalanche is driving." The chief looked Peter over as he, Tate and Chance joined her, then added, "Not you, either, Robak."

He took her point. Everyone who'd been buried in the snow—and him, since he'd been hip-deep in it, digging men out—were soaked and freezing. Although all he felt was miserably cold, the rest of the team might have had their core temperatures drop enough to make driving dangerous.

Last night, even after waiting until they'd warmed up some, Alanna had still been violently shaking as she'd navigated those mountain roads. Thinking about her made him anxious to get moving and he yanked open the back door.

Tate's eyebrows raised as they saw how crowded it already was. "I don't think we're getting two more men and a St. Bernard in there. Why don't you come back for us?"

The chief scowled at him, then the back seat, then finally nodded. "We'll be fast. The vehicles are less than a mile away. I want everyone who was in the avalanche checked out at the hospital."

When most of the officers grumbled, she snapped, "No arguments." Then the back door was slammed shut and the SUV was off, kicking up snow.

"Were you planning to surround me, Darcy and Alanna no matter what?" Peter demanded as soon as they were alone.

Tate turned to him, his lips still tinged blue, his face still too pale. "Are you kidding? Look what just happened here, man. *Your backup* hid and waited for your signal. Did you even see us out there?"

When Peter shook his head, Tate continued. "Yet somehow, Darcy knew. How do you think that happened?"

Anger heated him. He knew the rest of the team had already been thinking it. But he and Tate weren't just partners; they were friends. Tate should have trusted his judgment. "You're insinuating that Alanna tipped her off?"

Chance glanced from him to Tate, as if waiting for the reply, too.

Tate sighed, shaking his head. "She *stole* your truck. Why do you think she did that? Maybe she was trying to slow you down so you couldn't catch up to Darcy and she's mad you brought backup. Or she's been talking to Darcy from the start and she couldn't shake you, so she just brought you along and told Darcy what was going down."

Peter took an aggressive step forward and Chance, sitting between them, got to his feet, looking wary. The dog nudged his arm, as if telling him to calm down.

Peter absently pet Chance, trying to reassure him as he snapped at Tate, "Alanna didn't even know you'd be here. What happened to you thinking Alanna was genuine, that she was trying to help us?"

"Maybe she was," Tate replied, not looking at all threatened by Peter invading his personal space. "But maybe she had second thoughts. Let's be honest here. You cut her out by calling us in secretly. But that doesn't mean she didn't figure out what you were doing. Was she ever alone? Did she ever have a chance to warn Darcy before you two came out here? She probably didn't expect Darcy to shoot at us, but—"

"Alanna would *never* tip off Darcy. She'd never put those kids in danger."

"Wouldn't they have been in less danger if she'd told the police what she knew as soon as she found those locations? You have to admit it—she still loves Darcy. She's still trying to protect her. What happened to *you* thinking she had some warped loyalty to her kidnappers?"

"I got to know her," Peter said softly, backing up a

step as his shoulders slumped. If even Tate didn't believe in Alanna now, what would happen if they caught up to Darcy and Alanna was with her?

Tate nodded, the anger on his face softening as he stared at Peter. "You care about her." It was a statement rather than a question. "But look around here. She took your truck. She hasn't tried to contact you. She even left her dog." He gestured to Chance, who whined and lay on the snowy ground.

"She's not coming back."

Chance looked up from the spot he'd claimed on the floor of the Desparre police station and gave a low whine.

They hadn't heard from Alanna in five hours and Peter definitely wasn't the only one feeling anxious over it. He leaned down and petted the St. Bernard to comfort him.

"He really shouldn't be in here," Chief Hernandez said, but she sighed and petted him, too.

The chief couldn't be too stern with the dog who'd just saved half her force from an avalanche. The same couldn't be said of the way she was treating him. *Furious* was an understatement. He wasn't sure if it was because he'd tried to outpace them in the woods to reach Alanna first or because of everything that had gone wrong the moment they'd driven up to that tiny cabin.

She straightened and peered over his shoulder at his computer. "Any luck?"

Since they'd returned to the station, he'd been trying to figure out the other locations Darcy might have gone. Last night, he'd given Alanna a tiny notebook to jot down whatever she could remember of the list she'd found at the cabin. She'd spent over an hour writing things down and crossing them out until she'd finally gone to bed. While she'd slept, he'd slipped into the guest room and snagged the notebook off the side table.

He'd tried not to look at her at all, feeling like he was invading her privacy, but he hadn't been able to stop himself. The sheets had been twisted beneath her, her long hair tangled around her face, her eyes moving rapidly underneath her eyelids as she dreamed. Was she reliving the avalanche, he'd wondered? Dreaming of her past? Or worrying about Darcy and those kids?

In that moment, he'd had the absurd desire to curl up with her and chase away her nightmares. Then Chance had walked over and Peter had realized the big dog had been watching him from the floor beside Alanna's bed. He'd given the dog a quick pet, told him everything was fine and gone into the other room to copy the contents of the notebook.

The mix of odd symbols, numbers and blank lines— where presumably Alanna had been trying to remember what she'd seen—hadn't meant much to him last night. They didn't mean much more now. She'd translated some of the code, but not enough.

He shook his head. "Sorry."

"Luna police haven't had a single sighting."

Apparently they'd been notified about what was happening less than five minutes after Peter had contacted Tate. It made sense; the cabin was in Luna PD's jurisdiction. But it still bothered him that so quickly after he'd called for backup, it seemed like everyone knew what was going on. It made him wonder if there was some other reason Darcy had been tipped off, like she'd spotted Luna patrols driving by too often before the Desparre team had arrived.

Still, once the Desparre officers had headed to the hospital after the avalanche, Luna's had swept in. Their PD had set up roadblocks to search for Darcy. Although no one had mentioned it to him, Peter suspected they'd been told to stop Alanna, too. He hadn't protested. He would have been happy if they'd held her, prevented her from catching up to Darcy on her own.

By now, Alanna was either still following Darcy in his truck or she'd lost her and was back to following the list of coordinates. Peter refused to consider the other possibility: that she'd caught up to Darcy and the woman had hurt her.

Peter stared down at the notes he'd taken from Alanna's room. The truth was, he had a couple of guesses, coordinates he'd worked out based on what she'd written. But that was all they were—guesses that could be dead-on or hundreds of miles off course.

His chief narrowed her eyes at him, like she knew what he was thinking and wanted the specifics anyway. Before he could admit he had some possibilities, she told him, "According to the hospital, all of the officers are okay. Most of them are heading back to the station now."

"*Most* of them?"

"They're hanging onto Tate a bit longer. His core body temperature was a little low when he came in and they don't want to take any chances."

Peter swore and Chance came over to drop his head onto Peter's lap. Absently stroking the dog's fur, Peter realized how much Chance relaxed him, eased his worry over his partner and Alanna.

Chief Hernandez looked from him to the St. Bernard and back again. "Luna PD isn't too happy with how everything shook out today. I think they're wishing they'd said no to our request to handle it. They think it's time to put out a message to the public, enlist their help."

"Okay," Peter said slowly. "But I thought we were holding off on that in case it escalated things."

"It's been five hours," the chief reminded him. "Darcy got through our checkpoints, probably before we even had them up. If Alanna hasn't been in contact by now, she's not going to be."

"Maybe she can't. Her phone could have—"

"Peter." She said his name with a sigh and a tone of finality. "When Darcy fired into that mountain, Alanna made a choice. She *left* all those officers, including you."

"She went after the kids! She—"

"If she was on our side, we would have heard from her by now." Chief Hernandez put up a hand, as if to forestall the argument she knew was coming. "Maybe she's in trouble. Maybe she's already dead."

Chance whined and got to his feet. Peter's insides twisted until he felt himself hunch over from the pain of it.

"I'm sorry," the chief said. "You've gotten too close to this. At this point, we have to consider Alanna an accessory to kidnapping."

Peter jerked to a standing position, knocking his chair backward and making Chance step sideways out of the way. "She'd never actually *help* Darcy get away with those kids!" No matter how much he loved that woman, that would never happen.

"Peter, look around. Your partner is in the hospital and Alanna left her dog behind. She's gone."

"She's coming back. She'd never leave Chance. She hung on to him in an avalanche!"

"I'm sorry," Chief Hernandez repeated. "But it's time. We're going public with this and we're naming Alanna, too."

She gave him one last look, full of apology and residual anger and just a hint of distrust. Then she disappeared into her office and Peter sank back into his chair.

Chance promptly nuzzled up against him with so much force it pushed the chair backward, his whine a half growl, half cry.

"I know, boy," Peter whispered. "This is bad."

He stared at the chief's closed office door, then over at the few other officers in the station, who were studiously ignoring him. He blew out a long breath and stood. "Come on, boy."

Grabbing his coat, Peter strode for the door, trying not to run. Chance stayed right on his heels. With every step, he could feel the new career he'd fought so hard for slipping away.

But did he really have a choice? Alanna wasn't guilty. And he couldn't let her get hurt because she was trying to make amends for something that wasn't her fault.

It was time to break ranks. It was time to search for Alanna on his own.

Chapter 11

Maybe Darcy hadn't been as guilty as Alanna had feared.

Not that she was totally innocent. She'd escaped from law enforcement, fled across the country to hide. But for the first time, Alanna wondered if Darcy had been incorrectly blamed.

Had she really kidnapped those kids?

Alanna stared at the cell phone she'd been holding for the past ten minutes, at Peter's direct contact that he'd entered yesterday. She was sitting in his truck, the truck she'd *stolen*, with the engine running in a tiny back alley on the outskirts of Desparre as the sun began to set.

Five years ago, in the process of trying to find her, Kensie had run into trouble with a criminal. Alanna had first seen her in this alley, from the rearview window of a car as it drove away. For the second time in her life, she'd watched her big sister screaming for her, but in the alley, it had been Kensie who was in trouble. Until her sister had appeared at the cabin, Alanna had thought Kensie had been killed here. Things had turned out okay then, but would they now?

Her phone had rung repeatedly for the past five hours, Peter's name lighting up on her screen. When the first call came in, she'd been on Darcy's tail, too scared to take her eyes off the vehicle for a second. She'd caught up to it a few miles away from the cabin. She hadn't actually been able to see Darcy inside it, but the way the vehicle was speeding, taking corners much too fast, who else could it be?

An hour later, after she'd lost the vehicle—at that point not even sure it was Darcy she'd been chasing—she'd thought about calling Peter. But she hadn't been ready to admit defeat yet. And she'd been terrified to learn what happened to the officers who'd been buried under that avalanche.

When the snow had first started rushing down that mountainside, she'd considered staying for about ten seconds. Peter had already been running toward it, Chance outpacing him. She'd known Chance would be better help digging people out than she would. Darcy had been right in front of her, running back into the cabin, ready to grab those kids and make them disappear again. At least, that was what she'd thought.

Alanna had felt like she was those kids' only shot. She couldn't let Darcy take them again.

Now here she was. Alone. No Darcy. No kids. Afraid to learn what had happened at that cabin.

Setting the phone next to her, Alanna flipped on the

radio to a local station. Would this debacle have made the news?

"…officers are doing fine," the host was saying and Alanna relaxed against her seat, grabbing her phone to call Peter, to check on Chance and apologize for all of it. Tell Peter what she'd discovered.

She'd been so sure she could talk some sense into Darcy. Of course, maybe she would have been able to if there hadn't been officers hiding in the woods, signaling to Darcy that Alanna had already betrayed her.

She couldn't totally trust Peter. Not even now, after they'd seemed to connect on such a personal level back at his house. The realization hurt. A lot. But it wasn't the most important thing right now.

Alaska wasn't her home anymore. Soon enough, she'd be back in Chicago, Peter a distant memory. Right now, though, she needed his help. Maybe if she was lucky, if she was right, he could help her prove that Darcy wasn't a kidnapper at all. At least not anymore.

"Be on the lookout for escaped convict Darcy Altier," the radio host continued. "If you see her, contact police immediately. She is armed and dangerous. Police are also looking for her accomplice, Alanna Morgan. In case you don't remember the name, Alanna was one of five children kidnapped by Darcy Altier and her husband nearly twenty years ago. She—"

Alanna flipped the radio off, dropping her phone. The police had named her as an *accomplice*? After she'd told them where to find Darcy? After she'd run into that cabin, trying to rescue those kids, all without any police help?

And after what she'd found…

Darcy had been running out the back door. Alone.

At first, Alanna had thought she'd lucked out. That Darcy had decided to run and leave the kids behind, avoid putting them in the middle of a standoff.

But a quick search of the one-room cabin had shown Alanna that wasn't the case. Darcy didn't *have* the kids. Maybe she'd never had the kids.

Unfortunately, kidnappings happened all the time. An escaped convict—especially one who'd been in jail for a series of kidnappings—in close enough proximity to a new case would be an obvious suspect. Then, when another kid went missing in a part of Canada that was along a potential route Darcy could take to return to Desparre? Maybe that had been enough to cinch the investigation and Darcy had been innocent all along. This time, anyway.

Alanna would never know unless she found her. It was more obvious than ever that she couldn't trust the police, couldn't trust Peter.

She needed to do this alone.

"It's better to ask forgiveness than permission, right, boy?" Peter asked Chance as he sped them along the icy back streets of Desparre.

Chance's head swiveled in the passenger seat and the look in his eyes suggested he had doubts.

Since Alanna had his truck, Peter had taken his police vehicle. He wasn't sure how long he had before the chief noticed his absence and grew suspicious. Before she called him up and demanded he return to the station. Before he faced serious trouble for ignoring her orders.

Of course, she could track the police vehicle, too, have his fellow officers chase him down. But Peter hadn't had time to find something else. At this point, he was looking at insubordination at best, aiding and abetting a fugitive at worst. What was one borrowed police vehicle in comparison?

Even if he could get away without any charges being brought against him, he was probably finished in Desparre. He'd gotten the job because the department was desperate. Dozens of other applications around the state—even the country—had shown him how fast most police stations would eliminate him without an interview because of his hearing loss.

Unless there was drastic change, his career as a police officer was over. The idea made him nauseous.

Police academy had been brutal. He'd thought he was in good shape before he started, but he'd discovered that traipsing alongside soldiers in war zones hadn't prepared him for the full physicality of chasing suspects for long stretches. It hadn't prepared him for actually carrying his own weapon and learning not to flinch at the sound of it firing, which was just a little too similar to the *boom* of the explosion that had changed his life. It hadn't prepared him for all the small adaptations he had to make just to be sure his bad ear didn't put him or his fellow officers at increased risk.

He'd stuck it out, through the bruises and the flashbacks. He'd even worked through the bullying from an instructor who didn't approve of Desparre PD bending their applicant rules to get another recruit willing to live in their remote town. The guy thought Desparre PD was unnecessarily endangering him—and that Peter could endanger his future colleagues by not being up to the job.

He'd worked hard to be a good officer, to make sure his disability didn't impact his effectiveness. The day he'd graduated from the academy and gotten the official go-ahead to become a Desparre PD rookie, he'd felt a sense of accomplishment and joy headier than his first assignment as a war reporter.

Today he was throwing it all away.

Still, he didn't turn around. No way could he just follow orders when those orders were putting Alanna at risk. No, the only shot he had at saving the career he'd grown to love so much was to bring in Darcy and save those kids.

At least he had an idea where to start. Sure, it was an idea based half on coordinates Alanna had decoded from her memory of the symbols she'd seen, half on guesswork. He had filled in the blanks, considering what else made sense based on the numbers she had and satellite images of the area. But guesswork was better than nothing. It was better than sitting in that station, waiting to hear that police officers in some other town had surrounded Darcy and Alanna. That they'd considered both women dangerous and were willing to sacrifice them in order to save two kidnapped children. That they'd shot first, asked questions later.

The very idea of anyone training a weapon on Alanna made him punch down harder on the gas. The first location he'd worked out wasn't nearby. It was in the total opposite direction of the cabin in Luna, in a town even tinier than Desparre. A place that didn't even have their own police force. It seemed like the best option for his quarry.

After all, there was no way to know how long he could run these leads alone before his fellow officers surrounded his car and demanded he stand down. Demanded he hand over his weapon and his badge.

As if sensing his thoughts, Chance let out a sudden *woof* that startled Peter into jerking the wheel. Chance was jolted in the seat and Peter righted the car on the slippery ice. "I know, boy. You're my backup today."

Alanna had told him how the St. Bernard had been rescued from a cruel owner as a puppy, how she'd gotten him certified as a therapy dog so she could bring him with her to work. It was as much to help her own anxiety as it was to help the trauma survivors she worked with, she'd said. Chance had known exactly when to comfort him at the police station, even when to support Tate out in the cold by the cabin; it was clear he was a damn good therapy dog. And given the way he'd raced into action during the avalanche, he probably would have made a good police dog, too.

"We'll find her," Peter told him, hoping it was true.

Chance whined softly, turning his attention out the front windshield. The dog seemed as desperate to find Alanna as Peter.

And he *was* desperate. There was no other word for it.

Four days ago, he would have scoffed at the idea that he could come to trust Alanna Morgan, let alone that he would care for her so much. But at his house, they'd connected. It had lifted a weight off him to be able to open up about his past. And he'd come to admire her fortitude after everything she'd experienced. If she lived in Alaska, if she wasn't part of an ongoing case, he'd already be pursuing her romantically. The idea felt ridiculous and yet it made him yearn for something he hadn't realized was missing from his life.

Maybe it wasn't Alanna. Maybe it was just time for him to think about finding someone to settle down with, like all his older siblings. Have some kids, make a real home. Take down those pictures from war zones on his walls and move forward. Except how could he do that if he didn't even have a job?

He shook off the worries he couldn't be distracted by right now and slowed as he approached the coordinates he'd mapped out. He'd looked up the location online, zoomed in and seen what might have been a cabin. Perhaps it was a hiding spot for a desperate couple who'd known one day their crimes could catch up to them. Who'd suspected they would eventually be on the run again.

Adrenaline shot through him as he drove slowly past. It was hard to tell now that the sun was down, but up close, he realized there *was* a cabin. Tiny and tucked away from the street behind more woods, it looked a lot like the place in Luna from this afternoon. It was a well-built log cabin, similar in style to the house where the Altiers had lived in Desparre, the one they'd built by hand. Could Julian have built this place himself, too? Peter could see light through the windows.

This time he didn't slow down, didn't pull into the driveway. He drove right past and parked down the road where his vehicle wouldn't be visible from the cabin.

For one crazy second, he considered calling for backup. But even though he and Tate had developed a strong friendship outside of work, he couldn't ask his friend to risk his career. Besides, Peter didn't even know if Tate was out of the hospital yet. And there was no one else he'd trust to protect Alanna no matter what they saw, no matter what happened.

"It's you and me, boy," he told Chance, his breath puffing in front of him as he stepped out of the vehicle.

His boots broke through a top layer of ice with a noisy crunch, then sank down into more than a foot of snow beneath. He hoped he wasn't making a mistake letting the dog come, but he couldn't just leave him in the SUV, hidden out here in the woods. What would happen if Peter was killed and no one knew he was here?

Chance leaped out of the vehicle, sticking close and moving silently. His big body was hunched over, the fur on his back raised, like he was stalking something. Like he knew exactly what they were doing and he, too, was willing to risk everything for Alanna.

"Be careful," Peter whispered, simultaneously hoping that the dog understood and that Darcy wouldn't hurt Alanna's pet.

Chance glanced at him once, then looked back toward the cabin. The dog was focused and slinking forward as if he knew Alanna was in there.

Hoping he was right, Peter unholstered his pistol and crept slowly along beside Chance, toward the home. He moved from the cover of one tree to the next, cursing the wind that whistled past his ears as it limited his hearing even further. The snow was deeper here than it had been in Luna and the damp cold seeping through his jeans above the tops of his boots made him shiver. But at least the icy top layer was more melted here, his boots making a quieter *crunch* each time they broke through.

A shadow moved behind the curtains in one of the windows and Peter's pulse jumped. It didn't mean he'd found them, but *someone* was home.

He scanned the area and spotted something on the far side of the cabin, a brief reflection of light in the moonlight. Squinting at it, he realized with a start that it was his truck. Alanna was here.

Creeping closer, he reached the edge of the woods, then made a run for the side of the cabin, staying in a crouch. Chance raced along beside him, reaching the cabin first. But he waited for Peter, giving him a look that seemed to ask, *What's the plan?*

Flattening himself against the side of the cabin, Peter peered at the window, hoping for a gap in the curtains. There was nothing to see, so he tapped his thigh for Chance to follow and slunk to the back of the dwelling. He wasn't worried about Chance barking. The dog was well-trained and seemed to sense the need to stay silent.

The windows here were the same, but just like the last cabin, there was a back door. For a building this small, it didn't really need more than one entrance. Unless someone needed an easy escape route.

Peter tested the handle, expecting it to be locked. But it moved under his hand and he froze, hoping no one inside had seen it. For a moment, indecision gripped him, made all his muscles tense. Then he eased the door slowly open, angling his weapon so he could lead with it.

Though it probably wouldn't help; doorways were one of the most dangerous places for police officers. You didn't know what was on the other side, and the only way to find out if someone was standing there waiting with their own weapon drawn was to open the door and go inside.

He'd trained for this, Peter reminded himself. Sure, if he was here officially, he'd have a partner. But someone would still have to go through first. In police academy, you learned a simple series of steps to get you inside and out of a doorway as fast as possible. You learned the exact sequence your gun hand and your attention should move to eliminate any threats before they could eliminate you. Still, none of that changed the fact that dying as you came through a doorway was far too common for police officers.

He weighed calling out "police," but thought it too risky. If Darcy was holding Alanna and the children, he could put them in jeopardy by alerting her to his presence.

He glanced sideways at Chance, who was waiting in a crouched stance as if he planned to bound in after Peter, and held up a hand, telling the dog to wait. Then he steadied his gun hand, ignored the senses-dimming staccato of his heartbeat and pushed the door wide.

The tiny kitchen he stepped into was empty, but beyond an open doorway, he could hear voices. One of them belonged to Alanna.

"I *believed* in you," she was saying, the hurt palpable in her words. "After all this time, I really thought that if I could just talk to you, make you understand, that you'd—"

"What?" Darcy interrupted, the volume of her own anger and hurt dwarfing Alanna's. "Turn myself in? Go back to jail? *Die there*, like your father did?"

"That's the thing," Alanna said, her tone sad but strong. "As much as you wanted to be, as much as I loved you both, you weren't my parents. And—"

Darcy made a sound that was half furious screech, half wounded cry.

This wasn't going anywhere good. Peter darted around the doorway, handgun raised, hoping to find Darcy distracted and across the room from Alanna.

Before he'd fully entered the room, though, Darcy spun toward him, her own pistol raised.

"You shouldn't have come here," Darcy spat.

Peter aimed his gun at her head—instead of her center mass, like he'd been taught. He did a quick visual sweep—Alanna across the room, unarmed, her hands up in the air as if she'd been trying to calm Darcy down. But Alanna wasn't his problem right now.

It was the little boy on the floor, clutching Darcy's leg and staring at him wide-eyed. It was the little girl held in the crook of Darcy's arm, silent tears running down her face as Darcy used her as a human shield.

Chapter 12

"Please, just put the gun down," Alanna begged.

"Him again!" Darcy snapped. "What happened to all your promises that it was just the two of us talking? It's always lies with you, isn't it?"

Alanna swallowed the desire to snap back, to argue about who was lying to who. She'd never seen Darcy like this. All her life, Darcy had been full of smiles and ideas and plans she couldn't always see through. She was flighty and occasionally depressed, but she was always patient with the kids she'd called hers.

When Alanna had entered the second cabin in Luna, she'd been amazed. She'd thought it was a sign that things were about to go right. That even though Darcy had escaped from prison, she hadn't returned to kidnapping. That there was a chance to end it all peacefully.

She'd been so wrong.

Maybe Julian's death had unhinged Darcy. Or maybe Alanna had only seen what she'd wanted to see all those years she'd lived with her. Maybe Peter had been right and she'd been brainwashed by a pair of kidnappers.

"She didn't know I was coming," Peter said, his voice calm and soft as Chance walked slowly into the cabin behind him and came to a stop at his side.

The dog's gaze moved from Alanna to the kids, then back to Peter, as if awaiting instructions.

Tension knotted tighter in Alanna's chest. How had Peter found them? Why would he bring Chance into this?

She tried to tell him with her eyes to stay out of it, to let her try to reach Darcy. Her gaze darted to the kids, the small girl in Darcy's arms with dark, curly hair that reminded Alanna so much of herself as a child. The little boy clutching Darcy's leg with the deep brown eyes and the short dark hair. Both of them could have easily passed as Altiers.

"Do you know how much I miss you?" Darcy asked, her voice breaking as Alanna's gaze returned to hers. "Do you know how much I miss all of you? Do you know what it was like to have my kids ripped away from me?"

"I'm—" Alanna started.

"Do you know how badly it hurt to know it was *you* who set it all in motion? What it feels like to have you tell me I'm not your mom?" She let out a humorless laugh. "I know I'm not your mom. Not legally. I…" She shook her head, staring through Alanna now, her brow furrowed like she was peering into the past.

"I could never have kids," Darcy admitted softly.

She tipped her head against the child in her arms and the little girl hugged her neck.

She obviously felt safe with Darcy, despite everything. It was what Alanna had felt right from the start, too. Irrational, maybe, but she'd instinctively known she was loved.

A surge of hope hit, a gut feeling that she could still reach Darcy, still talk her into ending this peacefully. Because no matter what else might have changed, the Darcy she'd known for fourteen years was still in there. A Darcy who would never hurt kids she'd decided were hers. But Peter... If Darcy thought he was a threat, she'd fire at him the way she'd shot at Kensie all those years ago.

She hadn't done it when she could have at the cabin in Luna, a tiny voice whispered in the back of her mind. It was a voice Alanna couldn't trust, a voice that had been born from her past life. Still, it was a past life where Darcy had raised her to be strong, had hugged her every night before bed, had greeted her every morning with love.

"I'm sorry," Alanna said.

"My family never understood me," Darcy continued, not seeming to notice Peter as he shifted just slightly to angle his good ear toward her. His weapon, too.

Chance moved too, surprisingly stealthy for such a big dog, sticking to Peter's side as if they were a team with a shared plan.

Praying that Peter would just wait, that Chance wouldn't think she was in trouble and try coming to her rescue, Alanna nodded encouragingly at Darcy. She'd never met anyone from Darcy or Julian's families. When she was younger, it hadn't occurred to her to wonder why. When she was older, she'd assumed it was because of the kidnappings, because of the Altiers' constant reminders that it was the seven of them against the world. But maybe they'd been estranged long before that.

"They were all overachievers, every one of them. They couldn't stand failure," Darcy said. "Me? I had so much trouble learning. But Julian always accepted me just as I was. When we got married, I wanted our life to be so different from the way I'd grown up. We always talked about having a big family, raising them differently. So when we couldn't have kids, I was devastated. We tried to adopt. A little boy, the age Johnny would have been then. It was such a long process and we finally got to the end of it. He was supposed to come home with us over the weekend. Then that Friday, the adoption fell through. He went back to his biological family. They were drug addicts, in and out of rehab, in and out of prison, but somehow they convinced a judge they should get one more chance to be parents."

The sadness and loss on her face shifted to anger. "Four weeks later, he was dead. Killed in a house fire his parents had set while they were high. And we just couldn't do it. We couldn't go through it again. We gave up on adoption."

"So you took Johnny?" Alanna recalled what she'd read about his abduction in the papers years later. "From the park when his mom was distracted, right?"

"She wasn't even watching him," Darcy said, a new light in her eyes, the spark of a past joy. "Julian said it had been easy to pick him off the swings and bring him home to me. Johnny didn't even cry. It was like he wanted to come to us, like it was meant to be. But afterward…" She frowned, shook her head, glanced at Peter.

Her eyes narrowed and Alanna was sure she'd noticed that Peter was just slightly closer, that Chance was edging closer, too. "Afterward?" Alanna pressed.

"It was such a mix of emotions," Darcy said, happiness back in her eyes. "Probably what it feels like right after you've given birth to a child. Elation like you've never felt, but fear, too. Almost terror, really. And the guilt…" She leaned into the little girl she held and her gun hand, still aimed at Peter, shook a little.

She'd always known it was wrong. Alanna had wondered for years whether Darcy and Julian had felt any regret for taking her and her "siblings." If Darcy had felt guilty then, surely the guilt was intensified now, knowing that the kids who'd gone home to their families had missed them for years.

If she had any regret, felt any guilt, then Alanna could still reach her. She took a step forward, her hand out toward Darcy.

"A few years later, when we saw you…"

Alanna froze and her heart seemed to contract. It was a moment she remembered so distinctly and yet she'd never known how they'd picked her, or why.

"The first time I saw you, I just *knew.* You looked so much like I did as a child, but it was more than that. I just felt it, deep inside, that you were meant to be my daughter." Her eyes glassed over with unshed tears. "I still feel that, Alanna."

Alanna took another step closer until she could almost touch Darcy, almost reach out and push the gun down. "In some ways, I'll always be your daughter." The words were shaky with emotion, because they were true.

The smile Alanna had seen every day of her childhood blossomed on Darcy's face and the woman's rigid arm loosened, the gun angling downward, away from Peter.

Alanna slid forward just a tiny bit more. "But the Morgans weren't drug addicts. They loved me. They spent so many years searching for me. They were even called into more than one morgue for identifications that turned out not to be me."

The smile slid from Darcy's face. Alanna could see the guilt there as her "mom" glanced down at the little boy still hugging tightly to her leg.

"My older sister almost died trying to find me. My older brother turned to drugs and alcohol and anything else he could find because losing me tore my family apart. They didn't deserve that," Alanna said, sliding forward again. Just one more step…

"I know," Darcy whispered.

Hope erupted inside Alanna, a happiness that she hadn't been wrong about Darcy; that even though the woman had kidnapped her, there was still good in her, still reasons why Alanna had grown to love her.

Darcy was still a criminal. Once she returned to jail, Alanna would have to consider whether to see her again. She'd stolen the childhood Alanna had been meant to have. And yet, that fact didn't erase the fourteen years of love, the happy childhood Darcy and Julian *had* given her. It didn't change the fact that even though Alanna had gone home to the Morgans, even though she didn't regret it, she still loved Darcy, too.

Maybe that was something Alanna needed to stop feeling guilty about.

"You have to let these kids go," Alanna said.

Darcy's face immediately shuttered, the hand holding the gun shaking.

Alanna stepped closer, put her hand on the top of the pistol and said, "You know it's the right thing to do. Please."

The weapon shook violently underneath Alanna's hand, the fight happening within Darcy written all over her face. Then her shoulders slumped and Alanna smiled gently, knowing she'd won.

The sudden grumble of an old car engine from somewhere nearby startled her, made Chance let out a soft *woof.*

In an instant, the indecision on Darcy's face was gone, replaced by an angry determination as she took a fast step backward. The little boy stumbled along with her, the little girl lifting her head as Darcy stiffened her arm and leveled her gun on Peter.

"Don't," Peter warned softly. "I'm a trained police officer. My aim is better than yours."

Betrayal flashed across Darcy's face, but she didn't glance Alanna's way this time. Instead she stared directly at Peter, the guilt in her voice shifting to anger. "You want to find out? You're a bigger target than I am. At this distance, I could be a terrible shot and still kill you. You want to risk being slightly off your mark and hitting my girl?"

Chance let out a low growl, took a slow step forward with his front paw.

Alanna held up a hand and he froze. She didn't dare look at Peter.

She had no idea what Peter's training was like, how accurate a shot he was. She doubted he'd fire unless he had to with the little girl in Darcy's arms.

But five years ago, Darcy had fired at Kensie. And she hadn't aimed to wound.

Darcy's head tipped back slightly, her lips tightening as if she'd made a decision, and panic took hold of Alanna.

She leaped in between them, spreading her arms wide.

"Alanna!" Peter yelled, a mix of anger and fear in his voice as he shifted sideways and she moved with him. "Get out of the way!"

Alanna didn't take her gaze off of Darcy.

A ghost of a smile lifted one corner of Darcy's mouth, a sad understanding look in her eyes, before she spun and escaped out the front door with the little girl.

"Chance, stay!" Alanna yelled as she practically body-slammed Peter.

Peter slid his finger off the trigger, bracing himself to absorb her weight so he wouldn't get knocked to the ground. "What are you doing? She's getting away!"

"She could kill you!" The panic in Alanna's voice was unmistakable, the desperation clear in the surprising strength of her grip as she wrapped her arms around his waist and hung on.

He swore, angling his gun away from her as he tried to push her away with his free hand. Alanna was a lot stronger than she looked, with lean muscle in her arms and legs and a good knowledge of leverage that she used to her advantage.

He glanced at the closed door. "If she gets away now, how will we find her? She's got a child!"

"Darcy won't hurt her, but she'll hurt you," Alanna

said, her fingers digging into him, her desperation dangerous.

He didn't want to hurt Alanna. But the cough and sputter of a car's engine followed by the squeal of tires made him swear. "I'm sorry," he said, and twisted her arm as if he was going to push her to the ground and arrest her. The move broke her grip on him, prevented her from twisting back. Then he pushed her away and darted for the door, hoping he wasn't too late to stop Darcy.

Alanna ran after him and he spun back, holding his pistol away from his body, afraid it would accidentally fire as she grappled him. But she wasn't coming for him this time.

She reached for the little boy Darcy had left behind, who'd been crying since the melee had started and now ran toward the door, too, to follow the woman who'd kidnapped him.

Chance got there first, blocking the boy's way and plopping onto the floor. He knocked the boy down with him, but instead of crying harder, the little boy wrapped his arms around the big dog and buried his head in Chance's fur.

Alanna sighed, then looked up at Peter, fear and regret in her eyes.

She had to know he wouldn't hurt Darcy unless there was no other choice, didn't she? He wanted to reassure her that everything would be okay, but it wasn't a promise he could make, so he just broke eye contact and took off out the door.

The yard seemed empty, moonlight filtering through the towering trees and iced-over snow. But there were a lot of places to hide and no guarantee the engine he'd heard was actually Darcy's. Would she have been able to get into a vehicle that fast? He hadn't seen any other vehicles except his own truck when he'd arrived. The trees here were thick; there probably wasn't enough space to hide a vehicle except close to the road.

His heart thudded too fast as he tried to focus on any sound that didn't belong, any movement in his peripheral vision. But the woods were too dark, the diminished hearing in his left ear made worse by the stress of knowing Darcy could be hunkered down behind a nearby tree, taking careful aim at him.

A crunch that could have been someone stepping through the icy snow made him swivel his head right, toward the direction of his parked police vehicle. He squinted through the darkness, trying to spot any movement, then a quiet *snap* from the left made his head swivel. Animals? Darcy sneaking up on him, ready to eliminate the only other person with a weapon?

If he was shot in these woods, what would Alanna do? Rush out and try to help him while Darcy took aim at her, took her revenge for Alanna's betrayal, and then disappeared with both kids?

Furious to be in this position, Peter backed slowly toward the cabin, slipping inside. He shut the door, holstered his weapon and pulled out his phone.

"What happened?" Alanna demanded from where she was crouched on the floor, her arms around both Chance and the little boy.

"I can't see anything. Do you know where she parked?"

Alanna shook her head. "I didn't see a vehicle."

He pulled Chief Hernandez up on his phone, but Alanna was by his side, gripping his arm, before he could hit Call.

"What are you doing?" She sounded panicked, like she was still thinking with emotion instead of logic.

For a few brief moments, he'd thought her raw emotion and honesty were what would change Darcy's mind and end this whole thing peacefully. But that time had passed. Now they needed logic. And manpower.

He pulled his hand free and did the thing he should have done from the start. "We need backup."

When Chief Hernandez answered the phone, he gave her a quick rundown of their location and status, then turned back to Alanna.

She was staring wide-eyed at him, the shock on her face mixed with grief.

Knowing she'd just lost a piece of her childhood, he squeezed her hand gently as he told her, "Lock the door behind me. Stay here with the boy and Chance."

Chance stood at his name, took a step toward Peter, then looked at the closed door. As if he was ready to run out with Peter or stand between a threat and Alanna.

"Good boy, Chance," he said, then looked sternly at Alanna. "Don't let anyone in except the Desparre PD."

He didn't mention that they considered her an accomplice and might arrest her when they arrived. He and Alanna would have to deal with that if it happened. Instead, he let go of her hand and turned for the door when her fingers latched onto his arm again. When he turned back, there was regret on her face.

"Back at the other cabin, when I chased after her, I was so sure I could catch her. I thought if it was just the two of us, I could talk her down."

"I know," Peter said, peeling her fingers away. He pulled out his weapon again, glancing at her before he moved to slip out the door. The pink flush of emotion across her pale cheeks and the sadness in her dark eyes were a split-second image he knew would stick with him long after she was gone.

He'd risked his career for her. Risked his life for her. He had no regrets about that, but he'd still been wrong tonight.

If he'd let his team in on what he was doing, he would have had backup right now. There would have been a team waiting outside the cabin, ready to surround Darcy and talk her down, or follow at a distance until they could bring in reinforcements to take her out and protect the little girl.

Instead, Darcy was gone again. He and Alanna had the boy, but what about the little girl?

Peter forced himself not to look back at Alanna, at the sorrow and regret in her eyes. He closed the door behind him, his eyes slowly adjusting to the darkness. He hoped it wasn't already too late, but his gut told him it was.

He'd sacrificed his job thinking he was doing the right thing for everyone, Alanna in particular. But had his mistake just cost a little girl the chance to grow up with her real family?

Chapter 13

The subtle *clack clack clack* of metal against metal echoed through the woods and Peter froze, his arms tense as they supported his pistol. The noise was coming from his right, in the direction of where he'd parked.

In an instant, he realized what it was. The sound of someone trying to open the door to his police SUV. He didn't pause to wonder why Darcy would be trying to get into his vehicle instead of racing for her own. He just started running.

The deeper he went into the woods, the icier the top layer of snow got, crunching as he set each foot down, trying to suck his boots off as he lifted them back up. His breath puffed out in front of him in frigid blasts of air, his lungs feeling every degree that had dropped in the past few hours, every moment he'd spent earlier today digging his friends out of the snow.

As he got closer to the SUV, he slowed, knowing his heavy footsteps in the snow were telegraphing his approach. He couldn't hear Darcy anymore. But was it because she'd gone silent, listening to his approach and trying to line him up in her sights in the darkness? Or just because his hearing wasn't good enough to make out the soft noise of her slinking away over his own footsteps?

He ducked against the shelter of a big tree trunk just before the *boom* of a gun rang out. The muzzle flash told him she was standing behind his vehicle, using it as cover.

His heart thumped at the near miss, then with a realization. Darcy had run the wrong way out of the cabin. Unless he'd totally missed it, there was no other vehicle out this way. She must have left her car in the other direction. To get to it, she'd have to slip past him. Instead of taking the risk, she'd tried to take his vehicle.

He didn't need to rush her now, try to get close through the threat of more bullets. He just needed to pin her there, prevent her from flanking him and returning to her own vehicle. Then he could wait her out, because the rest of his team was on their way. With sirens and lights, they should arrive in less than ten minutes.

Sliding farther behind the tree trunk, Peter squeezed his eyes shut and focused on his hearing. He angled his good ear toward the vehicle, straining to hear any sound that would indicate Darcy was on the move. But he heard nothing.

The muzzle flash had left a temporary mark on his retinas and he waited, listening, until it went away. Then he opened his eyes again and shapes that had been indistinct before became identifiable. A stray branch, broken and dangling from the tree in front of him. Holes in the snow, distinctly paw-shaped, where Chance had stalked alongside him on the way to the cabin. Bigger holes where his boots had broken through in his frantic rush to get to Alanna.

Peter leaned slightly around the edge of the tree, leading with his gun, because if his eyes had started to adjust to the darkness, surely Darcy's had, too.

There was nothing. No top of her head peeking over the vehicle, no outstretched hand clutching a pistol, shifting to take aim. No crying little girl, cold and afraid.

A curse formed on his lips as he turned his head, angling his right side the other way to listen for Darcy. Had she given up on her vehicle to head deeper into the woods? Or maybe she had just kept going past his car and to the road, hoping to hitch a ride from someone who didn't recognize her? Was she able to move through the snow more quietly than he could, his hearing loss too great to detect her?

He didn't hear her. But suddenly, he heard sirens, approaching fast.

Then Darcy was racing away from his vehicle, desperation in the extended length of her strides, in the way the child was clutched in her arms.

She held the girl tight with both hands, Peter realized. It meant she didn't have a hand free to aim and fire.

He moved away from the protection of the tree to pursue her. He was taller than her, with longer strides, and he was quickly closing the gap between them. But he couldn't fire without risking the girl, so he holstered his gun.

Darcy glanced back, saw him gaining and put on a new burst of speed.

It wasn't going to be enough, though, and she must have known it, because she halted suddenly, spinning toward him, her arms shifting to juggle the girl and pull her gun.

He leaped toward her, going for her gun hand. He grabbed it before her finger could slip under the trigger guard and then he was tossing the weapon aside, twisting her arm up and back.

She yelped and the girl, still caught in her other arm, started to cry.

"Hand her over," Peter demanded. Then the sirens were suddenly on top of them, the flashing blue and red lights sweeping over Darcy's face and illuminating the tears there, too.

Chief Hernandez and Tate were running through the woods to meet them, weapons out. Peter felt a wash of relief to see his partner had been discharged from the hospital.

"She's unarmed," he yelled, even though as he said it, he realized he couldn't be sure she didn't have another weapon on her.

Still, he had a hard grip on her arm, had it twisted at such an angle that there was no way for her to move it without causing a break. If she wanted to go for a weapon, she'd have to drop the child. Staring at her now, at her tear-filled eyes, wide and panicked, he knew she wouldn't do it. Because even as she shook her head at the approaching cops, she made soothing *shh* noises under her breath to the child, slightly rocking her. Trying to comfort her.

"Hand her over," Peter repeated, softer this time, as

the chief stepped forward, holstering her weapon and holding out her arms. "It will be okay. We'll take care of her. I promise."

Then he heard the crunching of ice behind him, the sound of someone dashing toward them.

Tate shifted his weapon up and over, then returned his aim to Darcy.

Peter glanced over his shoulder and cursed as he saw that it was Alanna. Chance and the boy weren't with her, which meant she'd left them in the cabin. She'd probably heard the sirens, heard him yell to his teammates that Darcy wasn't armed anymore.

Darcy's gaze locked on Alanna and guilt flashed across her face before she dipped her head. Then her shoulders slumped. She stretched her arm with the girl in it toward Chief Hernandez.

The girl clung to Darcy's neck and Chief Hernandez peeled her arms free, tried to soothe her as she cried. The chief stepped backward, unzipping her coat and tucking the child into it as she nodded at Peter.

He grabbed Darcy's other hand and handcuffed her. Then he pushed her against a tree trunk and moved her legs slightly apart with his foot so he could pat her down for additional weapons. "I tossed a pistol that way," he told Tate, gesturing with the jerk of his head the area where he'd knocked it away from Darcy.

Alanna reached them just as he'd confirmed Darcy didn't have any other weapons on her. Alanna was panting from exertion, her gaze darting to Tate, to the pistol he still held as he swept the discarded one out of the snow, and tucked it into his belt.

Peter's partner didn't train his weapon at Alanna,

but as he straightened, he locked eyes with her, ready to take action if she rushed to help Darcy.

"She's no threat," Peter told Tate, hoping it was true. "The boy is in the cabin with Chance."

His partner gave him a tense nod.

Peter had definitely destroyed some trust tonight.

"Why did you run?" Alanna demanded, her focus entirely on Darcy. She stepped forward, getting too close, and Peter forced Darcy backward, toward the police car.

Tate holstered his gun and stepped in front of her, preventing Alanna from getting any closer to Darcy.

Chief Hernandez told Peter, "Put Darcy in my vehicle. You'll bring the kids back to the station. Take Tate with you." Her words were clipped and angry, telling Peter there was a reckoning to come.

Peter nodded and pushed Darcy toward the open door of the police vehicle at the edge of the road.

Alanna's voice trailed after them, gaining volume as she demanded over and over, *"Why? Why? Why?"*

Darcy didn't respond, didn't look back once as Peter put her in the SUV and slammed the door shut.

Then he turned back to the scene behind him. He took in Chief Hernandez smoothing her hand over the girl's hair, whispering quiet words as the girl stared up at her, her tears slowly drying. His gaze skipped to his partner next. Tate stood in front of Alanna, feet braced hip-width apart as if he expected he'd need to forcibly stop her from chasing after them. And then there was Alanna herself, frozen in place, her lips still parted from her last screamed question. The pain on her face was hard to see, but at least their chase was over.

Her methods might not have been ideal, but she'd helped them find Darcy. Ultimately, she was the reason they'd been able to rescue these kids. Without her knowledge of Darcy and how to decode symbols that had looked like nonsense to whoever had gone through the Altiers' home years ago, they never would have found this place.

The kids would be reunited with their families now. Alanna could go home to the family who'd waited so long for her return.

It was where she belonged. Back in Chicago, a town he'd never visited, never wanted to.

He belonged in Desparre, fighting for a job that had given him back his passion. For a team he'd grown to respect, a partnership that had become a friendship. A calling that spoke to him even more than being a reporter. A job that now might be beyond saving.

He hadn't even known Alanna for a full week and they'd spent most of that time at odds. He'd broken her trust by calling in his team at the cabin in Luna. She'd broken his by going after Darcy alone after the woman had caused an avalanche. But he had the sense that Alanna understood his actions, as he did hers. After everything they'd been through, he felt a connection to her that was undeniable.

It had been fast, and yet, he couldn't imagine her leaving. Couldn't imagine losing something he'd only just begun to realize he wanted in his life.

Chapter 14

Alanna drove slowly through downtown Desparre, taking in the snow-lined streets bracketed by a handful of buildings, looking like a postcard for peace and solitude. She was in a new rental car; her forgiving rental company had apparently lost other vehicles to avalanches. And yes, maybe they'd also been angling for juicy details of the new kidnappings from the mouth of someone whose involvement was still a mystery.

The police had given a statement to the press first thing this morning. Alanna had watched it in the darkness of her hotel room after a fitful night of sleeplessness. They'd announced Darcy's arrest and the rescue of the kids. When reporters demanded to know whether Alanna was still at large, the police chief had briskly shared that Alanna was no longer a person of interest, that she hadn't been involved in the kidnappings. Then she'd left the podium, ignoring the reporters' follow-up questions.

Technically, Alanna had been cleared of any wrongdoing. But she knew how this worked. The lack of details meant reporters would be clamoring to talk to her again. They'd start showing up on her doorstep, using creative methods to get into her building, asking invasive questions about her life and her emotions.

After watching the press conference, it had taken another hour for Alanna to get up the courage to leave the hotel and drive into town. But she wanted to see Desparre once more before she went home. She needed to make one stop before she drove to the airport and left Alaska behind, probably for good.

When she'd lived in Desparre, she'd only seen the downtown's main street from the back seat of a car. The Altiers had deemed it too risky to let her or her "siblings" walk around the more populated parts of Desparre, even if "more populated" meant seeing a dozen people.

The small town was beautiful, comforting. It was similar to the smaller section of streets nearer to the cabin where they'd lived, where she *had* been allowed to walk around sometimes. In a lot of ways, Desparre still felt more like her home than Chicago.

But it wasn't. And it was time to leave again.

Five years ago, when she'd stepped onto that plane with Kensie, she'd been terrified of what the future held. Terrified to leave behind everything she'd known for most of her life. But deep down, she'd known she'd done the right thing. This time, she wasn't so sure.

Yes, the kids were safe. But would it have happened sooner if she'd been more open with the police?

From the passenger seat, Chance leaned over and nudged her arm with his wet nose.

When she glanced at him with a fond smile, he gave her a forceful *woof,* like he knew what was going on in her mind and wanted her to forgive herself.

Darcy was back behind bars. This time, the woman who'd raised her had refused to see *her.* The children she'd kidnapped had been taken to the hospital to be evaluated. Their parents were flying in to be with them, joyous reunions that would get the reporters clamoring again.

They were safe. And they were young enough, the extent of their kidnappings short enough that they wouldn't attract the same kind of sustained media attention she'd faced.

There was nothing left for her here, no more guilt-ridden mission to fulfill. No reason to remain in Desparre any longer. If Darcy wouldn't see her, after everything that had happened, maybe that was for the best. And yet, Alanna felt unsettled, as if she still had unfinished business.

One last apology, she reminded herself, pulling into the parking lot alongside the Desparre police station. One last goodbye.

As if he could read her mind—and didn't like it—Chance gave a soft whine as she opened the door.

"I'm going to miss him, too," she whispered softly, realizing what was causing her anxiety. It wasn't the awkward apology, the thought of all those judging eyes inside the station. She was expecting that; she'd had practice dealing with it. No matter what the official line was, Alanna knew most of the police force was angry with her. For her part in leading them to the site where

Darcy had started the avalanche. For going off on her own afterward. For whatever role she'd played in Peter's decision to come to her aid alone.

None of those things were making her heart beat too fast, making dread lodge in her chest. It was the thought of never seeing Peter again.

"We have to do it," she told Chance, forcing herself to get out of the car. She was grateful there weren't any reporters camped out at the police station like they'd been at her hotel; she had needed to slip out the service entrance. But why would there be? They wouldn't expect her to come here.

She owed the whole station an apology. Her intentions might have been good, but when they'd come to help, someone she loved had tried to kill them.

She owed Peter an apology most of all. Even though they had never really been anything except reluctant partners in a search for a kidnapper, it felt like they'd created a friendship. It felt like they'd been on the path to something more.

Chance leaped out of the car to follow her up to the police station the way he'd done the first day she'd returned to Desparre. Had it only been five days ago?

When they'd arrived, his tail had been wagging at the adventure. He'd strode along beside her, then raced off briefly to pounce in the fluffy snow before returning to her side.

Today, his tail faced downward and even his chin was angled to the ground. Either he was catching her mood or he was sad to be leaving this place, too.

"We'll be home soon," she tried to reassure him. "You'll get to play with Rebel."

At the mention of Kensie and Colter's dog, Chance's

tail gave a quick wag, but then he was staring ahead again, intent and serious.

Alanna took a deep breath and closed her eyes, trying to relax. But her usual method for coping with anxiety didn't work. Instead, she pictured Peter's face, in turns furious, betrayed and understanding. She could almost feel his long fingers sliding through hers, offering comfort, even as distrust flickered in his eyes.

What might have happened between them if she had a reason to stay longer? If she'd come here for a different purpose entirely? If they were both different people, him without the trauma of standing too close to a hostage who'd blown herself up, her without the baggage of growing up with people who'd kidnapped her?

Maybe nothing. Maybe it was their pasts that had drawn them together, made them both understanding and wary of one another. Maybe the same thing that had created the spark between them would have ultimately destroyed it.

"I guess I'll never know," Alanna whispered, pushing open the door to the station.

The moment she was led into the bullpen where the officers worked, a dozen gazes flicked her way, started to turn back, then fixated on her. Angry, suspicious gazes from officers who'd dug their way out of an avalanche yesterday. Officers who, at minimum, thought she'd wanted a kidnapper to get away and at worst, thought she'd been helping Darcy all along.

"I'm sorry," Alanna said, her voice creaking out, little more than a whisper. She cleared her throat and repeated the words, louder. "I came here because I wanted to help. I came here because I thought I knew Darcy. I thought I understood what she'd do and how I could get through to her. I never wanted anyone to be hurt because of me."

When the officers just continued to stare at her, none of them making a move to accept her apology, heat pricked her cheeks and she ducked her head.

Then Tate was beside her, kindness in his eyes and in the hand he put on her arm. "It's okay, Alanna. It wasn't your fault. We all know that now." He shot a quick glance at his fellow officers, who grumbled agreement and went back to their work. "Besides," Tate added as he bent down to rub Chance's ears, "you brought along a snow rescue dog."

She gave him a grateful smile as Chance thumped his tail.

Tate stood again, looking more serious. "You should come with me, though." He headed through the station, toward the back, where she'd never been.

"I was actually hoping to talk to Peter," Alanna said, as she and Chance hurried after him. "I wanted to say goodbye."

"There's someone who wants to talk to you first." He gestured to the closed conference room door ahead of him.

Was Darcy in there? Had she agreed to talk to her after all? But why? And why would the police agree to it?

Or maybe it was the kids? Or their parents, wanting to know how to help them recover from the trauma of being kidnapped?

Even though it was part of what she did for a living, this was too personal. She was still too conflicted to offer the support they needed.

She shook her head, backed up a step, but then Tate pushed the door open for her.

On the other side of it, the police chief and Peter glanced her way. Then Kensie and Colter were there, hugging her, almost squashing baby Elysia between them.

Yet again, Kensie had flown across the country for her. This time, she'd brought her husband, five-month-old baby and their dog, too. She'd always been willing to do anything to protect Alanna. From the moment she'd wrapped her in a hug in Luna's hospital five years ago, Alanna had discovered her big sister always seemed to know exactly what she needed.

Rebel and Chance barked greetings to each other as Alanna breathed, "What are you doing here?"

"What are *you* doing here, sis?" Kensie asked her with a troubled gaze as she leaned back. "Why didn't you call us? We'd have come with you."

Peter looked at the police chief and said, "Let's give them have some privacy." The chief nodded and they left the room, keeping the door ajar.

In a quick burst, Alanna gave her sister and brother-in-law the short, ugly version of what had happened with Darcy.

Kensie stared at her a long moment, then asked, "What about the cop?" She nodded toward Peter in the other room.

Alanna glanced at him and blurted, "I owe him an apology." Kensie and her husband shared a smile over her head.

Then Colter announced, "Kensie and I came here to bring you home, Alanna. But I think we're going to spend the night at my cabin. We haven't been there in more than a year. I want to show the place to Miss Elysia here." He took his daughter from Kensie, bounced her in his arms and mumbled baby talk to her, then added, "It'll give you time to make that apology."

"But—" Alanna gestured to Peter, staring at her from beyond the conference room with his usual intensity, and Kensie took her hand.

"This time, when you come home, I don't want you to have any regrets, Alanna."

"I didn't—"

"It wasn't fair of us to think you'd want to leave this whole life behind, just walk away from everyone."

"You didn't," Alanna interrupted. "You encouraged me to stay in touch with Sydney and Johnny. You tried to help convince Drew's and Valerie's parents to let me talk to them. You've always supported me."

"But I should have understood how hard it was for you to leave the people who'd raised you, too," Kensie said. When Alanna tried to protest again, she pressed on. "You did a good thing, coming here to help find those kids. I know you're upset about how it all went down, but that's not your fault. And I can see that you found something else while you were here."

Alanna flushed and tried not to glance at Peter as Kensie winked and added, "Big sisters always know."

"It's not what you think," Alanna tried to explain. Her connection with Peter was forged from a situation that had ended. It would break as soon as she stepped on that plane.

"Maybe, maybe not," Kensie said, finality in her voice, a big sister tone Alanna had always secretly loved. "But years later, I don't want you thinking 'I should have, could have…' So, Colter is right."

"Happens sometimes," Colter interjected, making faces at Elysia as she squirmed and giggled.

Kensie rolled her eyes at her husband, then hugged Alanna once more. "Don't do it here. Go see him after work. Talk. Just be honest and at least then, whatever happens, you can move forward. Okay?"

Alanna nodded, unable to stop herself from glancing at Peter, who'd been staring at her as if he knew he was the subject of their conversation.

Alanna stared at the house in front of her, at the light shining through the curtains, the shadow moving inside. Her engine was still running as she debated whether she could go through with it.

Alanna could hear her sister's voice in her head from this morning, telling her she needed closure.

She'd never be able to have closure with Julian. The same was probably true of Darcy now, as well. It was too late to change either of those things. But she could find closure with Peter.

It had seemed like a good idea to go to Peter's house when Kensie had suggested it this morning. But ten hours later, she was having doubts.

Woof! Woof!

Chance's bark startled her and made the curtains part in the house's window.

"*Chance*," she chided as Peter stepped outside, wearing just jeans and a long-sleeved T-shirt in the frigid weather.

Alanna turned off the engine and got out of her car, an apology already on her lips as Chance leaped out after her.

"Come on," Peter said, cutting off her apology and

turning back for the house, his expression inscrutable. "It's cold out here."

Chance bounded up alongside him, accepting Peter's ruffling of the fur on his head before he jumped up the stairs and into the house.

Alanna followed a little more slowly, nerves building.

When she stepped inside, he helped her out of her thick winter coat, silent but not taking his gaze from hers. This singular focus made her flush and then he smiled.

His default expression was always so serious: his lips pressed together, his gaze steady, the sharp lines of his face making him seem even more intense. His was the face of a police officer. But his smile was a little bit crooked, a little bit shy. It made him seem younger, more approachable. It charmed her.

When he smiled, she could imagine walking beside him, tentatively slipping her hand into his. She could envision the giddy nervousness of a first date, the sweetness of a first kiss and then the smile on his face giving way to a thrilling intensity as he lay with her in front of the fireplace.

Awareness flickered in his eyes, then he stepped back, giving her more space than she wanted. "Let's sit by the fire." He headed that way, tapping his leg, calling, "You, too, Chance."

Her St. Bernard hurried after Peter, tail wagging. When Peter sat on the couch, Chance lay at his feet.

Alanna settled awkwardly a few feet away, angled toward him. She twisted her hands together, trying to remember the words she'd planned out on the drive to his house. But they wouldn't come and she turned away, her attention snagging on the bare wall across from her.

"You took down the pictures," she said.

"It's going to make my family happy. They're going to ask what prompted such a big change." His hand skimmed hers, then he shifted closer until they were sharing a seat. "I've been focusing on the wrong things. You taught me that."

"What? I did? How?"

The smile was back, amused now, less self-conscious. But those bright blue eyes were still laser-locked on hers, practically hypnotic. "You've had to make a lot of hard choices. Pretty much everyone around you— all these people who love you—they expect something from you. I see you trying to do right by all of them. I see you putting your own needs last. And honestly, with all the reasons you have to hate some of the people involved, you always seem to choose love."

Alanna shook her head, blew out the breath she'd been holding. Was that really how he saw her? She wished it were true. "I try to be fair to everyone, but it doesn't always work. It feels like I let people down a lot."

"You don't—"

"I let you down," she interrupted, flipping her hand over to squeeze his, trying not to fixate on how perfectly his hand seemed to fit with hers. "I owe you an apology. I shouldn't have run off without telling you where I was going. I shouldn't have forced you to make a decision that would hurt your career."

"I made my choice," he said, confirming what she'd suspected—his career as a police officer was in danger. "And I'd do it again." He lifted her hand, his breath dancing over her skin as he whispered, "If only we didn't live across the country…" Then he pressed his lips to her knuckles.

It was the briefest touch, but it made her skin tingle and her whole body warm.

"I wish…" Her voice came out so soft she wondered if he could even hear it.

He shifted even closer, pressed against her from knee to shoulder. "What?"

When she'd lived in Desparre, she'd been sheltered, isolated. She'd barely had the opportunity to talk to people outside of her own home. She'd certainly never dated.

When she'd returned to Chicago, Kensie had encouraged her to get out, meet people, join activities. She'd dated sporadically, but it had always felt awkward, tinged with a voyeuristic curiosity about her kidnapping on their part. She'd never developed a real connection with any of them.

Sitting next to Peter felt natural. It felt like she was supposed to be here. And now she was leaving again.

She didn't realize a tear had spilled from one eye until Peter swiped it away. His warm hand stayed on her face, turning to cup her cheek, stroke down the length of her neck. All the while, he never took his eyes from hers.

She couldn't seem to get a full breath as he leaned closer, so slowly, and his lips finally grazed hers. Then suddenly her free hand was clutching the front of his T-shirt and the fingers he had been resting on her collarbone moved into her hair. He took her upper lip between his, brushed his tongue against the seam of her mouth.

Pulling him toward her, she wrapped her arms around his back and held on tight, leaning into his kiss, demanding more. She didn't want to think about tomorrow, didn't want to think about leaving. She only wanted Peter, for as long as they had together.

He groaned, the sound somewhere between frustration and need, and then she was in a controlled fall until her back hit the couch cushions, her feet still dangling on the floor. Peter angled over her, his weight on his elbows as his lips met hers again, his kisses still unhurried even as she arched up toward him.

She slid her hands down his back, pulling him toward her, thrilling in the sudden contact as he lowered his weight more fully onto her, as she shifted so her whole body was underneath him. Running her hands through his hair, over his shoulders, she fused her lips to his. The world around her seemed to fade away until all she could think of, all she could feel, was *Peter.*

The phone vibrating in her pocket startled her, made her jerk. She yanked it out of her pocket, ready to toss it on the floor, when she saw the name on the caller ID. Kensie knew she'd come here tonight, probably knew she wouldn't want any interruptions. So why was she calling now?

As she squirmed to sit up, Peter moved off of her but stroked her hand.

Her voice was breathless as she answered, "Hello?" She cringed at how she sounded.

"Alanna?" Kensie's panicked voice made Alanna's head clear fast.

"What's wrong?"

Her older sister, who'd risked her life to find Alanna five years ago and come to her aid once again, burst into tears. "She's gone!" Her words were garbled over the tears as she rushed on. "Someone came into the cabin. Elysia was sleeping. Now, she's just gone. Alanna, she's been kidnapped!"

Chapter 15

"How is this possible?" Alanna paced in front of the fire, her skin still flushed from their embrace, her lips still slightly swollen from his kisses. With panic all over her face, she spun to face him. "How?"

"I don't know." Peter stood, used his free hand to pull her against his chest as he listened to the officer on the other end of the phone. "Are you sure?" he asked the officer, then swore.

"Well?" Alanna demanded.

Peter shook his head. "Darcy is still behind bars. They just confirmed it. She didn't escape again."

"And?"

"And nothing. She's not saying a word."

Alanna hurried across the room and picked up her coat, fumbling as she tried to get it on. Chance raced after her, barked once, then looked back at Peter.

He followed and grabbed the coat out of her hand. "Just hold on, okay? Let's not waste time driving around. Let's figure out what's going on here."

"This can't be a coincidence," Alanna said, her voice too high-pitched, panic in every shaky movement.

"I know." He pulled her back into his arms, held on tight. "I know. We'll find her."

He felt tension all through her body and wished he could rewind to five minutes ago, before Elysia had been abducted out of the Hayeses' cabin a mere twenty feet from her sleeping parents. Back to Alanna breathless and kissing him, back to a time when nothing else mattered.

He'd been expecting her at his doorstep, had known an apology was coming. He'd planned to cut it off to let her know how she'd impacted his life. He hadn't planned to tell her that he'd developed complicated feelings for her. He definitely hadn't expected anything to happen between them.

Now none of it could matter. Because somehow, from behind bars, Darcy Altier had orchestrated the abduction of Alanna's niece. "It could be a copycat," he theorized out loud. Maybe Darcy's media attention had spurred someone else into action.

"Really? Another kidnapper?" Alanna squirmed free of his tight hold just enough to look up at him from within the circle of his arms, her expression skeptical.

She was only a few inches shorter than him, and he was tempted to lean down slightly and kiss her forehead. He ignored the urge and agreed with her. "Probably not. But Julian is dead. Darcy's been in jail for five years. How likely is it that she managed to find a new partner while she was on her way here from Oregon?"

"There's no way," Alanna said, pulling away from him and starting to pace again, her hands curled into fists. "Maybe Darcy paid someone? I mean, it's Elysia." Her voice cracked and she swiped a hand over her eyes. "Darcy is trying to hurt me because I turned her in five years ago, because I came after her again. I should have stayed home. I should have made sure Kensie stayed home. I can't believe Darcy would do this! I can't believe—"

Peter pulled her back against him just as Chance ran over and pressed against her side, nudging her with his big head. "It's not your fault."

"Of course it's my fault!"

"Alanna—"

"Let's not argue about this." She spun in his arms to face him, staring up at him with desperation and trust. A trust he probably hadn't earned. "Let's just figure out how to find my niece."

"We will," he promised, praying he could keep his word.

To find Elysia, he had to figure out if Darcy had contacted someone. Who would help her? According to the station, Darcy hadn't made a single call since she'd been arrested yesterday. Maybe someone had acted without her needing to ask? Maybe they'd seen the news and taken their own revenge.

But who?

"Could it be someone she met in jail back in Oregon?" he asked. It was an odd thing to consider, but it definitely happened.

"Wouldn't that person still be in jail?" Alanna was obviously not following his trail of thinking.

"I mean, someone who visited her. You know those

women who marry men on death row? Or marry murderers while they're still in jail, then move in with them when they get released? It happens with female inmates and male civilians, too."

Alanna shook her head. "Darcy was already married. Julian—"

"Was in jail, too. They were separated, in two different prisons. Maybe someone started visiting her. Even if she wasn't interested, maybe they followed the news. They could have followed her here. Maybe it was their way of trying to win her over. Stranger things have happened."

Alanna looked skeptical, but it was the best idea he had. It made a lot more sense if it was someone who'd visited Darcy, who'd schemed with her. Someone whose trust she'd earned, someone who'd do anything to make her happy.

No matter what Alanna thought about Darcy and Julian's relationship, these were people who'd spent nearly two decades with kids they'd kidnapped. They were both capable of manipulation. Maybe someone desperate and lonely had visited Darcy in prison and she'd seen an opportunity. Then, when she'd managed to escape, he'd followed her here and taken revenge when she'd gone back to jail.

That actually seemed possible. No matter what Peter thought of Darcy's actions, he'd seen the love for Alanna in her eyes. He could absolutely picture her kidnapping kids she didn't know, trying to re-create what she and Julian had once had. But he wasn't sure he could imagine her intentionally hurting Alanna by having her niece kidnapped by someone else.

It wasn't her MO. Whatever messed up psychology

had allowed her to rationalize kidnapping children, she'd grabbed them with the intent of raising them. This was different. Elysia's kidnapping seemed malicious, angry, driven by revenge.

"I'm going to talk to the US Marshals she got away from back in Oregon," he told Alanna. "They've probably already looked into who visited her in prison. Hopefully they'll share that info with me. Otherwise, I'll try the prison."

Pulling out his phone again, he looked up the number for one of the US marshals who'd accompanied Darcy to Julian's burial. He'd spoken to the agent a few days ago to give her a heads-up that he thought Darcy could be in Alaska. At the time, she'd seemed overworked and overstressed and seriously doubtful that Darcy had made it so far north so fast.

When she picked up now and he explained the situation, there was a long pause. Then she admitted, "We can't be sure about this, but it's possible Darcy had help escaping us at Julian's burial."

Peter swallowed back words of frustration that he hadn't heard about this the first time he'd called. "Who?"

"We don't know. We don't even know if he was in on it. At the time, we assumed it was a coincidence. But given what you're telling me now, maybe we should have looked at it more closely. The distraction he caused, right when he caused it… He left right after, with the rest of the crowd. We never tracked him down."

"It's what gave Darcy a chance to run?" Peter guessed, as Alanna tilted her head close to his, listening in.

"Yeah."

"You have a description?"

"It was a man. Younger than her. Probably white."

Peter let out a noise that sounded like a laugh, but was all frustration. "That's it?"

"It was drizzling. He was wearing a dark raincoat. He wasn't particularly close to us and he wasn't our priority. There was a big crowd there, gawkers and press, plus mourners from another burial service nearby. He was in the wind immediately."

"Okay." Peter sighed, then said, "A little girl is missing. We think it's connected to Darcy. Do you know *anything* else about this guy that could help?"

"I'm sorry."

"Did you look into who visited her in prison?"

"Of course. But no one visited her. We confirmed with the prison that she received mail, but following procedure, they didn't read it. And whatever she received wasn't in her cell after her escape."

"What about phone calls?"

"Nope. She requested to have all the kids she abducted on her approved contact list, if you can believe it, but obviously, that was denied."

"Thanks." When he hung up, he saw how tightly Alanna's lips were pursed together, how her eyes were twitching like she was holding back tears. "I'm going to call my department. Whoever Darcy is working with, she had to contact that person somehow. If it was via mail, maybe one of her cell mates knows who was writing her. We'll find him. In the meantime, let's—"

The buzzing of his phone cut him off. He answered and told his partner, "Tate, I was just about to call you. Alanna's niece—"

"Has been kidnapped. Colter Hayes called us twenty minutes ago. You need to get in to the station right now."

"We're trying to run down leads," Peter told him, squeezing the hand Alanna had placed in his, watching her wipe away tears. "I think—"

"I've got a lead. I need you here right now," Tate interrupted, then hung up.

The moon was an ominous sliver in an angry gray sky when Peter whipped his truck into the Desparre PD parking lot.

Alanna leaped out as he put the vehicle in Park, Chance chasing after her. She raced across the lot to the station's door, sliding on a patch of ice and pinwheeling her arms until she regained her balance. Her frustration at the lack of information had grown unbearable on the way over. All Peter had told her after hanging up with Tate was that there was a lead.

Peter didn't live that far from the station—less than ten minutes at the near-dangerous speeds he'd been driving. But she'd felt every one of those minutes like they were hours. Elysia was out there somewhere, at the mercy of a stranger.

Alanna had never felt a joy quite like the day she'd gone to the hospital to meet her niece. She'd spent years agonizing over her choice to leave behind "siblings" she'd loved, so she could return to siblings she'd missed but who'd become vague memories. But that first moment she'd held Elysia in her arms, she'd been so overcome with love, she'd nearly burst into tears. That moment had been worth every doubt, every ounce of guilt she'd tried to psychoanalyze away.

Now Elysia was in danger. And it was because of her.

Yanking the door to the police station open, Alanna nearly stumbled as Chance raced in past her, barking a greeting that was returned immediately. Rebel was here. Which meant Kensie and Colter were, too.

The door marked Police Only was propped open and Chance bolted through it. Even though she knew Kensie and Colter would never blame her, Alanna's steps faltered. Her anxiety ratcheted up, but then Kensie was running toward her. Colter hurried after his wife, his gait uneven as he leaned on the cane he rarely used, his wartime injury obviously acting up. Before Peter had even finished slipping through the door behind her, Kensie and Colter had their arms around Alanna, a family hug that reminded her how much she'd missed in all her years away. Chance doubled back, running circles around Colter and Kensie's Malinois-German Shepherd, until the two of them pushed their way into the circle.

A short burst of anxious laughter broke through her threatening tears as Alanna pulled out of the tight embrace. She saw the panic and desperation on Kensie and Colter's faces and a sob burst free. "I'm sorry."

"Don't," Colter snapped, something deadly coming into his eyes that might have been his war face. "It's not your fault. We need to focus on getting her back, not on regrets."

Alanna nodded, swiping away the tears that had spilled despite her best efforts. "What do we know?"

At the question, Tate appeared, frowning as his eyes skimmed down the top page in a big stack of paper. "Not what we expected."

"What does that mean?" Alanna demanded, tired of all the cryptic information.

"Let's go sit in the conference room." Tate nodded briefly at Peter, then spun back the way he'd come.

Alanna hurried after him, alongside her sister, brother-in-law, Peter and the two dogs. Together, they all crammed into the little conference room and then Tate announced, "The parents of those two kidnapped kids arrived late this evening." He glanced at his watch and then amended his statement. "Technically, yesterday. Once they saw their kids, we sat down and talked to them about what happened."

"I'm sorry," Kensie interrupted, her hand clutched tight in her husband's, her eyes and nose bright red like she'd been crying fiercely not long ago. "What does this have to do with Elysia? Do you have any leads on where she is?"

Tate set the stack of papers on the table, rubbed the side of his hand against his forehead like he was exhausted. "We all assumed Darcy had kidnapped those kids."

"What?" The floor seemed to move underneath her and Alanna flung her hand out to steady herself on something. Before she could grip anything, Peter was holding her arm, keeping her upright.

"She *did* kidnap them, didn't she?" She looked from Tate to Peter and back again. "She had those kids at the cabin…" Or did she? They'd obviously been at the second cabin, but at the first one, Alanna had only seen her run out the door. Where were the kids then?

"It sounds like she was involved," Tate said, "but…" He glanced at them, leaning against the wall, holding onto each other, the dogs positioned in front as if standing guard. "Why don't you all sit?"

"Just tell us," Colter demanded, his arm tight around Kensie's shoulders. "What's going on?"

"According to the kids, Darcy didn't grab either of them. The little boy said it was a man, much younger than Darcy, who kidnapped them and brought them back to Darcy."

"I've been in touch with the Marshals who were watching her in Oregon," Peter jumped in. "It sounds like this could be the same person who helped her escape at the burial. We need to talk to the prison, try and see if we can figure out who was writing her there. She must have met someone through letters, convinced him to help her escape."

Was that really what had happened? Or was the answer much simpler? Alanna felt herself sway as Tate continued.

"Apparently, when you caught up to Darcy and the kids at the second cabin, this man was out. When you found her at the first one, he'd already taken the kids to the second location. Both times, he had their vehicle. Darcy had needed to start that avalanche so she could slip away and wait somewhere for this guy to pick her up. It's why she didn't have anywhere to go at the second cabin. Darcy was supposed to erase all traces of them and then call to get picked up again."

"Did they mention a name? Have we pressed Darcy on who it is?" Peter asked. "Or I can call the prison right now, light a fire under them, so that they—"

"You don't need to do that," Alanna said. "I know who it is." She looked at Kensie and Colter, shaking her head in disbelief, ashamed that it hadn't occurred to her before now that Darcy might have had help.

Darcy might see a child from a distance that she

wanted, that she believed should have been her child. But it had always been Julian who'd made it happen. With Julian out of the picture, there was only one person Alanna could think of who would try to piece together a new family for Darcy.

"It was my older 'brother,' Johnny."

Chapter 16

"Johnny is the kidnapper," Tate confirmed. When Kensie gasped and looked to Alanna, Tate said, "We don't have a recent photo of Johnny, but we showed the kids a picture from when he was rescued five years ago and they confirmed it was him."

"Why?" Kensie asked Alanna. She was flushed with panic and clutching Colter, whose expression had morphed into a fury Alanna had never seen before. "Why would he kidnap those kids? And why would he take Elysia?"

"He's—" Alanna choked on a sob, then took a deep breath to get control of herself. Focusing on all the mistakes she'd made, worrying about all the worst-case scenarios for her niece wasn't going to help right now. She needed to focus on what had happened to turn Johnny into a kidnapper. Maybe that would help them figure out where he was now and how to stop him.

"He was the first one the Altiers kidnapped," Alanna said, trying to work it out in her mind at the same time she tried to explain to everyone else. "He was five years old. As we grew up, he remembered his family, but barely."

"He refused to talk to you once you came to Chicago. He…" Lines appeared between Kensie's eyebrows as she squinted into the distance, into a memory. "He's the one who shot at me and Colter at the cabin five years ago, isn't he? That was him with the gun?"

Alanna nodded, wishing she could make it untrue. Wishing she could have gotten through to Darcy enough to get her to admit that Johnny was involved.

"He won't hurt Elysia," she blurted. Whatever Johnny had become, he'd never harm a child. Right now it felt like the only thing in her life she knew for certain.

"Alanna," Colter said, judgment and barely contained anger in his voice. "I know he was your big brother for a long time, but—"

"I'm not trying to make excuses for him." She cut Colter off, even though the thought of Johnny doing any of this made her chest hurt so bad she wanted to double over. He might not be her blood, but he *was* still her big brother. When she'd first been kidnapped, feeling terrified and alone, he had comforted her. He'd promised to always look out for her, look after her. He'd said they were brother and sister now and that would never change.

Except if he'd kidnapped Elysia, it *had* changed. There was nothing random about it. While the idea of Darcy grabbing Alanna's niece for revenge had seemed out of character, Alanna could imagine Johnny doing it far too easily.

The truth was, everything between them had changed five years ago. From the moment she'd left that note and brought the scrutiny of the FBI, Johnny's brotherly love had turned into confusion and then hate. When Kensie and Colter had tried to rescue her, Johnny had seen Darcy pick up a weapon, so he'd done the same. He hadn't spoken to her since that moment when the Altiers had been arrested, and he'd barely spoken to the rest of their "siblings," either.

"Drew's and Valerie's parents won't let them talk to any of us. Johnny won't talk to me, so he's only been in contact with Sydney since that day. Sydney said…"

Alanna frowned, wishing she'd tried harder to reach out to Johnny, found a way to get through to him. But every phone call had gone unanswered. Even her emails and letters had never gotten a response. Over the years, she'd all but stopped trying, reducing her attempts to a few letters a year she knew he'd never read.

If she hadn't given up on him, would it have come to this?

"*What*?" Kensie pushed, tears and anger mixing in her voice.

Alanna tried to focus. "Sydney said Johnny moved back to Alaska. When his birth family came to get him, he was already twenty-three. Initially, he went home with them to Colorado, but apparently it never felt like home to him. The last time Sydney and I talked about Johnny, she said he barely spoke to his birth family anymore. I think they gave up trying to build a relationship with him, because he didn't want one."

For Johnny, the Altiers had become his only family. When she'd left the note to tell the world she was still alive, she'd destroyed that family. From then on, he'd essentially been all alone.

"So this kid—man, since he's twenty-eight now—learned Julian had been killed. He was devastated, but saw it as his opportunity to help Darcy escape," Peter said, thinking quickly. "He went to Oregon for the burial, but also to create a distraction and help Darcy get free. They traveled to Alaska together and presumably hatched a plan to kidnap kids along the way. Or maybe they planned the kidnappings before that, when he wrote to her in prison, as soon as they learned Darcy was granted furlough for the burial."

"I think the recent kidnappings were spur-of-the-moment," Alanna said, remembering how Darcy had spoken of seeing her as a child and just *knowing*. She pictured those two kids in the cabin, so similar to the way she and Johnny had once looked. "I think Darcy saw a kid and felt a connection, felt like the child should have been hers. Then Johnny made it happen, like Julian used to do."

She flushed, realizing the one piece of information she'd held back five years ago suddenly mattered now. "Johnny knew how to do it because..." She squeezed her eyes shut, hating that her "brother" had been involved at all, wondering if he'd ever really had a chance to return to a normal life. Wishing she'd tried harder to help him.

"Why?" Colter asked, stepping closer. His dog, Rebel, who'd been in war zones with him as a Combat Tracker Dog, stuck close to his side, knowing when Colter needed him.

"When they kidnapped me and Johnny, they saw an opportunity and took it. But with all the other kids, they *created* opportunities. Darcy and Julian saw Sydney at a playground and they had Johnny lure her around a corner from where her parents were sitting, so they could grab her."

"*What*?" Kensie blurted, looking horrified but also distrustful, as if she wondered what else Alanna had kept from her. "You never told me that."

"It wasn't in the police reports, either," Tate said, his narrowed gaze on her.

To his credit, Peter kept holding her hand. She was afraid to look at his expression as she tried to explain. "Johnny was only thirteen when that happened. Did he really have a choice? I didn't want Johnny to get in trouble because he did what the people he'd called his parents since he was five told him to do. I didn't want him to get charged."

"He was a minor," Peter said softly. "He wouldn't have been charged." When she looked at him, her misery probably clear in her eyes, he asked, "That's not all he did, is it? What about Valerie and Drew?"

She could feel all eyes on her again, and she forced herself to look at Kensie and Colter. "For those abductions, Julian asked Johnny to distract the parents, pretend he needed help while Julian grabbed the kids." She ducked her head as Kensie and Colter stared back at her, disappointment and disbelief all over their faces. "I didn't know about it until after the fact," she added as if it mattered.

Ultimately, when she'd known anything related to kidnappings didn't really matter, did it? It's what Peter had been getting at the first time he'd met her. Yes, she'd been a kid, but she'd had fourteen long years when she could have spoken up, when she could have stopped this.

"He was older then," Tate said when she went quiet.

"He would have been seventeen with Drew and twenty-one with Valerie. An adult."

"Yes," Alanna admitted. "But he was a victim, too. They took him when he was five years old and raised him with love, but also raised him to be theirs. He reacted to it differently than the rest of us, maybe because when they kidnapped him, he didn't have anyone to reassure him, like the rest of us did." It had been *Johnny* who'd first gotten through to her, comforted her, made her feel safe when her whole world was turned upside down. He'd done the same for Sydney, Drew and Valerie.

"None of this was ever his choice. Drew and Valerie, they didn't remember their families, but the rest of us—we felt torn between these lives we sort of remembered and the life we had, the family who loved us." She swiped more tears away, begging Kensie to understand. "I'm so sorry. If I'd ever thought—"

"You were trying to protect someone you loved. I understand why you didn't tell." Kensie's voice sounded understanding, but her hands were fisted, betrayal in the depths of her eyes.

"I'm so sorry," Alanna repeated, but it felt like she was talking into a void, like it was already far too late. She'd tried so hard to do right by everyone and in the end, maybe she'd done right by no one.

Peter squeezed her hand, but she didn't look at him, didn't want to see the judgment there, too.

"So, what's the dynamic *now*?" Tate asked when the silence dragged on too long. "Who's in charge? Darcy? Now that she's behind bars again, Johnny is after revenge, right?" His gaze skipped to Colter and Kensie and he grimaced as he looked back at her. "What does that mean for Elysia? You said he'd never hurt her, didn't you? So what's his endgame?"

Alanna looked around the room, at four pairs of eyes all staring at her, waiting for an answer. It was an answer she didn't have.

He'd been right from the beginning.

Peter stared at Alanna, who was trying so hard to hold it together, and remembered the distrust and suspicion he'd felt when he'd realized who she was. Had that only been six days ago?

Despite everything that had happened since then, he'd been right. He just hadn't been right about Alanna.

When this all started, he would have felt vindicated that his theory wasn't illogical. He'd believed from the very beginning that the kidnapper could be someone who'd been kidnapped and raised by the Altiers, who'd bonded so closely to them, he was now willing to do whatever it took to protect them. It wasn't unusual. Feigning loyalty to stay safe in the beginning could easily shift over time into a warped need to protect the very people who'd kidnapped you. But Alanna hadn't been the one afflicted. Her "brother" had been.

Alanna remembered Johnny as a vulnerable and confused boy, and it was messing with her perception. Peter saw the truth: Johnny was dangerous to them all.

Peter should have felt sorry for him, but instead, it took him back to that war zone, covered in blood and sand and knowing everything he'd worked for as a reporter was over in an instant. He could feel his hand twitching, a strong desire to touch his bad ear. Ignoring it, he tried to focus on what he'd just learned and what it meant for the investigation.

Johnny had been the one kidnapping kids all along. Regardless of Darcy's involvement—which was identifying a kid she wanted—Johnny had actually taken action. What else was he capable of? And how far would he go to get back at Alanna for what he perceived as the ways she'd done him wrong?

He squeezed Alanna's hand tighter, not wanting her to get close enough to Johnny to ever find out.

Across the room, Tate's gaze dropped to their linked hands, then up to Peter's face. Tate's lips pursed slightly—assessing or judging, Peter couldn't be sure. Right now, as much as he liked his partner and valued his opinion, Peter didn't really care. His job was already in jeopardy. The fact that they'd called him at all, that they were letting him in on the investigation, probably had more to do with his proximity to Alanna than their belief in him as an officer.

After the debacle at the cabin, the chief had told him to take a few days off. He'd only been at the station yesterday because the chief had called him in to give him a serious dressing-down. He was lucky she hadn't immediately demanded he hand over his badge and gun. But he knew that wasn't the end of it. She'd all but told him she was still deciding if he had a future on the force.

He had a reckoning coming at the Desparre PD. He didn't want to think about it, couldn't afford the distraction of worrying what it meant for his future, for the very way he'd come to identify himself. Right now, his sole focus had to be on finding Alanna's niece. And on keeping Alanna safe in the process.

It was his job, but it had become more than that. Whatever his connection to Alanna meant, however long it was destined to last, he couldn't let her down now. Not with so much of her happiness at stake. Because if her niece *wasn't* okay, Alanna would never be okay again, either.

"What do you think Johnny was trying to do?" he asked Alanna, tugging on her hand until she turned to face him, forcing her to shut out the stress of her family's reactions and focus on what she knew about her so-called brother. "When he was grabbing those kids Darcy pointed out, are you sure that's how it happened?"

Alanna squinted at him questioningly, her free hand absently stroking Chance's fur. Her loyal dog scooted closer, lending support, as she asked, "What do you mean?"

"Didn't you say that you decided to reach out with that note five years ago because Johnny had met someone, started talking about getting married? Is there any chance he was grabbing these kids for himself, that maybe Darcy being there just gave him the courage to do it? What about this woman he wanted to marry? Who was she?"

Alanna shrugged. "I barely remember her. Darcy and Julian trusted Johnny more than the rest of us, gave him more freedom because they said he'd earned it. He met a woman when he was in town and thought it was love at first sight. Darcy and Julian were skeptical and warned him about keeping the family's secrets, but he started dating her. Once the truth came out and our faces were all over the papers, she wanted nothing to do with him."

"So, you don't think he's trying to build his own family? That grabbing Elysia was just a way to do it and get revenge at the same time?" It might be the best option, the version of events that made it most likely Johnny would take care of Elysia rather than kill her.

"No." Alanna's near-tears of a few minutes ago had turned into something hard and determined. "I think he wanted to re-create the family he had."

"But that was never going to happen," Peter said.

"No. He won't talk to me. Drew's and Valerie's parents won't let him talk to them—and from what I've heard in news reports, they're always watched over. That just leaves Sydney. She talks to him every few months, but growing up, she was the one who remembered her birth family best. The Altiers grabbed her when she was six—older than the rest of us were when we were kidnapped. She's the one that Darcy and Julian always worried would say something and put the 'family' in danger. Besides, she's twenty-one now. She's going to college. She has her own life. It's pretty different from our isolated existence in Desparre. She told me more than once that she'd never come back here. I'm sure she said the same to Johnny."

"So, he decided to find new siblings?" Tate asked, getting Alanna back on track.

"That'd be my guess."

"And then you showed up," Tate said. "You ruined his plan, so he snatched Elysia."

Peter frowned, wondering if his partner was right. Maybe it was enough for Johnny to know Alanna was suffering. But his gut told him otherwise. Everything Alanna had said about Johnny suggested he'd been deeply damaged by his experience growing up, that he had the psychology of someone who would misdirect all their anger and rage at the easiest available target. What good was rage like that if the target didn't know who was hurting her?

Peter looked at Colter and Kensie. "Did you see

Johnny at the cabin? Did he leave any indication that it was him? Some kind of message for Alanna?"

"Elysia was in her crib in the back room," Colter said. "Kensie and I had fallen asleep by the fire. We woke up because Rebel was going wild, trying to get into the bedroom. She might technically be a senior dog, but she still thinks like she's military. We ran back there and found it was locked. I was scared to kick the door in with Elysia in there, so I ran around outside. I found the window open." His jaw tightened, his lips turning inward. "Our daughter was gone."

"You didn't see anything? Not in the backyard or in the room? No note?" Tate pressed.

"If we had, don't you think we would have told you by now?" Colter snapped. He ran a hand through his dark blond hair, making it stick up. "Sorry. My daughter is five months old. We've just—" He choked on a sob, then finished, "I'm trying to hold it together here, but we have to find her."

Tate nodded, his expression saying he'd been in this room before with scared parents. He looked back at Alanna, and Peter was suddenly glad of Tate's extra years on the force, of his background as a police officer in a bigger city before he'd come to Desparre. "Are we waiting for a ransom note here, Alanna?"

Alanna shook her head, frustration and exhaustion on her face. "I don't know." Then that frustration morphed into angry determination. "But I know who does. I want to talk to Darcy."

Chapter 17

"I don't understand you at all," Darcy said, staring at her from across the table inside the Desparre PD's claustrophobic interrogation room.

Tate and Peter had brought Alanna here, insisted that Darcy had to remain cuffed and then left them alone to talk. Of course, *alone* was a relative term. Alanna's gaze darted to the camera mounted in the corner. Whatever was said in here, Peter and Tate were watching. She didn't know who else from the department was with them.

Darcy looked even worse than she had at the cabin. Her shoulders were slumped inward and the lines pulling at the edges of her mouth and eyes seemed even more pronounced.

"I'm not sure I understand you, either," Alanna said, clutching her hands tightly together underneath the table, trying to keep her tone even, keep the anger and blame out of her voice. Darcy knew her better than most people on the planet; it was unlikely she'd be fooled.

"You let me go at the cabin," Darcy said, real confusion in her eyes. "You stood in front of me, gave me an opportunity to escape."

Alanna tensed, resisted the urge to glance at the camera surely recording every word spoken in this room. That hadn't been her reasoning at all, but she clamped her lips together, let Darcy continue. She'd rather fight an accomplice charge than risk angering Darcy, risk losing the chance to find out where Johnny had taken Elysia.

"So, why did you bring police in the first place? Why did you turn us in all those years ago? It's like you're two different people, Alanna." A humorless smile flitted across her face, before morphing into a scowl. "I should have realized it sooner, I guess. You're torn between two worlds. I saw it over the years when you were growing up, this far off look you'd get on your face, like you were dreaming about the family you'd been born to, instead of the one you were meant to be a part of. I thought you'd grown out of it before you wrote that note. After all those years, we thought we could trust you."

This again? Alanna fought down her frustration. The guilt she'd seen in Darcy's gaze, in her words, when Alanna had told her how her kidnapping had affected the Morgans, already seemed forgotten. Right now, seeing Darcy wasn't about getting an apology. It wasn't about getting closure on her past. The fact was, she'd probably never fully have it. That was something she needed to manage. And it was something she *could* manage, with her degree in psychology and her job helping others overcome worse trauma.

What she *did* need was for Darcy to understand the hurt she'd caused. She needed to understand the further hurt she'd cause if she let Elysia stay with Johnny. It was the only way Alanna had a shot at getting Darcy to choose Alanna's happiness over that of the man she still called her son, the man who still called her Mom.

Alanna folded her arms in front of her on the table, leaned in.

Before she could speak, Darcy asked softly, "What happened to your ring?"

Alanna's hands twitched, her wish to keep them hidden under the table too late. Darcy had given her a worn ruby ring when she was sixteen years old. It was a family heirloom Darcy had worn most of Alanna's childhood. Alanna hadn't taken it off for three years. It was the only thing she'd taken with her when she'd left Alaska besides the clothes she'd been wearing the day police had split apart the "family."

The Morgans had all stared curiously at it when they didn't think she would notice, but they waited for her open up to them at her own speed. She hadn't wanted to hurt them, hadn't wanted to admit that she missed Darcy and Julian, that the ring felt like her final connection to them. Instead she'd taken it off, placed it carefully at the bottom of a drawer and hadn't put it on since.

"It's safe," Alanna said. "I still have it." She slid her hands back under the table, tried to get the conversation back on track. "You thought you could trust me? Well, you said you loved me. You said you wanted to raise me to be strong and happy."

The offense was as obvious on Darcy's face as it was in her voice when she insisted, "I do. I did."

Alanna leaned toward her again, closing the space between them, letting Darcy see the hurt and fear on her face. "Then why would you let Johnny take my niece?"

Darcy's mouth dropped open into a small *O*. She shook her head slightly, her brow furrowed, but she didn't quite meet Alanna's gaze.

"You didn't know?" Alanna demanded, not sure if the confusion on Darcy's face was feigned or real. Hope started to replace the fear that talking to Darcy was too much of a long shot. If she really hadn't known, she'd be more likely to help Elysia. But would she be able to? Would she know how to get through to Johnny?

"I— No. That wasn't part of the plan. I didn't even know your niece was here. Heck, I didn't even know you *had* a niece. It's not like you talk to me anymore." She scowled, then gave a quick, hard shake of her head. Her voice was sad and lost when she continued, "We just wanted what we had before. We weren't trying to hurt you. We weren't trying to hurt anyone."

"But you know you did, right?" Alanna asked softly, willing Darcy to look at her, to face what she'd done. "Just like you knew what you'd done to all of our families. You tried not to think about it, tried to convince yourself the families you stole from would all be fine, that the kids you ripped away from them were happy. But deep down, you knew. You *knew* it was wrong."

Tears filled Darcy's eyes and she blinked rapidly, clearing them away. She started to reach her hand out, then looked at the cuffs keeping them locked together and faltered.

Alanna leaned farther across the table, closing her

hand over the top of Darcy's linked hands, hoping she wouldn't fixate on the missing ring again. Not that many years ago, Darcy's hands had been smooth and soft, deceivingly small for how strong she was. Those hands had picked Alanna up hundreds—thousands?— of times as a child. They'd sewn her clothes and helped her build a desk for her studies. They'd wiped away her tears and wrapped around her in loving hugs that Alanna still missed.

Now those same hands felt paper-thin, dry and rough. They looked older, too, as if she'd aged twenty years in prison instead of five.

The guilt that was never far beneath the surface bubbled up. Normally, Alanna reminded herself that she had no reason to feel guilty, that she'd done the right thing. This time, she let Darcy see all of her conflicted emotions, hoped it would help Darcy admit to some of her own.

"Please," Alanna whispered. "Elysia is only five months old. Johnny doesn't know how to take care of a baby that young. Not alone. And my sister deserves to get her child back. Kensie has been through enough."

"I…" Darcy's cheek twitched, her lips twisting downward. Her gaze skipped away from Alanna.

"Johnny still has a chance to make a normal life for himself."

Was it true? Alanna didn't really know. Not only because he'd certainly be facing charges for helping a prisoner escape and kidnapping three children, but also because everything that had happened in the past week proved he was more damaged by their upbringing than Alanna had ever realized.

Still, there was one thing she knew for sure. Turning himself in, handing Elysia over unharmed, was the only chance he had.

Darcy looked up at her, eyes narrowed and unreadable.

"Please help me find them," Alanna begged, squeezing Darcy's hands under hers.

Darcy ripped her hands away and turned her gaze to the ground, but not before Alanna saw the regret there. "You're lying to me. I'm not going to help you relegate Johnny to the same life I've had, the life Julian had. I love my son."

She looked up at Alanna once more, finality in the hardness of her eyes, the clenched line of her jaw. "Goodbye, Alanna."

She'd failed.

Alanna stood outside the interrogation room, her whole body too heavy with dread to move. Even knowing that Peter and Tate had surely already seen everything over the camera feed, Alanna didn't want to face them. More than that, she didn't want to face Kensie and Colter, didn't want to have to admit that their best lead to find Elysia was gone.

The finality in Darcy's goodbye had brought tears to Alanna's eyes. Just as quickly, she'd blinked them away, vowing never to shed another tear over Darcy or Julian Altier.

Yes, they'd raised her with love. But ultimately, everything they'd done had been selfish.

Five years ago, Alanna thought she'd taken a huge step in regaining control over her own life. But maybe she'd just been living in limbo, stuck between two worlds, between two families.

Now, finally, she was picking sides. But she'd done it much too late.

Taking a deep breath to control her anxiety, wishing she had Chance beside her, Alanna forced herself to move back toward the station's bullpen, toward Kensie and Colter.

As soon as she rounded the corner, there they were, crowding around her, fear and hope in their eyes that quickly turned to disappointment when they saw Alanna's face.

Kensie swallowed hard and clutched her husband's hand. Then she reached for Alanna's hand, too, always the big sister, even when Alanna didn't deserve it. "We'll find another way," she croaked, but her voice was full of fear. "The police are already combing the woods around our cabin, looking for trails. They'll find something."

Chance, obviously sensing Alanna's distress, pushed his way through the crowd until he was beside her, his big head nudging her arm. Rebel hurried over, too, slipping in between, so she could press up against Colter and Kensie at the same time.

Alanna stroked her dog's fur, letting his calming presence relax her too-rapid heartbeat. She looked past her family to Peter and Tate, who were standing a few steps away.

Peter stared back at her with sympathy in his eyes, no obvious sign of the distrust he had to be feeling after all of the things Darcy had said about her. Beside him, Tate looked more pensive, but Alanna was surprised to see that he didn't seem angry or distrustful, either.

"What Darcy said—"

Peter stepped closer, cutting her off. "You did your best. I'm sorry she let you down."

She blinked back at him and for half a second, it felt like it was just the two of them in that station. She could see in his eyes that he understood, that he hadn't ever believed she was trying to let Darcy go. A smile trembled on her lips, remembering his frustration in that moment back in the cabin and knowing he'd chosen to believe her.

It faded just as fast as reality rushed back in. Elysia was still missing. Without Darcy's help, how would they find Johnny? Without Darcy's help, how did Johnny expect to care for a newborn while he was on the run?

"He never planned to," she realized aloud.

"What?" Kensie asked, leaning closer, probably recognizing the excitement in Alanna's voice.

"Without Darcy, Johnny's not trying to re-create a family anymore. He's looking for revenge."

Kensie and Colter shared a worried glance, maybe because they'd already decided Johnny had grabbed Elysia out of revenge. They were probably worried it meant Johnny saw Elysia as expendable.

It was more than simple revenge, though. Darcy was all highs and lows, lots of excitement followed by periods of depression. But she always acted with love, even when it was misguided. And until now, she'd stood by all of her "children," no matter what. Johnny followed her lead when it came to his mood swings, but his emotions were always all or nothing. Love or hate. Once the pendulum swung, it was hard to send it back.

He'd treated her like his best friend growing up, the little sister he was so happy to have by his side no matter what. When she'd left that note, all that love had twisted into fury. There was no in-between for him.

If Johnny had given up on rebuilding a family, then his entire goal was revenge. It meant Tate had been right when he'd asked what use revenge was if she didn't know it was Johnny. But with the kids rescued, of course they'd eventually figure out it was him. What Johnny needed her to know now was how to find him. What he needed was a reason to make her come. He'd found the reason. And she knew where to go.

Johnny had returned to where it had all started. He was at their cabin in Desparre.

Chapter 18

"Why are we out here?" Tate demanded, zipping his coat up to his chin.

Alanna looked around the circle of people she'd hustled out of the station and into the snow. Kensie and Colter had Rebel between them, and the dog looked as curious as her owners in the darkened parking lot. Peter stood beside her, absently petting Chance and waiting for her to speak, his narrowed eyes telling her he already suspected what was coming.

When she'd told them all she needed to go outside for some fresh air, she'd hoped Tate would stay inside. Some part of her had hoped Peter would, too. Because if either of them refused to go along with her plan, her niece could be in more danger.

"Maybe you should go in and warm up," Alanna suggested, trying to sound sincere.

"You figured out where they are, didn't you?" Tate demanded.

"What?" Kensie gasped, clutching her hand. "Really?"

Alanna stared back at the big sister who looked so much like her and nodded. "I think so. But…" Her gaze darted to Peter and Tate. "Johnny understands the Alaskan wilderness the way Darcy does. We grew up learning to shoot in case of trespassers or a rogue bear. Despite my carelessness a few days ago, we were taught how to spot signs of a potential avalanche. We learned how to use the wilderness to our advantage."

"Like firing at an overhang of snow and burying a team of police officers who thought they were well hidden?" Tate stared, assessing her like he was still trying to determine if the people who'd raised her were that in tune with their surroundings or she'd somehow given away their presence.

"Johnny was better than any of us," Alanna continued, ignoring the unspoken question—Tate was either going to have to trust her or she wasn't letting him in on her plan. "I can't have officers trying to surround him. Not with Elysia in the way."

Peter took her hand. "We'll be more careful about—"

"No." She turned toward him, Kensie's desperate face in her peripheral vision. "What I said before, about Johnny looking for revenge? I'm the one he thinks did him wrong."

"We're not going to let him hurt you," Colter hissed.

His loyalty brought tears to her eyes and she nodded a quick thanks to the brother-in-law who'd risked his life for her before he'd even known her to help Kensie bring her home. "I don't think he will. He's not trying to just lure me close enough to shoot me. He spent the past five years ignoring me. This is his way of reaching out."

Kensie let out a huffed breath, then leaned into her husband over Rebel.

Alanna kept her eyes locked on Peter, willing him to believe her, praying he'd have enough trust left with Tate to keep his partner quiet, too. "He wants to talk."

"Talk?" Peter asked, eyebrows raised. "And then what?"

"I know Johnny," she said instead of answering. "If we give him the opportunity to take me instead of Elysia, he'll jump at that deal."

"There's a better way than trying to make a trade," Peter insisted.

"Aren't we getting ahead of ourselves?" Tate asked. "Where is he keeping Elysia? Let's do some surveillance. We can—"

"You'll never get close to him," Alanna insisted. "But I can. I can go there and convince him to leave her behind. I just have to go with him."

"What?" Kensie stepped forward and Rebel did, too, giving a sharp bark in response to Kensie's distress. Kensie grabbed Alanna's arm, turning her so they were face-to-face. "I don't want to lose you again."

"You won't," Alanna said, forcing herself not to blink or shift her gaze. "He hates me right now, but I'm still his family. As long as I don't betray him by bringing the police, he'll go with me. He'll leave Elysia. I *know* he will."

"Alanna." Her name sounded like a sigh as Peter moved so he was in her line of sight, too. "You can't know how anyone from the Altier 'family' is going to respond anymore. Things have changed."

"You saw what happened in that cabin," she told Peter. "Darcy turned her weapon on you, but she ran instead of risking that she'd hit me. After everything that happened, Johnny is still her son. He'll do the same."

Kensie and Colter shared a worried glance and Peter's gaze lifted to Tate's, his forehead crinkled with doubt. Tate gave a short, hard nod and Alanna felt her whole body relax.

They believed her. They'd follow her plan. She let herself smile, because she knew it could work. Johnny had only grabbed Elysia to get back at her. He'd never hurt a baby. But no way did he want to raise one all alone.

"You can still go inside," Peter told Tate softly. "You don't know anything. You don't have to be a part of this."

Tate shook his head, the expression on his face a mix of anger and determination. "We've come this far because Alanna could predict what Darcy would do. If Johnny knows this place half as well as she does, he could disappear way too easily." His gaze darted to Kensie and Colter and then back to his partner. "Our department is good, but situations like this need one of two things—a good hostage negotiator or a full-time tactical team." He looked at Alanna. "I'll bet on our hostage negotiator."

"Thank you," she whispered. Then she took a deep breath and looked at her big sister. "He's at the cabin where we used to live. He must be. It's the only place he can be sure I'd know to look. I'll go up there and get in the car with him. We'll drive away and leave Elysia there. That way, he can be sure anyone coming after us will go into the cabin first. He's good at watching for tails. He'll see if anyone follows us."

"What happens if it doesn't work?" Peter demanded. "What happens if he tries to run with both of you?"

"I won't do it." Understanding that Johnny would probably be armed and there might be a situation where she had no choice, Alanna added, "If I have to get in the car with both of them, I'll signal you. Then you stop the car. Otherwise, you go in the cabin and get Elysia."

"What about you?" Kensie asked.

"Once we're far enough away, Johnny and I will talk things through. I doubt I'll be able to get him to turn himself in. But he'll know I won't stay with him forever, just like I didn't stay with the Altiers forever. He'll have to let me go."

They all stared back at her with worried expressions and she insisted, "I told you, he won't hurt me. He might take a while to let me go, true. Then he'll be a fugitive, because I can't bring him in if he doesn't want to go. But I'll be okay. I promise."

Chance whined, shoved his big head against her arm a few times, like he was begging her to be honest.

She stroked his fur and kept her expression even. Darcy would have been able to see through it, but the woman had raised her. Kensie had only known her for ten years, five of them as a little child and five as a woman torn between two worlds. But no longer. Today she was going to prove where she belonged.

If she didn't live through it, then at least she'd die looking after her niece the way Kensie had looked after her.

This was their best shot.

Peter believed it, but he didn't like it. If this were any other case, he'd bring in his team. He'd trust them to do their jobs better than a group of civilians. Proceeding by the book would have meant officers surrounding the cabin, bringing in a state SWAT team if they had time. It meant keeping higher-ups abreast of every single movement of the operation. It meant Alanna would stay safely outside, far away from danger.

As much as he wanted that last part, Alanna was right. They wouldn't have captured Darcy without her. Darcy and her husband had taught Johnny how to shoot, how to hide, how to fight. Right now, sending Alanna into danger was their best shot at getting Elysia back to her parents safely.

Since Kensie and Colter hadn't immediately nixed Alanna's plan, they knew it was true, too. From the way they were staring at each other—fear, hope and helplessness all over their faces—they didn't like it any better than he did.

Of course, they didn't have to do it completely Alanna's way.

Her plan was probably going to save Elysia's life. But it was probably also going to destroy what was left of Peter's career. It would take down Tate with him.

Thinking about either of those things put a pain in Peter's chest, but Tate knew what he'd agreed to, understood what was at stake. If it meant giving Alanna the life she deserved with the people who loved her, the way it should have been all along, Peter could accept giving up what he'd only recently discovered was his life's calling.

What he wasn't willing to do was risk Alanna's life.

She could be right. She knew Johnny best, knew what he was capable of and, hopefully, where he'd draw the line. Whatever their sins, the Altier "family" had loved each other. But love that had turned into hate was dangerous. It was unpredictable.

They could trade Alanna for Elysia, make sure the infant was safe. But they needed a backup plan, needed something to trade Alanna for, too. Peter wasn't willing to risk Johnny driving off with her and having her disappear again from everyone who loved her.

Peter's family could really annoy him sometimes. His parents still treated him like a teenager. Their encounter with Alanna at the coffee shop hadn't been the first time they'd seen him around town with someone, assumed he was on a date and told the woman how badly he needed to settle down. His siblings weren't much better. They were all older than him, all happily married with kids and certain that what they had was all that was missing from Peter's life. That if he would only hurry up and find the right woman, settle down and make a couple of babies, he'd forget all about the reporter job he'd left behind, forget how hard he'd fought over the past year to be accepted at the Desparre PD as an equal, rather than a possible liability.

No matter how little he sometimes felt they understood him, they loved him. They supported him. And he'd gotten their support his entire life.

Alanna deserved the same thing. She deserved to watch her niece grow up safe and happy and surrounded by her real family.

If he was being honest with himself, she made him see what his family was always insisting he needed. If she lived in Alaska, he could imagine dating her, could imagine one day marrying her and making babies, little miniature versions of her, maybe with his eyes.

It wasn't meant to be. But he wasn't going to let

Johnny decide her future. Even if it couldn't be with him, Alanna deserved to have her own babies and watch them grow up safe and happy, too, surrounded by the family that had waited and searched for her for fourteen long years.

"I have a plan, too," he announced, making everyone's head swivel his way. Even Rebel and Chance looked up at him expectantly.

"Colter and Kensie, you should drive Alanna back to my place. Drop the dogs off there and wait for my call. Then Alanna should take her rental and you two should follow at a distance."

Chance and Rebel looked from him to Colter and Alanna, as if waiting for their reply. When there wasn't an immediate rebuttal, Chance barked and Rebel followed suit, like they didn't approve of the plan.

"Sorry," Peter told the dogs, as a smile broke free, the first one he'd felt since they'd gotten the call from Kensie. "But you two need to stay home this time." He looked at Tate. "I'm going to tell the chief that Alanna has good reason to suspect the baby is at the first cabin we went to, the one where Darcy started the avalanche. I want you to go there with them, keep them looking. Keep them out of the way."

Tate shook his head. "I know what you're doing. You want to keep me out of trouble, hopefully save my career. But it doesn't matter. If you pursue this on your own and I looked the other way, it's the same thing as going with you. Face it. I'm in this. I'm with you."

"I want you to make sure the police go. I want you to make sure they're out of the way long enough for us to pull this off."

Tate crossed his arms over his chest. "Where exactly am I supposed to say *you* went?"

"Tell them I'm going to make sure Alanna and her sister don't try to get to Johnny first."

Tate shook his head. "You're trying to make things better for me and I appreciate it. But do you really think the chief will believe that I didn't know what was really happening? It would be better if I came with you. What if you need backup?"

"We'll be okay." He wasn't sure it was true, but this was about more than just doing whatever he could to salvage Tate's career. It was also about getting his partner out of the way. Because trying to take down a criminal without backup or following procedure was one thing. But what the rest of his plan entailed? Not even the closest partner would agree to it.

"I really don't think—"

"It's the best way," Peter insisted, knowing he needed to put this in motion fast before he thought better of it, too. He headed for the door, then pivoted back toward Alanna, Kensie and Colter, who were all standing immobile, like they hadn't absorbed his plan yet.

"Get moving," he told them. "Then wait at my place until you get my call that the rest of the department has cleared out. I want them far enough away that if anyone calls them to a situation at the old Altier place, they won't be able to respond quickly. But I also want to do this now, while it's still dark. Hopefully give us some element of surprise and keep Johnny off-balance."

His gut knotted at how badly this could all backfire and he tried to ignore all his training, all his common sense screaming this was a mistake. "Go," he insisted again, and finally Colter and Kensie nodded, heading for their trucks.

Rebel followed, but Alanna stayed where she was. She shook her head mutely at him, studying him too closely like she knew he wasn't telling her everything.

He wasn't going to give her time to figure it out. Moving in close, he looped an arm around her waist, pulled her to him and kissed her.

Her arms slid around his neck and she half leaned, half fell into him as Chance gave a sharp bark. Then she was kissing him back, the desperation in those kisses telling him that what he'd planned was necessary.

She pulled back first, stared at him a long minute, then spun and hurried to the truck where Kensie and Colter waited. Chance barked at him once more, then bolted after her.

"Let's do this," Peter told Tate, passing his partner and reaching for the door to the station.

Tate put a hand on his arm. "What are you really planning?"

"Trust me, it's better if you don't know." He yanked open the door and went inside before Tate could argue.

Then he was running toward the chief, pasting a frantic look on his face that wasn't completely feigned.

She was on her feet and met him before he made it halfway there. They met in the middle of the bullpen, all eyes on them. Chief Hernandez looked from him to Tate. "What's happening?"

"Alanna and her sister and brother-in-law just took off," Tate said.

"I told them they could leave their dogs at my place and get some rest, then come back to the station. I said we'd call if we had any updates," Peter jumped in, not wanting Tate too involved in the lie. "I think they are going to drop the dogs off, but I don't think they plan to stay there."

The chief's eyes narrowed. "Why not?"

"I overheard Alanna telling Kensie and Colter that she thinks Johnny took Elysia to the cabin over in Luna, where Darcy started the avalanche."

"Why does she think that?" Chief Hernandez asked. "I saw the conversation between Darcy and Alanna. Darcy never said anything about that cabin."

"Alanna spent fourteen years with that woman," Peter said. "She can read between the lines better than we can. Look, she might be wrong. But do we want to risk it? We need to go out there. Actually…"

The chief's narrowed eyes shifted into a scowl. "Actually, what?"

"I should go to my place, see if I can keep them there, keep them out of the way. I might be able to get Alanna to listen."

"I'll go with the team," Tate said. "I don't know what Darcy said to Alanna, but she seemed convinced they'd be at that cabin. We need to go now."

Peter swore inwardly at Tate's addition, because it made him part of the lie, rather than someone who'd trusted the wrong partner. But Tate's word seemed to be enough, because suddenly Chief Hernandez was nodding and waving her arms for the rest of the officers to gear up.

As they raced to the equipment room to gather the heavier weapons and protective gear, Peter ran out to his SUV and whipped out of the lot in the direction of his house. Around the corner, he turned off his lights and parked. He slipped out of the vehicle and pressed himself against the corner of the grocery store, waiting until the last police vehicle raced out of the parking lot.

Then he made one quick phone call, before he ran back to the station. He used his key card to get in the rear entrance, knowing there'd be an officer who'd stayed behind. They couldn't leave the station totally empty, not with a prisoner in a cell at the back.

Hopefully, that officer wouldn't check on Darcy for a while.

Peter ignored the voice in his head screaming at him. Yes, he was about to break the law. Yes, it was against everything he believed in. But he couldn't think of any other way to ensure the woman he loved wasn't heading willingly toward her own death.

The woman he loved. The words rang in his head, ridiculous after such a short time knowing her, yet they felt all too real.

He'd worry about it later.

Slipping the cell keys from their drawer, Peter unlocked the only occupied cell inside the Desparre station.

Darcy stared at him, unmoving even as he yanked open the door.

"Let's go," Peter said, striding inside and pulling her to her feet.

She resisted, staring up at him suspiciously.

"You want *both* your son and daughter to still be alive by morning?" he demanded.

She stopped digging her feet in and allowed him to lead her as he whispered, "You're my backup plan."

Chapter 19

A prisoner was handcuffed in the seat beside him; one he'd broken out of her cell. If his plan worked, she'd be back behind bars soon—and there was a decent chance he'd be headed there himself.

The whole thing sounded ridiculous, even in his head. When he'd first met Alanna, he'd seen her as his chance to finally find acceptance at the Desparre PD. Instead, he'd lied to the whole department and committed a crime inside his own station. How had this become his life?

Peter tried not to think too hard about the consequences as he maneuvered up the slick mountain roads toward a cabin well hidden in the woods that he'd only visited once before. Of course, his passenger knew the route from memory.

As soon as he'd gotten Darcy clear of the Desparre

police station, he'd hustled her down the dark sidewalk around the corner to his truck, praying no shop owner was watching from behind darkened windows. Then he'd slapped handcuffs on her and pushed her into the passenger seat of his vehicle.

For a brief moment, he'd considered cutting Alanna out entirely, just driving Darcy up to the cabin and trying to make the trade directly for the baby. But he'd reconsidered before he'd reached the base of the mountain. It would be too hard to manage it all alone. The safest thing for Elysia was to get her completely away from the line of fire. At least with Alanna, she could walk toward him. How would he hold a baby while keeping his gun trained on Johnny? Even cuffed, there was no way to predict what Darcy might try. And while Johnny probably didn't actually want to raise the baby, Darcy might.

Besides, Alanna had asked him to trust her. Maybe she'd be able to get through to Johnny and end the whole thing peacefully. Maybe he'd even be able to slip Darcy back into her jail cell without anyone noticing she'd been gone.

Yeah, and maybe he'd still have a job come daylight.

Still, there was a chance. Somewhere on the road ahead of him, Kensie and Colter were driving up in one vehicle and Alanna in another. Alanna was supposed to text them all once she'd reached the cabin, then wait for their confirmation before she went to the door.

Once Alanna left with Johnny, he would follow. Kensie and Colter were going to get the baby and take her to safety. When he'd called to tell them to get moving, he'd gotten Colter off Speaker. The man had a leg injury he'd sustained as a marine that had never fully healed, but he still had a military mentality. If needed, Colter had promised to get his wife and child down the mountain, then come back up with a weapon and possibly Rebel. While her specialty had been tracking bomb-makers and she was long retired, she'd been military, too. Peter had worked with enough soldiers to know: once military, always military.

Peter hoped he wouldn't need them, but he did feel slight relief at the idea of having backup if everything went sideways. Overseas, the deadliest thing he'd carried had been a pen. But he'd been with soldiers, who'd been armed and ready to protect. Now on the force, he worked with a partner. But right at this moment, he'd never felt more alone. And it might be Alanna's life on the line.

"You're in love with my daughter, aren't you?"

It was the first time Darcy had spoken since she'd let him pull her silently out of the station and into his truck. She hadn't even protested when he'd handcuffed her.

He glanced briefly at her, remembering the harsh words she'd spoken to Alanna in the interrogation room. "If you still think of Alanna as your daughter, then you'll help me convince Johnny to let her go and take you instead."

"So, that's your plan. I figured it had something to do with my son. I didn't think you actually planned to let me go, though. You must really love her if you're willing to break the law. Or have you always been a crooked cop?"

He darted another glance at her, trying not to show how her words stung. Her opinion of him didn't really matter. But he did wonder what she thought of their chances of getting both Elysia and Alanna out of there safely.

She just stared back at him, a mix of curiosity, distrust and anticipation on her face.

If this went sideways, he'd have to worry about more than just going to jail. If he couldn't find a way to stop Darcy and Johnny after he got Alanna to safety, he'd be letting two child kidnappers go free. He had no doubts she and Johnny would start up right where they'd left off.

A ball of dread filled his stomach and twisted angrily. Peter clutched the wheel harder as the icy dirt roads beneath him became even more rough; this was an area that the town's snowplows didn't go. Anyone who lived up the mountain was tough. They lived at the mercy of the Alaskan wilderness and they always had a backup plan, too.

Peter darted one last glance at Darcy, hoping she'd be worth enough to Johnny that he'd give up his dreams of revenge. Hoping he didn't have his own plan that would leave all of them at his mercy.

The phone in his cup holder buzzed, startling Peter, and he glanced at it. *Alanna*. She'd arrived and was waiting for their go-ahead. Less than a minute later, Colter texted that he was in place, hidden off the side of the road. They were just waiting for Peter.

He hit the gas and his wheels spun out slightly. As he righted the vehicle, Darcy warned, "Don't drive us off the side of the road now. Not when we're so close."

She sounded too calm, like this had been her plan instead of his, and he tried not to let it worry him.

Then they were near the top of the mountain, still deep in the woods, as the first rays of morning sunrise started to filter through the trees. In theory, there weren't many routes off this mountain, just the main roads that snaked their way up and down, and they were sometimes impassable. But Alanna had lost him up here less than a week ago and if she could do it, so could Johnny.

He pulled the truck off the side of the road, far enough away that Johnny wouldn't be able to see him from the cabin. Then he took a deep breath and sent a group text. I'm here. Be careful.

I'm going in, Alanna responded.

From where he was positioned, Peter could see the very end of the Altiers driveway. He watched as Alanna's rental pulled in and then disappeared up toward the house. Now all he could do was wait.

Time seemed to stretch out forever and Peter couldn't stop his fingers from tapping a nervous beat against the steering wheel. Beside him, Darcy kept craning in her seat, trying to get a glimpse of the house. But it wouldn't happen. Alanna had told him exactly where to wait to stay out of view from the house.

Maybe he should go in. In theory, he'd be able to hear a gunshot from here, but a gun wasn't the only way to kill someone. Alanna was fairly tall for a woman and much stronger than her thin frame suggested, but he'd seen pictures of Johnny from five years ago. The man was six feet tall, even back then, and made up of all lean muscle. Plus, he was full of rage.

Peter glanced at the clock, then at his phone again. Ten minutes and no word. It was too long.

He was just reaching for the gear shift when an engine started up. The *clunk clunk* was familiar and Peter realized it was the same sound he'd heard at the last cabin. He mentally flashed back to that moment. Alanna had been getting through to Darcy. He'd seen the decision flash across her face, the recognition that it was time to stop running. Then that car had driven by—the old engine sounds grumbling—and she'd changed her mind. Johnny must have been driving up to get her.

Peter shook the memory clear as an old sedan backed down the drive. He grabbed the binoculars he'd stuck in his truck when he'd tracked Alanna on his day off and peered through them as the vehicle backed onto the street.

Johnny was in the car, but he was in the passenger seat. He glanced around, paranoia in his eyes but a smile on his face. He held a pistol, pointed toward the occupant of the driver's seat.

Peter glanced right and saw Alanna behind the wheel, her jaw clenched tight. As she stopped in the street, she gave an unmistakable triple nod of her head: the signal that Elysia had been left behind. Then the car shot forward, racing out of sight.

Peter held his breath as another vehicle pulled into the Altier cabin driveway. Peter backed into the street, then braced his foot on the brake, waiting.

"Come on, come on, come on," he muttered as Darcy demanded, "What are you doing? Follow them! Follow Johnny and Alanna! When I was caught, he ditched his phone to be safe. I don't have a way to get a hold of him anymore. Hurry!"

Every instinct he had demanded he pick his foot up off the brake and stomp down on the gas, catch up to Johnny and Alanna before she drove right off the mountain and the two of them disappeared. But he'd promised.

"Come on!"

At his shout, Darcy jerked in her seat but went quiet.

Then his phone buzzed with a message from Colter. *We've got Elysia.*

Peter shifted into Drive and stomped on the gas, making the back of his vehicle fishtail as snow sprayed out behind him. Then he and Darcy were off, racing down the mountain, hoping to catch up to Johnny and Alanna.

This angry, snarling man holding a gun to her head as she drove was the "brother" who'd once carried her half a mile through the snow when she'd twisted her ankle playing. The brother who'd wiped her tears away when he'd caught her crying over missing the family she'd been taken from. The brother who'd told her he couldn't wait to watch her dancing at his wedding.

Every time the old sedan hit a bump on the pot-holed road down the mountain, Alanna grimaced, hoping Johnny's finger wasn't on the trigger.

Her plan had worked. She'd walked up to the front door and Johnny had opened it before she could even knock. He'd held the gun on her, then glanced past her at the driveway. When she'd offered to go with him if he left Elysia behind, he'd scoffed. Then he'd stared at her a long moment, nodded his head and let her look in on a sleeping Elysia, content in an old crib.

"I know you're not here alone. They try to come for me and I'll take you out first, you got that, Alanna?" he'd asked.

The coldness in his tone had dried up her mouth and all she could do was nod.

"Then let's go," he'd said, ushering her out the door. "I don't need the baby. And I'd never hurt her anyway. But you and I have a score to settle."

That had been five minutes ago. Hopefully by now, Elysia was cradled in Kensie's arms, on her way back to her parents' cabin.

Since then, Johnny had just looked over at her and demanded, "Are the cops coming?"

Alanna had shaken her head and stared back at him, feeling truthful, because the only cop around was Peter. And he wasn't coming until Elysia was safe. Even then, he'd have to catch up to them.

Johnny had always been able to read her. Maybe because he was older or he'd known her for so long, he'd always been able to tell when she was lying. This time, he'd just smiled and ordered her to head down the primary road off the mountain.

"I never wanted to hurt you, Johnny," she whispered, the fear she felt coming through in her voice.

He snorted, not moving the pistol away from her head. "Well, you sure screwed that up."

She darted a glance at him, taking in the new lines just visible across his forehead and the harsh line of his jaw, now shaded with dark stubble, that had still looked boyish five years ago. At twenty-three, there'd been something sad and pensive if you looked close enough into his eyes, but he had usually worn a smile on his face. Now there was nothing but anger.

An ache filled her chest, knowing her note had ripped his life apart and he hadn't been able to put together a newer, better one. Sadness followed, regret that she hadn't tried a note years earlier, back before Darcy and Julian had asked Johnny to lure Sydney away from a playground. Back when it might have made a difference to the life of the older "brother" she'd adored for so long.

Was the person she loved even in there anymore? Or had all the good in him been warped and destroyed?

She swiped at the tears that suddenly blinded her and Johnny snapped, "You don't get to cry. You caused this. You caused all of this."

She shook her head, wishing she could pull the car over, that they could just talk like old times. "Johnny—"

"Didn't you love us at all?" he asked, his voice suddenly softer, more uncertain, like the boy she remembered.

The boy she'd hugged tight while he shook with suppressed tears after Sydney had first come to live with them, had cried and slapped him, telling him she hated him. The boy whose skinned knees she'd helped bandage after he'd fallen on the roof they'd been building, skidding halfway down the side before catching himself. The boy she'd tried to keep up with when he took her snowshoeing through the woods.

"I've never stopped loving you," Alanna said, letting her foot lift off the gas a little, slowing their dangerous speed down the treacherous road.

He snorted. "That's a lie." But he lowered the pistol slightly away from her head and there was less fury in his tone.

The Johnny she remembered was still in there somewhere.

Her heart rate picked up, hope sparking through the fear. "There's another way, Johnny." She spoke fast, not wanting him to cut her off. "It doesn't have to be like this. It should never have been like this. But I still love you. You're still my brother."

"And what about our mother? What about our *fa-*

ther?" He lifted the pistol again and when she looked over, she saw the tears glistening in his eyes.

"I didn't want any of that. But you know what they did was wrong. What they made *you* do was wrong."

"They looked after us," Johnny said, but there was a tremor in his voice, as if he was trying to convince himself it was true.

She could get through to him. She just needed a little time.

Alanna lifted her foot a tiny bit more off the gas. She didn't know what the next stage in his plan was, but if she could stretch out this trip, where she had his undivided attention, then maybe she'd have enough time to get through to him. Convince him to put the gun down and turn himself in.

Her gaze darted to the rearview mirror and she pushed down on the gas again. She'd started out at dangerous speeds, speeds someone not familiar with the mountain roads probably wouldn't be able to match. But Peter was coming for her. She needed to stay far enough in front of him that she could talk Johnny down, but not so far that he'd lose her if she was wrong.

She loved Johnny. Despite the things he'd done, he'd been a victim once, too. He deserved the chance to rehabilitate, the chance to start a real life for himself. One that hadn't been built from lies, where he was surrounded by people who loved him without stipulations, who'd support him as he rebuilt something better for himself.

Still, if he refused to take this chance, she wasn't willing to give up her own life for him. She deserved a chance to really start over, too. She wanted to be fully honest with her parents, Kensie and Flynn, about how conflicted she'd felt for the past five years. She wanted the chance to travel to Kansas to see Sydney in person again. To talk to Drew's and Valerie's parents, explain that she didn't want to relive the past with their kids, but to build a future where they were still a part of her family, too.

And she deserved a chance to tell Peter how much he'd come to mean to her over the past week. If she survived this last drive with Johnny, she was heading home to Chicago. Three thousand five hundred miles was too far to build a romantic relationship. But it wasn't too far to build a friendship. It was less than she wanted, but it was better than losing him.

Before she could fight for Peter, she had to convince Johnny that everything he believed about Darcy and Julian was wrong, that everything he believed about her was wrong. She took a deep breath, then said, "They *did* look after us. But they stole from us, too. They stole our chance to grow up with other people who loved us."

He made another sound of disbelief, but it was quieter this time and the gun was lowering again.

"I met your parents, you know."

Back at the hospital in Luna, five years ago, Johnny's parents had shown up, tearful and excited to see their son again, just as she'd been ready to leave for Chicago. She'd shyly said hello and his mom had squeezed her arm and whispered, "Your parents are going to be overjoyed." Then she'd looked at her husband and added, "We couldn't even believe this was real."

"You did?" Johnny asked.

His gun was on his lap now, his expression a mix of suspicion and anger. But beneath it all, there was interest. Beneath it all, there was still hope.

Still a chance.

"Yes," Alanna said, her hand twitching to take his.

Then suddenly a truck flew out in front of her from a side road, making her slam on the brakes. Her head flew forward, the seat belt painful across her chest. The back end of the sedan fishtailed wildly, the vehicle not equipped to handle this kind of terrain. They continued to skid downward and she pushed the brake harder as the ABS activated, praying she wasn't about to crash into the vehicle stopped in front of her.

Peter's vehicle.

The car kept moving and Alanna heard herself scream, even though she didn't remember opening her mouth. Somehow the car finally stopped, with only a soft screech of metal as the front end scraped the side of Peter's truck.

Then everything seemed to happen at once. Peter scrambled out of his truck as Johnny's hand fisted in her coat, his other hand unhooking her belt. Then she was being pulled across the front seats, her body bumping every surface, surely creating bruises everywhere as she tried to help herself along. Suddenly she was outside the car, Johnny's hand still rough on her biceps, his pistol against the side of her head.

Across from her, Peter stood with his own hostage. Darcy's hands were cuffed in front of her, but the woman actually looked serene, a half smile on her face as Peter shouted, "I've got a trade for you, Johnny. Alanna for Darcy."

Chapter 20

Peter had destroyed his career trying to save her.

Alanna swallowed back tears as she stared at him standing behind Darcy, his gaze steady on Johnny, his finger resting above the trigger guard on his pistol.

The metal of the pistol barrel against her own head felt cold even in the ambient Alaskan temperatures. Johnny stood behind her, using her as a human shield, his grip painful on her upper arm, his angry breaths puffing against the top of her head.

She'd almost gotten through to him. But just like with Darcy, in the end, she hadn't been able to reach him. Not in time.

"Johnny—"

"Shut up," he snapped. Then louder, to Peter, he yelled, "What's to stop me from shooting you and taking them both?"

Alanna flinched, trying to twist in his grip despite the gun to her head. "No!"

"I'm a trained police officer," Peter said, his voice calm and steady. "You could miss and hit your mother. I won't miss."

She felt Johnny jerk at Peter's words, felt her own heart thud harder at the threat, at the idea of watching her older brother die right beside her.

"Your sister taught me something, Johnny. She taught me that love is stronger than hate. I know what you're feeling right now. You feel betrayed. You're angry with Alanna. But you still love her, just like she loves you."

"I don—" Johnny started.

"She doesn't want to go with you. She risked her life to protect her niece. You're her older brother. It's *your* job to protect *her*. It's your job to make sure she's happy. Let her go. You can take Darcy. The two of you can disappear. It's not right and you know it, but you can do it. Just let Alanna go. Please."

Johnny's hand loosened slightly on her arm and Alanna stared at Peter and the stoic determination on his face. It was probably all Johnny saw: a trained police officer who wasn't afraid, who'd be willing to shoot two kidnappers to save someone.

But she saw past that to the fear in his bright blue eyes. And she knew shooting Johnny would be his very last resort, something he'd only do if Johnny's finger started depressing the trigger on the gun to her head. She knew it was because she loved Johnny.

"Do it, Johnny," Darcy said. "Let Alanna go."

Alanna's gaze skipped to Darcy, saw the exhaustion on her face, the regret that said maybe she'd finally realized how many lives she'd hurt.

The hand squeezing her biceps released and the metal barrel against her head moved, redirecting to point toward Peter.

"Alanna, come here," Peter said, his gaze still entirely focused on Johnny as he let go of Darcy.

Alanna took a hesitant step forward, afraid any quick movement would startle someone, would make a nervous finger twitch against a trigger. Then she took another, her legs wobbly as Darcy moved past her in the other direction.

Darcy's gaze swung to her for the briefest moment, skimming over her face as if she was memorizing it. A sad smile flitted over her lips, then she mouthed something that might have been "Sorry."

Alanna took another step and then Peter's hand was on her arm, shoving her behind him as Darcy ran to the sedan and jumped in the driver's seat.

Johnny's gun stayed steady on Peter as he screamed, "Give me the key to the handcuffs!"

Peter tossed them over, his gun never moving off target.

Johnny caught them one-handed and jumped into the passenger seat. Then the sedan sputtered, the wheels spitting snow as Darcy, still handcuffed, maneuvered it around them.

Peter kept his weapon trained on Johnny and Johnny held his pistol in kind until the car was out of sight. Then Peter holstered his weapon and spun around, yanking her into his arms so hard she could barely breathe.

"I've got her," he said and it took her a moment to realize he'd pulled out his phone and was talking into it. After a short pause, he said, "Hurry. Darcy and Johnny are on their way down the mountain. They'll get off the main road now that I have Alanna, but we're close to the bottom. Come pick her up. I'm going after them."

As he hung up the phone and pulled back so he could look at her, Alanna asked, "How did you—"

"Darcy showed me a side road to get in front of Johnny's car. Colter and Kensie are only a few minutes behind us. They're coming to get you. I'm going after Johnny and Darcy. I've got to call in backup—I sent them all the way to Luna, but they might have figured out by now that it was a misdirect."

"Peter, you shouldn't have—"

"Don't worry. You're more important than a job."

Before she could reply, his lips crashed down onto hers. His kisses felt desperate, frantic, relieved.

She barely had time to wind her arms around his neck and kiss him back before he was pulling free. He smiled briefly at her, touched her cheek with his gloved hand and said, "I'll do what I can to bring them in safely."

Colter's truck raced up beside them and Peter jumped in his own vehicle. He waved a quick goodbye and then he was off.

Alanna stared after him until she couldn't see his truck anymore, then turned toward Colter and Kensie with tears in her eyes.

Was someone she loved still going to die today?

Alanna was safe. But there were two kidnappers on the loose and it was Peter's fault.

The law said so, but so did Peter's conscience. He had a shot at catching up to them alone, at getting Darcy back behind bars before anyone at the station realized what had happened, but it was a long one. He'd be more likely to capture Darcy and Johnny with help.

He didn't call Tate as he maneuvered down the slippery mountain roads, scanning any bisecting road for signs of Johnny's car. He didn't want Tate implicated any more than he already was. Instead, Peter called Chief Hernandez directly.

"Where the hell are you?" the chief demanded, her voice a tight hiss. "And where is Darcy Altier?"

"You're back at the station?"

"Heading there right now. I got a call from Sam, who was stationed in the front."

"We have Elysia Hayes. She's safe. But Alanna traded herself for Elysia and I—"

"You traded Darcy for Alanna." There was no surprise in Chief Hernandez's voice, just a quiet fury that told him unquestionably that his career was unsalvageable.

The grief tightened his chest, made it hard to breathe, but he forced it to the back of his mind. "I'm almost at the bottom of the mountain on the Desparre side, trying to catch up to Darcy and Johnny. They're in an old mustard-colored sedan. Plates are muddied and unreadable, but you'll hear the car before you see it."

"You'd better hope like hell we find it," Chief Hernandez said. "For your sake and your partner's."

"Tate had nothing—" he started, but the chief hung up before he could finish.

Silently cursing Tate for jumping into the middle of his lie, even if it had helped sell it, Peter pushed his truck harder. Hopefully he wouldn't pass Johnny and Darcy right by as he hurried to the base of the mountain. Because once they got onto flat ground, they had more options, more ways to disappear. Darcy and Julian had stayed under the radar for eighteen years. Even once police had suspected she was in Desparre, even with her face so well-known from the media coverage, Darcy had still managed to avoid them. She'd probably still be at large if it weren't for Alanna. If Darcy and Johnny got off this mountain, he'd probably lose them forever.

Then he heard it. An old engine turning over and over, but not catching.

Peter hit the brakes hard, certain they'd heard him, too. He eased his truck slowly forward, inching toward the break in the forest ahead that suggested a side street.

Before he reached it, he stopped the truck. He left it running as he climbed out. Maybe it would give him a slight element of surprise if they thought he was still creeping forward in his vehicle instead of on foot. He texted a quick location to Chief Hernandez, then messaged Colter, too, telling him not to come any closer until help arrived. Then Peter slid his pistol from his holster, hoping Johnny didn't already have a bead on him through the dense trees.

He couldn't see the car yet and suddenly, he couldn't hear it anymore, either. They knew he was here.

Hurry up, he willed his team as he slid against the closest tree, moving cautiously forward. He couldn't wait for them, couldn't risk letting Johnny and Darcy get away again.

Johnny's voice rang out. "I'm a better shot than you give me credit for."

Peter froze, pressed harder against the tree as he scanned his surroundings. Could Johnny see him or was he hoping Peter would respond, give away his location?

"I'm afraid I'm going to need your truck," Johnny

said as Peter twisted his head, trying to use his good ear to pinpoint the man's location. "Toss me the keys and I'll let *you* walk away. Otherwise, I'm going to have to take them off you."

He was straight ahead. Probably Darcy was too, although Peter couldn't rule out that she actually held the weapon. Johnny could be distracting him so Darcy could flank him and put a bullet in his head.

Except as Peter crept sideways, darting to the tree beside and slightly ahead of him, there was Johnny. He was scanning the forest, too, his attention mainly focused near Peter's still-running truck. Darcy was beside him, her hand on his arm.

As Peter lined the sight of his pistol on Johnny's center mass, Darcy's whisper carried through the woods. "It's over. You can't shoot him. Your sister loves him."

The weapon in his hands gave a violent shake before Peter righted it again, Darcy's words ringing in his ears. Why would she say that? Had Alanna said something to her when Peter hadn't been with her, made some calculated comment meant to help protect him that wasn't actually true? Or was it possible that Alanna was falling for him the way he was falling for her?

"We have to get out of here," Johnny whispered to her. "I'm not letting you go back to jail."

Darcy's hand pushed down on Johnny's arm, forcing his weapon to lower. "I don't want to go back, either. But I'm not letting you *kill* someone."

Johnny wrenched his arm free, lifting the weapon again, scanning the woods. But the expression on his face was conflicted.

Then sirens sounded, approaching quickly, and Johnny's pistol whipped in their direction.

If he fired at the police officers, they'd shoot back. Just like Peter, they were trained to shoot to kill.

This was Alanna's brother. And she still loved him.

Peter stepped out from behind the tree, keeping his weapon centered on Johnny. "Put it down. Please."

Johnny swiveled toward him, sighting his pistol on Peter's face, his gun hand shaking.

"Johnny, this is the moment that defines the rest of your life. If you fire that weapon, my team *has* to shoot you. Please don't make them tell Alanna you died here today. She loves you. She still wants a relationship with you. You still have a life ahead of you. *Please*."

The sirens ended as the police vehicles came to hard stop. Officers jumped out, using the doors as shields.

"Hang on," Peter yelled. "Just wait! He's putting it down. Right, Johnny?"

Peter stepped forward and lowered his weapon, knowing the team had Johnny in their sights. "Please. Please."

"It's over, Johnny," Darcy whispered.

Johnny glanced at her, then lowered his arm and tossed his gun in the snow.

Then Peter's team was swarming the woods, pushing both Johnny and Darcy against the cars, frisking and cuffing them. Tate was with them, but he stayed back at the edge of the woods, his expression pained as he stared at Peter.

The fact that Tate was here right now meant at least his partner's job was safe. But his expression told Peter everything he needed to know about his own. He looked right and suddenly Chief Hernandez was beside him, hand out.

"Give me your weapon, Robak."

Even knowing it was coming, the request hurt. With shaking hands, Peter unholstered his gun and handed it to the chief. He didn't make her ask for his badge and just handed that over silently, too.

She gave a sharp nod over his shoulder and then Charlie Quinn was behind him, yanking his arms behind his back.

The sound of the handcuffs snapping over his wrists echoed in the woods and then Chief Hernandez shook her head. "You're under arrest, Peter."

Epilogue

Three weeks ago, when those handcuffs had closed over his wrists, Peter had felt the life he'd worked so hard for slipping out of his grasp forever. He'd glanced over at Tate through the trees, grateful that his friend wasn't facing the same treatment.

He'd spent a week in the Desparre jail. He'd asked his family not to come see him and told Tate not to let Alanna back to the cells, either. The last time she saw him wasn't going to be through the bars of a jail cell. At least that way, when she climbed aboard the airplane with Kensie and Colter, her last memory of him would be the kiss they'd shared.

He'd been sure his arrest would make the news. There'd be no way to hide it from her. But he hadn't wanted her to see him, to try to help. Hadn't wanted to give her one more thing to feel guilty over when it had been his decision. And he'd do it again. Even if it hadn't turned out okay in the end.

Now Peter handed over his ID at the tiny airport a few hours outside of Desparre. The next flight to Chicago left in two hours. Along with the three legs of the flight and the layovers in between, that meant he'd land in Chicago eighteen hours from now. Maybe in that time, he'd figure out exactly what he was going to say.

Alanna had called the station a few times over the past few weeks, trying to get through to him, presumably not knowing the outcome of his arrest, since the chief had actually kept it out of the press. Alanna had even managed to dig up Tate's number and had Colter call Chief Hernandez. He'd asked them all to just pass on that he would be fine, without giving any specifics. He didn't want to give her false hope, didn't want to open the lines of communication if he was going to spend the next five to ten years behind bars. Didn't want to say anything at all until he was one hundred percent sure.

Nodding his thanks to the clerk who handed back his card and took his luggage, Peter headed to security, which was light as usual. It was a small airport, mostly jumper flights in and out of Fairbanks.

After passing through the X-ray machine, he went straight for the big window to stare out at the vast snowy expanse that represented Alaska to him. He'd be back, of course. His whole family lived here. When he had told them about his plans, they'd all looked at him like he was out of his mind and then erupted with arguments. Until his mom had simply held up a hand to silence everyone. Staring straight at him, she'd asked, "Are you sure?" When he'd nodded, she'd smiled sadly and said, "I expect you back here every two months, minimum. Got it?"

With the promise secured, he'd headed home and packed enough for a month. Hopefully in that time, he'd know.

Taking a deep breath, he turned his back on the openness of Alaska that he loved.

Then a loud bark made his head swivel and there was Chance, bounding toward him through the airport.

"What the—" Peter knelt down as Chance reached him and almost got knocked over for his trouble. "Easy, boy." He hugged the dog, looking over his head. "Where's Alanna?"

Then he spotted her, rounding the corner at a run, her rolling luggage making a *thunk thunk thunk* sound, her long dark hair trailing behind her.

He stood, running to meet her with Chance on his heels.

She skidded to a stop and he did, too, a foot away from her. Chance plowed in between them, walking through and back, punctuating each turn with a bark.

"Chance, relax," Alanna admonished, then stared up at Peter. "What are you doing here?"

"What are *you* doing here? Didn't you go home weeks ago?"

She settled her luggage next to her, slapped her hands on her hips. "Yes, when Colter and Kensie insisted there was no talking any sense into you, that you were never going to see me." Her eyes watered over, then she blinked the moisture away. "Why did you do that?"

He reached out, taking her hand. "I didn't know what my future held. I didn't want to tie you to it."

"I was already tied to it. It was my fault—"

"That's just it," he cut her off. "It wasn't your fault. And I don't want us to be connected by obligation."

She stared at him a long moment, then asked, "What happened? Last I heard, you'd been arrested."

"I was. But Tate talked the chief into filing things differently. *A police decision without proper documentation*, is I think how he framed it. That's not exactly how it ended up, but he saved me jail time."

Her shoulders relaxed, a smile lighting up her face. "So, your job is okay?"

"No." The smile faded and he squeezed her hand a little tighter, feeling awkward reaching across the space between them, but not willing to get any closer. Not yet. "I'll never be a police officer again."

This time, the tears did spill over. "Peter, I'm so sorry. I never—"

"Don't you dare apologize. It hurt, but it's not the first time I've left behind a job I loved. At least this time, it was a conscious decision. I knew what was on the line when I broke Darcy out. I got more than I deserved, because Tate is a damn good friend and Chief Hernandez can be nicer than she seems. And now..."

"Now what?"

He took a deep breath, suddenly nervous and very aware of how much he'd needed those eighteen hours to figure out what he was going to say to her. "I took a new job. It's a trial period, but I'm going back to reporting."

"Oh." Alanna's fingers twitched in his. "Back into a war zone?"

"No. I'm going to cover crime. With my background as a police officer and a reporter, they thought I'd be the perfect fit. It's not exactly where I thought I'd be right now, but I'm glad. I'm hoping you'll be happy about it, too."

"Well, yes. I'm sorry you can't be a cop anymore and I wish… Well, I'm glad you've found something else that excites you." She glanced down at their linked hands. "Peter, look, I came back here because I couldn't take all the silence. No matter what, I had to see you. I know we didn't have long together, but I…" She took a visible breath and Chance nudged up against her, as if to say, *Spit it out*, then sat at her side. "In the time we spent together, I've developed feelings for you. I want to see where that goes."

"Alanna—"

"Just hear me out." She stepped closer, almost close enough to kiss. "I know a cross-country relationship won't be easy. But I miss Alaska. I want to visit more. And I think you'd like Chicago. I really do. If we each travel to one another a few times a year, I really think—"

"Alanna, stop."

She looked at her feet, then back up at him. "I know you care for me, Peter. I—"

"I love you," he said, cutting her off. "I know it's fast. Too fast, maybe. But it's there and it's real and I'm not letting it go." He took a step closer, until he *could* kiss her if he just leaned down. "I'm not letting *you* go. I do want to travel back and forth a bit—my family insists on it, actually—but the job is in Chicago."

Her mouth dropped open and she just stared at him.

"I know you need to be there," he said softly. "It's right that you should get time with the family you were denied for so long. You deserve that. And I want to be where you are."

She continued to stare until he let out a nervous laugh. "Too much? I know—"

Before he could finish the sentence, she was up on her tiptoes, falling against him, her arms around his neck and her lips on his.

When she finally pulled free, her cheeks flushed and her eyes sparkling, she whispered, "I love you, too, Peter."

Then Chance pushed his way in between them and Alanna laughed.

Peter took hold of her luggage and her hand, then spun back toward the entrance.

Alanna hurried to keep up. "Where are we going?"

"I'm thinking back to my place. I'm hanging on to it for when we visit here. What do you say we stay here for a few days, then head home to Chicago?"

She stopped abruptly, making him pause, too. "Home to Chicago." She smiled, grabbing hold of him for one more kiss. "I like the sound of that."

* * * * *

Nicole Helm grew up with her nose in a book and the dream of one day becoming a writer. Luckily, after a few failed career choices, she gets to follow that dream—writing down-to-earth contemporary romance and romantic suspense. From farmers to cowboys, Midwest to *the* West, Nicole writes stories about people finding themselves and finding love in the process. She lives in Missouri with her husband and two sons and dreams of someday owning a barn.

Books by Nicole Helm

Harlequin Intrigue

A North Star Novel Series

Summer Stalker
Shot Through the Heart
Mountainside Murder
Cowboy in the Crosshairs

A Badlands Cops Novel

South Dakota Showdown
Covert Complication
Backcountry Escape
Isolated Threat
Badlands Beware
Close Range Christmas

Visit the Author Profile page
at Harlequin.com for more titles.

HUNTING A KILLER

Nicole Helm

For all those happily-ever-afters
that started as workplace romances.

Prologue

The tears leaked out of Kay Duvall's eyes, even as she tried to focus on what she had to do. *Had* to do to bring Ben home safe.

She fumbled with her ID and punched in the code that would open the side door, usually only used by a guard taking a smoke break. It would be easy for the men behind her to escape from this side of the prison.

It went against everything she was supposed to do. Everything she considered right and good.

A quiet sob escaped her lips. They had her son. How could she not help them escape? Nothing mattered beyond her son's life.

"Would you stop already?" one of the prisoners muttered. He'd made her give him her gun, which he now jabbed into her back. "Crying isn't going to change anything. So just shut up."

She didn't care so much about her own life, or if she'd be fired. She didn't care what happened to her as long as they let her son go. So she swallowed down the sobs and blinked out as many tears as she could, hoping to stem the tide of them.

She got the door open and slid out first—because the man holding the gun pushed it into her back until she moved forward.

They moved out the door behind her, dressed in the clothes she'd stolen from the locker room and Lost and Found. Anything warm she could get her hands on to help them escape into the frigid February night.

Help them escape. Help three dangerous men escape prison. When she was supposed to keep them inside.

It didn't matter anymore. She just wanted them gone. If they were gone, they'd let her baby go. They had to let her baby go.

Kay forced her legs to move, one foot in front of the other, toward the gate she could unlock without setting off any alarms. She unlocked it, steadier this time if only because she kept thinking once they were gone she could get in contact with Ben.

She flung open the gate and gestured them out into the parking lot. "Stay out of the safety lights and no one should bug you."

"You better hope not," one of the men growled.

"The minute you sound that alarm, your kid is dead. You got it?" This one was the ringleader. The one who'd been in for murder. Who else would he kill out there in the world?

Guilt pooled in Kay's belly, but she had to ignore it. She had to live with it. Whatever guilt she'd felt would be survivable. Living without her son wouldn't be. Besides, she had to believe they'd be caught. They'd do something else terrible and be caught.

As long as her son was alive, she didn't care.

The three men disappeared into the night, wearing the clothes she'd stolen for them. She hoped they froze to death. She hoped every bad thing befell them. As soon as her baby was safe, she'd help the authorities in whatever way she could.

She slammed the gate closed and locked it. She was sick with anger and terror, and her hands shook as she fumbled for her phone. She dialed her mother. Just because she couldn't sound the alarm didn't mean she couldn't make sure Mom was all right. Had they hurt her when they'd kidnapped Ben? Was she terrified too?

Or worse, dead? Mom definitely would have fought off anyone trying to take Ben, even if it ended her life.

Another sob escaped Kay's mouth, followed by a bigger, louder one when her mother answered sounding perfectly calm and cheerful. "Hi, honey."

She could only gasp for breath. Relief but new fears bubbling up inside her.

"What on Earth is wrong?" her mother asked, worry and confusion seeping into her tone. *New* worry. *New* confusion.

Kay blinked, taken aback by how calm her mom sounded. Did she not know? Had Ben been kidnapped without Mom even realizing? How could that happen?

"Ben…" she managed to croak.

"Shoveling in his mac and cheese like usual. We really need to work on getting this boy some vegetables. I know you don't want to give him a complex, but he can't subsist on cheese and pasta alone. Are you okay?"

"I'm fine. Mom… Everything is okay there? You're sure."

"Of course I'm sure. Ben's right here. Did you want to talk to him? Ben, here's your mom."

She closed her eyes, tears pouring over her cheeks. She heard her baby's voice, safe as could be, chattering about something in the background. She swallowed down the sinking, horrible realization she was a stupid, utter failure. "No, Mom," she croaked. "I have to go. I may be home late."

Her mother's words were little more than a buzz as she hung up the phone and slid it back into her pocket.

There was only one thing to do now—sound the alarm, own up to her mistake and pray she didn't end up an inmate herself.

Chapter 1

Selena Lopez yawned as she filed into the meeting room of the Tactical Crime Division—a specialized FBI team made up of experts from several active divisions in one small group.

Selena's specialization was currently back home asleep in her crate. Lucky dog. Of course, if Selena was deployed into the field, she'd be waking her German shepherd and taking her out to track regardless of the time.

She yawned again. She was used to middle-of-the-night calls, going on little to no sleep, but her neighbors had been having one hell of a party. *Again.*

She was really getting tired of apartment living.

In the boardroom, half the team were in various states of disarray already situated around the large table. Sleep-tumbled hair, casual clothes and desperate looks at the cups of coffee in front of them were all typical signs of a middle of the night call.

Selena knew once their director walked into the room, they'd all sharpen into the tools they were. But for a few more minutes they could be human.

Axel Morrow walked in behind her. He looked like he'd somehow had the time to take a shower, comb his hair and get dressed in fresh clothes without a wrinkle in sight. Casual though the jeans and long-sleeved tee were, he could have walked in at two in the afternoon looking like that. His blond hair didn't appear sleep-tousled at all, and his green eyes were perfectly alert.

How did he look perfect at two o'clock in the morning? When she knew he'd driven in farther than everyone else, since he lived on an old nonoperating farm outside town.

She frowned at him when he took the seat next to her. God, he smelled good. And when he flashed her a smile, that obnoxious fluttering she got whenever she saw him spread deeper and flirted way too close with serious attraction.

Which was *not* allowed.

She knew exactly where those kind of thoughts led. To poor choices and embarrassing breakups. The TCD team was pretty tight-knit, and she wouldn't jeopardize her good standing here over attraction. Not when everyone liked her.

She glanced at her sister across the table. Okay, maybe not everyone. Opaline had been here longer. She hadn't exactly been hostile toward Selena joining the group, but she hadn't been welcoming either. Their continued standoff remained as it always was.

Tense and mostly silent. But they worked together when they had to.

Selena had hoped coming here might help bridge the gap between them, but she'd yet to figure out *how*. They were so different. What they believed and how they felt about their family… How could it not keep them at odds?

Dr. Carly Welsh entered the room and sat down on the other side of her. "You look rough."

Selena slid her friend a look. "You try living in party city. I bet they aren't even allowed to have parties in your swank place, and I'm guessing Noah's isn't prone to loud raves into the night."

Carly rolled her eyes, but the smile she always got when anyone mentioned her fiancé spread across her face. "You could live somewhere nicer," she pointed out.

"Who's got the time to find a nice place when we're getting called in at two in the morning?"

Carly didn't answer because Alana Suzuki walked in. Director of TCD, she looked put together in her smart suit. It didn't matter that it was the middle of the night. She carried a folder, and her face was grim.

Which made Selena fidget. Alana was *all* business, and while their business was serious, there was something…discomfiting about the way Alana specifically looked at her.

Then Opaline.

"Selena, Opaline, could I see you outside for a moment?"

The discomfort settled into full-on dread in her gut, but she got to her feet and walked out of the boardroom with Opaline.

Alana stopped in the hallway and looked at both of

them with some sympathy. "I wish we had more time so that I could put this delicately."

"No need," Selena replied, careful to keep her voice even and calm. "Lay it on us."

She heard her sister huff, but Selena couldn't look at her just now. She had to keep it together. Doing her job required being able to compartmentalize. Opaline had never understood the fine art of pushing things away, let alone dealing with things at appropriate moments. She always reacted. Oftentimes when it got both of them in more trouble.

"I'm afraid you have a personal connection to this assignment," Alana began.

Selena closed her eyes. She knew she couldn't outwardly react, but in this moment, just the three of them, she gave herself a moment to breathe. "Peter."

When Selena opened her eyes, Alana's expression was empathetic. "Yes, your brother has escaped prison with two other convicts. We need to stop them before they cross the Canadian border."

Alana was a good boss, an excellent director. The perfect mix of personal and business. She knew how to take care of her people. Selena appreciated that beyond measure.

Which meant she wouldn't let Peter jeopardize her job here. She'd do whatever she had to do to complete the mission that involved her half brother. She'd bring him to justice, no matter what it took.

"We'll go over the details inside, but before we head in there, I wanted to give you both a chance to bow out. We can replace either or both of you for this mission if you feel your relationship with Peter would keep you from being able to do your job. Conversely, you can take some time to think about—"

"I don't need any time," Selena said, keeping her voice devoid of any and all emotion, no matter how it battered at her on the inside. "If we're tracking, you need me and Blanca."

Alana nodded, then turned to Selena's sister. "Opaline?"

Selena finally glanced at her. Opaline looked at her like she was some kind of monster. She'd never understood you couldn't save people who didn't want to be saved. And seemed to blame Selena for the fact their half brother did not want to be saved.

"I can handle it," Opaline said, glaring daggers at Selena. Her voice was rough, and her eyes were bright with unshed tears.

For a half brother they hardly knew, who'd refused help, again and again. Whose very existence had caused such a rift in their family, it still hadn't healed.

Selena would never understand it or Opaline. She turned on a heel and walked back into the boardroom. No one looked directly at her, but she could feel their consideration all the same.

She slid into her chair, keeping her expression neutral. Carly was friend enough not to say anything, but of course Axel would be obnoxious.

"You okay?" Axel asked.

Selena raised her chin, keeping her gaze on where Alana was taking her place at the head of the boardroom table. "Just fine."

Selena was definitely not just fine, but as Alana walked back into the boardroom, Axel Morrow had to focus on the task at hand. TCD business, and the challenge Alana Suzuki would lay out before them.

"Team, I appreciate you all coming in at such an hour, but we need to get started as soon as possible. Opaline?"

Where Selena was completely blank, Opaline was outwardly shaken by whatever Alana had told them. It didn't take a special agent to deduce whatever the mission was involved the sisters on some kind of personal level.

Still, Opaline went to the front of the room and took over the computer. As the tech specialist for TCD, it was always her job to run through the slideshow.

"Three inmates have escaped a maximum-security federal prison this evening. Because of the nature of their crimes, the way they've escaped and where we think they're going, TCD has been tasked with stopping them and bringing them back before they cross the border to Canada. Police have set up roadblocks on routes to the border since they likely stole a car, but so far, no sightings to give us an idea of their route." Alana nodded at Opaline, who brought up a mug shot on the screen at the front of the room.

"Leonard Koch is the presumed leader of this little trio. He's in for life for the murder of a family, among a litany of other charges."

Alana didn't look directly at Axel, but he felt the consideration all the same. Murder was part and parcel with his job as special agent, even in his supervisory role. He still considered himself part of the team more than some kind of leader.

But the murder of a family was…well, it hit close to home. Families being murdered was why he was here.

As an FBI agent, as the person he was today. To stop men like Leonard Koch before he hurt any more people.

Alana nodded at the screen, and the mug shot changed to the next slide, which included a list of charges.

Max McRay, special agent and explosives expert, let out a low whistle next to him. "That's quite a rap sheet. How'd this guy get out?"

"He and his cohorts convinced a prison guard they had her son. Unfortunately, since they had a lot of personal information and were threatening her son's life, she fell for it. On the bright side, the child is fine. So, right now we're just focused on apprehension." Alana pointed at Opaline to bring up the next slide.

"Steve Jenson is our number two. A history of battery, assault, but he's in for his role in an armed burglary that went south when a security guard was killed in the resulting shootout. Though we don't have any concrete idea of what kind of access they have to supplies, we're considering them both armed and extremely dangerous."

"And the third?" Aria Calletti asked. She was the newest member of TCD, but she'd proven herself extraordinarily capable last year when she'd been instrumental in bringing down a murderous smuggling ring. Axel had been with her when she'd gotten their best lead to talk. She was a go-getter, that was for sure.

But Axel wished she hadn't pressed so quickly when it clearly upset Opaline. The woman let out a shaky sigh before she brought up the next picture.

"The third escapee is Peter Lopez," Alana said with more gravity than she'd used to announce the other two.

As it was a group of highly trained FBI agents, no

one immediately looked to Selena or Opaline, but that didn't mean everyone in the room wasn't paying attention to the reactions to the two women who shared a last name with the third man.

Opaline wiped at her eyes and shook her head. Meanwhile, a surreptitious look at Selena showed a woman with no reaction at all.

"Peter is Opaline and Selena's brother, and they've both been briefed in advance and given the option to remove themselves if they felt like they couldn't do their jobs, but both agreed to stay on."

"We're not close," Selena said, her voice even. "He's our half brother, the product of an affair our father had. Don't feel like you have to walk on eggshells around me. We might share some genetic material, but I don't know the guy."

Alana nodded, and Opaline glared daggers at her sister, but she didn't argue with the assessment.

Axel found he wasn't sure which reaction made more sense. The complete lack of emotion had to be hiding *something*, but if they were so removed from the man, why was Opaline so upset?

Something he'd get to the bottom of before the day was out, but for now, they had to decide on a course of action.

"Opaline, would you bring up the map?"

The screen changed from Peter's mug shot to a topographical map of the area between the prison in northern Michigan and the Canadian border.

"We have reason to believe they're heading for Canada. We want to catch them before they do, and before they hurt anyone. The first wave of that will fall to Selena."

Selena nodded. "I'll take Blanca up to the prison and we'll start from there. Unless we have new known whereabouts?"

"Rihanna will keep in close touch with local authorities," Alana said, referring to TCD's police and press liaison. "If we get any updates on location, that will be relayed to you and Axel."

Selena straightened next to him. "Axel?"

"He'll partner with you on this. No one works alone. Aria and Carly will work together as well, and we'll bring in Scott Fletcher from the FBI to pair with Max to keep things even. We'll station the teams of two along the Canadian border. While Selena and Axel track, you'll set up a perimeter where hopefully if they don't catch up to the trio, you guys can stop them. You'll want to stay in close contact, and adjust as necessary. Axel will be lead on this."

He nodded at Alana before sliding Selena a look. She continued to show absolutely no reaction. She was a statue.

"We might be in charge of tracking," Alana said, "but the local police will be helpful resources, especially if the escapees cause any trouble in some of the smaller towns or more remote areas. This is a true team effort. The six of you tracking, Opaline working on tech—she'll get you all the maps you'll want to download onto your phones. Rihanna is working with local authorities in case we catch wind of them somewhere. No one acts alone."

"And we bring them all in before anyone else is killed," Axel added. Maybe it didn't need to be said, but there was an urgency that had to be heeded. He stood as Selena did.

"I'll follow you to your apartment in the Jeep. We'll go from there."

She didn't say anything, just gave the slightest nod and then walked out the door. Axel looked back at Alana, but her expression was neutral.

This wouldn't be as simple as bringing three fugitives to justice, that much was for sure.

Chapter 2

Selena pulled her personal car into the parking space of her apartment complex. The partiers seemed to have finally dispersed—since it was nearing four in the morning at this point.

She trudged up the stairs to her top-floor apartment and thought about Carly saying she could move if she didn't like where she was. Selena was sure there wasn't time, nor did she have the energy to look for a new place. But she realized she'd been doing this for four years now. Saying she didn't have time. Saying she didn't have the energy.

Was she going to settle into this crappy apartment complex forever and just exist? She put a lot into her work at TCD, and enjoyed it, but that didn't mean the rest of her life had to be…this.

She shook her head as she unlocked her door and

then the dead bolt she'd installed herself. There really *wasn't* time to deal with her living quarters right now—but she promised herself when this assignment was over, she'd really start looking into a more permanent living space.

For now, the focus had to be getting her dog and tracking the three escapees.

One of whom you know.

Didn't matter. She hadn't lied to her team and friends. She'd had limited contact with Peter. She'd tried to help him over the years. Not because she'd wanted to, but because her father had insisted her position in law enforcement made her the perfect person to reach his son.

His son. With a woman who had not been his wife at the time. Yet he'd expected Selena to step in and…

Selena couldn't let herself go down these messy emotional paths. She'd attended Peter's trial in some silly attempt to understand how a man related to her could go so wrong, and what she'd realized sitting there watching him answer questions belligerently was that she couldn't allow herself to take responsibility for her father's mistakes. Or Peter's.

She'd been in the midst of her own stupid personal drama, surprised at all the ways she could screw up her own life. All the ways she could fail.

Then and there she'd promised herself to stop letting other people run her life. She wouldn't feel guilty about Peter, she wouldn't keep helping her father when she didn't want to and she certainly wouldn't let herself get so wrapped up in a man that her entire career could be threatened.

No, she'd come to a lot of conclusions in that courtroom. Her life was her own. Peter being involved in this bite her tongue to keep from knee-jerk sniping at him on a personal one.

Hardly his fault she thought he was hot. Definitely not his fault she'd already learned her lesson in that department. She moved into the passenger seat without a word.

He climbed into the driver's seat and turned the key in the ignition. Blanca had already settled herself into the back—specially designed for tactical dogs, so Blanca wouldn't be too jostled by any off-terrain driving.

"No word on any new sightings?" Selena asked, pulling out her phone and bringing up the map of the area Opaline had sent all members of the team. By the time they got to the prison, the escapees would have a significant head start. They could head toward the prison, but what they really needed was someone to report seeing the fugitives.

"Afraid not," Axel said pulling out of her apartment complex's parking lot.

"I don't know how we're going to catch up with them at this rate."

"I imagine they'll hang low during the day. They won't want to be spotted—not before they cross the border. That should give us a few hours to minimize the distance. There's only so many ways to get to Canada, and the prison guard was sure that's where they were headed."

Selena wasn't so sure. There wasn't much in terms of towns or people between the prison and the Canadian border. Lots and lots of wilderness and lakes, though. The kind it was easy to disappear into. Even crossing by water could be done with the right amount of money.

They might not have had any leading the prison, but that didn't mean some wasn't waiting for them.

They drove for a while. Selena was grateful Axel didn't try to fill the silence with chatter. He was good at knowing when to do that and when not to. He read people well.

It was one of the many reasons she avoided being alone with him. The last thing she needed was him *reading* all that went on in her head when she looked at him.

Axel's phone rang, and he used the Jeep's Bluetooth system to answer it. "Morrow."

"Hey, guys," Rihanna's voice greeted them. "I just got off the phone with local police in Winston. There's been an incident, and it looks to be our guys."

"What happened?" Axel demanded. With a glance at the lane next to him, he moved over to get off at the exit, immediately altering their course to head toward Winston instead of the prison.

Selena studied her map, but Rihanna's pause on the other end had her gut clenching in dread as she calculated their new driving distance and how much of a head start the escapees had.

"Local wildlife officers found two poachers who'd been shot," Rihanna said at last. "One was capable of telling local law enforcement a little about who'd shot him. They'd stumbled upon three men, who fired without pause. They left our witness for dead after stealing guns and money. His description of them matches our escapees."

Axel's grip on the steering wheel tightened. "You said one was capable of talking to law enforcement," he said, his voice abnormally cold. "What about the other poacher?"

Again, Rihanna paused, and Selena watched Axel's expression get harder…and harder. She wasn't sure why he cared about the other poacher. Another set of eyes? Two stories instead of one? More witnesses meant more information and—

"He was dead when the wildlife officers arrived."

The coldness in his voice spread into his gaze on the road. The clear *fury* pumping off him was an emotional response Selena wouldn't have expected from him. He was always so controlled. So *cool* under pressure.

"Get us the location," he said, the words having a sharp bite. "We'll meet local law enforcement there."

"I'll make sure they know you're coming." Rihanna hung up.

Axel increased the speed of the Jeep. The roads were mostly empty this early in the morning, but he was taking exits too fast, and curves even faster, to the point Selena was actually afraid they'd wreck before they got where they needed to be.

"Getting there faster won't change the fact the man is dead," Selena said, gripping the handle of the door as tight as she could.

"But it might stop another innocent man from being killed."

Though it grated, Axel slowed down. It was possible he was pushing things just a little too hard. Yes, it was a failure a man had been killed. A failure he felt deep in his bones. But if he did something foolish because of that feeling of failure, that would also be his fault.

And if it hurt Selena or Blanca…well, no. He had

to get a hold of himself. They'd get to Winston soon enough.

"I don't like being too late," he muttered, the closest to an apology he was going to get.

"Who does?" Selena replied, too flippantly for his tastes. "But I can't blame myself for every criminal who does the wrong thing. I'd never get out of bed in the morning."

Axel knew he had to control his emotions, knew he couldn't compare this to all those years ago, but his temper strained at how unaffected she was. "Even your own brother's wrong thing? Because I think that'd mean *something* to you."

She whipped her gaze toward him. There was fury in her dark eyes, but she'd paled a bit. Like he'd landed a blow.

Hell. He'd screwed up. He could blame it on lack of sleep or what have you, but the bottom line was he should handle loss of life better. He had to. "I'm sorry. That was uncalled for."

She slowly looked away from him, her eyes on the road before them. The sun was flirting with the horizon, and she said nothing. Not that it was okay. Not that she accepted his apology. Not even telling him where he could shove his apology.

Which was somehow worse. He squeezed the steering wheel, then forced himself to loosen his grip. "Look. It bothers me."

More silence, because it bothering him was hardly an excuse for being a jerk.

"Which isn't an excuse. I can't excuse it. I shouldn't have said it. I shouldn't have let the emotional response take over. But I've been the survivor in that situation, so there *is* an emotional response. Better to get it out now rather than let it bubble up later." Or so he'd tell himself for the time being so he could focus on getting the job done.

Selena's eyebrows drew together. "I don't remember hearing anything about that."

"Not on duty. Not... I was a kid."

Her silence in response made his skin feel too tight. While there were members of the team who knew about his past, he didn't trot it out to discuss for fun. If people knew, fine, but he'd rather not have to get into it too often.

Still, he'd been the jerk. This was his penance.

"My family was killed when I was seven. The FBI had been after the guy for months and were closing in, but they didn't make it in time. He killed my parents, my brother. He shot me, but by that time they'd surrounded the house. I was transported in enough time to save my life. I got into this so some kid didn't have to be the one with the murdered family members, and yeah, I can't save everyone. But I don't like to lose a life on an active case I'm on, knowing if we hadn't sat around in a briefing meeting we might have gotten there."

"I don't know what to say," Selena said softly. "I guess there really isn't anything to say."

Most people said they were sorry, which he hated. Or went on and on about how awful it must have been. How brave he was to survive it. To go into the FBI. He appreciated the fact she knew there wasn't anything that would actually help.

"Except briefing is necessary to know who, how and what. We could have been on the road to the prison sooner, but it wouldn't have saved that guy's life."

Axel pushed out a breath. "I guess not."

"There's enough hard stuff in this job without heaping guilt and blame on yourself or your team that doesn't belong there. You start questioning—"

"I'm not questioning. I have the utmost confidence in our team."

"Okay, well…" Both their phones pinged at the same time. He let Selena deal with the information.

"We're meeting the local police force at a cabin near where the incident took place," Selena said, tapping a few keys on her phone. "GPS isn't going to be much help once we go off-road, so I'll navigate once we're in Winston."

Axel nodded wordlessly. He was glad they were moving on. They had a job to do, not pasts to obsess over.

"Is that why you have a scar on your jaw?"

He slid Selena a look. Her gaze was on the road in front of them, but the scar was faint these days. Hardly noticeable. Unless someone had been looking.

Which of course, he knew she had. Four years they'd worked in the same department. He was aware there was…chemistry. It was why he kept his distance. Clearly he had enough of his own baggage, he didn't need to add the complication of romantic entanglements.

Still, he wasn't *unaffected* that she looked.

"Yeah. The guy shot me, but mostly missed. Didn't have time to check I was dead before he ran."

"And they caught him? The FBI?"

"Before he'd even gotten out of the neighborhood."

"That's rough." She shifted in the seat and slid her arm back to give Blanca a pet, all the while keeping her gaze on the road. "Turn here," she instructed. "We want to go in on the west side of town."

Axel only nodded and took the turn she instructed him to make.

"I got into law enforcement because of family too. Because of Peter, to be specific. Some part of me thought if I became a cop, I'd be able to talk him out of being hell-bent on destroying his own life."

"I thought you didn't have a relationship."

"We don't. Doesn't mean I wasn't aware what was going on with him. Mom complaining about Dad's deadbeat son. Dad washing his hands of any kind of trouble because heaven forbid he try to help his own kid." She shrugged jerkily. "Point is, we've all got our stuff, right? Sometimes it pops up and gets the best of us for a minute or two, but we're pros. I've never seen you falter when it mattered. I haven't either."

She was saying it so he didn't think too much about the moment before. That was obvious, but he thought she was saying it a bit for herself too. She might act unaffected, but Peter meant something to her. They both had their baggage that might affect them as they went through the assignment.

But in the end, regardless of feelings of failure or brotherly attachment, they'd both do their jobs.

They had to.

Chapter 3

Early morning light filtered through the trees as Selena followed Axel toward the flashing lights of a police car and the low hum of conversation. She held Blanca on her leash, keeping her close.

The air was frigid, and Selena was grateful for the thick tactical boots she wore as they hiked through the snow. It was packed down from many sets of footprints. Were any of them her brother's?

It didn't matter. She couldn't think of Peter like her brother. She had to think about what he really was: a stranger she was tasked with bringing to justice. She didn't know him. And he most certainly didn't know her.

So, he was a stranger. She would work with Axel to apprehend him, because regardless of what genes they shared, he was responsible for killing a man. Maybe he hadn't pulled the trigger on the poor poacher who'd come across the wrong men at the wrong time.

But maybe he had.

Axel's strides were long, and she didn't bother trying to keep up. Blanca sniffed the snow and trees and oriented herself to her new surroundings—in order for her to be ready to track, she needed that time. Selena refused to admit she was giving the time to herself, as well.

She needed a little distance from Axel Morrow. She hadn't gotten into the FBI and this special unit by being soft, by showing compassion and empathy for her partner. There wasn't time for that. A teammate had to be understanding and forgive their partner's mistakes, or you'd never keep moving forward.

But that wasn't what she'd done. She'd given him a piece of herself. When he'd apologized for snapping at her and using her brother to do it, she should have accepted it. The end.

But *no*. She'd had to tell him she'd gotten into law enforcement because of Peter. She'd *shared*, when she knew that was professional suicide as a woman in a tough field. Oh, she'd worked with Axel long enough to know he wasn't one of those guys who used every weakness a woman showed against her, but that didn't change the fact she was on dangerous ground.

Dangerous ground she'd walked on before, and lost far too much of herself in the process.

By the time she caught up with Axel, he was already deep in conversation with the local police officer.

"I think they'd planned to stay at this cabin for the day," the officer was saying. He gave Selena and Blanca a brief nod. "But the poachers came in and… Well, you can read the statement."

"I'd like to talk to the survivor first, if you don't mind."

Again, the officer nodded. "We've got him in the car. We've already taken his statement, and we'll drive him home once things are good on your end."

The officer started walking toward the police cruiser, but Selena stopped Axel with a light touch of the arm. It would be impossible to get through this mission without touching him like this—lightly, casually—but that didn't mean she had to like it.

"I'm going to search the cabin," she said, maybe a little bit sharper and more authoritatively than she needed to.

His expression was flat. She'd worked with him for four years, and she'd learned—whether she wanted to or not—to read Axel's moods on a case. The murder bothered him, plain and simple, and now she knew why.

She wished she didn't.

"Cops said they left everything as is," Axel said quietly, his green eyes searching the woods around them. "Blanca should be able to pick up something. We'll track from here with her."

"We shouldn't take too much time. The snow will make tracking harder, and they've already got a head start."

"Yeah, but this poacher might have overheard something. Search the house while I talk to him. We'll head out from there as soon as we can."

They parted in silent agreement, and Selena urged Blanca to the cabin. Since she had winter gloves on, she opened the door and stepped inside. There was no electricity, and very few windows, so the interior lighting was dim at best. She pulled the flashlight off her utility belt and began to search.

"Stay," she ordered the dog. Blanca settled into a seated position by the door while Selena moved forward.

They couldn't have been here long, and Selena had to wonder why they'd rest at night. Wouldn't they want to get as far away from the jail as possible? On foot, they hadn't gotten more than twenty miles from the prison. Which meant they hadn't stolen a car.

Yet.

It had been cold last night. Temperatures dipping well below zero. Even if they'd stolen some supplies, they wouldn't be well equipped for a trek across the northern Michigan wilderness in February. Maybe they hadn't stopped because they'd wanted to, but because they simply hadn't been prepared for what lay in front of them.

But the escape had been so well planned, executed perfectly. Why had they decided to escape in the dead of winter? What more was at stake here aside from simply freedom?

Too many questions. It wasn't her job to imagine answers. It was her job to find facts to bring them to answers. Or if not answers, the men themselves.

Selena let her flashlight roam the area of the small, rustic cabin. It was sparse. Clearly a space used simply as a base for hunting or fishing in the wilderness rather than any kind of cozy vacation home. There were quite a lot of these types of cabins in the area the police had been searching. Hunting spaces, or the nicer lake houses probably closed up for the winter, family cabins. If they knew where to look, the escapees would be able to find shelter here and there. Most of it empty in the middle of February.

But this one hadn't been. On first sweep, she saw nothing in the main area. There was a couch, a table and a fireplace to one side, and then a kitchenette to the other. There was one door besides the front door, which Selena assumed was a bathroom. If anyone slept here, they likely slept on the couch or on the floor.

Selena wrinkled her nose at the floor. It was hard planks of wood, no carpet or rugs to soften anything up. This wouldn't be the place she'd want to spend some free hours.

The windows had thick curtains that looked like they'd been collecting dust for years. She approached the fireplace. Though there was no fire, not even a glow of embers, she could smell the trace of smoke in the air. When she squatted to hold her hand over the blackened wood, the air was warmer than it had been closer to the door.

They'd come in here. Made themselves comfortable, then been surprised into moving again.

Selena glanced back at the door. Blanca still sat dutifully, waiting for the order. But if Selena didn't find anything that might have a good scent on it, there wouldn't be much for Blanca to go on. They'd have to get a look at the tracks outside and make a decision from there.

Selena got back to her feet, and as she stood she noticed something slightly different colored than the blackened wood in the hearth. A gray fabric. She leaned closer. It looked like a glove.

There was no way to tell whether it belonged to one of the men they were searching for, or the owner of the cabin, or another passerby altogether. But it was *something*.

"Blanca. Come."

Axel prided himself on the fine art of compartmentalizing. Senseless murder always tested that ability, but he muscled through because that was what this job required of him.

He loved his job. The structure. The clear goal. Sometimes cases dealt more in the gray area, but when it came to murder, the task was clear—stop the murderer before he could do any more damage.

Axel frowned at the surviving poacher. There was more to his story he wasn't telling. Axel slid a look at the cop next to him. From what Axel could tell, he was a good one. But tired and ready for this to be over.

Axel couldn't blame him. Even with the sun inching up in the sky, it was bitterly cold. The snow was fairly deep, and despite waterproof clothing, the chill of having your feet surrounded by snow wasn't for the faint of heart.

The poacher sat in the back seat of the cruiser with the door open. He looked at his hands. When he answered Axel's questions, questions the cop had already asked him before they'd gotten here, he mumbled.

Axel nodded away from the cruiser, and the officer followed him. "I want five minutes alone with him."

The officer scratched his cheek and sighed. "Poor guy's friend is dead and he's been out here for hours. Let me take him in."

"He's got more information than he's letting on. Come on. You know he's afraid of the poaching repercussions."

"I've told him—"

"Just give me five minutes alone. That's all."

The officer sighed but gave a short nod and then moved stiffly away. Axel turned back to the poacher. He'd said he didn't know which way the escapees had gone. That they hadn't taken anything.

"What aren't you telling us?"

The man looked up, noted the cop had moved away. Still, he shrugged. "Nothing I can think of."

"Your buddy is dead, and it's my job to stop these guys from killing anyone else. The local's gone. Anything you tell me? Stays between us. Whatever illegal hunting you were doing? I don't care about it. I want these guys. So, tell me. What are you leaving out?"

The man looked at the cop, then back at Axel. He blinked and looked down at his hands. "Earl didn't deserve to die."

"I'm sure he didn't. So, why don't you help me get Earl a little justice."

"Justice," the man repeated. Then he sighed. "They took some stuff."

"What kind of stuff?" Axel demanded.

The guy fidgeted and shook his head. He scowled out the back window of the car. "Guns," he finally muttered. "Cash."

Axel didn't allow himself to swear, though that's what he wanted to do. "And why didn't you tell him?" Axel said, jamming a finger toward the officer. "Or any other law enforcement."

"The guns aren't registered to us, and I didn't tell my father-in-law I took them. The cash?" The poacher licked his lips, and his eyes darted back and forth.

The man was not good at lying. Likely the cash was

from some underhanded dealings. Ones Axel didn't have time to care about. "That all?"

The man scrunched his face up. "They made me give them my car keys. It's not parked here, but I told them where it's parked a few miles out."

"A car? They stole your car and you're just now telling us?" Axel knew his voice was a little too sharp when this man had just lost his friend, but he couldn't bring himself to care.

"Just the keys. They'd have to get to it first. I... The car is my wife's, and she's going to leave me if she finds out I got caught poaching again."

"I want the make and model of the car," Axel bit out. "License plate number. You don't know it? You're going to be breaking the bad news to your wife a lot sooner than you'd like. Then you tell me exactly where you left it."

The poacher rattled off the information, still staring at his hands. Axel noted everything down in his phone and sent a quick text message to Opaline, Rihanna and Alana. Between the three of them, the information would get out to all the necessary authorities.

The difficult part was that the men were now confirmed as armed. They'd killed together, which meant they would kill again, given the chance. Authorities had to be extra careful.

Axel had to hope no one did anything stupid before he and Selena could track them down. Axel glanced back at the cabin. Selena was still inside with Blanca. If she'd found anything, they should head out.

He gave one last look at the poacher, who appeared as miserable as possible. Axel didn't think there was any information left to get from him, so he turned to walk away. It was time to move.

"You're going to bring those SOBs in?" the man asked.

Axel stopped and glanced at the poacher over his shoulder. The shock he'd been under when Axel had first arrived had worn off and shifted into anger. Axel understood. "That's my job."

The man nodded. "Good. Well, I'd cooperate in whatever it took to get them behind bars. Earl didn't deserve to die. He wasn't perfect, but he didn't deserve to die. Not like this."

Not like this. Yeah, Axel knew that feeling all too well.

He headed for the cabin, instructing the local cop that he could take the poacher into the station. He opened the door. Selena was crouched by a rudimentary fireplace, Blanca sniffing something.

He rubbed his hands together. "A little warmer in here than out there," he offered by way of greeting.

"A little. Looks like they had a fire going. There's a glove left behind, but who knows if it belonged to the guys we're looking for." Selena pointed to the glove Blanca was sniffing.

"We know they're in the area," Axel said. "We know they were in here, and the poacher said this cabin was his friend's and they hadn't been up here in a month or so because of the snow. His buddy was shot before they entered, so I think the likelihood of it belonging to or at least used by one of the escapees is high."

"Agreed," Selena said, standing up from her crouched position.

"Stole a car, guns and cash."

Selena swore.

"My thoughts exactly. Poacher said the car was a few miles out. They took his keys. I imagine that's what they headed for."

Selena nodded, motioning for Blanca to follow her to the door.

"Why don't you drive? We'll track, make sure the glove is one of theirs. I'll keep in touch and meet you at where this car was parked."

Axel studied her. She was dead serious. And out of her mind. "Nice try."

She puffed out a breath, her distractingly full mouth curving slightly. "It was worth a shot," she offered.

"Was it?" he returned, working hard to keep his voice light and even. Close quarters with Selena Lopez was not high on his list of ways to torture himself. "You know you're not going to work alone."

"I'm not alone. I have Blanca."

Axel looked up at the dog, waiting patiently by the door. Then at her again. He raised an eyebrow.

She rolled her eyes. "Yeah, yeah. We're in pairs for this one. So, you want to drive to where the car was?"

Axel nodded. "I've gotten the information out, so hopefully someone will catch sight of them in the car."

Selena frowned. "If not, Blanca isn't going to be able to track a car. Certainly not in time to stop them from crossing the border."

Axel nodded. "They won't stay in the car long. They'll assume it'll be tagged. My guess is they find some place to stay, then get a new car. But they're going to want to stay as rural as possible to avoid detection. At some point, they might even camp."

Selena looked out the open door dubiously. "You

couldn't pay me to camp in the dead of February." Her expression went thoughtful. "You know, I was thinking about that. Why plan this escape in February? Why not wait till April or May when you might have more survivable weather?"

Axel considered. He'd been focused on the poachers and hadn't thought about the time of year. Selena was right. If it was just about escape, they would have waited for a better time of year.

"So, there's more to it."

"Has to be. Don't you think?"

Axel nodded. "Come on. Let's get to the Jeep and see if we find anything where they took the car."

"Got it, boss," Selena said, stepping outside, Blanca at her heels.

"Don't call me that," he muttered, following her.

"What?" she said, grinning over her shoulder at him. "Boss?"

He didn't scowl, didn't allow himself to. He kept his expression as neutral as possible. "Yes."

"But are you not, technically, my boss?"

"I'm not—"

"Your title is *supervisory* special agent, right? That seems to imply, or perhaps even straight out say, you are something of a *supervisor*."

Axel didn't say anything to that. Though it *was* his official position title, it was more about seniority and the chain of command than wanting to place himself above anyone in the team. They had to be a *team*. Not boss-employee. As full supervisor, Alana felt the same way. It was why they were a successful FBI division. They'd worked hard to foster a community of teamwork and equality, to avoid any politicking or grandstanding to get positions over each other.

And mostly, he didn't want Selena thinking of him as her *boss*. It made his shoulders tense in a way he didn't want to analyze too deeply.

"That's what I thought," she said with a sultry chuckle. She sauntered off toward the Jeep, and Axel tried *very* hard not to watch her.

Chapter 4

Selena watched the forest pass as Axel drove to where the poacher had said his car would be. Sun glinted off the snow, glittery, white and beautiful. She wasn't sure how long they'd have the luxury of heat blasting from the vents, so she tried to soak up all that she could.

Finding the escapees in a car was going to be more difficult, especially with their head start, but she didn't mind avoiding a hike through the woods. No matter how the sun shone, the air was *cold*.

More to it. Why would three men escape prison in the midst of this? Why would that be the plan? "Do we know if they have any connections in Canada? Maybe it's not the final destination. Maybe it's stop one."

"Maybe. Maybe it was just a…chance. Happenstance. They saw a moment of weakness to escape and they used it."

Selena shook her head. "No. It was too coordinated. And the three of them… There has to be something they have in common. The briefing didn't say anything about them knowing each other on the outside."

"No. They didn't, as far as we know."

"There's a piece we're missing."

Axel nodded grimly. "I agree. But right now our job isn't the pieces, it's tracking them down."

Selena didn't say anything to that. She wasn't so sure they shouldn't be trying to figure out the puzzle. Sure, some of the people back at headquarters were doing that, and as an agent she specialized in tracking and suspect apprehension, not investigation, but that didn't mean investigating wouldn't get them closer to apprehension.

Axel slowed the car, squinting into the midmorning sun. "It's still there."

"You're sure that's the car?" She could only see a flash of silver—not enough to make out the model yet.

"Silver sedan. In the exact place he said." Axel came to a complete stop. "If it's still there, they might be too."

Selena studied their surroundings, as Axel did. She didn't see a sign of anyone, but that didn't mean they weren't out there. Waiting.

"I'll get Blanca out and we'll track using the glove. You search the car."

She waited for Axel to argue. To say they should stick together. With the potential for attack, they couldn't split up.

"Vests," was all he said.

They had their tactical gear in the rear cargo space, so when Axel slid out of the car, Selena did the same.

They moved quickly and silently, watching and bracing themselves for a surprise attack.

But they met at the trunk with no hint that anyone else was near them. Axel held out her vest, and she took it. They both shed their jackets, pulled the Kevlar vests on, tightened the straps and shrugged back into their coats.

Then, in nonverbal agreement, they went completely still and silent, listening to their surroundings.

The wind whistled through the trees, and snow blew so hard it sounded like pebbles being tossed in the wind. Any slight noises made by anyone else would be lost.

There would be no way to *hear* if anyone else was around, though the wind might have also drowned out the sound of their car approaching, depending on how close the men were to the silver sedan. Maybe she and Axel would have a chance to sneak up on them.

Selena nodded toward the car, a signal she was going to let Blanca out and begin to track.

Axel nodded his head, green eyes cool and assessing. He had many sides to him. This was the man back in the car this morning who'd driven too fast to stop a murder that had already happened.

They both crouched behind the car, guns drawn and ready, and Selena knew she had to say…something to keep his focus on the task at hand, not the life they'd lost.

"We take all three in alive, they'll fold on each other. They'll go back to jail for a very long time."

His gaze met hers, green and cold. She might have shivered, but there was something about Axel. She didn't know what it was, didn't *want* to know what it was, only that it always had things shifting around in her chest. A flutter. A sense of…not just wanting. Something far more complicated than that.

The worst part was, she got the impression he felt it too. The way their gazes held just a little too long in moments like this. When they should be moving forward. Acting.

And where did you end up the last time you thought a guy felt the same thing you did?

She held his gaze out of her own warped sense of spite, but she struggled to find her equilibrium here, in the depth of green that reminded her of a spring forest rather than the winter white they were surrounded by.

"Got it," he said.

She'd forgotten what point she'd made, but she wouldn't dwell on that. She gave Blanca a quick pet, then held out the glove. Blanca sniffed. Moved ahead a few feet, came back to sniff again.

Selena kept her gun drawn, her eyes scanning the area around Blanca. Blanca did her job, sniffing and inching forward. She was struggling to find the scent. Selena knew they had to get closer to the car, but she wanted Axel to clear the area before she moved Blanca in.

"Clear," Axel called after a few minutes.

Surprised, Selena jogged over to the car.

"They were stuck," Axel said, pointing to where the tires were lodged deep in the snow and, below that, mud. "Ran the car till the gas tank was empty, probably trying to get out. Engine is still hot, but they're gone."

"If they did that, I can't imagine they're too far ahead of us."

"No, they can't be. We'll grab our packs and follow

Blanca. I imagine the car should give her a good scent to go on."

Selena nodded. "You get the packs. I'll search the interior."

Axel nodded, and Selena jerked the driver's side door open. There was the smallest hint of warmth still in the interior, but it dissipated quickly as Selena leaned inside. She wanted clothing, preferably. Nothing in the front seat, but as she moved to look into the back, something on the floorboard caught her eye.

She was already wearing gloves, so she reached down and picked it up. It was a prisoner ID card.

Peter Lopez.

She looked at the face of a man she didn't know. One her father had expected her to save. How had he gotten tangled up with murderers and batterers? He'd been arrested during a drug deal that had gone wrong, but his sentence was shorter because in the trial it had been proven he hadn't been carrying a weapon.

He was still responsible for fleeing the scene of a murder, and for dealing, but if there was anything Selena had ever comforted herself with—and likely why Opaline still thought Peter could be saved, and expected Selena to *help* save him, just like Dad did—it was that he wasn't in prison for a violent crime.

Or hadn't been. Maybe he'd been the one to pull the trigger on the innocent poacher back there. Maybe this was the end of the line for Peter. And there was no doubt in her mind that Dad *and* Opaline would blame her for that.

"Selena?"

Selena didn't startle—she was too well trained—but she closed her eyes and immediately chastised herself.

She'd told Alana she could handle this case without her personal feelings getting in the way, and she *had* to make certain not to make a liar out of herself.

"Prison ID left behind," she said, reaching backward to show Axel, who stood outside the car behind her. "You were right, they were definitely in the car."

Axel took the ID. "Anything Blanca can track?"

Without moving and giving away the fact she hadn't fully searched the car yet, Selena looked into the back seat out of the corner of her eye.

"Clothes in the back. But even if they sat in here, this isn't their car. Too many competing smells. Give me a few minutes to use the glove around here to see if she gets a trail scent."

Selena scooted out of the car and stood, Axel way too close for comfort. Luckily he wasn't looking at her. He was frowning into the woods.

"They got guns, a car and cash from the poacher. The car is stuck."

Selena worked with Blanca while Axel mused aloud.

"They warm up, then take off again. There has to be a plan to get supplies. They can't make it to Canada on foot without food and water."

Selena held the car open while Blanca sniffed the back seat. "Plenty of hunting cabins and the like scattered around. Could be they expect to find shelter and food as they hike along."

Axel's frown deepened as he pulled his phone out of his pocket. "I wonder if Opaline could get us an idea of where the cabins on the route to Canada are."

"Maybe, but how would they have anything like that? As far as we know from the prison, they got clothes and the security guard's gun. That's it." Selena looked at the winter landscape around them. "Unless they had more help than that."

Axel's expression was grim. "That's what I'm afraid of."

Blanca moved forward, gave one bark, then sat and waited for further instruction. "She's got a scent. We can pack up and follow?"

Axel nodded. "I'll update the team."

Selena waited by Blanca. The dog would wait for the signal to search, though she all but vibrated sitting there in the snow. It was a good sign. She had a good scent on at least one of the fugitives, but Selena worried about the snow. It wouldn't stop Blanca from tracking, but melting snow could hinder their progress.

"I guess I have to be grateful it's so darn cold," Selena muttered.

Axel brought their packs to where Blanca waited to search. A cold, isolated landscape.

Selena was right. There were a few threads that didn't make sense, and Axel knew their priority had to be this search. But when there was a mystery, a puzzle, what he really wanted to do was sit down and sort through it.

"We've got teams of two moving in from the Canadian border," he told her. "Local police notified of the information we have. It'd take some serious planning and skill to evade capture." Or help from a bigger, stronger threat.

Selena secured her pack on. "Ready?"

Axel nodded and she gave Blanca the *search* command.

Blanca immediately moved forward. There were

some footprints, but the wind had blown snow over them so they were just little indentations in the snow. Likely they'd be completely gone before they followed the dog for a mile.

They walked in silence for a while, pausing when Blanca paused, then following behind her again when she moved forward. "I'm not sure how much of a head start they've got, but she'd be moving faster or signaling if they were close. She does either of those two things, we'll want to pause and draw our weapons."

Axel nodded. He'd never worked this closely with Selena and Blanca before. While he prided himself on being a team player who didn't use the "supervisory" part of his title to take over any assignment, it was an odd sensation to be completely beholden to how Selena decided to use her dog.

Axel watched the time as they walked, routinely checked to see if there were any updates from the team and mostly tried not to think about the subzero wind chill.

"Let's take a water break," Selena suggested, and it took Axel a moment to realize she meant for the dog. "Pause."

Blanca immediately stopped. Selena shrugged off her pack and got out a water bottle and a dish. The dog eagerly lapped up the water, and Selena took her own swig. When their gazes locked, Axel didn't look away.

He should. He knew he should. They didn't need to constantly be staring at each other a little too long when there was work to be done. But he wouldn't be the one who looked away first. She was the one who'd always avoided this...*thing* between them. Not that he pressed the issue, but she'd set the precedent to ignore it.

And now was *not* the time to play these mind games with himself.

Selena looked down at her pack, dug around until she came up with a dog treat. She tossed the Milk-Bone at him, Blanca's eyes following the treat even as she stood completely still.

"She's still not sure about you," Selena said casually.

Axel frowned at Selena, then at the dog, whose focus was on the treat in his hand. "Excuse me?"

"She likes you, but she's not sure about you. Just in case you need to give her commands, you need to suck up to her a little."

"I need to suck up to your dog?"

Selena nodded. There was humor in her eyes, but her expression was serious. And Axel wasn't comfortable with the serious nature of the reasoning. "Why wouldn't you be able to give her commands?"

Selena shrugged. "We're law enforcement, Axel. Don't pretend like you don't know what could happen."

No, it was never far out of his mind, but there was something about the dog that added a weird weight to all the things that could go wrong in their profession. He shook his head and crouched, holding out the treat. "Come."

Blanca trotted over and took the treat from his fingers, then she stood in front of him and let him scratch her behind the ears. "There's a girl. I miss having a dog," he murmured, more to himself and the dog than Selena.

"You don't have one out on that farm of yours?" Selena replied, packing the supplies away. "What's the point in space if you don't have a dog?"

"I'm gone too much, so I've had to settle for animals

that don't need constant care. Chickens. Cows. I was thinking about getting a goat."

She laughed. It wasn't something she did a lot around him. Sometimes he'd hear her talking to Carly, and she'd laugh like that. It hit him a little too hard out here in the snowy wilderness, just the two of them.

"A goat?" she said, somewhat disbelieving as she adjusted the pack back on her shoulders.

Axel shrugged, trying to keep a casual grin on his face. "Sure. They're good at keeping a lawn tidy."

She shook her head, her mouth curved into a smile. She seemed relaxed enough, and he'd never gotten much of that with Selena. "Search," she commanded Blanca.

They set out again, and Axel couldn't help wanting to let the moment stretch out a bit. "You know, I was reading this article about a former NHL player who raises llamas. Maybe that's what I'll do in my retirement."

He got another husky laugh out of her. "Llamas. You've lost it, Morrow. Besides. You? Retire?"

"Sure. We all have to sometime."

"I don't know. You seem like one of those guys who'd just transition into the guy in charge. Not retire and putter around at your farm."

"Lots to putter around with on a farm, no matter how old or small. It's peaceful. It's home. Sometimes I look forward to it."

"And the other times?"

"I'm glad I have a challenging job that keeps my mind occupied." Though the older he got the more he wondered if keeping his mind occupied kept him from fully dealing with things he'd have to face eventually. Or maybe he wouldn't. Maybe he'd let the loss of his family define him and keep him from ever building new, deep bonds that went beyond work friendships. It didn't seem so bad when he was working.

Only when he was home on his farm. Alone.

"Now, keeping a mind occupied I understand," Selena said, stifling a yawn. "I don't think we're going to catch up to them at this pace."

"No, but we'll stay close. And unless they've magically found supplies somewhere, we should be able to keep going longer than they do."

But that *unless* hung between them, because they both thought there might be more to it. Help somewhere. A plan TCD hadn't figured out yet.

"Tell me about Peter."

She clammed up immediately. The easy curve of her mouth gone, any light in her eyes vanishing in a second. He might have regretted focusing back on the task at hand, but the tightening in his gut wasn't at all appropriate for the situation. Better to focus on what they should, even if it made her uncomfortable.

"I've told you all there is to tell," she said, her voice as cold as the world around them.

"So, why was Opaline so upset?"

"Opaline's…emotional. I know you guys see the happy, bubbly side of her, but there's the other side of that. She feels things…deeply. It's just who she is."

"And you aren't emotional?"

"I'm an FBI agent, Axel. That's what I am."

"Last time I checked, FBI agents got to be human."

She snorted derisively. "You can say that because you're a man."

"Fair enough. The point I'm trying to make, though, is… You get to have some feelings about this. Even if once we catch up to them, you push them aside and do the job."

"Or I can handle it my way. Thanks all the same."

"It might help the case, Selena."

She whipped her head around to stare daggers at him. "I'm not sure how my father and Opaline thinking I should be able to save Peter, convince him to follow the straight and narrow, has anything to do with the case. I don't know the kid. I've been responsible for him for half my life and I don't *know* the guy. I don't know his friends. I don't know what he's capable of, and if you think Opaline might, that's a laugh and a half, because she thinks she can save anyone if she forgives and forgets. Well, I don't believe in forgiving and forgetting betrayal, and I don't believe in ignoring that people have their own free will. Peter made his choices. I don't know how or why. I only know I'll make sure he pays for them. And if that makes me a crappy person? So damn be it. Because my *job* is what I care about. It's who I am. The end."

Axel didn't say anything to that. She wouldn't listen anyway. Still, it was hardly *the end*. That was a lesson he'd had to learn the hard way, and no doubt she was in the midst of learning it.

She wouldn't appreciate his understanding, so he kept it to himself. Just like attraction. His own doubts and conflicting emotions about the assignment. *Keep it to yourself. Bury it down deep.*

And hope the dam that kept it all inside never broke.

Chapter 5

Selena didn't mind losing her temper when the situation called for it, but this was not that situation. She'd been...hurt. God, she was an idiot. But they'd been talking. She'd actually been enjoying his company without being too worried about the whole attraction thing.

Then he'd asked her about Peter. Like sharing genetic material made him *her* responsibility.

Why did everyone in her life want to make Peter her responsibility?

She blew out a breath slowly, willing her anger to cool, her heartbeat to calm. She'd spewed all that at Axel, and that had been a mistake. She knew this was going to be an assignment fraught with them. She would deal with that by promising herself those mistakes would only be here, in these quiet moments.

When they had to act, really act, all of this conflicting, ancient history garbage would be shoved aside to do her job. If she lost her temper in the *waiting* that was so much of her job, well, she'd forgive herself. She *was* human.

So was he.

"I don't know him," Selena said calmly. "I don't have some secret understanding of who he is as a person, who he might be connected to. Fair or not, everyone in my life has expected me to in a variety of ways. I'm not here because Peter Lopez is my estranged half brother. I'm here because Blanca and I make a good team apprehending suspects. I need you to understand that."

Axel was quiet as they walked. When he finally spoke, she got the feeling he'd really *thought* about what she'd said. "Understood," he offered.

She thought he might…actually do just that. An odd feeling when she'd felt misunderstood and maligned for a really, *really* long time. First with her family and their insistent need for her to be the one who handled *everything*, and then at her last department when…

Well, it didn't do to dwell on all the ways she'd been humiliated and embarrassed. She snuck a glance at Axel. Maybe it was good to remember that sleeping with a coworker, especially in law enforcement, never ended well for the woman.

Blanca paused, scenting the air, her body vibrating in a way that spoke to an excitement. Either they were close, or the scent trail was clear enough she wanted to take off. But Selena had a feeling they were quickly catching up to the escapees.

Who were armed and dangerous.

Selena held up her hand and drew her weapon. Axel did the same. Instinctually, they moved so they were almost back to back, protecting themselves from being surprised. A unit that could see in both directions.

"Close?" Axel asked quietly.

"Within shooting distance," Selena murmured, eyeing the trees around them. Blanca's positioning meant the three men were not all in one direction. Were they fanning out to surround them?

"We're easy pickings right here. We need cover," Axel said. "See anything?"

Selena scanned the area in front of her. "Some dead trees. We'll have to lie in the snow, but they'd give us some cover." Not enough. Not from all sides. But that was the risk of the job.

"You go first. Then call Blanca. Then I'll follow."

"Got it." Selena moved slowly and carefully, on full alert. She studied the pile of logs, tried to adjust and rearrange them in her mind to give themselves the best tactical advantage. They'd still have to lie in the snow, and dead trees weren't exactly bulletproof shields, but it was something. She crouched and said softly and forcefully, "Blanca. Come."

There was a moment of hesitation from the dog—she wanted to do her job, track—but she obeyed Selena's command. Selena pointed to the spot she wanted Blanca—behind both the tree cover and Selena herself. If they had anyone sneak up from behind, Blanca would sound the alarm.

"Clear," Selena said to Axel.

He started moving toward her, and almost immediately a shot rang through the quiet air. Selena flinched, and Axel dived to the ground. Selena felt her heart leap to her throat.

"Hit?" she called out, hoping her voice didn't sound as panicked as she'd felt.

"No," Axel replied through gritted teeth. He was army crawling through the thick snow, which couldn't be comfortable.

Selena couldn't see anything. Wherever they were was either too far away or too well camouflaged. Another shot rang out. She ducked. When she peeked her head over the dead tree, Axel still had his head in the snow.

"Morrow," she barked.

He shook his head and started crawling again. Each inch seemed to take forever, and she had to fight back the need to jump out and pull him into the makeshift cover.

He was fine. Not shot. Just trying to avoid it. He was a skilled agent. They might be a team, but it wasn't her job to *protect* him, just to have his back. The fact that *protect* seemed to be an instinctual need inside her was perplexing.

Luckily, she didn't have time to think about it. After what felt like hours and was maybe minutes, Axel crawled over the logs and laid himself next to her. He faced the same direction she did.

"Two shooters in front of us," he said, his voice low but not a whisper. Too deep and authoritative to be called a whisper. "If there's a third, he hasn't fired yet."

"How do you know it's two shooters?"

"Sound of the gun. Angle of the shot." Axel lifted his own gun and rested it on the log in front of him.

"What about the third? Coming from behind?"

Axel glanced over his shoulder. "Blanca will warn us, don't you think?"

"I know. She'll bark, once, the minute anyone's within forty feet of us."

"Good. So, they're still a ways off."

Another shot rang out, and they both ducked again. Selena couldn't tell where the shots were hitting.

"Bad aim?" she asked.

Axel shook his head. "They're just too far away to get a good shot. They're trying to keep us far away, though. Don't get me wrong, they get the chance, they'll kill us, but right now these are warning shots."

"Why not come and kill us?"

Axel was quiet for a moment, clearly considering. "I suppose the risk they'd get shot in the process. They're more worried about escape than adding more crimes to their rap sheet?"

"Escaping prison isn't going to do them any favors. And they already added another murder to their rap sheet. Axel, there has to be something more they're trying to do than escape. I can't imagine all this is just to be free."

"Men have done far less just to be free."

But it didn't set right. These were career criminals. Her brother had been in trouble with the law since he'd turned thirteen. A prison sentence was hardly unexpected. It was a risk he was well aware of—a path he'd chosen to go down knowing full well what the consequences might be.

Another shot, but Axel and Selena had their heads below the logs so there was no ducking this time.

"They're retreating," Axel noted.

"How can you tell?"

"Sound of the gun. The direction they're coming from isn't so spread out. They'll keep shooting, even out of range, in the hopes the sound of the gunfire will keep us off their tails. Only two are shooting—which leads me to believe one is doing everything he can to hide their tracks."

"They can't hide from Blanca's nose."

Axel nodded.

"We shouldn't fall for it. We've got vests and we're trained FBI agents. Sitting here being scared of a little gunfire doesn't complete the mission."

"They're heading right toward the rest of our team. All we have to do is keep behind them like this, make sure they don't slip through any cracks. Eventually we'll have a tight enough circle to bring them in without a dangerous shootout."

Selena didn't particularly care for the slow, patient approach. It meant more days out in the wilderness alone with Axel. But she knew his plan was one that would be best to safeguard the team.

Trying not to scowl, Selena settled into the cold snow around her. "How long?"

"Until we don't hear the gunshots any longer."

It took far too long. Axel was doing everything to keep his teeth from chattering. Even in layers of tactical gear, lying in the snow was cold, uncomfortable business. Once they'd gone a good ten minutes without hearing a gunshot, Axel motioned for Selena to sit up.

"How's Blanca in this cold?" he asked. The dog had remained alert and still the entire time.

"She'll need a break eventually, but she's good for a few more hours yet."

"Good. I think we're safe to get up out of the snow now, but let's call in."

"And give them more of a head start? Let's get going and call on the way."

She was too impatient. It wasn't her usual MO, so Axel had to wonder what was driving it. The cold? Her brother's connection? The same things that bothered him about being out in the expansive wilderness with only her and her dog?

Best not to think too much on it. Focus on what needed to be done. What he'd really like to do was find somewhere warm to change into dry clothes, but that wasn't an option.

He settled himself on the log, Selena beside him. Blanca would warn them if the escapee trio doubled back. Axel pulled out his phone and started a conference call with Aria and Max.

They popped on, seated next to their respective partners. Both screens showed two people, perfectly warm and indoors.

"I hate you all right now," Selena said grimly.

Aria grinned from the screen. "Got a nice fire going. Some hot chocolate ready for marshmallows. It's actually so warm I might have to take off my sweater. What do you think, Carly?"

Selena snorted in disgust as Carly smiled ruefully next to Aria on the screen.

"You're going to have to move out of the cozy digs," Axel offered, not above a little jealousy himself. "We want a tighter circle."

"Something happen?" Max asked.

"We got too close, and they took a few shots," Selena said with a shrug. "Too far away to do any damage."

Carly frowned, and Aria's humorous expression got very serious.

"Do you have the map of cabins in the area Opaline sent?" Axel asked.

They all had the partner not holding the phone pull up the maps on their phones.

"Right now we've got a triangle of sorts, with our trio right in the middle," Axel confirmed. "We need to make our triangle smaller, keeping them in the middle. They're armed and they're going to shoot, so we want to be slow, steady and careful."

"There has to be something more to this," Selena said, hugging her arms around herself. "It's miserable out here. No one *plans* to escape prison in the middle of February unless they've got to accomplish something in the here and now. In whatever downtime you guys have, see what you can come up with."

"But first, we want everyone moving in closer," Axel said.

Selena tapped the interactive map on her phone as Axel looked over at her screen. There were three cabins they could use to try and surround the fugitives.

"Axel and I will move to the one I've marked three." Selena said, glancing at him for agreement.

He gave a nod.

"Aria and Carly, you'll take cabin two. Max and Scott, you'll base at one. Our escapees are currently closest to three, but heading toward one and two. As Axel and I head for three, we'll be following them toward one and two. Think of your cabins as bases. You'll want to take turns patrolling the area in between. We've got Blanca, which means we'll be able to stop any backtracks. Our main concern is them taking a longer route to the east or west rather than the straight shot toward the border."

"We'll call Rihanna and see if there are some local law enforcement who we could get stationed in the east and west," Max said, all business. "Small departments in these parts, if any, but maybe we can get a county to lend some manpower beyond the APB."

"Good idea," Axel agreed. "I think they'll take the straight shot, but we can't be too careful. Armed. Dangerous. I want everyone to understand that. Leonard Koch has already killed someone. Cold-blooded. We have to assume anyone associating with him has the same capability. We want these guys, but we want to be smart and safe."

"They can't do much damage in the middle of nowhere, upper Michigan, can they?" Aria offered. "I haven't seen a soul around this cabin."

"One man is already dead," Axel replied flatly, trying not to sound too much like a superior dressing down a subordinate. Aria was a rookie, but she was good at her job. Still, lives had already been lost, and they all needed to remember that. "A man who had nothing to do with any of this. Keep that in mind."

They all nodded their assent, then closed the call. Axel could *feel* Selena's steady gaze on him. He didn't look toward it. He put his phone away.

"Will it bother you forever?" she asked quietly.

Axel frowned, turning to glance at her. "What?"

"That a man died. A man you didn't know, that you had no responsibility to. It bothers you now. I'm just curious if that sticks with you forever." She was too close, her dark eyes too discerning.

Axel wasn't sure he was comfortable with the question, and he definitely wasn't comfortable with the answer. Especially when she kept talking, right here sitting hip to hip on the log.

"Innocent people have died during assignments I've been on," she said, her gaze never leaving his. "I've never felt responsible. They don't haunt me. So, I'm just wondering if I'm cold-blooded, or if you get over it."

"You're not cold-blooded," Axel muttered.

"How do you know?"

"You care about your brother, that much is clear." Her expression shuttered, and she looked away. Which, yeah, he'd been going for. "You care about Opaline. You hide it all, compartmentalize it all, but you've got family issues up to the hilt, Selena, and you wouldn't if you didn't care. If you were cold."

She stood abruptly, adjusting her pack and ignoring him completely.

He blew out a breath. He should let it go at that. Keep his mouth shut. But she'd asked him a question, and he felt some...*need* to answer her. To try to make her understand what he felt.

"It's not the individual deaths that haunt me. It's the feeling of being too late. When you lose your family the way I did, when you survive, you start to realize that timing is everything. And it's the one thing beyond your control. You can be the best damn FBI agent out there, and you might still be two seconds too late."

"So why be an FBI agent at all, knowing that you'll be faced with the uncontrollable timing part of things?"

"Because if you never face the things that haunt you, Selena, they eat you alive."

She stared down at him a moment, something that looked a lot like shell shock in her expression. She frowned, shook it away and then held out a gloved hand.

It was an offer of teamwork. Help him up off the log though he didn't need it. But it put them back on equal, mission footing.

Or it was supposed to. Even though they both wore gloves, fitting his hand into hers, letting her help pull him to his feet, it ignited a dangerous warmth that spread through him. He should have immediately let her hand go once on his feet, but he didn't.

He held on, stood far too close and looked down at her face. Dark eyes, cheeks and nose pink with cold. She was a complicated woman with a complicated past, and they were on a *very* complicated mission. Everything was dangerous and required a delicate balance.

But here they were, in this side moment, separate from everything else. Touching hands. Looking at each other, and he thought, most dangerous of all, *understanding* each other.

She didn't pull away. He didn't let her go. They didn't speak, and they didn't move. They simply looked at each other, breathing in time with one another. He could imagine what it would be like if he did. If he stepped closer, if he pulled her to him, if he fitted his mouth to hers.

It was like a mirage in front of him, one he wanted to lean into.

Her phone buzzed in her pocket, breaking the moment.

Thank God.

Chapter 6

It took a moment for the buzzing to break through the odd static in Selena's brain. A static she didn't understand. She'd been made stupid by lust and inexperience once. This was neither. It was something far...bigger.

Far scarier.

But the phone buzzed incessantly in her pocket, and she finally thought to drop Axel's hand and dig out her device. It was her sister calling.

There were so many reasons she didn't want to deal with Opaline right now, but it very well could be about the task at hand. The task at hand being searching for and apprehending criminals, *not* having weird out-of-body experiences with Axel.

And, wow, what would an in-*body experience with Axel feel like?*

"Hello," she greeted too harshly, trying to get the image of *anything* with Axel out of her mind.

"Selena. You were shot at?" Opaline demanded. Her voice reminded Selena of their childhood. Opaline was older. She'd taken that role seriously, but something about their parents' divorce had seemed to flip their roles. Opaline had turned emotional and needy and at sea. She'd thrown herself at people, men in particular, always looking for safety. For shore. Selena had to take over being the one who could handle anything and everything their mother and father threw at them.

Selena had gotten away from that as soon as she'd been able.

But this sounded like concern, with a hint of scolding, which was far more big sistery than Opaline had acted in over a decade. It made Selena's heart twist uncomfortably with a hope she thought she'd eradicated a long time ago.

"Shot at is probably an exaggeration. There was shooting, but it was far away." She couldn't help but try to soothe. After Dad had ruined everything, Selena had been the one to pick up the pieces. But maybe they were adult enough now that they could find a way to bridge the gaps in their relationship.

"Do you think Peter was the one shooting?" Opaline asked in a hushed whisper.

The bubble of hope burst in an instant. It was always that. Always about Peter. Never about her. Why did that still hurt? She'd kept herself separate and away, and still Opaline could cut her in two. Over their *half* brother. "I don't know," Selena said flatly.

"I hate that you're out there as enemies."

"His choice, Opaline. Did you call about something in particular?"

"He's our brother."

"I'm your sister."

There was a silence, charged with hurt. But how was that fair? "You don't need my help, my support. You never did," Opaline said softly—the opposite of her usual loud demeanor. "But Peter did."

Selena didn't know what to do with that, even less so when she could practically *feel* Axel watching her, listening to her side of the conversation. Picking it apart. No doubt thinking of all the ways she should be responsible for Peter.

"You gave up on him," Opaline said, sounding more like herself. Overemotional. Laying the blame on Selena's blameless shoulders.

Or does she just sound like Mom?

Selena was in the middle of an important assignment. She couldn't cry. She couldn't indulge in self-pity. She had to set this aside and move on. Ignoring all the feelings it churned up. "I'm sorry you feel that way," Selena said robotically. It was how she talked to her mother too. "Maybe at some point you'll understand that while you were all so busy trying to save Peter, some of us needed help and support too." She tried to hold her tongue, ice out the emotions, but those words…

You gave up on him.

It hurt because it was true. She had given up on Peter. She didn't know how to keep believing in someone so dedicated to ruining their own life.

And when she'd needed her sister, when everything had blown up at her last job, Opaline had been so obsessed with Peter's trial and him going to jail, she hadn't bothered to ask Selena if she was all right. If *she* needed anything. Peter was her project. Selena was on her own.

They both were still on the line, in a weighted silence

neither knew how to fill. Maybe Selena should just accept they never would.

"You never let me help," Opaline said, hushed and pained.

"When did you ever try?"

"When did you ever ask for any?"

Selena didn't know what to say to that. She was sure she'd asked, or at least hinted... Hadn't it been obvious to anyone after Tom had ruined her reputation that she needed someone to hold her hand—just for a little while? Someone who understood what it was like to feel betrayed by someone you'd loved, or thought you had.

"I have important work to do," Selena said. Her voice was so cold it matched the air around her. "And so do you."

"The difference, Selena, is I can care about both." The call ended with a click and echoing silence.

Why did she always handle things so badly when it came to Opaline? If she'd kept her feelings out of it—a lesson she'd been trying to impart to Opaline since their parents had started the divorce process—everything would be okay.

A lesson life had reinforced, over and over again. *So why are you still struggling?*

It was just Peter. Opaline. The perfect storm of things she didn't want to deal with. In a few more days, after they tracked him down and Peter was in jail, Selena could leave all this *feeling* behind.

Because if you never face the things that haunt you, Selena, they eat you alive.

Axel's past was a lot more haunted than hers, so she should ignore that he'd said that. That it had clamored around inside her like church bells, too close, too loud. *Too right.*

"Everything okay?" Axel asked gently.

"Just fine." Certainly none of his business.

"It's not unnoticeable, you know," Axel said softly, almost sympathetically. But she didn't want his softness or sympathy.

"What?"

"The tension between you two."

Which was the worst thing he could have said to her. She worked so hard not to let those feelings show. The cracks in her armor. She knew the people they worked with could tell they weren't close, but to have him stand there and say it was obvious…

She would have preferred a slap to the face.

"Yeah, I'm pretty well aware," she returned, wincing at the acidic note in her own voice. Which only made her angrier. At him. At Opaline. At Peter. But mostly just herself. "And Aria made sure to let me know the tension between *us* isn't exactly unnoticeable."

Axel could admit that she'd shocked him into silence. It wasn't the information that surprised him—Max, on occasion, had asked what on earth was up with them. Axel had always played it off, but he knew people…sensed it. Much like sensing issues between Selena and Opaline.

But for a good four years there'd been a tacit, silent agreement between him and Selena that they would not speak of that tension. If they ignored it, it wouldn't go away, but, well, they could avoid it.

Now she'd laid it out between them. He wasn't *op-*

posed to that exactly. Clearly ignoring it hadn't done them any favors. But the timing was less than ideal.

"We should move out."

She laughed. Bitterly. Though he got the sense her bitterness wasn't just aimed at him, but at everything. Hard to blame her.

They got their stuff together. Selena ordered Blanca to search, and they started moving forward again, following the trail of the escapees while keeping an eye on the map and the cabin they'd try to reach by nightfall.

It was a cold, quiet and mostly miserable hike. Occasionally Blanca would pause and they'd wait, weapons drawn, ready for the next round of gunfire.

Axel began to dwell on that, to turn it over. His job right now was apprehension, but the puzzle pieces were irritating. "Why not stay and take us out?" he wondered aloud after they'd started again after another stop that yielded no gunfire.

"Oh, lots of reasons, I suppose," Selena said. All the emotions she'd had before and during Opaline's call were now wrapped up and hidden under the veneer of professional detachment. "If they kill us, there will be a bigger task force working to stop them. They might now know our numbers and don't want to risk the chance."

"Bottom line, it's clear their goal isn't just escaping to escape. It's bigger than that. Wouldn't you say?"

"I'd leave the profiling up to you," Selena replied. "That's your expertise."

It was, and Axel felt like he had a good picture of the men as individuals. It was the combination of the three men that didn't make any sense to him. Leonard Koch was a cold-blooded killer. Steve Jenson not quite as clever, but just as interested in violence. Motivated by it, in fact. Peter Lopez…he was the loose thread. The one that didn't tie in.

He glanced at Selena. Her gaze was on Blanca. They'd stopped to water the dog a few times, but Axel knew Selena wanted to get them to some shelter so the dog could rest in some warmth.

She didn't know Peter. Axel had to believe she wasn't holding anything back on that front. She cared too much about her job to thwart it. Alana had questioned Opaline herself after he and Selena had left, but the answers she'd passed along to Axel didn't help him any.

"Your brother was the getaway car driver in a murder."

"You could call him the escapee, the perp, the criminal, the suspect, et cetera, et cetera."

"Noted."

"So, he's weak. The weak link you pressure into doing something stupid."

"But what would they need him for? What does he bring to the trio?" Axel continued. Alana had sent the police report from the security guard who'd let them go, and Axel had reviewed it. Once they got to the cabin, he'd need to go over it again. Or even request new questioning for the security guard.

"It's the bigger thing we're missing. Career criminals don't escape from jail in the dead of winter unless something better is waiting for them," Selena said. "A sure deal. But there's no evidence the three men were connected in any way. They all were involved in different groups."

Axel glanced at the map, noticing how low the sun was in the sky. They should be getting close to the cabin. They were equipped to continue to hike through the night, but they'd need a rest for Blanca and a meal for him and Selena. He wanted to get to that base before true night descended.

"So, we need to look beyond the groups." But where? The problem with being on the tracking trail was he couldn't study the evidence the way he'd like.

"What about the victims?" Selena offered. "Maybe the victims of the crimes they committed connect in some way? Remember that case we had two years ago? The trafficking case that looked so similar, but we didn't find the thread until you connected the two missing people."

Axel nodded thoughtfully. "Once we get to the cabin, we'll talk to Alana. It's a good thread to pull."

"We should be getting close."

Axel nodded. They kept walking. Axel tried to work through all the angles of the case that he knew. Leonard had murdered someone. Steve had been part of a group of thugs who'd beaten another man to death. Peter had been the driver in fleeing a murder scene. They were different crimes, but all involved a dead person one way or another.

Would the three dead people connect?

Blanca stopped, barked twice.

Selena frowned. "That's not one of our signals."

Which was when Axel's nose began to burn. "Do you smell that?" he murmured. The world was dusky, the sun setting somewhere behind the trees. The faint hint of...

"Smoke," Selena said. "Surely they didn't start a fire knowing they've got a trail."

"Maybe they're trying to draw us out."

Selena crouched next to Blanca, running her hands

over the dog's furry coat. She murmured encouraging words to the dog, scanning the trees herself. "What do you think, Axel?"

He really didn't know what to think. "How's Blanca holding up?"

"She'll keep going if we need to."

Axel considered that. In the dark, they could sneak up on the trio if they really were just…sitting around a fire. But he couldn't ignore the possibility it was a trap. The men had shot at them—they knew they were being tailed.

"Why doesn't any of this add up?" Axel muttered. He frowned at the eastern horizon. Something flickered. "Do you see that?"

Selena looked to where he pointed. "That's no campfire."

No, it wasn't. So what was the fire? A diversion? An attempt to hurt them? Something else altogether?

"Blanca, follow," Selena commanded her dog. When Axel fell into step next to her, she spoke quietly and started moving toward the fire, weapon drawn. Same as him.

"I think we should see what's going on. If she follows rather than leads, she'll alert us to any ambush from behind."

Axel nodded, and they crept forward. The smoke in the air got thicker and thicker, the flickering light in the distance bigger and bigger. Until they both stopped in their tracks.

A cabin was ablaze. The cabin on their map that they'd been hoping to find for a rest.

"Why on earth would they do that?" Selena asked.

But Axel didn't have an answer for her.

Chapter 7

Selena lifted her sleeve over her mouth. The air was choked with smoke. They hadn't just set fire to the cabin. They had to have used something for it to be completely engulfed in flame like this.

"I'll get Max on the phone."

Selena nodded. Max was their explosives expert. He'd have a better idea what could have caused the fire. She didn't know what he'd be able to tell them over the phone, or if it mattered, but it was a reasonable next step. At some point the information they gathered had to lead them to some answers.

"We've got a situation," Axel said into his phone. "The cabin we were headed for is on fire. Not just a little fire. It's completely engulfed in flames."

Selena stared at the blaze, frowning as she thought back over the past few minutes. "We didn't hear anything. Everything has been quiet," Selena said more to herself than to Axel, since he was on the phone.

But he turned to face her. "You're right," he said, then relayed the information to Max on the line.

Axel held the phone to his ear so Selena couldn't hear Max's reply. While Axel conferred with Max on the phone, Selena studied the flames. They were on every side of the cabin. The chilly wind seemed to feed the blaze, and even with the snow Selena didn't foresee the fire going out any time soon.

What on earth could be the point of this?

"Max says if we didn't hear anything, explosives are unlikely," Axel said, sliding his phone back into his pocket. "The advanced blaze could have more to do with the use of accelerant, but he'd have to discuss it with someone with more expertise in fire over explosives."

"What's the point?" Selena said. "This doesn't stop us following them. In fact, it slows them down. It had to have taken time. We can't be that far behind now. We could catch them and—"

"And they could shoot us both dead. We have to be more careful than that."

Selena knew he was right, but it tested her patience. Though, that's why they did this kind of thing in pairs. To balance each other out. To work through the problems with a plan. She was trained specifically in search and apprehension, and she was very well aware of the necessary role of caution.

But I want this over.

She took a moment to breathe—though she couldn't allow herself a deep inhalation when there was so much smoke in the air. Still, she needed to remember her calm, remember her center. Her job over feelings. Her assignment over herself.

"Why did they burn it down, Axel? We can keep following them, we can even apprehend them, but there's something to that. They did it for a reason, and I think it's important we figure out what it is."

Axel studied the burning cabin grimly. "You're right."

"That's two 'you're rights' in under twenty. Should I be concerned?"

He gave her a sardonic smile, which produced an unnecessary and untimely flutter in her chest. She looked back at the blaze. "What about the owners of the cabin? Could they have a connection?"

"Opaline is on it."

She could feel his considering glance at that. She refused to fall for the bait. She kept her expression neutral. Because her sister was part of the assignment too, and she would do the work she needed to do while Selena did the work she needed to do. "Good. Now, what are we going to do about shelter? It's nearly dark."

"Wasn't there another cabin in the vicinity?"

Selena pulled out her phone and brought the map onto the screen. "Not confirmed as a cabin. A structure of some kind. No known owner."

"Some shelter is better than none, yeah?"

"Agreed. But let's follow our crew a bit beyond the fire. Make sure we've still got an idea of what direction they're heading in."

Axel nodded and shrugged off his pack. He pulled out a headlamp. Selena wrinkled her nose. "Those look ridiculous."

Axel chuckled. "It's dark, we're tracking three escapees and you're worried about your appearance?"

She didn't snap at him about not understanding. She preferred people think her vain when she talked about appearances rather than have to explain that being a woman meant things were different. You had to look the part too. If someone *knew* you were trying to look authoritative, it undercut the effect.

So she said nothing and pulled a flashlight out of her own pack. Even in the dark she didn't miss his eye roll.

That was fine. Let him. She knew what she was about.

"Blanca. Search."

It took longer than before because the odors of the fire interfered with Blanca's sense of smell. Selena had to get out the glove and use it a few more times to ground Blanca in the search.

"Could they have set the fire to interfere with the dog?" Axel wondered aloud.

"A lot of work to go through for one search dog." They moved away from the fire, getting Blanca back into clearer air. Another sniff of the glove and she was moving at a better pace again.

Axel kept an eye on the map on his phone, determining if they were getting closer to their potential shelter or farther away.

Selena let out a sigh when Blanca lost the scent again. "It's too much. She needs a break."

"We could use one too," Axel said, clearly holding no blame for the dog, which soothed Selena some. "We'll head for the shelter. Food and rest for everyone. Our counterparts up north will keep the escapees from crossing the border. They'll likely have to stop too. They can't keep going on forever without food supplies."

But Selena wasn't convinced they didn't have access to *something*. They'd ventured out into the bleak winter. They'd burned down a building. Both things required supplies or the promise of supplies.

So many things didn't add up.

Still, they marched on through the dark and the cold and the snow. Axel navigated with his phone until they found the structure Opaline had dug up on some far-flung map.

Selena and Axel stopped in their tracks, his head-lamp and her flashlight illuminating the…teeny, tiny shack. It'd be a tight squeeze for the three of them, and even with the close quarters, the gaps in the wood wouldn't give them much shelter. There was a roof with a crooked chimney, and if their shafts of light weren't creating an illusion, there appeared to be a foundation, which meant flooring without snow.

"It's better than nothing?" But Axel's voice was hardly one of certainty or relief.

"We might want to make sure there aren't bodies in there."

Axel snorted. "Allow me."

He moved forward. He didn't draw his weapon, but he kept his hand on the butt of it in its holster. He toed the door open with his foot. It creaked and groaned like it might fall off its rusty hinges at any moment.

He swept his beam of light inside, taking his time to examine the opening. So much time Selena eventually moved forward, pointing her own flashlight inside the doorway above Axel's shoulder.

There was a small, ancient stove in the corner of

the rectangle of a building, connected to that crooked chimney she'd noticed on the roof. The floor was concrete and cracked, bits of ice and snow here and there, but that could be brushed off.

If anything it had maybe been some sort of rustic hunting shelter. For one. Not two and a dog.

But the stove was a potential for warmth. "Think that thing works?"

"Only one way to find out."

They both ducked into the shack. Axel went about examining the stove while Selena pulled some of Blanca's supplies out of her pack. A blanket that would be more comfortable to lie on than the icy, cracked concrete floor.

There wasn't much room to maneuver. Occasionally they bumped hips or elbows, and Selena focused on Blanca, ignoring that the person she kept jostling into was a very large, very attractive man, and eventually got the dog situated. She was curled up in the far corner, resting on the blanket Selena had brought. She'd drunk some water, eaten some kibble and now rested her head on her paws and watched the fire be slowly brought to life by Axel.

Selena didn't have much of a choice of what to watch, but she just knew it couldn't be Axel stoking a fire. She settled herself on the cold ground next to Blanca and distracted herself with getting the food out of her pack, a water bottle, arranging it all in her lap. By the time she'd arranged and rearranged and driven herself slowly insane, Axel had the fire glowing in the stove.

She could feel its warmth on her face, though her body remained cold. She had to focus very hard not to shiver or let her teeth chatter since Axel looked perfectly comfortable.

The jerk.

He settled himself into a seated position as far away from her as he could manage. It still meant she could reach out and touch him, but at least she knew better than to do that.

He got his own food supplies out of his pack and began to eat. Selena tried to focus on the fire, but her gaze kept drifting to Axel.

"We shouldn't stay here too long," she offered. Not because she couldn't handle it, but because the escapees were moving forward.

"No. How long do you think Blanca needs?"

Selena looked at her dog resting next to her. "An hour. Maybe two."

Axel nodded, the flickering light of the fire giving his chiseled features a dangerous cast. Silly to let that flutter through her stomach. She knew better than to be attracted to danger.

"While Blanca rests, we can check in with various members of the team and do some of our own research about the victims, or what might connect these three and so on."

"Sounds good," Selena said. "What kind of research are we going to do from here, though?"

He turned his gaze to her, and she had to fight the tide of embarrassment from the knowledge that she'd been staring at him, not the fire.

"I know Peter is a sore spot."

Embarrassment gone, Selena turned her expression to stone. "Not sore," she replied. "Complicated."

"Use whatever words you like, but no matter how little interaction you've had with him, you know his past. You know what's shaped him, even if you don't know how. The other two men, I've only got rap sheets on. With Peter, I have a connection with you and Opaline, who know his whole background."

"Get to the point, Morrow."

"I want to know about Peter. Maybe if I do, I can make some connection to how he'd get wrapped up with these two much more violent characters. Their rap sheets don't add up. *They* don't add up. But maybe if I get a better picture of Peter, something will."

Selena stared at the flickering flame through the slats in the stove. What she knew about Peter wasn't much, but she believed Axel was right. As a gifted profiler, the more information he had, the more he could paint a picture and develop theories. Theories that could lead them to the answers they needed.

She just…didn't want to go here. Didn't want to remember, rehash or share.

But it was her job. So she'd just have to suck it up.

Testing the waters, and what Axel knew of Selena, he shrugged. "I can ask Opaline if you'd prefer."

Her jaw tightened. "What kind of things do you want to know?"

He bit back a smile. She couldn't always be maneuvered, but when she could it was a little too satisfying. "Everything. Just start from the beginning."

She clasped her gloved hands together, then rested one of them on the dog next to her. "We didn't find out about Peter until he was about two. His mom brought him to our mother to drop the bomb about their existence. I don't think Peter would remember that. He was a little thing."

Her expression was bland, but there was a hint at some emotion in her voice.

"Where was your father for that?"

She shrugged. "Work, I think. I don't remember the whole thing. Opaline and I walked in from school and Mom and this woman were yelling at each other and crying, and there was this little boy between them. He wasn't crying."

"So, he was used to emotional outbursts at that age?"

"I suppose. I don't know."

"How old were you?"

"Ten. Opaline was twelve."

Axel knew what it was like to have your life pulled out from under you at a young age. Sure, death was a little more traumatizing, especially when you'd been a witness to it, but trauma was trauma, no matter the severity.

"After Mom divorced Dad, Peter and his mother lived with my dad for a while." She paused, picking at a thread on her coat. She took a deep breath. "Sometimes Dad would show up and take us to his house. Mom would tell him he couldn't. Dad would insist we had to. It was ugly, and the only reason I'm telling you that is because when we'd then go over to Dad and Mariane's, we were always…upset. Then Mariane would get upset."

"And Peter?"

"I never remember him crying. I never remember him doing much of anything except watching us." Her hand curled into a fist and then released. "I wasn't very nice to him."

"How so?"

Selena shrugged jerkily. "Opaline always played with him, read him stories. I kept my distance. Rebuffed him if he tried to play with me. At that age, I didn't understand he wasn't to blame for what my father had done. I'd only known Peter had showed up, and my life had changed irrevocably."

"You were young." Too much for a young girl to try to sort through.

"Yeah, I was. It went on like that for years. When Peter was about eight, Mariane was diagnosed with cancer. Dad got clean—I didn't realize until that point he'd been an alcoholic. Maybe drugs too. I didn't really get it until he stopped."

"Mariane died, right?"

Selena nodded. "When Peter was ten. I was in the police academy at that point. Dad did okay for a while, but I'd say by the time Peter was thirteen, Dad was drinking again. Peter was getting into trouble. Opaline was married to her first mistake in a line of many. I was working on the road, taking classes for K-9 handling, and once Dad started drinking again, I cut him off. Which cut Peter off too."

"You feel guilty." It surprised him. She'd imparted how much they weren't connected, and he'd believed they really had been separate, but there was a heavy, sad guilt in her voice that couldn't be ignored.

"He had his mother's family. He preferred them. When Dad begged that I help Peter, I tried a few times. Peter rebuffed me at every turn. I did what I could. He wouldn't have it. That's Peter. That's the thing you need to know."

But there was guilt there, whether it was warranted

or not. Still, Peter was his target, not her. So, he should focus more on the information she'd given him. A few extra details to what he'd already known about the criminal.

"How was his relationship with your father?"

Selena's expression was grim. "Volatile."

"Violent?"

She took a moment, eyebrows drawing together as if she was deep in thought. "I guess not. A lot of yelling. Throwing things. But they never got into a fistfight or anything like that. At least, not that I ever saw or heard about."

"That's the part that's stumping me. There's nothing violent in Peter's record. Everything he's been in for has been mostly aiding and abetting."

"And don't forget, selling drugs."

"Sure, but Leonard and Steve have a violent bent. Where does Peter fit in?"

"We need to know who owned that cabin. There has to be a clue in there."

She was right. Still, Axel brought up the file on Peter he had on his phone. "Gangs. Peter was involved in a lot of gang stuff. So was Steve. But not Leonard Koch."

Selena's expression went thoughtful. She looked… gentler in the firelight. Softer. He was under no illusions she was either, but he had to wonder if there was this side to her, just hidden deep down under the professional, put-together facade she seemed to need.

"No ties to gangs at all?" she asked.

"No. Leonard Koch's misdeeds were almost always done on his own. He's not a man who works with a team, but he has one now."

Selena tapped her own phone, frowning over something. "The security guard's statement, did you read it?"

"Yeah. She says Leonard was the ringleader in the escape, in threatening her."

Selena tapped her fingers on her knee and Axel brought up his Leonard Koch profile while snacking on the nuts he'd pulled out of his pack.

"There is one arrest on Leonard's record where he wasn't working alone, but the charges were dropped," Axel said as he skimmed the information.

"Who was he working with?" Selena asked.

Axel kept reading. "A man named Bernard McNally."

Selena tapped a few keys on her phone. "Bernard McNally." She let out a low whistle. "Well, he's clean as far as I can tell. Nothing since that incident."

Axel was already typing a text to Opaline and Alana. "We'll get a full background check from headquarters on him. See if something adds up. Connects." He grinned over at her. "See, a little rest did us good."

She grunted. "We'll see."

Chapter 8

Selena dreaded leaving the shelter they'd found. It was uncomfortable, she was way too close to Axel Morrow and the subtle smell of his soap or cologne or something male and a little too enticing, but it was warm in these four walls.

Still, keeping up with their escapees was of the utmost importance. So, once they'd given Blanca an hour's rest, they started gathering their things again, Axel dousing the fire, Selena putting Blanca's supplies back in her pack.

She adjusted her hood on her head, and Axel placed the silly headlamp over his stocking cap. Why didn't it look silly on him? Something about the square jaw or sharp nose. *Or just the fact he's a hot guy.*

"How long do you think they can last out there without supplies?" Selena asked. Maybe the cold wouldn't be so bad. She wouldn't be tempted to study his face when the wind felt like knives against her exposed skin.

"We don't know what they might have taken from that cabin," Axel said, adjusting the pack on his back, then eyeing the shack to make sure they hadn't left anything behind.

"Could something have been *left* at the cabin for them?"

Axel was quiet as he opened the door and they stepped back out into the icy chill of a February night.

"Interesting thought," he said after a while. "I'm hoping the owner of the cabin gives us some clues as to that, but for now…"

"For now, we march."

"You know, some people do this for fun."

"Chase criminals through the arctic tundra?"

Axel chuckled, a low, grumbly sound that had no business making her stomach flutter helplessly. What *was* that? She was a sane woman. A sane woman who'd gone down this particularly stupid road before. She'd learned her lessons, sworn an oath to herself up and down, and she *loved* her job more than anything else.

So, why did it feel like Axel Morrow threatened all that?

"Winter night hikes. Full moon. Starlight. Some people find it exhilarating."

"Some people need their heads examined. It's *freezing*." She'd thought the cold would be bearable, but her feet felt like ice blocks, and when the wind blew just hard enough, it made her eyes water and her teeth want to chatter.

Pretty? Sure. The stars through the bare tree branches were something else—something she didn't see in town—and the dark of the forest was an eerie kind of moody that she got a kick out of. But she'd much rather be cozied up next to a fire looking at it all through a window with heat blasting over her feet.

Blanca sniffed the ground. It took a few tries for her to pick up the trail they'd left behind. With the snow and the wind and the dark, it was harder to keep track of. But the rest had done the dog some good, and though they had to pause and reset on occasion, they were continuously moving forward. Selena following Blanca, Axel behind her.

They were quiet as they walked, which Selena knew was for the best. They had to listen for potential danger, pay attention to Blanca's cues. But she wished she could talk to him if only to keep her mind off the cold.

It was a trick of the trade when it came to long, monotonous searches, stakeouts and waiting. So much waiting in this job. But she didn't usually have to be quite so cold.

Look it as a challenge, she ordered herself. She liked a challenge. Relished proving to herself she could do more than she thought. She could be silent, frozen and strong.

She listened to the whistle of the wind, Blanca's panting, the crunching sound of their feet on snow. "Do people really find this exhilarating?" she muttered.

Again that dark chuckle. "There's no accounting for what people find exhilarating."

He really had to stop saying that word. It made nerve endings she'd purposefully forgotten about spring to life, all crackling energy. Wanting to be *exhilarated.*

They stepped into a clearing, both slowing their pace and listening and watching with great caution. Clearings could be dangerous. Without discussing it, they each clicked off the lights they were carrying.

Selena heard nothing. Saw nothing as she turned in a slow circle. She was about to suggest they turn their lights back on.

"Wait," Axel said, so authoritatively she stopped moving immediately, and Blanca did too, even though Selena hadn't uttered the command.

"What is it?" Selena moved for her weapon, but Axel's large hand closed over her arm. "The northern lights."

She looked up at the fathomless sky to see the pale greenish sparkle that seemed so otherworldly it took her breath away.

They were silent, still for a few moments.

"Haven't you ever seen them before?" he asked, standing way too close since she could feel his breath on her ear. Yet she couldn't pull her gaze from that rippling, colorful light in the middle of the night sky.

She shook her head. "I don't spend much time out of the city." Why not? Why didn't she get away from the buildings and the crowds every once in a while and just…breathe?

"I can see them from my farm sometimes," Axel said, his voice low and sensual in her ear. She could feel warmth emanating from him, which she knew meant he was too close, but she didn't move. She didn't say anything.

"Getting out of the city would do you some good, Lopez," he continued. "And *that* feeling you've got going on—the awe, the peace, the idea that the world is bigger and more amazing than you'd ever imagined—

that's why people take a night hike through the frozen tundra or whatever you called it."

She didn't fully absorb his words—she was too busy looking at the sky and absorbing the feel of standing here watching this. With him.

"Is it like this all the time?" she wondered aloud before she could think to censor herself. "You just live out in the middle of nowhere and feel this awe?"

"A lot of the time. Other times it's just…quiet. There was a time in my life I didn't want the quiet. The noise, the push, it was better. But you get old enough…"

She scoffed, turning to look at him though he was only a shadow above her shoulder. "You're hardly ancient."

"I've lived a lot of years in thirty-four."

"Mmm." She knew he meant what he'd been through as a child, and she had to admit sometimes he *felt* more than three years older than her. It was the way he held himself. That supervisory part of his job. He was a man who'd either been born older or had come to it honestly after losing his family in such tragic circumstances.

The thought of a boy who'd had his family murdered around him, who'd somehow survived, living alone as a man out in the middle of nowhere on some nonfunctioning farm felt…wrong all of a sudden.

"You need a dog, Morrow. You make that quiet sound far too lonely."

Though she couldn't make out his face, she could sense he stared down at her. She could sense them measuring each other up, even in only shadow.

Maybe that was why she didn't move away. It was dark. She could pretend that this spiraling, *exhilarating* feeling inside her chest wasn't about him—a man she worked with. But instead just a shadow. Someone removed from TCD and the FBI.

"Maybe I need more than a dog," he murmured.

Her breath caught, and it felt like her heart mirrored the movement. A sharp beat followed by a holding moment where she thought about all the implications of what that might mean.

But she'd been here before. All those what-ifs used like promises. She couldn't believe them, no matter how different Axel felt. Older, wiser—she didn't make the same mistakes twice.

She just wished he'd *feel* like a mistake, instead of something she wanted.

"Selena."

His voice was a velvety promise, the northern lights all around them, Blanca waiting patiently in the dark. Their work was hardly done, but it would hardly be ruined by one…

The vibrating buzz of a phone interrupted the quiet, and thank *God* it interrupted her break with sanity. Again.

"Saved by the bell. Twice," she muttered. Because both times his phone had gone off, interrupting these *moments*, she knew she'd been far too close to giving in. When she'd promised herself never to give in again.

"Morrow," Axel answered his phone, sounding terse and gritty.

It soothed her a *little* that he didn't sound his cool, collected self.

"Well, we've got our lead," Axel said after talking in low tones on the phone. "The cabin belonged to a shell company, but Opaline did some digging and found a connection to Bernard McNally."

"The guy Leonard was arrested with way back when?"

"One and the same. Now to figure out who and where Bernard is."

Axel couldn't say what the hell was wrong with him. Working with Selena for four years had been a challenge at times, but it had never truly tested him. Granted, they'd never been quite so alone, so isolated.

He knew all sorts of things about her, but there was something intimate about watching a person see the northern lights for the first time.

Maybe he was delirious from smoke inhalation or some sort of brain hypothermia.

"Friend or enemy?" Selena said into the quiet.

They'd resumed their walking, following Blanca in a line through the clearing and toward another thicket of trees. Axel had to remind himself they were in the middle of an assignment and bring his mind back to what they'd been discussing.

Instead of how easy it was to forget what he was doing the more time he spent around her.

You make that quiet sound far too lonely. The soft, gentle way she'd said that seemed to infect him. He couldn't help but picture her...at his farm. Watching the stars come out on a pretty spring night.

Yeah, right.

"Axel?"

Get it together, man. "Yeah. No. I don't know. Foe seems more likely if they burned the guy's cabin to the ground."

"Why take the time? That's what I can't get over. We'll catch up by morning even with our break. They took time to burn that place down."

"Must have been important."

"To Leonard."

"Seems that way."

They fell into an easy silence, following Blanca through the woods. She seemed to have a good trail now, and he knew that Selena was listening to the world around them just as he was. How far back were they? How much longer would they chase, just out of reach, before they acted?

He checked his phone and the map. Both teams of TCD agents were still a good fifty miles away. The trio couldn't have made it that far yet. As long as they kept it up like this, they'd be able to surround, outnumber and take down the trio without anyone getting hurt.

He hoped for that outcome, even with all the questions about the case still bothering him. He could hope for easy.

Slowly, after hours of walking, a faint hint of light creeped into the woods around them. Selena had turned off her flashlight, and he'd taken off the headlamp and thrown it in his pack. It was still early, dawn just a pearly promise, but it gave them enough sight to walk.

This time it was Selena's phone that buzzed.

"Yeah?" There was a pause. "Opaline, calm down." The words were spoken with some impatience, but also a certain authority that was interesting to note. She was the younger sister, but she was the one more...in control of the situation.

He thought about what she'd said about everyone in her family wanting her to take responsibility for Peter. She was the rock there, and she didn't want to be. Still, when push came to shove, they all turned to her. No matter the bad blood, or the tension, Opaline was calling her with a problem.

Family. A bond even bad feelings couldn't erase. Did Peter have that? Axel knew he himself didn't. He'd watched people have that, wondered how his life might be different if he'd had a family. If he'd had that connection no matter what happened.

But Peter's family connections weren't simply lost by losing his mother. He still had family, but it had been fractured by his father's actions with another family. Gangs were notorious for attracting people who wanted a sense of family, community, purpose.

Had Peter simply fallen into this trio to belong? To feel a part of something? And if that was true, could he be convinced to do worse things than he'd done before? Or was there some breaking point for him?

"They don't know who?" Selena asked carefully, something a little bleak in her eyes, and if the light wasn't playing tricks on him, she'd paled. Quietly he commanded Blanca to stop so they could stop walking for a minute while Selena finished up the phone call.

She stood there, still as a statue, blinking at the ground. When she spoke, she had to clear her throat first. "They found a body in the fire."

Axel's mind flipped through a hundred different scenarios, but he kept his expression neutral. "And there's no ID?"

"Not yet."

She was trying to be strong, but they both knew the body could be Peter's. Unfortunately, the profile he had of Peter Lopez only supported the possibility. A man desperate for family, but not desperate enough to get violent. With two violent men, who'd likely leave him behind in a heartbeat if he didn't fall into line.

"It'll take some time to get the ID. We should keep walking," Selena said. She ordered Blanca to search and started following the dog without waiting for his response. Still, he followed, but he wasn't totally ready to let it drop.

She, on the other hand, was good at letting things drop, burying them under layers of professionalism and cynicism. But he'd seen underneath all that these past few hours more than he ever had.

"Was Opaline upset?" he asked, keeping the query casual.

"In Opaline's world everything is worth getting upset over. Every bad possibility is one to indulge. Instead of just waiting and seeing and dealing with the reality, she has to drama her way through it."

There was a simmering anger there, but Axel could see it was covering up Selena's own fear. A grief she didn't even know for sure she had to feel yet. So, he decided to help her. To focus on the things that made her angry. If Opaline was one of them, so be it.

"Four years you guys have worked together. And unless I'm mistaken, it was your choice to make the move."

"You *are* mistaken, hotshot."

"What? She forced you to take the job?"

"No, of course not. It's nothing to do with her or here. The last department I worked for…" She shrugged, her shoulders jerking restlessly. "Things were messy. Someone was making it messier. I had a choice, I guess. Take Alana's offer and work with my sister, or keep fighting a losing battle. Opaline won out."

"Messy how?"

Selena shrugged again.

"Romantic messy?"

She laughed, but it had a sharp edge of bitterness to it. "There was nothing romantic about it."

"What exactly does that mean?"

"It means I made a stupid mistake, slept with the wrong guy who then used that against me."

The thought of someone using something personal against her, in a professional situation, had his fingers curling into fists. Maybe when they got back after this assignment he'd do some digging into whatever waste of space thought messing with Selena was a good idea.

But for now, he had to focus on the task at hand. Keep Selena's mind off the body until they knew for sure whose it was. "Sounds romantic to me."

"Maybe it was all mean-spirited lust."

"Not for you, it wasn't."

She stopped following Blanca and whirled on him. "How do you know?"

"Because I've got a pretty good handle on you."

"Oh, have you made a little profile about me, Morrow?" she demanded, angling her chin and putting her hands on her hips. All the fear was gone. She was nothing but anger and irritation now.

He probably shouldn't find that attractive. "What's more," he said, ignoring her irritation and demand, "it wouldn't still bother you if there hadn't been feelings attached."

"It doesn't still bother me."

"Then you wouldn't be afraid to kiss me."

The noise she made was neither a laugh nor a shriek nor a grunt. It was some mixture of all three. "Afraid? To *kiss* you? You're accusing me of being afraid to kiss you while we're tracking three escaped criminals, one of whom happens to be my brother?"

He flashed a grin he knew would piss her off—and that would result in one of three things, she'd haul off and hit him. A potential he could live with, though he no doubt she packed a punch. Two, she might kiss him out of spite. He wouldn't complain. Three, she'd march off and they'd keep following Blanca. Not his favorite option, but he'd deal.

"If the shoe fits," he offered, and he decided to add insult to injury and follow Blanca himself, leaving Selena gaping behind him.

Chapter 9

Selena wanted to strangle him with her bare hands. Or she wanted to kiss the living daylights out of him and saunter away completely and utterly unbothered.

She knew *that* wouldn't happen. No matter how much she prized her control, kissing Axel would be... Well, she'd prefer to consider her other options rather than risk losing herself to *that*.

She considered trying to murder him. Satisfying, but it would take too much time when they had an assignment in front of them.

So her only option and recourse was to find a way to be calm.

Which was part and parcel with her job that she loved. Remaining calm in high-pressure situations. His ridiculous statement was hardly high pressure, but everything surrounding them was.

Too bad it was a lot easier to ignore the barbs of a perp over a man who seemed to have been created *specifically* to torture her in any number of ways.

Because he wasn't like Tom. If she gave in to the buzz of electricity between them, no matter what happened, she *knew* he wouldn't use it against her like Tom had done. It wasn't who Axel was. Even when she tried to convince herself she'd ruin her career by letting any of the feelings she had for Axel come to the surface, she just…couldn't.

He wouldn't do that to her.

But that didn't make giving in to those feelings safe or right by any means. She didn't want to analyze too deeply all the ways she thought it would be far more dangerous than the disaster with Tom at her last department.

Maybe because your heart would be more involved than your pride this time?

Yeah, she was definitely not thinking about this right now.

So, she walked. She allowed herself some inward fuming, just as she allowed Axel to be the one to follow the closest behind Blanca. Focusing on anger had gotten her through a lot of tough situations. Anger could be controlled. Sadness, grief, worry…those things spiraled out of control.

With anger there was a clear line. She might say the wrong thing, even do the wrong thing, but as long as she wasn't using her fists on someone, she knew she hadn't gone too far. Anger was a safe box within which to act, up to a certain point.

You never knew when you'd gone too far with hurt. With hope. With loss. Life just came and shoved them in your face regardless. You couldn't predict it, fight it, control the tide of it. Which was why she did everything in her power to channel all of those things into *anger*.

She looked at the man hiking in front of her. His broad shoulders, strong back, the easy strides through the snow. He had his hat pulled low against the wind, and still he walked with a strength of purpose as if it wasn't freezing and miserable.

Kiss him? That was hardly all she wanted to do with the man. Which was why she held herself back. Under all that made him nice to look at, and the easy way he had with people wasn't the Napoleon complex, weak-willed, nasty streak that Tom had wallowed in once she'd broken things off.

She was terrified there'd be no breaking *anything* off when it came to Axel. Like loss and grief and hope, wanting someone completely was out of her control.

She wanted no part of it. Even while her body told her all the things she *did* want part of when it came to Axel Morrow.

So, no. No kissing. No more bringing up her past—Peter, Tom, who and whatever. No more looking at the northern lights and hearing that thread of loneliness in his voice and wanting to do something about it.

No. More.

His pace slowed, and Blanca stopped abruptly, a low growl emanating from within her. Selena came to stand next to Axel, ready to think about the real problem, not the stupid ones in her brain.

He pointed at the ground. "Tracks," he murmured.

Selena looked down at them. They weren't just following the scent anymore—they were close enough to see tracks not altered by the wind. It *wasn't* as windy today as it had been yesterday, but the clear indentations spoke to being right on the escapee's heels.

Selena crouched down. She studied the footprints, forced herself to think dispassionately about what she thought she saw. She got down, measured the different marks with her hands, squinted around to determine the wind's effects. She knew how to track people like this—Blanca made it easier, but Selena knew what she was doing even without her dog.

She looked up at Axel, doing everything in her power to mask the relief and hope she felt swelling in her chest. "This is three different sets of footprints."

His eyebrows raised, but that was the only reaction. There was no doubt there, but she felt the need to prove to him she wasn't reaching anyway. Wasn't trying to prove Peter was still alive when that's what she desperately wanted to do.

"Look," she said, pointing out the three different sizes and treads. "One. Two. Three."

"We have to be close," Axel said, scanning the woods around them.

Selena nodded. "Very close." She wanted to rush forward. She wanted to take them down now. She wanted to find Peter and *demand* to know he didn't have anything to do with the body in the burned cabin.

And she hated herself for that very Opaline response. She wanted to let Peter go. He was an escaped convict. She didn't care about him. For years and years she'd tried to convince herself she'd done her part, he'd rebuffed it and she didn't care. She'd washed her hands of it and moved on.

But there always seemed to be a glimmer of that toddler, quiet and sad, standing between her mother and his, while they screamed at each other.

Because if you never face the things that haunt you, Selena, they eat you alive. She hated that Axel's words would come back to her now. That they'd make something shift inside her, a sad realization she'd been fighting for a long time now. She was too hard on Opaline, always, because she was trying to forget that little boy, and Opaline always wanted to bring him to the forefront. And while they fought those things they never addressed, never dealt with, it continued to haunt them both.

"Selena." Axel's voice was gentle, as was the hand he placed on her shoulder.

"I'm fine," she said, probably too sharply, getting to her feet. "It doesn't mean anything. Not really. He could be the murderer. Hell, it could still be him charred to a crisp and his friends picked someone else up along the way. I know it doesn't mean much. I just…" There was a lump forming in her throat. She'd never give in to tears, but she couldn't stop that lump from lodging there.

"It's okay," he said, his hand still on her shoulder, giving it a squeeze that infused her with a warmth she couldn't afford. Not here. Not now. Not with a damn lump in her throat.

She shrugged his hand off. "I don't want you to understand or absolve me," she said, because that was exactly what she wanted. Too much. For *someone* to understand, to tell her she wasn't…all the things she was so afraid she was. Cold. Mean. Wrong.

He shrugged, unbothered. "Too bad. I absolutely understand you, and I absolutely think it and you are *okay.*" He looked around again. "Let's fall back a little bit and conference call with the team."

She opened her mouth to argue. *This* close to the escapees, to finding out if Peter was still alive, they should act, but his expression was stone. The kind even an FBI agent didn't get to argue with.

"Two people are already dead on this little path of destruction," he said in that cold voice from before, when the poacher had died. "I won't add either of us to the tally. Fall back."

It was an order. A sharp, decisive one. He could say he wasn't her boss all he wanted, but that was Mr. *Supervisor* right there.

She wished it bothered her more.

Blanca started following him back in the direction they'd come without Selena giving her the command. Selena frowned at both retreating figures.

But there was no recourse here. Much as she *wanted* to move forward, Axel was right. They had to employ caution. The men were armed. Dangerous. She and Axel might have vests and their own guns, but the trio—whoever they were—likely had a better vantage point and certainly knew they were being tracked.

They might not know people were waiting to stop them, so to keep following and lead them into that surprise would be best. Safest.

So all she could do was follow Axel.

Axel backtracked until he found a tight grove of pine trees. He contorted his body, ducking his head against the sticky, snowy needles. "This'll work," he said. Inside the thicket there was a small space. It wasn't much protection, but it would keep them out of sight.

He heard Selena murmuring to Blanca before she shoved her way into the space. She wrinkled her nose. "Smells like Christmas," Selena commented. The haunted look she'd been sporting out there had dissipated back to professional stoicism. It was what the moment needed, but unfortunately it didn't eradicate his sympathy, his...very visceral need to make this okay for her.

"Blanca will guard," Selena added, nodding at the trees. "She won't bark if she senses something, she'll either come in here or let out a low growl depending on the level of threat."

"She's some dog."

Selena's mouth curved slightly in pride. "Yeah."

Axel got out his phone and set up the conference call. It took a while to get everyone connected. He'd patched in Opaline and Alana along with Carly and Aria, and Scott and Max.

"We're tight on their heels. Going to keep giving them space until we've made a good circle around them. Selena found something that we'll want to keep in mind."

"There are three separate tracks in the snow." She looked at the screen in Axel's hand, and Axel could tell she was staring at the little box that was Opaline. "Don't know what it means, of course, but there are still three of them. Whether it's our original three or a new one, we'll have to get close enough to find out."

Opaline let out a long breath. Clearly she wanted to believe the third track was Peter, and Axel found himself wanting to believe that too. For both sisters.

"After this call I want you to do just that," Alana said. "Don't act unless you have a surefire way of bringing them down without injury to yourself. Your purpose this morning is to get close enough to see who our new trio is, if it is new. The better idea we have of who we're dealing with, the better choices we'll make."

Axel nodded, though he didn't like the idea at all. Did it matter *who* was out there *now*, when they'd find out when they all met together? But you never knew what kind of advantage knowing who someone was could give you.

Still, he'd rather keep Selena safe and sound right here until they were ready to act. Which wasn't his job. His job was to be Selena's partner. Not her protector.

Why was that getting harder?

"I already marked our location on the map," Axel said. "Carly and Aria, Scott and Max, you'll want to adjust your locations accordingly and make sure there aren't any holes in the direction they're headed toward."

"I think we're good," Aria said, looking down at what he assumed was the map. "If they keep heading in this same direction, we should be able to have a tight circle around them by...tomorrow morning?"

Axel nodded. "They've taken some breaks, but I'm not sure any of them have stopped to rest. They'll have to eventually."

"I imagine they got some kind of foodstuffs and possibly more weapons from the cabin they burned down," Selena said from beside him. "Enough food and water, they might be able to go on without sleep if they have a destination in mind and someone to meet."

"It's possible," Alana said, her voice cool and calm even over the phone. "From what Rihanna has relayed to me from local law enforcement and fire department, the cabin was well stocked. And purposefully burned to the ground."

"We're still looking into Bernard and what his connection might be to Leonard," Opaline said. Axel gave a sideways glance to Selena, since he could tell Opaline was searching the screen for signs of Selena being in distress.

Did Selena notice that? Did Opaline notice the heartbreak in Selena's eyes? It seemed more and more wrong to him that these sisters would be so antagonistic toward each other when the things that had caused their rift were beyond their own control.

"When do you think we'll have an ID on the body?" Selena asked, and Axel knew she was doing everything in her power to sound robotic and unmoved about the potential answer.

"Hopefully soon," Alana said. "Rihanna will send out an alert to all of you the minute she's got the information. She's at the morgue now waiting. We'll want to reconvene and discuss the information, of course, but I'm hopeful the identity gives us a clue as to what we're dealing with." And if Axel knew his director, which he felt like he did, she knew Selena and Opaline needed to know right away without having to wait for a conference call.

"It doesn't make sense they took the time to burn the cabin," Selena said. "There has to be something more to it."

"I agree," Carly chimed in. "I've read the arson investigator's initial notes—not a formal report yet—but the time it would have taken them to burn that cabin in the way that they did, it's considerable. And seemingly pointless."

"So, there's a point," Max said. "What's the usual reason for arson?"

"Insurance money," Aria offered.

"Kill someone," Selena pointed out.

"Or," Max returned, "destroying something. Sometimes even evidence. Could be there was something there our escapees didn't want anyone to find."

The call went quiet for a few seconds. "Definite possibilities," Alana agreed. "We'll work on that on our end. Those of you in the field, let's concentrate on getting these three men without any injury to us. Axel, Selena, find out who we're dealing with, but don't act until you're close enough to the others for all six of you to move."

"Yes, ma'am," Axel and Selena murmured at the same time the others on the call did. They offered brief goodbyes, then the phone went dark. Axel shoved it back in his pocket.

He knew what he had to do. He knew Selena wouldn't like it. So, he had to figure out how to play it.

Ah, screw it. "You'll stay here with Blanca. I'll sneak close enough to see who we've got. Then I'll meet you back here." Then he walked out of the tree enclosure before she could argue.

When Blanca began to trot after him, he turned and held out a hand. "Stay. Guard." He had no idea what the actual commands were, and Selena seemed to act like Blanca would only listen to her, but the dog planted her rear in the snow. Looking just like what he needed her to be. A guard dog.

Now, he had to find out what trio they were dealing with. Weapon drawn, Axel moved for the tracks.

Chapter 10

Selena could take an order. As a law enforcement agent over the years, she'd had to take her fair share of them. And Axel was her superior, no matter how much he didn't want to label it that way.

Still, his order was tough to swallow. He was doing a simple reconnaissance mission. It made sense only one of them went, and it made sense it was him since she should stay with Blanca.

Selena was frustrated, angry and trying to convince herself those were the only two feelings twisting her stomach in knots. But there was an anxiety over Axel's well-being underneath that. One she couldn't afford.

"What the hell *can* I afford these days?" she muttered to herself. And her own voice broke her out of her trance of worry enough to focus on the moment in front of her.

She was going to stand here and wait for Axel because that was his order, which he had given because Alana had ordered him to find the ID of their third man before they went any farther.

Chain of command. There was no getting around it.

Since she was waiting, Selena needed to use the time wisely—give Blanca a drink, a treat and maybe even a rest. She whistled for Blanca, who pushed through the tree branches. If the dog's expression was anything to go by, she wasn't too thrilled by her current circumstances.

Selena got out the waterproof blanket from her pack, the water, the treats. She set up a nice little rest area for Blanca in the middle of the circle of trees. Blanca circled the blanket, then plopped herself down in the middle.

She looked at Selena with the haughtiness of a queen—at least that was Selena's interpretation. Which gave her a smile and helped her keep her mind off how long Axel had been or would be gone.

Blanca drank, ate the treat, then scooted her body closer to Selena. Selena crouched down and scratched the dog's ears, looking into her dark eyes. "I don't know what I'm doing," she whispered to the dog. "Everything feels all jumbled up, and I don't have time for that. I have to keep it together."

Blanca gently licked Selena's face. Some of the tension inside her chest unwound. There was nothing quite like laying all your problems on a dog. Who couldn't talk back and couldn't hold anything against you either.

"I don't even know what to hope for," she murmured to her dog. At the end of the day, Blanca was her *best* friend. The dog was the only being in her life she was totally honest with. Even as close as Selena had become with Carly working together, she still held herself back.

She'd learned a long time ago the only way to sur-

vive was doing that—holding parts of yourself back.
Hiding them away.

And what had it gotten her? A job she loved, sure.
But a lonely apartment. Distance from every member
of her family. Surface relationships.

Selena blew out a breath and plopped her butt onto the
blanket next to Blanca. She had to fight the urge to go
after Axel just to avoid all these thoughts and feelings.

*Because if you never face the things that haunt you,
Selena, they eat you alive.*

She thought she'd been strong. Tough. She'd with-
stood a lot of challenges and setbacks and considered
that enough.

But no matter how strong her outer shell, she had the
sinking realization those things she'd pushed away and
never really dealt with *had* eaten her alive. Everything
in her life outside TCD was a shell.

Blanca whined, not in communication but in com-
miseration as she laid her head on Selena's lap.

Selena felt shaky, but she was on a job. She couldn't
indulge in tears. She didn't have time for personal
epiphanies.

Do you ever?

"I don't want it to be Peter," she found herself saying.
No one was here except her and Blanca. Maybe there
could be something cathartic in laying it all out for her
dog. Who wouldn't judge or ask for more. Who would
just sit there and absorb. "I don't want him to be dead
in that awful way. I don't want him to be a part of any
of these murders. I want to go back in time and *force*
him to take my help. But you can't do that. You can't
force your help on someone, no matter what Opaline
or Dad think."

She blew out a breath. She still had a lot of guilt when it came to Peter. She hadn't always been nice or loving like Opaline had been, but she *had* tried. Selena knew in her heart she'd tried. And Opaline had tried in her way.

So maybe she needed to let it go. Peter. Guilt. Expectation. Hope. Maybe when it came to her arguments with Dad and Opaline about Peter, she needed to accept... She'd done everything she could. It was up to Dad and Opaline to accept it.

It wasn't that easy, of course. She stroked Blanca's ears. She couldn't just *accept* it or she already would have. But there was something about…thinking it over, speaking the words out loud even if Blanca had no response, that made the problems take shape.

And with a shape, there was the need to actually solve them. Not just avoid them.

"I want my sister to stop blaming me for Peter. I want her to…care about me as more than just the guardian of things." She thought of what Opaline had said on the phone. Wondering if she'd ever asked for help.

No, Selena wouldn't. Asking for help was like baring your soul. It was admitting you couldn't do it on your own.

She didn't believe she was the sole cause of this problem, but she shared some responsibility. She'd never told Dad or Opaline how she'd felt. She'd either been too angry, or more likely too upset and wanting to lean into anger, or she hadn't wanted to feel…vulnerable.

She never wanted to feel like she had the afternoon she'd walked into her normal childhood and seen her mother screaming at another woman, a little baby with her father's eyes between them. She'd never wanted all that *emotion* choking the room.

Emotion. Betrayal. Hurt. She'd found it anyway. She'd gotten involved with Tom because he was charming and because, she realized uncomfortably, she'd thought he was the kind of guy who couldn't hurt her.

In some ways, he hadn't hurt her heart. But he had hurt her pride. Which very unfortunately led her brain to think about Axel.

"And Axel." She looked out through the tree branches. "I don't want this feeling, but it's there." She nuzzled her cheek against the top of Blanca's head. "Why couldn't he be an accountant or something? Why couldn't we have met at the gym? At a bar?" Not that she spent much time at either—rarely bars, only the gym at work. Maybe if she did she'd find some other person who'd make her feel…

Right. This feeling had persisted for four years because it was ordinary, forgettable, and someone else could inspire it.

It just wasn't an option. Surely Axel thought so too, considering he'd kept his hands relentlessly to himself. Sure, he'd made that crack about her being afraid to kiss him, but it hadn't been so much a dare as…

As…

He'd been trying to keep her mind off Peter. Off her personal connection.

Her heart fluttered obnoxiously in her chest even as her stomach twisted at the thought he knew her, understood her *that* well. And cared enough to use that knowledge and understanding to help her get through the harder parts of this assignment.

Selena swore into Blanca's fur. "I am so screwed," she muttered.

* * *

Axel heard the raised voices after he'd been walking maybe ten minutes. There was some relief to that, that he wasn't spending hours distanced from Selena. They should stick together, but this was a one-person job.

All he had to do was make the ID. That was it. So he paused and listened to the murmurings. Carefully, he moved toward the sounds. He kept himself calm, present, focusing on getting closer to the voices without being heard himself.

He thought of nothing else. Not what it would mean when he identified the trio, not what he might do if caught. Not even the cold that seemed to seep into his bones. He could only let his brain focus on the mission and completing it.

Eventually he eased close to a line of trees. He thought he saw movement but got the impression the men were carefully dressed in camouflage. He stopped behind a tree thick enough to hide him, then carefully peered around the side.

He could make out three men now. They stood close together, making it harder to distinguish between them. Still, Axel was sure they were the fugitives.

"Would you shut up?" one voice demanded in a censoring command. "We know they can't be far behind. And with that damn dog. I don't want to stand here arguing when that dog is on our heels."

"It's a search dog, not an attack dog," a bored voice said. "Calm down."

There was incoherent grumbling. Axel stayed exactly where he was. It would be imperative to observe them without being detected. All three men were likely armed, and though he could probably pick all three off without a problem, that wasn't his assignment. Nor his duty.

As a law enforcement agent, his job was to *enforce* the law, not take it into his own hands. Or take the easiest way out. Apprehension was the goal here. Using his weapon to cause injury was a last resort.

When dealing with murderers, he sometimes had to take the moment to remind himself of that. He didn't believe in rehabilitation when it came to cold-blooded murder, but his job wasn't about his belief. It was about following the law.

He drew his weapon for his own safety and then crouched low. He moved toward the voices, keeping himself as hidden behind tree trunks as he could. He just needed one good visual, then he could retreat and head back for Selena.

Axel was beginning to make out the shape of them. The exact location. He crept closer still, keeping his breath soft and even. It puffed out in front of him, but he finally found a good vantage point behind another tree. Not as thick as the last, but if Axel kept his body angled, it was still good cover.

They were indeed dressed in camouflage, including stocking caps in the same pattern. These weren't the clothes they'd left the prison in. Which meant somewhere along the way they'd had help. Or they'd found clothes at the cabin they'd burned down? Something to file away to think about later.

"Why not kill them?" one of the men said. "Why bother with this chasing game? It's cold and miserable. Kill them. Bad enough we had to mess around with that fire, now—"

"You can't kill them," another voice interrupted, sounding panicked. When he spoke again, he was calmer. "Right now we're just escapees. You kill federal agents, they won't rest until they hunt you down. We just have to evade. Then we really can just…disappear. That's what we want, yeah?"

"You got that info from your sister yet?" the bored-sounding one asked. But he wasn't bored anymore. He was sharp. A leader demanding info from a subordinate.

Axel sucked in a breath, heart ramming against his chest in surprise. *Sister.*

"She's working on it," the voice said. There was a defensiveness to his tone, but that didn't do anything to put Axel at ease.

"What does that mean? It's been too long. She was supposed to give us the intel so we'd know where to go and more important, not go, after we escaped. You're the one who told me that." The angry one. Could that be Steve Jenson?

"That's the whole reason you're here even though I doubted your…mettle." Bored. Leonard Koch?

"She's just in computers, man. Besides, it's going to take her some time to make sure it doesn't come back on her."

Computers. Sister. Opaline?

"I don't care if it comes back on her."

"You should. I have someone in the FBI in my pocket. You should care she stays there." It had to be Peter Lopez. Who else had FBI connections?

"What about the other one?" This was the voice who'd expressed concern over the dog, and who Axel was moderately sure was Steve.

There was a cold silence. Axel couldn't see their faces, though he could see the three of them standing in a circle.

"What's this?" the leader said, his voice deceptively amused. "Secrets? Shame on you, Peter."

Axel had his confirmation. Peter was one of the men here. Sisters and the name weren't a coincidence. He couldn't make out the faces of the other two, but talking about escape, plus the heights matching the descriptions he'd been given, made it clear that these were the original three. Whoever was dead back in that cabin was someone else entirely.

"Pete's been keeping an ace in the hole," the taller man said. Steve Jenson. "He doesn't just have one sister in the FBI. The other one's an actual agent. She's not as easy a mark as the computer one, but I bet we can make her talk."

"And you both kept this from me because why?" The question was calm, even pleasant, but no one—neither the two men standing there nor Axel himself—seemed fooled by the tone. Yeah, this man was clearly the leader. Which meant he was Leonard Koch.

The man Axel assumed was Peter sputtered and stuttered but didn't actually say anything to defend himself.

"Hey, we all need an ace in the hole," Steve said with a shrug. He had a gun in his hand. Leonard had one in each hand. Both of their fingers were on the trigger.

They didn't trust each other. That was good. A fractured team didn't always make the best decisions. Information Axel could use. Or maybe they'd just kill each other right here and end it.

Guilt swept in. Selena could say Peter didn't mean anything to her, but Axel knew the kid did. If he got killed in all this, she'd blame herself. Maybe her family would even unfairly blame her. Axel couldn't hope for it to end in a hail of bullets. He had to work to make sure cooler heads prevailed.

"I could kill you right here, right now for lying to me," Leonard said. Then he jerked his chin toward Peter. "Keep him alive because he's the one with the connections."

Steven paused, seeming to consider Leonard's threat. "Come on, man. I convinced you to bring the kid, didn't I? Because I knew he'd be of some use. Yeah, I didn't give the whole story, but have you given us the whole story about your brother?"

Brother. Axel frowned. There hadn't been any information about Leonard Koch having a brother.

"So, these sisters." Leonard turned slightly toward Peter. His fingers remained poised on the triggers, even if the guns still pointed at the ground. "One is helping you?"

Axel felt shock, true, utter shock slam through him. *Helping* him? No, Opaline was just talking to Peter. Not *helping* him. Had to be.

"Yeah, yeah. She, uh, she's trying to get their game plan. But she's just like a computer geek, you know? It takes her time to get the information."

"Time's up. Call her. Get the info now. From her. Or the other one. I don't care. I want to know exactly where the feds are—not these morons following us, but the one's they've no doubt got set up at the border. You don't get me that in ten minutes, you're dead."

Axel stayed where he was as Peter fumbled with a phone.

It couldn't be true. Surely Opaline wasn't helping Peter. She'd been with TCD for five years. She was...

Peter's sister.

Axel let out a careful breath. He had to push away any emotions he had about the possibility of Opaline betraying them, about making sure Selena's brother didn't end up dead at Leonard's hands. Bottom line, they didn't know where the FBI agents were, so it was possible Opaline was just pretending she was going to get him the info, setting a trap. Maybe Alana even knew about it.

God, he hoped.

"Well?" Leonard demanded when Peter pulled the phone from his ear.

"She didn't answer," he said, sounding…scared.

Axel refused to feel sympathy for him. Maybe he was young, but a man knew the difference between right and wrong.

And Opaline?

He couldn't think about it.

"Try the other sister."

"I don't know her number. I don't remember it. This isn't my phone, you know." There was a mix of whining and anger in his tone.

Leonard shrugged. "Then I guess you're of no use to me. Steven? Take care of him."

Steven stepped forward, lifting his gun to point at Peter. Axel lifted his own. He couldn't let this man kill Selena's brother.

So he pulled his own trigger before Steven could.

Chapter 11

The gunshot was a clear, decisive sound in the otherwise quiet landscape. Selena jerked, and Blanca jumped to her feet.

Immediately, Selena grabbed her weapon. She left the pack. There was no time. She was out of the tree shelter in seconds flat, but she skidded to a halt as she realized Blanca was at her heels.

Whatever was going on, it was no place for a search dog. Swallowing down the fear and nerves, Selena had to find her authoritative and commanding tone. She crouched down and grasped Blanca's collar with a definitive hold.

"Stay," she said clearly, without any waver or shake. "Stay," she repeated. She would have given the command one more time just to be clear, but she knew her voice wouldn't hold.

Another gunshot rang out, quickly followed by another. Selena's heart lurched and she ran toward the sound.

The cold was like needles against her lungs, but it helped center her. It helped all that training she'd had kick into gear. This wasn't about Axel. It was about getting to and defusing the situation. It was about doing her job. Which involved helping people. Saving people.

Making sure Axel is okay.

He was wearing his vest. He was an excellent agent. If there'd been shooting, it had been…

He wouldn't have shot first. That wasn't the assignment. An agent like Axel being caught? It seemed impossible.

But things happened. Not just mistakes. Bad timing. Wrong place, wrong time. Not enough information to make the right choice.

And she knew the three trying to reach the Canadian border wouldn't hesitate to kill a man. Not when they'd already killed two. Not when freedom lay on the other side. And a Kevlar vest didn't make someone invincible.

A sob tried to fight its way through her throat, but she refused to let it win. She would get to him. Everything would be okay. She was a damn FBI agent—she would make sure of it.

But only if she thought rationally, calmly. She slowed her pace, though it killed her. But going half-cocked into the situation wouldn't help anyone.

She'd run toward the shots, but she hadn't *thought*. She slowed to a walk, surveying the world around her. Trees and white snow. She could see her tracks behind her. Axel should have left some too. She should have followed them.

She could backtrack, but there wasn't time. She sucked in a slow breath of the icy air. She moved forward, because this was the right direction. She kept her pace at a walk, but quick. She slowed her ragged breathing so she could listen.

But the world had gone quiet again. Three gunshots and now quiet.

Selena squeezed the handle of the gun. No use thinking about all the might-have-happends. She had to take this one step at a time.

She slowed, paused, frowned. Were those…footsteps? She looked in the direction she thought she heard the sound. Crouched, and had her gun ready to aim and fire.

But the figure that materialized was solitary. Dressed in black. Tall. Broad.

Axel.

He was running, but not crazed like she had been. He wasn't exactly moving at a leisurely jog, but hardly a life-or-death run.

When he saw her, he didn't stop until he'd moved next to her, crouched in a similar position that she was in and scanned the world in front of them. "No sign of them?" he asked.

But she could only stare at him. Relief might have swamped her, but there was a streak of blood across his cheek, dripping gruesomely down his jaw. His right hand was in much the same shape. Torn-open skin, dripping blood, and he was holding his gun with his left— not his dominant hand.

"You're bleeding." It was perhaps the stupidest thing she could have said in the moment, but it made her heart twist. He was hurt. Maybe not dead, but he was still hurt.

"I'm on my own two feet," he said, his voice calm. Reassuring. But blood was dripping *off* him. "I took one of them down, and the other two took off after getting a few shots on me. I could have followed, but they had a better vantage point. Would have been too easy to pick me off."

"The other…" But she couldn't make sense of that when he was crouching next to her, breathing hard and *bleeding*. "Your face. Your hand."

He finally turned to look at her. "I'm alive, Selena. And so is Peter."

She wasn't sure what she felt at that news. Relief wasn't the right word, but disappointment wasn't either. Besides, feelings didn't matter. Not when Axel was bleeding.

She stood to her full height, scanning the woods around them. "Shelter. We need shelter."

"If we follow—"

"No." Her heart hammered in her ribs, her pulse a painful throb in her neck, but the word was authoritative and calm. "We have to assess your injuries before we move forward."

"Selena—"

"It's protocol and you know it," she snapped. Though she managed to keep her voice steady, her hand shook as she pulled the phone out of her pocket. There had to be a cabin around here somewhere.

"Selena, I shot one of them. Took him down. We need to update the team and then get back to the scene." He moved to put his hand on her, she was pretty sure, but he seemed to realize it was torn up and bloody and stopped himself. "You can't tell them about my injuries."

"Axel—"

"They'll pull me. You know they will. All I need is a few bandages and I'll be fine."

"Your shooting hand... Axel, you could have some serious damage."

"Do I sound like I'm in agonizing pain?"

She didn't say anything, because she didn't *want* to admit he *seemed* fine, even when she could see he most assuredly wasn't.

"We'll go back and get the packs and Blanca. You'll call Alana while we do. We'll update them, see if they can get local law enforcement out in case the one I shot needs medical attention. I imagine we'll still get there before they do."

"Axel..." She didn't know what to say. She didn't think he should be hiking around with blood dripping off him, but he was right about acting like it was just... scratches at most.

Still, when Axel started walking back toward the way Selena had come, Selena had to follow.

"Tell me what happened."

There was nothing but silence as they walked, following Selena's hurried footsteps in the snow.

"Axel. Tell me what happened."

"A lot," he muttered. "Call Alana. Don't mention my injuries. Tell her we had a run-in. I shot one of their men—"

"Axel, she's going to want that information from you."

"Then we'll wait until I can slap a bandage on my

face," he muttered, still striding purposefully through the snow.

She grabbed his arm, making sure it was his left, and whirled him around to face her. "You need to get bandaged up. You need to tell me what happened."

His expression was… Well, not as in control as she'd thought. Something had rattled him back there, and she didn't think it was shooting one of the men.

He gestured helplessly. *Helplessly.* It made her heart twist and dread sink like a rock in her stomach. "What is it, Axel?"

"Peter's been in contact with Opaline."

Selena blinked at the ragged note in Axel's voice. "In contact… Since…?"

Axel nodded. "At least that's what he made it sound like. They were using him because he had connection to people who worked with the FBI. They expected him to call Opaline and get information on where we were located so they could avoid us."

Selena couldn't wrap her head around the words. "She wouldn't…"

"No, she wouldn't," Axel agreed. But neither of them sounded convinced.

"We need…" She had to push away all the uncertainty, all the fear and worry. The gruesome look of Axel's bloody hand. There was only thing that could matter right now.

The assignment.

They walked in silence from then on out. When they reached where Selena had left their packs, Blanca was waiting patiently. After Selena motioned, giving her the permission to move, she bounded toward Axel. She pressed her furry body against his legs and whined.

Axel could only stare down at the dog. Expressing some kind of sympathy or concern…for him.

Selena disappeared into the trees, then returned with both their packs. She was already rummaging around in one, likely for the first aid kit. When she pulled it out, she still didn't look at him.

He tried not to think too deeply at how much his minor injuries seemed to bother her. What that might mean. In the moment, it couldn't mean anything.

"Patch up my face so we can call in," he said gruffly.

She frowned and gestured at his throbbing hand. "Your hand—"

"Patch up my face so we can call in," he repeated. "We'll go from there." The damage was painful, and he'd likely need some professional medical attention eventually, but he could deal for a few days. He had to.

"I want you to walk me through it. Step by step," she said, opening the kit and getting out what she would need. When she had everything, she stepped toward him and then hesitated.

"You're too tall."

His mouth curved. "Not a complaint I usually get."

It got an eye roll out of her, which was nice.

"Get on your knees. Put that hurt hand in the snow. I don't know if that'll help any, but the cold can't hurt."

He did as he was told, kneeling before her and plunging the injured hand into the icy cold of the snow. He sucked in a breath and tried to enjoy the interesting position of kneeling in front of Selena Lopez.

But she touched his face with a disinfectant wipe and the burning pain was the only thing he could pay attention to. Since he didn't want to embarrass himself by cursing up a blue streak or wincing away from what had to be done, he focused on his breathing. On the blue of the sky above them.

He told her what happened in quick, succinct summary.

"This might need stitches," she said, unwrapping a bandage with hands that weren't quite steady. "You were shot in the *face*."

"The bullet *grazed* my face. And, hey, it's not the first time. I'm old hat at this."

She paused, then instead of smoothing the bandage over his wound, gently touched her hand to his good cheek. Her expression went heartbreakingly sad. Not just sympathy or pity—that he could have ignored, shrugged away.

This was care. It tightened his chest, and for a few seconds the radiating pain in his body seemed to dissipate.

"Ax…" She squeezed her eyes shut, pulling her hand away. She swallowed, wiping at the cut again. "Why would you take a risk like that?"

"I don't plan on witnessing any more cold-blooded murders in my life, Selena."

"You didn't have to—"

He reached up and curled his fingers around her wrist, needing her to understand that this didn't lie on her shoulders. Not the way she was thinking. "It would have been wrong to let them kill Peter. No matter the circumstances, it would have been wrong. It's what I had to do."

She let out a shaky breath, then nodded. He released her hand, and she smoothed the bandage over his cheek.

It hurt all over again, but he'd survived worse. He'd survived a hell of a lot worse.

"Now—"

But he was silenced by her mouth on his. Her lips were soft, her hands cupping his face softer. This wasn't the sexual attraction that often crackled between them that they were so good at ignoring. The kiss spoke of fear and relief, care and...

He would have said hope, but she ended the kiss abruptly, stepping back and away from him. Her usual wariness was back in her expression, even as his body struggled to catch up.

Selena Lopez had *kissed* him, and not in the sort of way he'd rarely allowed himself to fantasize about. No explosion. No argument that led to the bedroom. She'd cleaned him up and kissed him like he mattered to her.

Then she shut it all away, assessing him coolly. "Well, your face is bandaged up. I don't know what to do about your hand. We need to call it in and then get you to some shelter."

His heart was beating so loudly in his ears it was a miracle he heard her at all. But since he did, some of that emotion and reaction faded quickly. He got to his feet. "I don't need—"

"We need to get your hand seriously bandaged. I can't do it out here." She handed him some gauze. "Try to hold that to the worst of the bleeding. We need shelter, and you need a meal and some rest. That's final, or when we call in, I tell them to medevac you out."

His eyes narrowed. "You're not in charge."

She cocked her head, fisting her hands on her hips. Her eyes flashed with temper and something else he couldn't pinpoint. "I didn't think you were either."

"Touché."

She shrugged her pack on, then held his out for him. When he tried to take it from her, she shook her head.

"You don't need to help me with my pack."

"Have you seen your mangled hand?"

Muttering irritation to himself, he turned around and let her help slide the pack onto his shoulders without jostling his, yes, big, mangled hand.

He moved to get his phone out of his pocket, but he reached with the right hand and hissed out a breath. Nothing was going to be easy without his dominant hand.

"I'll call. I'll say Blanca needs a break and we need the closest cabin they can find. Then I'll hand the phone over to you and you can report what happened." She already had the phone out.

He wanted to argue, to put himself back into the lead in this, but he also needed to keep his injuries as much a secret as he could. He wouldn't be pulled off this case. Not now.

Selena marched, following their footprints, back to the scene of the shooting. Blanca stayed close to Axel.

"Alana, hi. A few updates. First, Blanca needs a rest. A couple hours of real rest. Axel overheard them fighting, and we know that they know we're on their tail. Let's give them a chance to make their own mistakes. Can you get Opaline to track our GPS and tell us the closest available shelter?"

Whatever Alana said in response, Axel couldn't hear. Axel didn't bring up they couldn't trust Opaline. He wasn't any more ready to deal with it than Selena. But, he'd discuss it with Alana once it was his turn to talk.

"I'll hand it over to him to give you a heads-up on

what he found." She handed the phone back to him without looking at him. Her jaw was set, her expression fierce.

She was going to march him to a cabin if she had to force one to materialize out of her own sheer will.

"Alana," Axel greeted. He launched into an explanation of what he'd seen, heard and done, leaving out only the fact he'd been shot and the conversation about Opaline. He made sure to emphasize there was dissent among the ranks. No one was following Leonard blindly, and there was a lot of mistrust among the three. They could use that in their favor.

"You're hurt," Alana said flatly.

Axel was taken aback that she had somehow ascertained that. But he couldn't let his surprise show or she might figure out just how much. "It's just a scratch. And it's worth it for the information I got. Alana, I'd like to speak with just you on the line. Just you."

There was a pause. "All right. Hold on." The line went dead for a few minutes, and Axel continued to tromp after Selena.

"All right. I'm in my office. No one else is on the line. What's so important and private you can't tell the team?"

Axel explained everything he'd heard about Peter and Opaline's potential involvement. It was hard to get the words out. Hard to fight for objectivity.

"It's possible Peter was lying," Alana said. She masked her reaction quite well, but there was something about the careful way she spoke Axel knew was a reaction in and of itself. And she certainly wasn't aware Opaline had been in contact with Peter. "To seem useful or valuable to the other two?"

372 Hunting a Killer

"It's possible," Axel agreed.

Alana sighed. "But less probable."

"They didn't seem to know where we were. Peter acted like Opaline was low on the totem pole and didn't know anything, when we know that isn't true. It's possible Opaline has talked to him but downplayed what she knew."

"It's possible. But she didn't inform me."

Axel slid a look at Selena. Her gaze was on the terrain in front of them. He knew she was bothered, concerned, hurt and a whole slew of other things, but her expression was mostly stoic.

But that couldn't matter. "There's more. Steve mentioned Leonard had a brother. We don't have any intel on that, do we?"

"No. I'll put Opaline…" Alana trailed off. Though she didn't sigh into the line, there was a pregnant pause. "I'll have Amanda look into it," Alana finally said, speaking of her assistant. "And I'm going to sit down and have a conversation with Opaline, but until the situation with her is satisfactorily handled, no one moves on this group. We keep them in our sights, but absolutely *no one* moves. Got it?"

It was like a series of blows that kept landing. That one of their team might be working against them, and now they had to take precautions for that over finishing the mission. Still, there was no other choice when the safety of the team was at stake. "Yes, ma'am."

"Axel… If Opaline tells you where this cabin is, we don't know for sure you and Selena will be safe there. Nothing is for sure until we get to the bottom of this possibility."

Axel eyed Selena's back, so straight even as she struggled to walk through the deep snow.

"We'll take that chance. Can you get local law enforcement to check out…" Axel trailed off as they came to the clearing where the trio had been. There was a body, seated against a tree. He didn't move, and his open eyes saw nothing.

"You'll want to mark our location and send out a medical examiner," Axel said flatly. "The man I shot is dead."

Chapter 12

"You shot him in the head?" Selena said, blinking at the man in the snow. She'd seen her fair share of dead bodies, but she couldn't believe...

"No. I shot him in the leg." Axel pointed at the man's leg, where there was indeed another wound. "Leonard must have executed him."

"But why..." Of course she knew the reasons why. She just couldn't wrap her brain around them in these first moments.

"Couldn't keep up with them with a bullet in his leg," Axel said, his voice devoid of any emotion or inflection. "His use didn't outweigh his holding them back." Axel frowned, turning in a slow circle and scanning the trees around them. "They ran away when I shot. They were shooting at me, sure, but they were retreating. Why come back?"

It was Selena's turn to verbalize the answer they both already knew. "He'd talk. He knew their plans. They had to come back and make sure he couldn't."

Axel nodded grimly.

"It's not your fault."

"No, it isn't," he agreed, but his agreement didn't *feel* like one.

"So why do you look like you're blaming yourself?"

"Have you ever taken a life, Selena?"

She inhaled sharply, the words hitting their intended target. "No. But you didn't either. Leonard or Peter killed him. Not you."

Axel shrugged. "I think it could be argued that I started the chain of events that led to it. Justified or not, it has an effect. It's a part of it."

"A mangled hand also has an effect," she said crisply. She wouldn't let him linger on this. They had to move, or he might as well have been medically removed from the assignment. "There's nothing we can do here. Alana will send in the ME. Come on. Amanda sent me coordinates for a nearby cabin. She said half-hour walk, tops." Which Selena knew meant Alana hadn't trusted Opaline enough to handle finding them potential shelter.

Selena looked at Axel's hand. She didn't know what to do about it. He needed…stitches for sure. At the *very* least. There was no way to effectively field dress it to stop the bleeding. "You're losing a lot of blood."

He looked down at the bloody gauze he clutched in his hand. "Some of it's stopped."

She didn't believe him, at all, but they had to get away from the lifeless body of Steve Jenson. So, she looked at her phone and the map Amanda had programmed into the GPS for her. Instead of Opaline.

Opaline. She didn't want to think about her sister. So she focused on each step. She glanced back at Axel. Blanca was walking by his side as if she was protecting him. Some doggie sense that he was hurt.

It was easy not to think about kissing him back there. There were dead men, the possibility her sister was *helping* Peter, and even if she wasn't expressly helping him the very real possibility Opaline would lose her job over whatever she *had* done and kept to herself. Then there was Axel's hand. And the interminable walk to shelter.

So, no, whenever her mind drifted back to that ridiculous, *intimate* touch of lips that she'd initiated in some fit of…softhearted stupidity, it was easily shoved away again.

No matter how much she worried about Axel's hand, she couldn't imagine partnering with anyone else at this point. There was too much… He understood. The shock of Opaline being involved. The thorny connections between her, Opaline *and* Peter. Besides, he'd heard everything the men had said. Infighting and Leonard having a brother. It all added up to someone who was in the thick of things, who'd know how to proceed.

She kept herself from looking back at him. Examining his still-injured hand wouldn't change anything. They had to keep moving forward. It was the only way to end this.

They were silent as they hiked. Selena followed the directions on her phone, Blanca kept close to Axel's side and there were no sounds in the snow-covered forest except the occasional rustle of animal or bird.

It was almost meditative. Like the sun and trees worked together to make her breathe easier. Like the physical exertion outside had some special element she'd never find in the gym. She could breathe…deeper than she had in a long time. Despite the danger, frustration and worry around them, she felt more in control. As though she'd been granted new clarity.

When the cabin on the map came into view, Selena stopped short.

"Whoa," Axel said beside her.

This was no rustic hunting cabin, but a pristine, gleaming two-story *getaway*. The wood was a rich reddish hue against the bright white of the snow around it. The shutters were green, and they matched the door. There was a wraparound porch, liberally covered in snow. So, despite its gorgeousness, it wasn't being used right now.

"I think I'm afraid to go in." But that was silly, of course. They had a job to do, and if it meant commandeering this cabin, so be it. Her phone chimed, and she read the message on her screen aloud.

"Owners notified. Okay to break in. Our office will cover damages and cleanup."

"Know how to jimmy a lock?" Axel asked as they moved up onto the porch.

"I'm not going to waste my time with that," Selena muttered. If TCD was footing the bill, she'd get inside the quickest way possible. She eyed the door, then gave it her best skilled kick. Something splintered, but it took another two kicks to get the door swinging open.

"That was hot."

She snorted out a laugh, which loosened the tightening vise in her chest. Everything was a mess, but at least they could still laugh. "You're twisted, Morrow."

He shrugged, and they entered the cabin. Selena immediately slipped off her pack while Axel moved into the dim interior and turned on a lamp. Blanca padded inside after them.

"First things first. We need to get your hand washed up and sanitized." She looked around. The layout was open, and she immediately found the expansive kitchen and nodded him toward it.

Axel let out a low whistle as they passed a giant stone fireplace and hearth. "This makes my house look like a shack."

"It makes my apartment look like a prison." Selena turned on the tap, flipping it toward hot. She'd half expected the water or electricity or *something* to be shut off, but everything was working. "Must be nice to be loaded, huh?"

Axel didn't respond to that. He was eyeing the water dubiously. "How hot are you going to make that?"

"Hot as it can be. Scared?"

"Survived worse," he muttered, but he clearly wasn't too excited about surviving this.

"Stay put," she ordered, waiting for the water to get a little hotter. She searched the lower level of the cabin, found a nice mudroom off to the side. There was even a dog bed in it. A little small for Blanca, but it would do for now. "Blanca." The dog padded over, and Selena pointed to the bed. "Lie down."

The dog obeyed, and Selena knew she'd take a good doze for as long as Selena let her. When she woke up, or when they needed to leave, Selena would feed and water her again. Ideally the rest would do them *all* some good.

She returned to Axel in the kitchen. "Lose the bandage."

"Sure, Nurse Ratched."

She batted her eyelashes at him. "I'm a lot prettier."

"Yeah, you're all right," he grumbled, unraveling the makeshift dressing. He winced as he pulled it completely off.

Selena ignored the lurching of her stomach at the sight. The bullet had passed through the pad of his palm, ripping the flesh open and leaving a gruesome sight of blood, tissue and perhaps the hint of bone. She didn't look close enough to ascertain for sure.

She lowered the pressure on the water, then gingerly took his wrist and moved it under the slow, gentle stream.

"I'm not even sure how you managed to only get shot on the pad of your hand and a graze on your cheek. That's some luck."

"Yeah, some invisible force field of luck since the day I was born."

Her heart pinched at that. She couldn't possibly begin to imagine what he'd been through, and at such a young age. Still, she knew he wouldn't want her to *express* that. He'd survived close to thirty years since, and she imagined he had a handle on his own ghosts.

But that didn't mean she could just turn off the compassion she felt toward him because of it. Because of who he'd become in spite of it.

She blew out a breath and studied the hand, now that the water had washed away a lot of the dried blood. She held his wrist and forearm gently, trying to work out how to wrap the bandage, and lifted her gaze to his. "You know you need medical attention on this," she said, all joking aside. "Lucky or not, been shot and survived before or not, you need serious medical attention."

He held her gaze, a steely glint of determination in

the green depths. "And I'll survive a few more days without it."

She pursed her lips. "Can you shoot with your left?"

"Can. Wouldn't risk a sniper situation or anything, but I do all right. Besides, we keep a tight enough circle, if we need that kind of help, Max is the best shot out of all of us."

His hand now disinfected and dried, Selena began bandaging it from the wrist up. She was as gentle as she could manage. Every time he hissed out a breath, she strove to be even more careful. She wrapped layer after layer, wanting not only to stop the bleeding but to make as much padding as she could so he wasn't constantly making the wound worse.

"I look like a mummy," he complained, the first signs of fatigue and grumpiness edging into his voice.

"You want me to kiss it and make it better?" She grinned up at him, hoping to lighten the mood.

But his gaze was serious. "I wouldn't say no."

Her heart bumped unsteadily against her ribs. Because she wanted to. Just like the moment before when she'd let down her guard because emotion had swamped all rational thought. She'd just wanted that…thing she'd been holding herself back from.

It couldn't be now. Maybe…she could think about it after the assignment was done, but it couldn't be now. She finished with the bandage and gently let his hand go.

"We need to conference call. Then we can grab a meal and some rest." Maybe if she stalled here enough, the other two teams could apprehend Leonard and Peter. She'd never once shirked her duty, or hoped someone else had to do the hard parts, but with Axel hurt…

"Don't get soft on me, Lopez."

Irritated he'd seen right through her, she lifted her chin and glared at him. "I wouldn't dare." She jerked her phone out of her pocket and pulled up the app to videoconference with the two teams to the north.

Axel ached inside and out. Bullet wounds. Heart. Other…places. Everything hurt or throbbed or wanted with something he couldn't have…or at least right now. The mission came first.

Max came on the screen, followed by Carly and Aria in their little box. Selena held the phone so Axel himself was out of frame. Clearly she knew he had to keep the extent of his injures as much on the down low as possible.

Max let out a low whistle. "Where the heck are you two?"

"Finally lucked out," Selena said, and despite the fact Axel could see her knuckles were white from the tension in them, she spoke lightly and easily. "You all talk to Alana?"

"Yeah. Told us to stay put unless we make a visual, and even then to only approach if necessary. You guys got an idea what the holdup is?"

Axel could only see Selena's profile, but she didn't seem to give anything away. "We found one of the men dead and left behind. I think Alana wants to get the body taken care of and a verified ID before we move forward. This just proves how dangerous they are. Not just to us, or passersby, but to each other."

"Right. But what's all this about filtering all info requests through Amanda instead of Opaline?"

This time Selena betrayed *something*, though Axel

wasn't sure anyone would be able to notice the minus-
cule wince on the tiny conference-call video screens.
"Opaline was a little overwrought about Peter's involvement and thinking he might be dead. She just needs a
break. Have you guys seen anything?"

"Scott's out patrolling the gap we've got between us.
He hasn't seen anything."

"By my calculations, they shouldn't be close to us
until tomorrow," Aria said. "I'm not sure I understand
why you guys don't just take them down now. Down a
man. Surely you two could handle it."

"Alana wants to be more safe than sorry," Axel said
decisively. "Leonard has already left a trail of bodies."

"Why are you creeping around out of screen, Morrow?" Carly asked with some suspicion.

Selena gave him a questioning look. Axel sighed.
He'd keep his hand behind his back, but there'd be no
hiding the bandage on his face. It didn't *look* as bad as
it probably was, so that was something.

He gave Selena a little nod and scooted closer to
her as she angled the phone to get them both in frame.

"What happened to you?" Max demanded of Axel.

"A scratch. Our focus now is on two things. One,
tracking down Bernard McNally. And two, figuring
out this mysterious brother of Leonard's that I found
out about when they were arguing."

"Funny you bring that up," Carly said calmly, and
though she studied Axel through the screen, she didn't
let Max or Aria butt in with any questions about his
injury. "I was doing a little digging on Leonard while
Opaline researched Bernard, then Alana mentioned the
brother angle. I dug at the potential connection between
the two. I'm still working on irrefutable proof, but so far

all evidence points to Bernard McNally being Leonard Koch's brother. Not sure if it's a half brother, stepbrother or just foster situation, but they're connected through family. Somehow. Brother would fit."

Selena shared a look with Axel. Even without proof, it did fit. But even knowing the relationship still didn't help them figure out what Leonard was trying to accomplish.

"And do we have anything on Bernard McNally or the body found in his cabin?"

"No body ID yet, and not a lot on Bernard. We think there are aliases, but tracking them down has been difficult. Opaline's been working on that arm. I suppose Amanda is now."

"Let's all work on it," Axel said. "There's no way they get to the border by nightfall. Even if they hike through the night, it's unlikely. If they go off course, we'll use Blanca in the morning."

"Resting like this seems…" Aria trailed off.

"Necessary. Smart. For the good and safety for all of us," Axel said, bringing out his rarely used authoritative, brook-no-questioning voice.

Aria looked a bit chagrined, but Max didn't appear convinced. "Something is pretty off here," he said.

Axel didn't want to lie to his friend, wouldn't lie to his colleagues, so he could only give them reassurance, not fact. "Everything is as it needs to be. We'll plan to sit tight tonight unless Alana directs otherwise. Agreed?"

"Agreed," Carly said quickly. Max and Aria were a little more hesitant but eventually concurred.

At some point they might need to know about Opaline, but Alana would want to handle that herself. So, Axel would let her.

If that helped Selena out, so be it.

"Bernard McNally is our primary focus right now. I want to know all aliases, who he is, who he pretends to be. I want us completely armed with everything we can by morning. The more we know, the better chance we have of stopping this before Leonard kills anyone else."

He didn't usually bark out orders like this, but he supposed there wasn't anything *usual* going on right now. "Understood?"

Everyone agreed, and then gave half-hearted good-byes as they cut off the call. Selena shoved the phone in her pocket. Her brows were furrowed, and she seemed to be deep in thought.

"Penny for your thoughts," he offered.

She lifted her gaze to his. Sad and serious. "I want to approach Peter. Alone. Just me and him."

Chapter 13

He didn't laugh. She half expected him to. It was not the smartest plan she'd ever concocted.

But it was *something*.

Axel held her gaze, but he didn't say anything, and it felt like he could see right through her. Like he *knew* this didn't have anything to do with the mission and everything to do with the fact Peter was her brother and she wanted to save him.

Even now.

Are you any better than Opaline?

She couldn't hold his gaze after that popped into her head. She turned to the mess they'd left in bandaging him up. She threw away trash, found a dish towel to wipe the wet counters and desperately tried to find some way to get her professional shell back.

But he'd dissolved it, back there, when he'd let her kiss him as if they hadn't been avoiding it for *years*.

"How do you propose we go about letting that happen?" Axel asked.

She wasn't fooled by his even tone. His eyes said everything his voice didn't. *No way in hell.*

"You have good reason to rest. And do all those things you were talking about with the team. I'll take Blanca and—"

He held up his bandaged hand. "This is what happened the last time we split up."

She wanted to say it wasn't the same, but of course it was the same. Splitting up left them far more vulnerable, especially when her plan was just…personal. She could pretend it was about the assignment—that somehow getting a message to Peter would allow him to escape Leonard's clutches, or bring Leonard down and somehow redeem himself—but deep down she knew she was just grasping at the same old straws. Drowning under the weight of other people's expectations.

"You said they were all fighting. That they didn't trust each other. If we can use that—"

"I get what you're saying, but why not just keep closing in the circle until the six of us can apprehend them without anyone getting hurt?"

Anyone else, she wanted to say, looking at the bandages on his hand and face.

"We might get more information about this Bernard McNally and what he has planned. I've been saying from the beginning, escaping prison in February when you're in northern Michigan just doesn't make sense."

"And you don't think we'll get that information if we apprehend them?"

Selena wanted to present a calm, decisive front. The stoic agent who didn't care—that woman she'd been back at the offices. But Opaline being involved, Axel getting shot…it was poking holes in all her defenses. In all the ways she usually kept her feelings buried and to herself.

"You said Leonard was going to kill Peter. Because he didn't have a use," Selena managed to choke out. "If Opaline was his use…"

Axel scrubbed a hand over his face. "Listen. If Leonard was going to kill Peter, he would have done it then and there with Steve. He escaped *with* men, when it likely would have been easier to orchestrate alone, for a reason. Just like they broke out now for a reason. I'm not saying he won't kill Peter if it helps whatever his end goal is, I'm just saying I don't think it fits with Leonard's goal right now."

Selena tried to let that ease her worry. Axel wasn't the type of agent to say something simply to mollify her. It had to be the truth. The problem was the truth wasn't *certainty*.

Axel reached out, his hand touched her face. She didn't spend much time dwelling on how much larger her male coworkers were than her. She focused on herself, on being strong and capable regardless of size. But now… His hand was big, and he was so much taller with those broad shoulders and…

She was a federal agent. Not a woman. Not here. Not now.

But his fingers brushed her cheek with the gentleness of a…a… She was afraid to let her brain finish that sentence. Like thoughts would materialize in the ether and she wouldn't be able to fight for herself anymore.

"If you really feel like you need to do this," he said, his fingers on her cheek, his words low and serious.

"If you take some time and really work through how and what you hope to accomplish, I go with you. Non-negotiable."

She blinked. *With her*. That was most definitely not what she expected from him, and she didn't know how to… She didn't know…

"But for the next few hours, we take the time to eat and rest. You come up with a plan and we'll go from there."

She swallowed, but it didn't dissolve the lump in her throat. He sighed, fingers sliding off her cheek and then very carefully reaching around her and pulling her toward him. Carefully, gently.

A genuine, friendly, sympathetic, comforting *hug*.

He was warm, steady and still smelled like the fire they'd had in the shack last night. She couldn't seem to hold herself stiff like she knew she should.

When was the last time she'd let someone just hold her, comfort her with nothing more than the shelter of their arms?

She didn't have a clue, and it brought the sting of tears to her eyes. She wouldn't let them *fall*, but it was impossible to fight them completely off. She left her hands at her sides, afraid of what they might do of their own volition if she brought them up to touch. He had the palm of one big hand on the small of her back. He rested his chin on her head, and that had a breath shuddering out of her, sounding far too loud in the quiet room. But she didn't stiffen or pull away. She felt like the warmth of his body was some kind of drug lulling her into complacency, and in that complacency, she rested her head on his shoulder.

She didn't know how long they stood like that. She

was half convinced they both dozed off, there on their feet, for a few minutes anyway. In that hazy place, she'd somehow raised her arms to wrap around him, to hold him tight and close as though she could hide away from all that needed to be done.

"You need to rest," she said, not sure why her voice was so thready, why she felt…shaky.

Oh, you know why.

She lifted her head up and dropped her arms. She tried to step away, but his hand remained on her back, a strong, steady pressure keeping her exactly where she was—leaned against him.

"Then we both need to rest," Axel said, his voice a rusty rumble that had her nerve endings tingling to life.

She looked up at him, convinced she would lecture, not get lost in the green of his eyes and the stubble now dotting his jaw. "I wasn't shot," she said, managing—just barely—not to sound like a breathy fool.

"We haven't slept in a long time."

Why did that sound like some kind of sensual invitation when it wasn't? It *wasn't*.

They needed a meal, sleep, and she needed to figure out a way to get to Peter. To hand him a lifeline. If he didn't take it, well, that was his choice. She just…had to offer it. And if Axel was by her side…

She sucked in a breath. It shouldn't feel good. It shouldn't feel necessary. He was her partner on this assignment. She knew how to work with a partner, but that didn't mean she had to depend on them to make her feel like she had a handle on things.

She'd only ever been able to depend on herself for that. Which felt sad with Axel's big hand on her back, holding her so close to him she wanted to give in and lean against him again.

But if she did, she'd lose. She'd lose everything. If she gave in…

What could you gain?

She couldn't listen to that voice. It was the voice that always got her in trouble. That had her trusting people. That had her offering Peter help against her better judgment. That had her moving to TCD thinking she and Opaline might have some sisterly relationship again.

It was the voice that broke her heart, again and again.

So when Axel touched her face again, she shook it off. She couldn't let it linger like some half-reached promise. "I'm not going to pretend we aren't attracted to each other. We've been dancing around that for years, but—"

"I'm not going to pretend attraction is all it is."

She sucked in a breath, and then another. Panic, she convinced herself, was all that she felt. The warmth around her heart, squeezing her chest painfully and beautifully at the same time, was just *panic*.

Not hope.

Even if he felt what she did, that didn't mean it could…mean anything. Go anywhere. She wasn't suited to any of that. She was bad at communicating. She was hard, mean.

Unlovable.

But this wasn't about love. It couldn't be.

And still she didn't move away from his hand on her back, or the soft look in his eyes, or all that *yearning* welling up inside her.

They shouldn't be doing this here. Now. But he was to blame, and Axel didn't know how to stop it.

They had been ordered to stand down, and yes, his hand and cheek throbbed in a mind-numbing kind of pain that was perhaps exacerbating his lack of control.

So damn be it.

"There's more here between us. You know it. I know it. We've pretended there isn't for a long time, but it doesn't go away." He'd kept thinking it would, so much that it had become a habit. Just keep assuming they'd hit some magical point where it didn't feel like some invisible cord tethered them together. "It doesn't go away, Selena. So maybe we address that in the here and now."

She let out one of those shuddery breaths that seriously tested what little control he had left. She was a strong, poised, controlled woman who had almost never showed any signs of weakness in the four years he'd known her.

To see it now sent a powerful bolt of need through him, to match all the other needs tangled up inside him.

"I don't know what you expect to *address* about it." She even tried to lift her chin, do one of those go-to-hell looks she was so good at unleashing on the world. But it fell flat. The only thing it served to do was crack his leash on control.

"This." He hooked his good hand around her neck and pulled her up to meet his mouth. This kiss wasn't soft as hers had been. It spoke more of frustrated attraction than *care*, and any of the many reasons he'd held himself back for *years* dissolved. Into heat. Into need.

Into the strangest, most disorienting sensation that this was exactly what he'd been waiting for, when he hadn't known he'd been *waiting* for anything. Exactly what he needed when he prided himself on being quite self-sufficient. But they were locks clicking into place. Bodies made to fit together. Her and him. Just them.

She didn't resist. That wall was gone. No doubt she'd fought to keep it erected, but some things were meant to be destroyed, and some people were meant to do the destroying. Which was okay. He'd be careful, he promised himself that. No matter what happened, he wouldn't be what her ex had been. *No matter what.*

Her hands came up to his shoulders, her fingers digging into the tense muscles there, as she lifted to her toes and kissed him back with the same need and frustration he'd initiated the kiss with.

It wasn't possible to think about anything else except the feel of her mouth on his, her body pressed up against his. She was soft and sweet, underneath that outer shell of strength and steel. It was the combination, both twined into one woman, that made it feel like this was…unavoidable.

At *some* point the dam was going to break, no matter what they did. It just so happened, the time was now.

He slid his hand down the sexy curve of her back, urged her closer, as if there was any space left to be closer.

Even if one of their phones rang at this point, he didn't think they'd hear it. He certainly wouldn't care. Not when the taste of her melted through him, rearranged something inside him.

He gentled the kiss, not sure he could have articulated *why*, only that he wanted more than just heat and need. Something softer. More lasting. His hand traveled back up the length of her spine to rest on her neck once more. Light. He kissed her with a gentleness he hadn't known himself capable of, his fingers trailing up and down the side of her neck.

His entire body was heat and tension, twined with a pleasure so big and different, he was almost afraid of what came next. Not afraid enough to stop. No, he wanted to wade into this new *thing* and explore it until it was his whole existence.

But that was clearly a mistake, since she pulled her mouth away from his. He could feel the war inside her, because her fingers still dug into his shoulders. She'd found some semblance of reason, but it was fleeting.

He wanted to eradicate *all* sense of reason. Here. Now.

"This is a mistake," she breathed. She kept her gaze averted, her breath coming in uneven puffs. But she held on, and he held on to that.

He wished he could agree with her, make things easy on either of them, but the word *mistake* landed all wrong. A discordant note in a strange new world that was all harmonies. Her in his arms, kissing him with all she was… He could find no mistake in there. Maybe someday he would, but for now, it was only everything. "Selena." He gave her neck a gentle squeeze, trying to get her to look up at him. But she refused.

He pressed a kiss to her temple. "What part of this feels like a mistake?"

Her gaze whipped up to his, arrested. She opened her mouth as if she had an answer, and he braced himself for it.

But none came.

Chapter 14

Selena searched for an answer. An excuse. Anything she could throw at him, or convince herself to let go of him. Anything to douse the curling need inside her.

She tried to think about their assignment, about Opaline, about Peter, but nothing took hold. There was only this man who'd given her some understanding.

"It isn't a mistake," he said, his voice low and grave, like he was delivering bad news. And it *was* bad news. Terrible news. But he kissed her temple again, then her cheek, and no matter how she tried to hold on to the thought that it was bad, feelings crowded thoughts away.

It felt good. It felt right. He was right. Always had been.

She shook her head, trying to remind herself of all the ways this would end badly for her. "We shouldn't. Not here. Not now."

"Probably not," he agreed equitably, but his mouth

touched her neck, trailed down the slope of it, and all those protests and reasons and rational thought slid through her mind like smoke.

Her hands were still on his shoulders, holding tight, as she tilted her head to give his mouth better access to her neck. She'd never felt this… It wasn't just that haze of lust, or the want of companionship, touch. There was something deeper.

It scared the hell out of her, and had for a very long time, but he was carefully kissing his way through all her defenses, all her fears. When his mouth returned to hers, she was shaking. She'd have been embarrassed by that show of weakness if she could think straight. But his kisses were like a drug, his hand traveling her body a spell.

It hit her that this wasn't—couldn't be—Axel's norm. He was an agent who prided himself on control and professionalism, and he was shoving that to the side. For her. Because of her. With her.

In that realization, something cracked for her. And then him. The kiss became frenzied. The soft touches were gone, replaced by desperation. They pulled off each other's vests and tumbled to the floor. She tried to be careful of his injuries, but even with only one good hand, it seemed he touched her everywhere, stoking fires, driving this insanity to a fever pitch.

She managed to get his shirt off, then had to help him get hers off. They kicked off their pants, neither quite caring if they were fully divested as long as skin touched skin, body met body.

When they came together, a tangle of clothes and limbs, they both stilled.

"Finally," he murmured into her ear.

Finally. Finally. It echoed in her brain like a chant while he moved inside her, driving her to a waving crest of pleasure she would have thought impossible. But it pulsed through her like light. Like *right*.

She rolled on top of him, seeking more.

They found that more, that release, together.

Selena tried to roll off him, but he only rolled with her, not letting her go. She didn't know how to fight the need to cuddle into him, to hold on to this. She'd been fighting it for so long. *So* long. It had happened. What was the point of still fighting?

His breathing was heavy and steady, and while his arms were still tight around her, as though he hadn't fully drifted into sleep yet, she knew he was getting close. And if she let him fall asleep, she'd give in to the need to fall asleep. Tempting, but tangled in a mix of their clothes, half-naked on the floor of a stranger's cabin in the middle of an assignment, just wasn't going to work for her.

"Come on. You're dead on your feet. Let's get some rest." She wiggled out of his grasp and he finally let her.

He muttered something she couldn't understand, but she pulled her shirt and pants back on while he did the same. Then, with a hesitation that irritated her because it spoke to making this a bigger deal than it could be, she took his hand and led him to one of the bedrooms.

It was odd, using some other person's cabin as their own, but they both needed some food and some rest, and the strangers would be compensated. So, she had to get over her unease. She pulled the covers on the large bed back and gestured Axel to climb in.

He frowned at the bed, but she gave him a little push

and he obeyed. He yawned, fumbling with his phone. "Half hour should be good, yeah?"

"Yeah," she agreed, slightly amused at how he fumbled to set his alarm. She stood there. Her body was still warm and lax and relaxed, but her brain was whirling.

Until he reached out and took her hand. He scooted over in the bed, then pulled her down next to him. "Get some sleep, huh?" he murmured, tucking her firmly against him.

It felt so *nice* and *normal*, she wanted to cry. Instead she blinked back the tears and focused on keeping her breathing even. She thought about it—*in, out, slow, calm*—rather than all of the other emotions tumbling through her head.

Axel was asleep in seconds, each moment the tight hold he had on her loosening until it finally went lax. She slid out of his arms and off the bed, pausing to make sure he didn't stir.

He'd set his alarm for thirty minutes. She shook her head. That was hardly long enough after he'd been shot. She carefully took his phone and turned off the alarm. Then she slid out of the room.

She'd eat something, do a little work, then slide back into bed before Axel woke up. Maybe she'd catch a fifteen-minute nap. Let him think she'd slept longer.

Out in the kitchen, Selena poked through the cabinets. She didn't allow herself to think about what had transpired on the floor. It had been…stress relief. A blip. They'd go back to normal.

Her stomach flipped as she thought of the way he'd tucked her against him in bed. Why couldn't she have that with someone she didn't work with?

Because no one would do a very good job of un-

derstanding your job, or your strengths, without doing similar work.

"I really don't need that kind of clarity right now, self," she muttered. She found peanut butter and a frozen loaf of bread. She took a few slices out, used the toaster to thaw them, then went to work making peanut butter sandwiches.

When her phone buzzed, she pulled it out of her pocket and answered without looking at the caller. "Lopez," she said quietly so she didn't wake Axel. She licked peanut butter off her thumb as only silence greeted her.

"Selena," Opaline's voice finally ventured. It sounded scratchy and weak.

Selena blinked. She hadn't expected a call from her sister. She didn't know what to do with it when…

"I asked Alana to let me call you and tell you everything rather than you getting it from her," Opaline continued. Selena wasn't sure she'd ever heard her sister sound so…beaten down.

"All right," Selena managed, feeling as though her heart was in a vise.

"I wasn't helping Peter. I need you to know that up front. He thought I was, but I didn't give him any information. I wasn't going to. I just thought if he trusted me, he might tell me what was going on and I might be able to…make sure he didn't end up dead."

"But you didn't tell anyone."

Opaline let out a noisy breath. "No, I didn't. I didn't… I just thought it would be better if I handled it so…"

"So we didn't get involved and use him to end this?"

Selena demanded, though she couldn't find her usual anger with her sister.

"I just wanted him to be safe," Opaline whispered.

Selena swallowed. The usual wave of frustration and anger didn't materialize. Selena wanted the same thing. She tried to pretend she didn't. Tried to be over Peter. Tried to blame Opaline for bringing up those feelings she wanted buried. But no matter how she tried, he was still that little boy to her, and she knew that was true for Opaline.

Opaline had been wrong, but she'd done it out of love and care. Love and care. Selena hadn't put much stock in those things in a very long time. Too often, they burned.

Axel's words had dug their way into her soul, though. *If you never face the things that haunt you, Selena, they eat you alive.* She didn't want to be eaten alive anymore. So it was time to stop burying, fighting, ignoring. Selena sucked in a breath. Being truthful, vulnerable with Opaline felt a bit like asking someone to shoot her in the face.

But maybe it was better to face the pain and the hurt, rather than to keep running from the things she couldn't outrun. "I don't blame you," Selena managed.

"You...don't?"

"You made a mistake. You shouldn't have done it. But I can't blame you. I know you want to help him and he's... He's our brother."

Opaline was quiet on the other end for a while. She clearly didn't know what to say to Selena's change of heart. "Alana's sending me home. I don't know what's going to happen. She said she has to think about it, but I'm not allowed back until she makes her decision."

Selena shouldn't feel sorry for Opaline. She'd made

a very big mistake, but maybe instead of holding everything against her family, she could start…cutting them a break. No, not even that. Stop feeling guilty for *wanting* to cut them a break. Maybe she didn't need to hate herself for never fully being able to harden her heart to Peter and Opaline.

"We'll figure it out. We will." And Selena knew Opaline was their best chance to find something when it came to digging through digital files and information. "But while I'm finishing this, I need you to do me a favor. You can do all that tech stuff you usually do from home, can't you?"

"Not all of it, but some of it."

"Keep researching Bernard McNally. He's the key to all this."

"But what am I supposed to do if I find anything? Alana won't like me…butting my nose in."

"If the ends justify the means, she'll be hard-pressed to hold it against you. You find anything, you email it to *all* of us. Immediately. Okay?"

"O-okay. I guess. Okay. It'll help?"

"I think so."

"Okay. Yeah, I won't sleep till I find something."

Selena breathed out slowly. "And we'll get through this, Opaline. I promise." Because it was time to stop fighting her demons through her family members, and instead work on fighting them together.

"I am sorry, Selena. Really."

There was more to say, but now wasn't the time to say it. "I'm going to do everything I can, okay?" *For both of you.* She always had, but she'd kept it under wraps. Under a layer of blame and guilt. "And when this is all over, we should talk. Really talk."

"Then I guess you'll have to make sure you don't get yourself killed."

"I'll do my best."

"I know we...don't see eye to eye. I know... I've been blaming you, but we're both to blame."

"We are. I agree."

"I love you anyway," Opaline whispered fiercely.

Selena didn't think she would have been able to accept that even a day ago. But something inside her had changed today. "I love you anyway too. 'Bye, Opaline."

"'Bye."

Selena ended the call and closed her eyes, breathing carefully through all the emotional upheaval. When this was over, she'd give herself leave to cry, but for now, she had to stay in control. She had to get this done.

She forced herself to eat, though she didn't feel hungry. She hunted up a plate and put the other sandwich on it and returned to the bedroom Axel was sleeping in.

She put the plate next to his phone on the nightstand and stared down at him in the inky dark. He looked no less strong or big in sleep. In a stranger's bed. He looked more like a statue, something carved to bring out the best features of the subject.

Except his best feature was that good heart of his, and it was definitely going to get her into trouble.

She shook her head and pulled her phone out of her pocket, setting her own alarm for thirty minutes. It'd give him over an hour and her a quick, refreshing nap. Then it would be back to work.

She stared at the bed. Back to work. Except she'd broken all her personal rules with this man, and the way her heart was still all *fluttery*, it really was *all* her personal rules. But that would have to be dealt with later,

on her own time. For now, she slid into a stranger's bed,
next to Axel Morrow, and slept.

Axel woke up disoriented and starving. His hand and
face throbbed, but it only took him a second or two for
his brain to lurch into gear. to remember where he was.
What had occurred.

He was in a stranger's bed and there was a woman
beside him. She was curled away from him, her dark po-
nytail a tangled mess on the pillowcase. Her body rose
and fell with the slow, steady rhythm of her breathing.

Axel rubbed a hand over his chest where a tight sensation seemed lodged. He'd crossed a few lines he'd
never imagined he'd cross, and he didn't even know how
to feel badly about it. It had built up too long.

Timing was a hell of a thing.

But it wasn't simple, that was for sure. He wasn't con-
ceited enough to think she'd wake up ready and willing to just *be together*. No, that wasn't Selena's way.
She might have given in for a moment, but she'd build
that wall back.

And you'll just have to tear it down again.

There was a part of him that didn't want to. That
wanted to let her build her barriers, and step back into
his own walls. They were comfortable. He figured he
was a little more aware of his than Selena was of hers
if only because he'd had to deal with a lot of his stuff
head-on and she'd clearly avoided, denied and compart-
mentalized her stuff. But awareness didn't mean a person didn't *like* the safety of their own walls.

But there was something here, something he didn't
fully understand and didn't have the time to parse, that

made returning to the way they'd been ignoring each other seem impossible.

She would not agree.

Carefully, he swung out of bed. He frowned at his phone. He'd set the alarm for… He glanced at the woman fast asleep next to him. She'd turned it off. He might have scowled, but he was more interested in the sandwich next to his cell. Peanut butter wouldn't have been his first pick, but it was better than the trail food he had in his pack.

He tucked his phone under his good arm, used his good hand to grab the sandwich and left the plate behind as he quietly moved out of the bedroom. He downed the sandwich, dumped his cell on the couch, then frowned.

She'd turned his alarm off so he could sleep longer. She'd clearly taken the time to make sandwiches, to clean up after herself. He'd bet money on her having done some work too.

"Two can play that game," he muttered. He went back into the room, careful that his footfall was silent and that he moved like a ghost. He picked up her phone from the nightstand on her side of the bed and typed in the department code. He turned off her alarm.

See how she liked it.

He didn't let himself linger. They would, at some point, hash this all out. Linger in some of the feelings they'd indulged, but this assignment needed to be finished first. He'd make sure it was soon.

Back in the living room, he decided to make himself comfortable and then do some of his own digging. They'd gotten some new information on all the players, and if Axel could take some time to really comb through it, he might be able to come up with deeper profiles of

the three men who'd escaped. It wouldn't magically
explain what the endgame was until they understood
more about Bernard, but it would help predict Leonard
and Peter's movements.

It wasn't too much later when Selena's alarm was
supposed to go off, that he heard a quiet, irritable curse
and grinned. He was smart enough to wipe the grin off
his face as he heard her shuffling around, then walking
out of the room. He looked down at his phone and pretended to be absorbed in the information on his screen.

"You turned off my alarm," she accused.

"You turned off mine first." He slowly looked up, and
then wished he hadn't. She was…rumpled. Even on the
trail she tried to look if not sleek, put together. Rum-
pled Selena made something painful in his chest catch.

They stayed there, regarding each other, both clearly
grappling with emotions. He didn't think Selena was
ready to let hers go, and maybe he wasn't either, because he didn't press the matter.

She swallowed hard. "Before we focus on work, we
should clear the air."

"Clear the air?" Axel repeated blandly, though nothing inside him felt particularly *bland* at the way she was
obviously trying to handle him. Put him into one of her
neat little compartments.

I don't think so.

"You won't tell anyone about this."

He tried very hard not to be offended she was *ordering* him not to tell anyone, like he was some randy teenager who'd spread it across school after prom. Or worse,
her ex, who'd used a relationship against her in her job.

"Look, I'm not saying you're going to be like my ex
or anything," she said as if reading his mind. She even

waved a flippant hand, but there was nothing flippant in her eyes. Anxiety and maybe even a little fear. Because some wounds certainly hadn't healed yet.

"I just don't think guys fully understand what it means for a woman. You tell the boys, and things change for me."

Maybe he should let her have her delusions, but surely she understood... "They're going to know, Selena. They're all going to know." She paled, so he hurried on. "Our *friends* are highly trained observers. They're going to see something between us changed."

"It was just once. There's nothing to—"

He stood then, because if he moved maybe he could control his reaction. "Like hell it was."

Chapter 15

Selena's pulse pounded in her neck. Which was stupid, of course. She'd faced down men with guns and all manner of criminals. She wasn't afraid of Axel, of the feelings twirling inside her.

Of everything, some little voice in the back of her mind whispered.

No. She would not be afraid. "Look—"

"No, before you insult me, I want you to think about what you're saying."

"I have thought about what I'm saying," she snapped as he approached her. How could she think about anything else? When she was *supposed* to be thinking about everything else. And how could he want...

Me.

She swallowed at the lump in her throat. She wanted to tell him the truth. *All* her truths, but she couldn't do that and then turn it off and do her job. So, this just couldn't… It just…

Axel fitted his palm to her cheek, and his eyes were too much. She wasn't a coward, but she couldn't quite meet his gaze and stay…strong. She needed to be strong. She had a *job* to do.

"There's something here," he said quietly. "We could go back to ignoring it, but I don't think we'd last as long as we did the first time around. Not knowing how right it feels."

She felt absolutely lost at sea and hated that feeling, that weakness. His bandaged hand came to her other cheek, and it felt like an anchor. How could she let him be her anchor? Hadn't she learned she didn't get one of those?

"Maybe we both need some time to think about it," he said gently. "What it means. How it looks. What we want."

She nodded, a little too fervently, but God, she wanted time. *Needed* time. Away from him, and she wasn't going to get that any time soon.

His hands fell away from her face, and she didn't know why it made her feel downright bereft.

"I've been thinking about the three of them," Axel said, going back to the couch and his phone and his completely normal way of acting. "How they're connected. Why they'd have left together."

She would have been devastated that he could change channels so quickly, so easily, but he rubbed a hand over his chin, something he only ever did when he was agitated.

Thank God.

She let out a long breath, working to change gears

too. Later. They would deal with them later. She didn't look forward to it, but at least it gave her the space to breathe.

"You have Leonard," he said, taking a seat on the couch. "A loner for all intents and purposes. Steve, a serial group criminal. He never did anything alone. Then you have Peter…"

"Who desperately wanted to be part of a group." She stood where she was, across the living room. Physical distance would be best for as long as she could manage it.

Axel nodded. "I think Steven and Peter were the group. Friends. Partners. Whatever. Leonard needs more than one guy—for reasons yet to be determined—so he goes to Steve, and Steve makes a case for Peter to go with them. Leonard needs men, so he says okay."

"Then why would Steve go through with killing Peter?"

"Because Leonard told him to. Leonard's the leader. Steve isn't a leader. He does what he's told. He *likes* doing what he's told. Or should I say, *wasn't* a leader, *liked* doing what he was told."

She heard the guilt in his tone. Even though he hadn't killed Steve, who was nothing but a criminal to Axel, he hadn't worked through the blame he felt. She didn't understand why he'd hold himself responsible. She wouldn't *let* him hold himself responsible. "You shouldn't feel guilty."

"Guilt's a tricky thing. I've learned how to deal with it, but it takes time. Luckily I've got about twenty-five plus years' worth of learning to take that time."

Twenty-five plus… Surely he didn't mean the murder of his family. But more than twenty-five would have put him at a child and… "But you couldn't possibly feel guilty about what happened to your family."

"Of course I did."

"You were seven."

"And I was there. I really have…moved on from that. It took a lot of therapy and maturing and whatnot, but… The thing about guilt is it allows you to think there was some way to make the world make sense, if you'd only moved through the right steps. Things wouldn't be this bad, you wouldn't have to feel this awful, but at some point you have to accept you had no power."

It shouldn't hit close to home. Not when he was talking about his family being murdered around him and she'd just had to survive some family drama and betrayal, but something about his words made things in her chest shift, rearrange. Things that had been heavy and uncomfortable for a very long time.

"Sometimes the world is just…not fair for random reasons you couldn't have predicted or changed or fixed. No matter what you think about that situation, you have to live with the effects. There's no going back." He looked up at her. "I think you might understand the guilt thing a little more than you're willing to acknowledge."

She wanted to be something instead of more wrapped up in him. But he understood. Even though his childhood had been so much more tragic than hers, he didn't act like he won the bad childhood Olympics. He put them on the same level of understanding and didn't make her feel small.

He made her feel understood. She'd never wanted that. Still didn't. Or so she tried to convince herself.

"There's a lot of guilt involved for kids of broken homes," he said gently.

"Broken homes," she echoed. "It wasn't…broken."

"Your father had an affair that resulted in a child, which, once the news got out, caused your parents to divorce. You had two families, parents who used all three of you as pawns, death, uncertainty and emotional upheaval. No one looked out for you guys."

"We looked out for each other."

"Not good enough. Sorry. Kids aren't emotionally capable of handling all that with aplomb."

"I don't know what this has to do—"

"Peter is a part of that dysfunction. He's searching for the remedy. The thing that fills the holes it created. You went into law enforcement, and so did Opaline, in a way. That didn't fit for him, or he didn't want it to. So, he's looking for the thing that balances the scales."

She didn't like him reading everything so easily. Putting her family into neat little packages. Especially since he was right. "I really don't like when you put on your profiler hat."

He smiled a little. "Noted."

"But if he's…searching," Selena said, thinking of her conversation with Opaline. "He can still be reached. He isn't a lost cause."

"No, I don't think Peter is." Axel tapped his fingers on his leg. "You want to talk to him."

Selena nodded. "A note? A text message? Something. If he knew… If he knew he had some place to belong, even if he had to go to jail for what he'd done…"

"I'd leave the last part out of it and go with the first part."

"So you agree?"

"Sort of," Axel said, pulling a face. "But I think—

and you don't know how much I hate myself for thinking this—you need to do it face-to-face."

Undiluted shock crossed her expression before she blanked it out. "How do we manage that?" she asked, sounding like she'd put her agent hat back on.

"First, we have to catch up to them. Separate them somehow."

"You're really going to..." She didn't finish her sentence, just studied him with her eyebrows drawn so hard together her entire forehead puckered.

"It was your idea," he pointed out.

"Right, but to separate them, *we're* going to have to separate. Which, you know, you got shot up the last time we did that."

He frowned a little. "I'd hardly call it *shot up*."

"Well, whatever you'd call it, I'm having a hard time wrapping my head around you thinking it's a good idea."

"It's not. It's kind of terrible." He wished he could lie to her, pretend this wasn't *about* her, but there was no point wasting energy to lie. "I agree with you that Peter isn't a lost cause. And there aren't a lot of ways not to shove him into lost cause territory. So, we have to get him away from Leonard and into your orbit. I think we can do that without splitting up. If we come up with a good plan."

Selena seemed to mull that over. She looked around the room, then went over to the kitchen and grabbed something off the counter. She returned with a little pad of paper and a pen.

She drew some circles and some x's. "If we get close enough to everyone," she said, pointing at the circles, "we can use them to create a diversion to Leonard, while I approach Peter and you can be my backup," she said pointing to the x's.

Axel considered it as Blanca padded into the room. She sniffed Selena, then came over to him and rested her head on his leg. "Your dog loves me."

She grunted irritably. "My dog *pities* you and your mangled hand."

It was Axel's turn to grunt irritably. "The plan is solid," he said after working it around in his mind. "But we'll need to get back out there. I imagine they'll stop to rest at night, but we don't know for sure."

Selena nodded, but before they could begin to pack up and move out, both their phones vibrated.

"Alana," they both said together.

Selena blew out a breath and then took a seat next to him. They both held up their phones for the videoconference that was about to happen.

The entire team popped onto their screens. Everyone except Opaline.

"I wanted to give everyone an update," Alana said without preamble. "And get any new information from the team, if there is any."

"I've done a deeper profile of the two remaining men we're dealing with," Axel said to the screen. "I'll be sending it over momentarily. Bottom line, Leonard is the leader of this whole organization, no doubt. Peter Lopez is a pawn at best. I don't think he's dangerous."

Alana's face was expressionless, but Axel felt a bit like an insect being sized up. "You're sure about this?"

And he realized Alana suspected, just a little, that Selena or his feelings for Selena might have impaired his judgment. It would have been insulting if he weren't a little worried about it himself. Still, he was a good profiler. A good agent. He'd connected the dots. "The facts support it, Alana."

When Alana said nothing, Axel continued with his theories. "My primary concern is why Leonard, someone who clearly prefers to work alone, took two men with him to escape prison. Being on his own would have been quicker and been easier to avoid detection. Especially in the wilderness."

"It has to connect to the brother," Selena told the team. "None of their choices make sense unless they're working for someone else, who's working toward a goal we don't understand."

"I agree," Carly said.

"Same," Aria chimed in. "Hiking through this weather is no joke, and I don't think they're stupid enough to think it would be."

"But we're hitting a brick wall on the brother," Max said, frustration simmering in his tone. "Unless Opaline's found something?"

"Opaline has been taken off the case until further notice," Alana said briskly. "Amanda is doing some digging while also finding someone who can replace Opaline for the time being."

A silence descended. No one asked why, but Axel slid a glance at Selena. She didn't look surprised, only a little sad. As if she'd already been informed that Opaline was off the case.

"Axel and I were discussing the need to move," Selena said, all business. "We've rested. Refueled. Blanca's ready to go. We tighten the circle, all of us. Instead of pushing them toward you guys, we all tighten."

"In the dark?" Carly questioned.

"Yeah, in the dark. We don't know what they're planning, or why they're doing this now. Let's not give them the chance to show us. How long do you think it will take if we all start moving in?"

"A couple hours," Max said.

"So, we move out now. In a couple hours, our circle is tight enough to apprehend both Leonard and Peter, and then one of them will surely be able to turn over on whatever this Bernard McNally is up to."

"They're armed and dangerous," Max pointed out. "We have to acknowledge the fact we may need to use deadly force, *especially* in the dark. In which case we wouldn't get any information."

Axel kept himself from looking for Selena's reaction out of sheer force of will. "Like I said, Leonard's armed and dangerous. Peter isn't. We'll try to split them up as Selena and I come up the rear. We'll want you guys to the north to see if you can get Leonard to follow one path, while we try to get Peter to come back to us."

There was a silence that spoke of dissension, or at least doubt, but no one voiced it. They were trusting Axel to make the call.

Anxiety tightened his chest, but he breathed it away. It *was* the right call. The facts supported the theories, and yeah, feelings were involved, but feelings weren't always the enemy.

"You all have your plan," Alana said, her voice cool and calm and authoritative, but Axel noted a hint of strain in her eyes and figured it had to do with Opaline's choices. "I agree the brother, Bernard, is the missing piece, and we're working on finding it. You'll all be notified immediately of what we find. Make sure you use the walkies once you're in range of each other.

Communication is key. It goes without saying we want to avoid loss of life, but if we can't find anything on Bernard McNally on our end, apprehending Leonard Koch and Peter Lopez alive is going to be of the utmost importance to figure this mess out."

Selena let out a slow breath, clearly relieved Alana's orders prioritized keeping everyone alive.

"Let's get this done and get you all home," Alana said firmly.

Everyone agreed and hung up. Axel scratched Blanca's silky ears. "Back out into the cold," he murmured.

Chapter 16

Back out in the cold was right. Night was falling and the temperature was dropping. After their few hours in the nice, heated cabin, in an actual bed, no less, it felt like a cruel slap to be back hiking through the snow.

Still, there was a clear plan now. An end in sight. God, Selena hoped.

They had to hike back to where they'd been when Axel had been shot, then hope Blanca could pick up a scent in the snow. Selena still had the glove from the very first cabin, but it'd be better if Blanca could pick up something new.

"You knew about Opaline," Axel said without preamble as they walked with only the light of his headlamp and her flashlight to guide them.

It didn't *sound* accusing, but she felt accused. Still, she tried to keep her response easy rather than defensive. She didn't have anything to be defensive about. "She called while you were sleeping. With Alana's permission."

"And you didn't think to mention it?"

Selena was glad to be in the dark, because she visibly winced. Maybe she should have told him, but her thoughts had been on ending this. "We were focusing on what was next. It didn't come up. I would have, but Alana mentioned it first."

"But didn't explain. And you'll note, no one asked her to."

"Yeah, because as you pointed out, we're all agents highly trained in observation. I'm guessing they knew it had to do with Peter. They didn't need to ask." And Selena couldn't help but wonder if they found Selena *herself* suspect now too, by association. Maybe the only thing keeping her on the case was being paired with Axel.

Maybe she'd been paired with Axel for *exactly* that reason. She couldn't be trusted with her half brother being one of the escapees no matter what Alana claimed.

"Your brain's working so hard, I can hear it," Axel said, not unkindly. "No one's blaming you, Selena. I doubt anyone's blaming Opaline. The thing about being in law enforcement is it isn't our job to be judge and jury. Your coworkers and friends are going to wait until they have the whole story."

Selena hoped that was true. She wanted to believe it was. She puffed a breath out into the cold. "I don't know what to do with these doubts," she muttered. "I feel like a rookie all over again."

"Dealing with a case that involves your family isn't exactly easy." Before she could be offended or doubt even harder, he continued, "That doesn't mean I think you don't belong here. It just means it's a more complicated situation, and that means it's going to have extra challenges. I happen to have all the faith in the world that you can meet them."

It shouldn't mean so much to her, but it did. His faith. His reassurance. Whether she'd been assigned with him as partner to make sure her association with Peter didn't affect her choices or not, she was glad she'd been partnered with him.

Sex aside, and it had been really good sex.

And it was really not the time to think about it.

"Now, what happened with Opaline?" he asked, gently.

She told him about her phone call with her sister. What Opaline had said. She thought about leaving out the part where she told Opaline to keep investigating Bernard, but then thought better of it. He was her partner out here. She had to trust him and...

She did. He understood her in a way she didn't think anyone in her life did. She cared about him, God help her. And she had to figure out a way to believe he cared about her too. Because Axel Morrow was not a careless man. He didn't do or say things he didn't *mean*.

He wasn't perfect, by any means, but he was a good man.

And once this was all over, maybe she'd figure out what that meant for her, but for right now, she had a job to do.

"Alana didn't fire her right away."

"I'm sure that's a process with a lot of red tape," Selena replied, trying not to let hope choke her.

"Sure, but she would have given Opaline some kind

of notice. Just sending her home? I think she's hoping to find a way to just do a suspension or a write-up or something. Which would make sense. This was a specific set of circumstances. Ones that likely won't repeat themselves."

"God, I hope so."

He chuckled at that. They made their way to where he'd last seen the three men. It had been taped off by local authorities and Steve's body had been removed. She could see Axel staring at where Steve's body had been while she worked with Blanca to pick up the scent of their escapees.

She understood Axel too. That was the thing that couldn't be ignored or shoved away no matter how much she tried.

Axel held himself responsible for things. He'd learned how to work through that, but it was a process for him. Of letting that responsibility go. She understood that, because she knew it was something she needed to do when it came to her family.

"He was a man who was going to get himself killed one way or another, Axel," Selena said quietly as she let Blanca sniff around the area, trying to find the right scent. "By his own choices. I know you know that, but I think it helps to hear someone else say it too."

"It does," he said, finally looking away from where Steve's body had been. He didn't look at her, she figured because his headlamp would blind her. But he came to stand next to her. They watched Blanca work, but as they did, his gloved hand slid into hers, their fingers curling together quite naturally.

It felt good and right, and yeah, a little scary, but

Selena was used to fear and facing it on the job. Maybe it was time to start applying that to her personal life too.

"One step closer," Axel said quietly as Blanca sniffed a particular spot, and then another, in the way she did when she was getting ready to move. "Eventually, we'll have taken all the steps."

"And then what?" Selena asked.

Axel inhaled. She could tell he wasn't so sure and certain as he liked to pretend. But the pretending gave her some measure of comfort.

"I guess you should come over for dinner."

She wrinkled her nose. "Like…at your farm?"

"Yeah, like at my farm. A dinner, like a date. And maybe some advice on what kind of dog to get. You can bring Blanca and the wine. I'll handle the food."

"Are you seriously…asking me out on a date right here in the middle of the night on assignment?"

"Seems like. So?"

She wanted to laugh, and it felt good to want that. "So, I guess we have to take that one step and then another to get to that bridge."

Axel nodded, and in the faint glow of their lights, she could see his mouth curve. "I guess we should hurry up then."

This time Selena really did laugh. And though her toes were about frozen through, the rest of her felt warm, and it all centered on where Axel's hand held hers.

After a few more minutes, Blanca gave a short yip. "She's got the scent," Selena announced once Blanca gave the signal.

Axel nodded. "Then, let's move."

He dropped her hand, and that felt like a loss. Especially as they walked and walked and walked in silence, in the dark, and the cold dug deeper and deeper. They listened to the sounds of the night around them and just kept walking no matter how cold or dark it got.

She wasn't sure how many hours they'd walked when Axel held up a hand and pointed to his beam of light in the snow. Footprints. *Clear* footprints.

Selena gave Blanca a touch command to stop, then crouched down to study the footprints with her flashlight. Clear indentations with no sign of the wind softening the edges. The pair couldn't be too far ahead of them. She explained that to Axel, and he nodded.

"I wish we could wait for daylight," Axel muttered. "Too many things can go wrong in the dark."

"Thanks for the pep talk, boss," Selena returned in the same quiet voice.

He gave her a slight grin in the odd light of his headlamp. "Follow?"

She nodded. They couldn't wait for daylight. They simply couldn't wait. This had to end. Because the more it dragged on, the less chance of survival Peter had.

"We stay completely radio silent. I lead, then you and Blanca follow. If we caught up to them, that means they took a rest. By the way these footprints look, I'd say they're back on the move."

Axel pulled out his phone and typed in a message, likely telling the other agents what they'd found while also pinning it on the map, so they kept their circle around the right area. Once he was done, he nodded at her flashlight. "We stay close. We only need one light. Mine's hands-free."

"Mine's easier to turn off if we need to go dark. Plus,

it makes a pretty darn good weapon in a fight. You turn yours off and follow me."

She could tell he didn't like that, but after an internal struggle, he clicked off his lamp. He got behind her. Selena gave Blanca the quiet orders to follow Axel rather than search. The footsteps would be all she needed for right now.

She felt the usual calm wash over her. This was her job. She was good at it. Peter aside, she knew what she was doing with a flashlight in one hand and a gun in the other tracking something. Dark or light, she knew how to come out on the other side of an assignment with all her goals achieved.

The calm led to confidence, and the confidence reminded her that she was a good agent. Maybe she'd been a crappy sister, and maybe she was an uncertain... *whatever* with Axel, but this was something she knew how to do.

She saw bobbing lights ahead and clicked off her flashlight.

"Walkies on," Axel whispered.

They both shrugged off their packs and pulled out the walkies and earpieces. If everyone was in range, they'd be able to move forward. Selena fastened hers to her vest so it was in easy reach. She had to help Axel with his since his right hand was incapacitated and his vest was under his coat.

She didn't let that shake her. He could still shoot with his left, and if everything went the way it should, there would be no shooting needed. Axel with only one good hand was still better than half the agents she knew with both hands in good shape.

They both turned their walkies on and kept their

voices low enough not to echo across the quiet forest night.

"Team three in range," Axel said quietly into his comm unit.

"Team two in range," came the first reply.

"Team one in range."

"We want a split," Axel instructed. "Two different diversions. Bigger one from teams one and two. Smaller one from three, so ideally the two escapees split. Team one and two should be designed to attract Koch, and team three set to attract the smaller threat of Lopez."

"We'll turn on all our lights," Aria said. "Between the four of us, it should attract enough attention for them to move closer. Try to determine how many we've got."

"Good, and Selena and I will try to have a conversation that's overheard. We'll take our earpieces out, let the walkie static give us away."

Selena thought about what Axel had told her about Leonard ordering Steve to shoot Peter rather than do it himself. It might have had to do with Steve being the one to convince him to bring Peter, but Selena wondered if it had to do more with power. Or even not wanting to be the person accused of murder. "He'll send Peter toward the voices and tell him to take care of them, yeah?"

Axel nodded. "I think so. He might not come for the lights, but he's not going to come for the voices either. He'll send a subordinate. So, with your lights on, team one and two move in on Koch. We'll stay where we are and try to draw Lopez out."

"Clear," Max's voice said, the other team echoed his clear.

Axel nodded at Selena. They took their earpieces out and adjusted the walkie volume low, so the sound might

also draw Peter without being loud enough for someone to make out the words unless they were very close.

"We'll want our conversation to be about Leonard,"
Axel said. "I think the more we talk about getting him,
the more likely he'll be to send Peter to check it out."

"He wouldn't come himself?"

Axel shook his head. "Overhearing the conversation with Leonard, Steve and Peter was more enlight-
ening than any profile could be. I could hear what he
said and the way he said it. The way he interacted with
the other men. He liked wielding his power. He wants
to feel in charge. Like whoever is following him has to
jump when he says jump."

Out in the woods, lights began to pop on. Flashlights,
clearly carving out swaths of light. It was time to act.
Axel started walking toward the center of the circle
they'd determined on their maps, motioning Selena to
follow. Blanca trotted behind them, still heeding Selena's earlier command to follow.

"I think it's interesting Leonard has clearly taken
great pains to distance himself from the brother," Axel
said. He didn't shout it, didn't even sound particularly
loud, but she could tell he was projecting.

"Are we supposed to be scared of this brother of his?"
Selena improvised. "Seems like a penny-ante thief if
you ask me. What was on his record? Like one arrest?"

Axel grinned at her. "Agree. My expert profiling
skills tell me he's just another weak, ineffectual criminal. Not even sure he's worth the jail time or all this effort. But we might as well check it out while we're here."

She pretended to roll her eyes at his boast at expert
profiling skills.

"I've got a visual through the night-vision device,"

Max's voice said from the walkie. "They're arguing. Leonard's pointing in your direction. Keep it up, whatever you're doing. I think he's going to send Peter your way."

They continued to disparage Bernard, sometimes throwing in a few scathing remarks about Leonard's intelligence. The relationship between Bernard and Leonard beyond brothers of some sort was a mystery, but Axel threw in a few made-up criticisms of Bernard that wouldn't give away how little they knew about the mystery man.

From what Axel understood about Leonard, he wouldn't stand for it. But he'd want someone else to do the work. He wanted to be the head honcho, not the minion.

"Coming your way," Aria said over the walkie. "We're closing in on Leonard."

"Once you're in place, you'll wait for my signal," Axel ordered. They needed to play this carefully. So Peter didn't bolt, so Leonard didn't have a chance to call for reinforcements. But most importantly, so no one got hurt.

Selena made a hand motion that had Blanca sitting on her haunches in the snow. She leaned into him, whispered into his ear. "Listen."

Axel held himself still and did just that. The snap of a twig. A little sigh of breath. So, Peter wasn't carrying a flashlight or anything to help him move through the dark, but he was definitely coming for them.

"You should stay here," Selena said quietly, clearly not trying to be overhead now. "Out of sight with Blanca. So he thinks it's just me."

"He heard both of us."

"I know, but you said yourself I should talk to him alone. I'm not saying you should go away, just stay put. I'll keep my flashlight on, you'll keep us in sight."

"And what do you plan to do?"

"Just try to talk to him. Maybe I can get him to surrender without a fight. I take him, the team of four takes Leonard. Everyone's safe."

Axel hissed out a breath, realizing belatedly he'd curled his injured hand into a fist.

"If he didn't have anything to do with the string of murders…"

Selena trailed off and Axel knew he didn't have to remind her that it was a big *if*.

"Just stay here."

She said it like an order, but there was a question in the way she paused. Axel gave a slight nod. "No more than twenty yards, Lopez. No more."

She began to immediately move. Blanca whined next to Axel, and Axel felt a bit like doing the same. He just wasn't sure this was the right course of action, but he knew Selena needed it. She needed this chance, and she was a good enough agent to know that if it didn't work out, if Peter wasn't persuaded, she'd take him down.

Maybe not with as much force as she would have for a man who wasn't related to her, but she'd still do it. Axel had to believe she would.

Axel kept his eyes on the light, moving carefully in the dark of the woods. She took her time, which gave him some comfort. She wasn't hurrying in, guns blazing, trying to play hero to everyone. She was taking precautions.

His phone buzzed in his pocket, and Axel pulled it

out, figuring it would be Alana with an important update on Bernard or even Leonard. He fumbled a bit trying to answer with his bandaged hand, but he wasn't
about to put his gun down.

"Morrow."

"Didn't want to put this out over the walkie," Max's
voice said, low and determined. "But I can get in place
to take Peter out should the need arise. Just as a pre-
caution."

Axel trusted Max's judgment, but it just didn't feel
right. He wasn't one hundred percent happy with Selena
over there meeting up with Peter, but a sniper in place
felt all wrong. "We want them alive."

"We want us alive too."

"Six of us, two of them. We don't need a sniper."

"Selena is awfully close. It wouldn't take much for
him to take her hostage, or worse."

"He's not going to hurt her."

"How do you know? I've seen family members do a
lot worse than just hurt each other. Haven't you?"

"I've got a gun and I'm closer than you four. If Peter
tries something, I can take care of it. That's why I'm
here." Of course, he didn't have the night-vision devices
the rest of the team had or his best hand available. Still,
he trusted Selena to handle this. And if Leonard started
toward them, the rest of the team would stop him.

"I'm just saying it wouldn't hurt—"

Axel cut him off. "Sometimes you listen to your gut,
Max. A sniper in place is asking for trouble we don't
want. Stick with the team and arrest Leonard."

There was a slight pause, as if Max was determining what exactly to say. When he finally spoke, Axel

knew it was as a friend, not as a coworker. "*Is* it your gut? Or is it something else?"

It landed like the jab it was, though Axel knew it was concern not accusation. Axel couldn't help but entertain the doubt Max's words brought up. Was he letting something happen because of his feelings for Selena?

But he had to reject that thought. "If this was about that something else, I'd have her locked up in a room while I took care of everything. I'm not going to pretend I didn't have the urge, but we need information, and with Steve Jenson dead, Peter is going to be the best source of that. We can't just think about apprehension—we have to think about handling this in a way that creates an open-and-shut trial."

Max was silent for a few humming seconds again. "All right," he eventually acquiesced.

"Focus on Leonard. We know they were trying to get across the border. They had to be meeting someone there. We have to make sure whoever is waiting for them won't get antsy and come get them. And we have to make sure we can keep Leonard from taking Peter out if he thinks Peter's going to give us information."

"Got it," Max said. "Take care of yourself."

"You too."

Axel was about to shove his phone back in his pocket, but it buzzed again, a text from Opaline that read, UR-GENT. Axel read the rest of the message, his stomach sinking as though it had turned to lead.

Bernard McNally. Think he's a serial cop killer. Emailing the evidence. BE CAREFUL.

He could see she'd sent the message to everyone. The entire team on the ground, Alana and Amanda, as well.

Axel didn't have time to read the email or the evidence. He looked up at Selena. Her light hadn't moved in a few minutes. He followed where it pointed, and though it didn't illuminate much from this distance, he thought he could make out a pair of shoes in the beam.

She'd found Peter and was talking to him.

"Lopez, we've got a situation," he said into his walkie.

"I thought Opaline was off the case," Carly said, her voice followed by a blast of static. "What's this text and email about? Should we really—"

"Someone tell me what the email says," Axel interrupted, keeping his gaze focused on Selena. Had she turned off her walkie? She certainly wasn't responding as she talked with Peter.

"Opaline tied each of his aliases she found with the murder of a police officer," Aria said, clearly skimming the email and giving the main points. "She says the cases have a pattern. He started with small-town, low-level sheriff's deputies, then moved up to bigger cities, higher ranks." Even over the walkie Axel caught Aria's harsh intake of breath. "The body in Bernard McNally's cabin was an ATF agent."

"No known whereabouts," Carly said. Her voice was hard, which meant she was rattled. "Which means he could be anywhere. Especially if that cabin was his."

"Clear," Axel muttered. This had just gotten a hell of a lot more complicated. He had to believe Bernard was in Canada, that Leonard and Peter were trying to get there. But the fact the dead body in Bernard's cabin was a government agent…

It spoke of escalation, and it suddenly made Peter—

who had two sisters who worked for the FBI—and his involvement with Leonard seem a lot more sinister.

Then, more sinister by far, Selena's light bobbled, jerked and went dark.

Axel stepped forward then forced himself to think before he acted. His light was off, and he'd keep it that way. Without light, he could only make out his team, not Selena or Peter.

Blanca whined from behind him, and Axel crouched next to the dog, focusing on the cool calm of a man on assignment. He couldn't afford to be anything else. "Blanca, I sure hope you're going to listen to orders from me, because you've got to find Selena. Now."

Chapter 17

Selena approached Peter's antsy form. He looked like he was trying to sneak toward her, but he was too… fidgety. Everything a little too jerky to be smooth, undetectable movements.

She turned down the volume on her comm unit. It wasn't exactly standard operating procedure, but she needed to be able to focus on Peter. Besides, Axel would keep her in sight, and if something changed, he or the team would handle it.

She had to handle this. Everything would be fine. It had to be. And she had to give this one shot. If Peter refused, she'd let it go. She'd have to let it go, and the guilt with it. She'd arrest him herself if she had to. That was a promise—to herself, and to her team.

"Peter."

He came up short. She didn't know if he recognized

her voice, was surprised to see her here or what. She could just barely make out his face, but surely he knew she'd be one of the people after him. Maybe he just hadn't expected her to catch up.

"Er, where's your dog?"

It wasn't the question she would have expected, and it made her wish she'd brought Blanca with her. She'd feel a bit like a safety net at the moment. Instead of out here in no-man's land alone with her brother, who was acting like they'd just happened to run into each other during a walk in the park.

Peter's gaze dropped to the gun in her hand. She lifted her flashlight so the beam would illuminate him and give her an idea if he was carrying a weapon.

"Did he really send you out here without a light or a gun?" she asked dubiously.

Peter didn't respond. He just looked around, still fidgety and...strange. She wasn't sure how she'd expected him to act, but she didn't understand this.

There was no time to. She moved a little bit closer. He didn't back away, just eyed her warily.

"Peter, I want to help you. I think you know Leonard would throw you under the bus the second he could. *If* you survive. Let me help."

His expression didn't quite curl into its normal sneer, but it was close. "You always say you want to help."

"So, why won't you let me?"

"I don't need your pity help. I'm taking care of things on my own."

She bit back the bitter laugh and tried to keep her tone moderate, without judgment. "Are you?"

He inhaled sharply at that, but he didn't answer or say anything else.

"You're going back to jail. For longer this time. You had to understand that when you escaped. You might be in there for the rest of your life. But if you come with me, if you give us what you know about Leonard, you've got a chance. A *real* chance to have a life."

"I don't have any chances," Peter said bitterly. But his expression went lax, almost…sad. "Steve was going to…" Peter trailed off, shaking his head. "He would have been fine if not for you guys."

"You mean if not for Leonard Koch. *He's* the one who killed Steve and you know it. Blame Leonard, not us."

Peter didn't shake that away. If anything, his expression kind of crumpled, like a little boy about ready to cry. But he didn't cry, and the sadness was quickly replaced by an edgy anger.

Selena didn't let it fester. She didn't have time to anyway. "Opaline got kicked out of the FBI because of what she did for you," Selena said. It was a slight exaggeration as Opaline hadn't been officially fired, but Selena figured she had reason to exaggerate a little. To try to reach Peter however she could, even through guilt.

Peter's expression shuttered. "She didn't even help me. She just pretended."

"Doesn't matter so much when you keep that pretending a secret from your boss. She's done nothing but try to be there for you. I've tried to help you." But that was anger and guilt talking, and she had to find something else, *hope* something else would get to him. "We're your family, Peter. We've all made mistakes, but I can help you now. If you let me."

"You don't want to help me."

"I am standing here, my team far away. It's just me

and you. If I didn't want to help you, we'd all have surrounded you already and arrested you. We have more men than you. We know where you're headed. It's over for you and Leonard, but if you cooperate, Peter, I *can* help."

"You've got a gun," he said.

She didn't point out that she was a federal agent so of *course* she had a gun. This was dangerous, and God knew even if she let herself trust Peter, she wasn't going to trust Leonard. But this wasn't about her or reasonable action. This was about getting Peter to *listen*.

"You want me to put it down?" She started to crouch to lay the gun down on the ground. Axel and the rest of the team would have her back, and she had to show Peter some evidence of trust. Besides, she could and would fight if she had to.

"No! No, don't do that," he hissed, surprising her so much she paused midcrouch. "You have to get out of here," Peter said. He was scowling, but there was fear under all that bravado. His eyes darted around the woods as if he thought anyone might jump out. Maybe he was afraid of being arrested, but Selena thought maybe…just maybe…he was afraid of Leonard.

"If you surrender yourself, come with me—"

Peter shook his head emphatically. "Too late for that. You have to get out of here. Now. Please."

Her eyebrows drew together as she stared at Peter. She didn't see the little boy she'd known right now. She saw a fidgety, scared guy who'd gotten into something *way* too deep. Who was begging her to get out of here. "Why?" she demanded.

"It's you they want."

He couldn't have said anything that would have confused her more. "Me?"

"Not you specifically, but—"

"That'll be enough, Peter."

Selena whirled at the voice, gun at the ready. But she didn't see anyone. Only darkness.

"D-don't hurt her," Peter said, his voice shaky and pleading. "She's… She won't… There's other ones out there. More important ones. You want an important one. The boss guy. That's who you said you really wanted."

Selena didn't understand what was going on, but she immediately clicked her flashlight off, plunging the entire world around them into darkness. Whoever was out there, Leonard or someone else, was definitely going to kill her if they could. The light gave her away, but not now.

She'd have to disappear into the shadows, find her way back to Axel. *And leave Peter behind?*

And who was the voice? Leonard? But her team was supposed to have their sights on Leonard.

The boss guy. That was Axel. They wanted to kill Axel?

It didn't make sense, so she had to focus on what did. Getting away from that voice. Getting to Axel and warning him.

With everyone so close, everything so tense, she couldn't risk turning her walkie back up, but she had her earpiece in her pocket. If she could get far enough away that a few rustling noises and clicks wouldn't give away her exact location, she could get that situated.

She tried to give herself a second to orient. Peter had been in front of her, a few yards away. She hadn't been able to tell where the voice had come from. Neither direction nor vicinity to Peter or herself. It felt like it had come out of nowhere.

But thinking like that wasn't going to get her out of this situation. She could see where the rest of the team still had their lights on. Which meant she just had to slowly turn until she saw the slight beam of Axel's light.

If he'd turned it on. If she could get there without making too much noise. If—

Her phone buzzed. She bit back a curse, immediately moving as stealthily as she could in the direction she hoped would lead her to Axel. She pulled the phone out of her pocket, focusing more on those quiet, stealthy steps than the phone at first.

But it buzzed again, the screen brightening up. She fumbled with the switch to completely silence the damn thing, turn it off so it couldn't give off any light, but the message on the screen distracted her for one moment.

URGENT! Bernard McNally. Think he's a serial cop killer. Emailing the evidence. BE CAREFUL.

"You're going to want to heed that warning."

She couldn't bite back the scream that escaped her, or stop herself from fumbling her phone, which then thudded to the ground. She had to run, but the blow came out of nowhere instead and knocked her to the ground.

But she wouldn't go down that easily.

Selena's scream made Axel's blood run cold.

"Move," Axel yelled into his comm unit. "All bets are off. Just get Selena out of there," he ordered into the walkie. He didn't listen for the answers. He immediately moved in the direction Selena had gone, Blanca at his heels.

Axel kept following Blanca, hoping to God the commands were right or at least enough for Blanca to lead him to Selena.

"Scott has Leonard. We're going dark." It was Aria's voice over the walkie. The lights went out, one by one, until the entire woods were pitched into darkness.

So Axel had to focus on the sounds of the dog moving, focus on following her in the complete and utter black.

Seconds turned into minutes, but Axel only focused on movement. On listening and following. He didn't let his brain go anywhere else. One thing at a time. One step at a time. They'd get to Selena. The dog would get to her owner, and then Axel would get her out of this mess.

He didn't let himself blame himself for allowing her to get into it in the first place. He'd save that for later, when they were both okay. Each next step would need to be assessed in the moment, so he kept his mind blank of everything except *this* step.

Blanca slowed and gave a slight growl. Axel gripped the gun harder in his left hand. He tried to squint through the dark, but it was no use. He thought of asking for an update from the team, but Blanca had stopped completely.

Surely they were close. To Selena. Or Peter.

Before Axel could decide on the next move, light flooded his surroundings in a blinding flash. Axel instinctually squeezed his eyes shut and flung his arm over his eyes before fighting back the reflex. Where was the light coming from?

Axel blinked through the painful brightness until his eyes adjusted. He frowned at the structure in front of him. Some kind of platform that looked newly constructed. Almost like a stage in the middle of the woods.

He raised his gaze to the figures on the stage, where four poles with bright stadium-esque lights blazed down, illuminating a large man standing at the center, Selena next to him.

"Drop your weapons," the man shouted. He had a gun pressed to Selena's temple. Her expression was furious and defiant, but her arms were behind her back and a trickle of blood dripped from her temple and her mouth.

She'd given him a fight, that was for sure. But her hands must be bound behind her back. Peter stood a few feet away, fidgeting. Axel couldn't see them, but he knew his team would be approaching, slowly. Tactically.

"You must be Bernard," Axel said, forcing his voice to sound calm. He didn't know this man or how to handle him, and if he got off on killing law enforcement, there'd be no *reasoning* with him. They just had to get Selena out of there, then take him out. Beginning and end of story.

"Axel Morrow, there you are!" he greeted jovially. "I'd drop the gun before I blow her brain matter everywhere."

That wasn't the example he wanted to set for the rest of the team. Still, it would buy him time. Slowly he crouched, making a show out of gently placing his gun on the ground as he spoke into his comm unit. "No matter what he says, at least one person keeps a gun on him. No matter what."

Slowly, Axel stood back up, and looked at Bernard, who was smirking.

"It's your lucky day, Axel Morrow, *supervisory* special agent. Why don't you come join us on the stage?"

"Suicide by cop," Aria said into the walkie. "This is about body count. Not survival *or* his brother. He knows we're out here. He knows even if he kills the both of you, he can't get out of here without going through us."

Axel agreed with the assessment. If he got up on stage, even if he put his weapon down, he'd have a chance to take Bernard down. But surely Bernard wasn't stupid enough to think two FBI agents couldn't stop him if given the chance.

He'd either shoot Axel before he got up on the stage, or there was more here. A bigger, far more dangerous plan.

Keeping the movement as discreet as possible, and his gaze firmly pinned on Bernard, Axel muttered into his comm unit, "Max, check for explosives." It would be a way to kill them all. If Bernard was already resolved to his fate, blowing up the whole area would be a way to kill a bunch of agents.

"Got it," Max said. "I'll check under the platform first."

Axel didn't say anything, but he figured Max was right. The platform could be hiding explosives. What other reason was there for it?

"Come on now," Bernard said, the gun still dug hard into Selena's temple. "Don't be shy. Let's get this show on the road. I've been planning for it. Thank you, all, for falling so perfectly into my plan."

Axel kept his expression bland, though fury bubbled under the surface. He wasn't sure how they could have possibly seen this coming, but he couldn't help wishing they'd taken some other tactic here.

But there were no do-overs. There was only now, and getting Selena and the rest of his team safe and sound. He couldn't order them to back off, even with the threat of explosives, until they got Selena out of there.

He took a careful step toward the stage, hoping Blanca would read and obey his "stay" hand command. For the first time, he let his gaze turn fully to Selena. The gun dug into her temple, and the blood was now dripping off her chin.

But when their gazes locked, she winked. *Winked.*

Axel didn't know what on earth to do with that.

Chapter 18

Axel's shock at her winking was visible in his expression for approximately one second before he went back into FBI agent mode.

She couldn't verbalize to him that he was more of a target than she was. She was the bait. But she could give him at least a hint that she wasn't totally out of her element.

Not that Bernard wouldn't kill her. From what she could tell, murder was his only goal. Even if he died in the process. Maybe *especially* if he died in the process. As long as he took out a bunch of agents on his way.

Peter was the outlier. She didn't think he'd hurt her, not when he'd tried to warn her away. But he wasn't helping her either. He was too afraid. Too certain he had no hope.

Or maybe he just didn't care that the big psychopath had beaten up his sister. Maybe he'd even enjoyed it.

Didn't matter.

Selena had kept her head. Bernard had gotten a good few knocks in, but when he'd tied her hands behind her back, she'd managed to keep the bonds looser than they should be. It was taking time to wiggle her hands out because she had to make sure she didn't move any part of her body that he could see.

Once they were free enough, she could kick Bernard's legs out from under him. As long as he didn't catch her wiggling her way out of the bonds.

Right now, Bernard's gaze was firmly on Axel slowly making his way onto the stage. In return, Axel eyed Bernard warily. He moved slowly, and Selena was grateful for it. It gave her more time to work at the bonds on her wrists.

She took a quick look around now that her eyes had adjusted to the light. She could make out Aria and Carly far off in the trees, guns drawn. She didn't see Max or Scott, but they were around somewhere. Probably with Leonard.

"Take all the time you want," Bernard said cheerfully, clearly talking about Axel's interminable approach. "It's not going to change the outcome. Nothing can change the outcome."

Selena fought off the shudder of dread. Her team was out there. They wouldn't shoot Bernard as long as he had a gun to her head. But with two team members missing, it meant they were somewhere out there getting into place. Unless Leonard was posing more of a problem than they'd anticipated.

But Selena wouldn't let herself think like that. Sometimes hope was all a girl had. She'd cling to it.

"Peter?" Bernard yelled, even though Peter was only a few feet away.

Peter shuffled in front of Bernard. He kept his gaze down, patently refusing to look at her. For the first time, Selena felt the true pain of betrayal. He was actually going to let this man kill her if she didn't get out of it herself.

"I tried to help you," she whispered. "You only have yourself to blame for whatever happens."

"Oh, shut up," Bernard muttered. "This boy knows who really cares. Who's really going to help him. Cops and agents and the like just send people to jail. They don't care. They all deserve to die. Peter understands that. Don't you, Peter?"

Peter cleared his throat, still not looking at her. "Yeah, yeah. I do."

Selena couldn't give in to the tears that threatened. Too much was at stake. But it hurt. Even when she should be past it.

"Get the rest of the rope from the bag," Bernard ordered Peter. "Tie Axel Morrow up. You hear that, Axel Morrow? He's going to tie you up. You fight him off, she's dead. Right in front of you. Her blood on your hands, Axel Morrow."

"Why do you keep repeating his name like that?" Selena muttered. "Obsess much?"

Bernard laughed, which made her lungs contract in fear rather than resentment. She didn't think *amusing* him was a good thing in any way, shape or form.

"You and your kind are scum of the earth. This isn't obsession, it's *justice*. And you led me to it. You and your useless brother have given me exactly what I needed. How does that make you feel?"

Selena hid her revulsion, guilt, fear and every other negative emotion swirling inside her. She kept her expression carefully blank.

"Peter! Stop messing around and get it done!"

Selena winced against the sound of his bellow in her ear. Bernard's hand fisted in her hair roughly, keeping her head still so the gun dug into her temple. "Don't go moving on me. My trigger finger might slip and splatter you all over your friend over there."

His hand tightened, pulling at her hair until she saw stars. Still, she bit back the moan of pain. She'd withstand it. Find a way out of it. Six against one, basically. They had to find a way out of it.

"You know, I might enjoy that," Bernard said, contemplatively. "Watching his expression when it's your brain matter splattering all over him. Yeah, I think—"

"She untied her rope," Peter said, sounding small, but it interrupted Bernard's terrifying string of thoughts. His grip on her hair loosened for a second, but that did nothing to ease the pain.

Peter had just ratted her out. Selena felt the full blast of betrayal. Her one hope and Peter had taken it away from her? She would have glared at him, but she couldn't move her head with Bernard's hand in her hair.

"Untied her... You little..." He didn't let her go, but he didn't pull the trigger either. "No, we'll stick to the plan. Stick to the plan. You'll all die. All of you. Blaze of glory."

Bernard sounded insane, and Selena had to accept there was no reasoning with him. He wanted them dead.

Not because of anything they'd done. Simply because of what they were. What they'd dedicated their lives to. Men like him didn't listen to reason.

And it very rarely ended well for the cops at their mercy.

Her only hope of escaping this was taking Bernard down and out. She was going to have to get his hands out of her hair. If she could do that, she had a chance. She could fight him. If he took her out, she could deal with that—if it saved her team.

"Should I tie them back up for you?" Peter asked Bernard, sounding fully subservient. "I think Morrow knows not to move, but she might try to fight you with her hands untied."

"Yes, good job, Peter. Fix her bonds. Then take care of Axel Morrow."

Peter scurried to do just that. He came up beside her, pulled her hands over to him. Which was weird. She didn't know why he wasn't standing directly behind her. This angle wouldn't allow him to tighten them enough.

Then he bent forward, his mouth practically on her ear. She would have headbutted him, but the gun was on the other side of her head and kept her from having any range of motion.

He fiddled with the rope, but he spoke into her ear, his voice an almost inaudible whisper. "I'm going to push you off."

Push her off? The shock slammed into her like a blow. Push her off the stage? *Save* her?

Hope she shouldn't entertain bubbled up inside her. If he pushed her off, that would be her chance to take Bernard out. If he pushed right, she could be close enough to Axel's gun to grab it and shoot Bernard first.

A risk, but a chance.

It would leave Axel vulnerable in the interim, though. When Peter pushed, who would Bernard target? She needed to communicate with Peter. Tell him which angle to push her out, tell him to give Axel some kind of signal.

Except she couldn't do any of that when Bernard was literally standing right next to them with a gun to her head. If Peter took much longer, Bernard would know Peter was talking to her or he might at least suspect something.

"I've got her," Peter said to Bernard. "Nice and tight now."

"Good," Bernard said. He seemed to pause and consider, then finally let go of her hair. "Good, Peter. You've been an undeniable asset in this. Forget Axel Morrow over there. Bring me the whole bag. It's time to begin."

"Yeah, okay," Peter mumbled, fumbling with Selena's rope as Bernard fully let her go. Though the gun was still pressed to her temple, if Peter gave her a good push, Bernard wouldn't be able to shoot in time. Not at first.

She felt the ropes loosen fully rather than tighten. Peter's mouth was still next to her ear, and he spoke once more.

"He's got a bomb. Run away from here."

A bomb. But she didn't have time to argue, to come up with a better plan that wouldn't get Peter *and* Axel blown up, because Peter gave her a hard shove that had her sailing off the stage and onto the hard, cold, snow-covered ground below.

* * *

Axel watched Selena tumble off the stage, as if pushed. Pushed. Peter had purposefully pushed her off.

She landed on a tuck and roll, then was quickly up on her feet, holding out her hand. Axel realized she was warning Blanca off running to her.

Peter had pushed her off the stage to *help*. To save her life.

It gave Axel a surge of hope.

But in the next second Bernard's gun whirled on him and before Axel could act, the gun went off. Pain slammed into him and exploded across his chest as he fell backward and crashed onto the stage with enough force he heard some of the wood crack beneath him.

Head pounding, brain rattled, Axel struggled to get a breath in. The pain was excruciating, and he couldn't seem to suck in enough oxygen at first. He gasped and gasped for it before he could remind himself to calm down.

Calm down.

He wasn't dead. Thanks to the vest he wore. Because the bullet had hit him right in the Kevlar vest. He counted off breaths, doing everything to calm himself. He was alive, which meant there was still a chance to get out of this in relatively one piece.

Bernard must not know he was wearing a vest, or maybe was just a bad shot. Either way, it didn't make Axel invincible. He had to get out of here before Bernard shot him in a place that wasn't protected.

He barely heard the voices in his ear. They sounded far away, but his team was yelling words. He tried to make sense of them and move at the same time. Move and breathe. Listen and act.

Focus. Calm. Breathe in, one, two, three. Breathe out, one, two, three.

"No explosives under the stage that I can find." Max's voice.

"There's a bag on the stage," Aria's voice said. "Peter got the rope out of it. But it's big and there's more in there. He's dragging Peter to the bag now. I can't shoot without hitting Peter."

Axel could give no orders, no insight. He could only try to roll off the stage and away from Bernard. He had to get himself out of harm's way and make sure Selena was, as well.

Peter had saved her. Axel hadn't thought it in that moment he'd seen Selena tumbling into the snow, but it had only taken a few seconds—before the bullet had slammed into him—to realize Peter had been getting Selena out of Bernard's grip.

Though Axel was still in excruciating pain, the fog of the wind being knocked out of him started to lift. Someone was yelling. Raving.

Bernard.

"I'll kill them all! I'll kill you all. You'll all die. We'll all die!"

Cop killer. Suicide by cop. There was no getting out of this one without someone getting hurt. Axel would make sure it was Bernard.

"I've got the visual. He's got a bomb in that bag," Aria said. "Take him out. Someone take him out. I can't get an angle."

"Peter's in the way," Max said disgustedly. "From

every angle. Bernard knows it, that's why he created that little corner on the stage to hide in. Peter is his body shield."

Axel knew they'd consider going through Peter. Why not? He was part of this after all, but he'd saved Selena. Hard to overlook that.

"I'll get Peter out of the way," Axel managed to rasp into the comm mic. He wouldn't let them consider taking out Peter too. Not when he was right here.

There was arguing, but Axel didn't have time for it. Maybe he wasn't one hundred percent, but he was the closest to Peter. If Max could take out Bernard in seconds, that was all Axel needed. He ripped the earpiece out of his ear and got to his knees.

Bernard was rummaging through the bag, holding Peter in front of him. Max was right. Bernard had built this stage just for this.

It was chilling, how well planned out this all was. How little they'd understood about what Leonard's trio was doing. Not trying to escape. No, they'd been a lure. Bait.

It explained everything Selena had questioned. Why February. Why let them catch up time and time again. Why kill Steve. Hard to lay a trap if someone informed the police about it.

But Axel couldn't dwell on that. They hadn't made mistakes. They'd fought with the information they had. Now they had more. And now they would end this.

He glanced at Selena. She was crawling across the snow and toward the gun he'd left behind. Good. The more guns on Bernard, the better.

Axel got to his feet in a crouch. He moved to one

side to get a better view of how Bernard was using Peter as a human shield. He had a gun to Peter's chest. Peter was still as death. Axel reminded himself that no matter how little Peter was fighting now, he'd saved Selena's life. At peril to his own.

And now Axel would do the same for Peter.

Chapter 19

Selena got to Axel's gun and immediately grabbed and whirled, looking for Bernard. But all she saw was Peter, huddled over a corner. And Axel, a few yards away, looking like he was about to rush him.

Selena flipped on her radio. "Fill me in," she demanded to whoever was listening.

"Axel's going to get Peter out of the way so we can take Bernard out," came Carly's calm reply.

"Bernard's got explosives back there," Aria added.

"Some of the team should fall back," Max said authoritatively. "I've already got Scott taking Leonard to some backup agents, but we don't *all* need to be in the potential blast zone."

"We're a team," Carly said, sounding offended.

"We're not leaving Axel behind," Aria added forcefully.

"Damn straight," Selena said into her unit. Max was the one with sniper training, so if he didn't think there was an angle to get on Bernard, she'd believe it. "Morrow?"

"It's no use," Carly said disgustedly. "He pulled out his earpiece."

Selena cursed him silently, keeping her gun trained on the area where Peter was huddled. Bernard was behind him. She would take him out. She would damn well take him out given the chance.

Axel moved. A swift blur. How he managed to run across the stage making almost no noise was beyond her. Axel lunged, and both Axel and Peter crashed onto the stage, but they rolled—Selena couldn't tell who rolled who—nor could she watch them roll. She had to take out Bernard.

She fired, her gunshot echoing with at least one other. Bernard crumpled immediately.

Max's voice came out over the walkie. "I'm headed in to check the explosives. Someone follow and make sure Bernard is dead."

"I've got it," Axel said. His voice was rough. The man was hurt and still doing all the work. But he was closest to Bernard.

Selena dared look at him as he got up from Peter's still body. Axel stumbled a little, but he managed to push himself back up on the stage. As if he sensed the rising fear in Selena, he spoke as he checked Bernard's pulse.

"Peter's been shot," he said. "Fall knocked him out, I think, because the only wound I found was in his shoulder. He's going to need medical attention and a stretcher even if he does regain consciousness."

Selena moved forward carefully, gun still trained on Bernard, just in case. She couldn't think about Peter. She had to think about handling this the right way. So no more mistakes were made.

No more people shot. Hurt. No. This would be the end.

"Dead," Axel announced into the walkie.

Selena rushed forward and immediately searched Peter's body for the bullet wound. "Right in the shoulder," she muttered. But she didn't find any other wounds except a trickle of blood from his temple. Likely, as Axel had said, from the fall.

Bernard was dead, but there was no sense of relief. Peter was seriously injured, and there were explosives.

"Status of the explosives?" Axel demanded.

"There's a timer on these," Max said from where he was crouched over the bag of explosives. His voice gave away no hint of if he could handle that or not.

They weren't done yet, Selena thought grimly.

"Carly or Aria or someone with a pack? I need tools," Max said into the walkie.

Though Selena was close enough she could hear Axel and Max without the walkies, Selena barely registered their words. She did what she could, used what she could, to put pressure on Peter's wound. But his head was bleeding too. There wasn't anything she could do about that.

It was over, but it didn't feel over. Especially as Carly and Aria rushed forward. Aria dropped a pack next to Max, then crouched beside him taking orders to help stop the bombs.

Carly came up next to her. "Here's my first aid kit. What do you need?"

"I wish I knew," Selena muttered, but they worked together to patch Peter up. "What about you, Morrow?" Selena yelled at him. She was still bandaging Peter's shoulder, but she couldn't ignore Axel might have been hurt too.

"Fine," Axel gritted out.

"Liar," she returned. She took the brief moment to look over her shoulder at him. He sat on the stage, Blanca next to him. His face was bloody, both from his previous injury on his cheek and new ones. The bandage on his previously injured hand was a mess.

But Blanca sat next to him, and he rested his good hand on her furry head. Something in Selena's chest eased. Like maybe this was all over and going to be okay.

"Ambulance is on its way, but it's a ways out," Carly said quietly.

"He can hang on that long, don't you think?"

Carly nodded. "He's young and strong. He'll be okay."

Selena held on to that reassurance from her friend, even if that's all it was. She almost relaxed, but she couldn't ignore the fact there were explosives directly behind her. Max was an expert. He would—

But he stood abruptly and jumped away from the bag. "I can't stop this timer," Max said. He didn't bother with the comm unit now. He shouted. "We have to get out of here. As far away as you can get. Now. Move!"

Carly stumbled to her feet, but before she could help, Max grabbed her and was pulling her toward the woods, Blanca running after them, presumably on Axel's order.

Then Axel was on the opposite side of Peter. "Help me get him over my shoulder."

She might have argued that Axel was hurt and she

should be the one to carry Peter, but Axel was bigger. He'd be able to move faster with Peter than she would.

Aria jumped next to them, lending a hand, even as Max yelled at all of them to move. They got Peter over Axel's shoulder and immediately began to head out. They ran as fast as they could into the woods, away from the impending explosion.

"You can run faster than this, Lopez," Axel said through gritted teeth, his pace hampered by the weight of another human.

"We're not separating," Selena replied, keeping her pace even with Axel's. If something happened, she… She just had to be here. With both of them.

"Take cover," Max yelled. "Find some cover!"

But before they could find any, the first explosion sounded.

They weren't far enough away, that was all Axel could think as the explosion reverberated around them. Heat, the tinny sounds of metal falling all about them. The blast of air that had them all pitching forward and hard into the ground.

Peter's weight landed awkwardly on his own head, which was another rattle his brain certainly didn't need today. The biting cold was opposite to the heat on his back, and as much as he was aware of being alive, he couldn't seem to shift past that one and only thought.

"Cover your hard head, Morrow," Selena bit out.

He listened to her, folding his arms over the back of his head, but also lifted his head to see her pretty much bodily shielding her brother from the flying debris.

It didn't last long. Small bits and ash still floated in

the air, but the thuds of large pieces of wood and other things hitting the ground had stopped.

Static blasted out of Axel's walkie, which must have somehow gotten turned up to max volume during his fall. Max's voice came out booming. "Everyone okay? Carly and I are good."

"I'm good," Aria's voice echoed.

Axel fumbled to roll over to turn the volume on his walkie down.

"Morrow and I are still breathing," Selena said next to him. Her voice was calm and cool and like some kind of balm. They were okay. They were all okay.

"Peter needs an ambulance stat," Selena said firmly.

"There's an ambulance waiting, but we've got to get to it," Aria responded. "Are we clear, Max?"

"Yeah. There were a series of explosives in the bag, but all set to go off at the same time. So, there shouldn't be another explosion unless he had more stashed elsewhere, but my bet's on that being it. Biggest concern now is falling debris, but we seem to be past the worst of it."

"We need help with Peter," Selena said. "He's still unconscious. We're not going to be able to carry him ourselves."

"I'm good," Axel insisted. He pushed out of the snow and onto his knees. The world spun, but he could breathe through that. He'd get used to it. He didn't feel pain. Everything was kind of numb, so surely he could get to his feet. But as he tried, the world didn't just spin, it seemed to tilt.

"You're really not," Selena said, grabbing onto him before he toppled over. "And I messed up my knee a bit. Can you guys find us? Blanca? Where's Blanca?"

"We've got her," Max said.

Selena let out a sharp whistle that felt as though it split his head in half. As if on cue, his entire body started throbbing in pain. Instead of letting Selena hold him up, Axel went ahead and lay back down on the ground.

Selena's face swam above him. "Don't you lose consciousness on me too," she demanded.

"Won't," Axel bit out, though it was a close thing. He could feel his vision graying, his body wanting to retreat from the pain. But he fought through it. Selena was here and they were all right. The team was all right. Somehow.

He heard panting, then felt the rough wet of Blanca's tongue moving across his face. He winced, which sent more sharp lances of pain through his body. But he was awake. Alive.

He reached out for the dog, and Blanca licked his face again. "Not sure that's sanitary." But it was a nice reminder they'd all made it out okay.

"Up and at 'em." Max's voice, then Axel was being hefted to his feet. Things were still spinning, but Max held him upright. Then Carly stood next to him and wound her arm around his waist.

Aria was helping Selena, who limped. Max had moved over to Peter and was gingerly lifting him.

"Bit of a hike," Carly said next to him. "Just lean on me."

"I'm fine," Axel grumbled, but he ended up needing the support as they moved forward. He watched Selena in front of him, hobbling with the help of Aria, Blanca at their heels.

It *was* a hike, and all Axel wanted to do was lie down

in the snow and go to sleep. But he kept moving and eventually the ambulance and a hive of paramedics and cops came into view. The medics rushed forward, immediately to Max, getting Peter onto a stretcher.

"Him too," Carly said, and Axel didn't realize she was referring to him until another paramedic came over. The man glanced at Selena. "You need medical attention too?" the paramedic asked.

Selena shook her head. "No. Just twisted my knee. I'll grab a ride in the cop car and get checked out without bogging down emergency. These two are the ones who need an ER."

Axel tried to argue with Selena, then the paramedic, but he was ushered into the ambulance and wasn't too pleased with himself that he didn't seem to have the strength to stop anything that happened. Somehow he was on a stretcher in an ambulance being rushed to the ER.

He didn't need an ER. He was conscious, wasn't he? The pain was bad, the dizziness was almost worse, but he was *alive*.

Axel looked over to the opposite side of the ambulance where the paramedics worked quickly and efficiently on Peter, clearly the worse off between the two of them.

Axel tried to pay attention to what they were saying so he'd be able to assure Selena Peter was okay, but the words kind of jumbled and it took most of his concentration just to fight the gray fog that wanted to suck him under.

The paramedic leaned over him, studying his face. He lifted the bandage on his cheek, poked and prodded, then did something horribly painful to his hand.

"I'm all right," Axel grumbled, trying to roll away from the medic's attentions.

The paramedic shined the light in his eye and kept examining him as if he hadn't spoken at all. "Concussion. Your hand is a mess. You're in better shape than him, but it isn't getting you out of a trip to the emergency room. Good news is, you'll both survive."

Survive. Axel blew out a breath. Yeah, he had a lot more planned than just *survived*.

Chapter 20

Selena had lost all sense of time and place. She'd been right about her knee, though. She'd just twisted it, which was good. They'd given her a pair of crutches and told her to stay off it and to go home and rest. It had taken hours, and maybe she should have listened.

But she couldn't. She'd found her team in the ER waiting room. A bit banged up here and there, but mostly just waiting to make sure Axel was released.

Axel. She couldn't think about Axel yet. She had to deal with her family.

She found Opaline in the OR recovery waiting room. Opaline immediately jumped to her feet. "You should be home," she scolded, but she rushed over and nudged Selena into a chair. "You've got to rest that."

"I will. I just had to…"

"He's okay. He's okay. The doctor said I could even

go back and see him in a few minutes. He'll recover just fine."

Selena nodded. She'd known as much, but it was good to hear hope and reassurance from Opaline. Then Opaline's arms wrapped around her. "I'm so glad you're okay."

For the first time in something like twenty years, Selena let herself feel comforted by her older sister's hug. She wrapped her own arms around Opaline and just sat like that for she didn't know how long.

"I need you to believe I really wasn't helping Peter," Opaline whispered fiercely. "I didn't even consider it. I just thought if he trusted me, if he thought I *would* help, I might be able to help everyone else." Opaline pulled back, though she kept her hands on Selena's shoulders. Her eyes were dripping with tears. "I need *you* to believe that, Selena, even if no one else does."

Selena took a deep breath. She'd done her fair share of trying to help Peter in this, in ways that wouldn't meet with Alana's full approval, that was for sure. But more… Peter had made mistakes. Mistakes he'd pay for, but at the end of the day he'd helped. He'd *saved* her when her team couldn't.

"I believe it. And what's more, I believe in Peter. He's going to have to go back to jail, no getting around that, but he tried to help all of us. He… He saved my life." And Axel had saved his. Selena couldn't dwell on that yet. "I'm going to fight for him."

Opaline gripped her hands. "We'll fight for him together."

"And you… You saved us too. Finding all that information about Bernard. We couldn't have handled it the way we did without your information. I'll fight for you too. With Alana or whoever else I need to." Selena sucked in a breath. There were so many old hurts, but at the end of the day, they were family. Family who'd try to save each other when they could.

They'd have a lot to work through, but instead of convincing themselves they were all uniquely misunderstood, maligned or not cared about enough, they had to try to save each other. Instead of doing everything they could to protect themselves from all the ways their parents had hurt them.

Selena stuck around long enough to see Peter. He was mostly out of it, but she got to thank him for saving her, and to promise to do better for all of them in the future. She thought he'd murmured his own promises, but it would take some time before he was lucid enough to fully deal with everything.

Dead on her feet, Selena still tried to argue with Opaline, who insisted she go home. But eventually Carly came in and ushered her outside against all Selena's protests.

Once there, Selena was surprised to find it daylight. She'd lost all sense of time. All sense of anything. But when she saw Blanca waiting patiently in Carly's back seat, Selena felt like maybe everything was going to be okay.

Selena crawled right back in there and cuddled with the dog while Carly drove.

"We'll have you both home in no time," Carly said. "I can stay with you if you need help."

"That's sweet," Selena said through a yawn. "But actually… Don't take me home, Carly. There's somewhere else I need to be."

* * *

"I really don't like being chauffeured around," Axel grumbled.

"You don't say," Max replied blandly. "And here I thought being injured and fussed over was your favorite thing. You've been so gracious about it."

Axel glowered at Max. He knew he should be grateful he didn't have to spend the night at the hospital, but they'd given him those damn pain meds that made him feel fuzzy without *fully* eradicating the dull ache in his head and hand, insisted someone else drive him home, and left him with a list of instructions on how to care for his injuries a mile long.

He was in a filthy mood, and he wanted to be alone. "You're not staying."

Max chuckled. "Wasn't planning on it."

Axel eyed him suspiciously. He wasn't convinced his friend was truly going to let him be alone, at least for the first twenty-four hours, but Max didn't appear to be lying.

He stopped the car, didn't kill the engine, and let Axel step out. Axel frowned. The lights in the kitchen were on. He didn't leave lights on before he went onto an assignment. Weirder still, Max did not follow. Didn't turn off his engine. Just sat there and gave Axel a wave.

They were really going to let him be alone?

Then, breaking through the engine of Max's car in the quiet of a winter country late afternoon, there was a bark, and then Blanca bounded off the porch. Axel stopped midstep and just watched the dog run up to him, tongue lolling out of the side of her mouth.

She circled him, yipping and whining and wiggling happily.

"What on earth are you doing here?" he muttered at the dog, scratching her behind the ears before moving forward.

Max was driving away and Axel had no choice but to step forward. When he reached his front door, it was unlocked. So, he walked inside.

Selena was standing in his kitchen, fooling with something over the temperamental stove. Her hair was a little damp and piled on top of her head. She wore sweats—*his* sweats—and there were crutches leaning against his counter.

"Did you…break into my house? Are you wearing my clothes?"

She didn't even look over at him. "More or less," she replied cheerfully. She looked around the kitchen. "A little sparse, but I like it. It's…peaceful. Be a good place to recover."

"I…"

"I found the instructions you left the animal babysitter and followed them too."

Axel frowned. "He's a caretaker, not an animal *babysitter*."

"Right, well, all handled," she said with an easy shrug. "I liked the cows. The chickens, though? Mean as all get-out. The horse is a sweetie. You'll have to tell me their names in the morning. But for now, all you have to do is sit down and eat." She put a plate—*his* plate—on the table—*his* table—with a flourish. Said *in the morning* like she belonged here.

It slammed into him, as hard as all the blows he'd received in the last few days, that this was exactly where he wanted her.

"Come on now. You have to be starving."

He didn't know what he was, but he managed to move forward and sit himself at the table. Blanca padded after him, then curled into a ball at his feet, resting her head on her paws.

The plate was filled with spaghetti. That she'd apparently made. In his kitchen. In his clothes. Was he hallucinating? But her crutches were right there.

Crutches. "You're the one who should be sitting down."

She waved that away, pouring milk into a glass. "Too antsy." She set the milk next to his plate, then stood there, all her weight on her good leg. She brushed fingers over the bandage on his cheek. "You got hospital paperwork? You once called me Nurse Ratched—well, just you wait."

She tried to move away, but he slid his arms around her and held her there. Just held her. God, they were both okay, and the relief hadn't fully washed over him until just now.

She stilled, rested her cheek on the top of his head. Then merely held on. "You saved Peter," she said, her voice cracking with emotion.

"He saved you."

She let out a shuddering breath. "He did. I didn't expect it."

He loosened his hold enough to look up at her. "You're not feeling guilty for that, after everything we went through?"

She looked down at him. Brown eyes swimming with emotion. "I don't know. I really don't know... I talked to Opaline. I visited with Peter. I think…things will be better between the three of us. That's good. I've needed that and was too…afraid, I guess, to try for it. Risk it." She shook her head, blinking back unshed tears. "You better eat before it gets cold. We can talk after—"

"I'm glad you're here. And not just for the food. I'm glad you're here. It feels like you belong here." She inhaled sharply. Then she shook her head, trying to pull away. But he held on tight. There was no more pulling away. No matter how tired or injured or hungry they were. "There's not going to be any more of that. We're going to deal, here and now, with this. With you and me."

She didn't struggle to get out of his grasp anymore, but she did keep shaking her head back and forth. "I don't know *how,*" she said, sounding lost. "You think I understand this?"

"What 'this' are you referring to?"

"How I *feel.* I thought I'd come take care of you and figure it out, but it just… I really don't know what to do about it."

He tugged her down and onto his lap. "I know what you can do about it."

"Oh, don't go thinking with your—"

"Stay, Selena. That's what you can do." He pressed his mouth to hers, just a gentle pressure. Just a promise. "Stay."

She searched his face, and he saw what she didn't want to feel. Fear, uncertainty and, yeah, that guilt they both needed to work through. Then she cupped her hands to his cheeks.

"You know you want to," he added, trying to sound

cocksure, but it only came out serious. Hushed. "I know you're afraid. I'm not exactly steady on my feet here, but it's what we both want. What we both feel. You know it as well as I do. But we also came through life or death on the life side of things, so let's let the fear go, huh?"

She swallowed, still searching his eyes, still holding gently onto his face. She took a deep breath. "You're really afraid?"

"Of course I am. I know far more what to do with a gun in my face than I know what to do with a woman and a dog in my house. Doesn't mean I don't prefer the latter."

She smiled a little at that. "Okay," she said, in something no more than a whisper. "We'll stay," she said, giving a glance at Blanca, who sat on the floor, looking up at them with intelligent eyes. "That's where we'll start."

"She'd like it here," Axel said. "Room to run."

"You've got a home here. I've been…wanting a home for a long time. But—"

No, there wasn't going to be any buts. "I'm in love with you, Selena. I think I have been for a while now."

She nodded, those tears swimming back. He'd have thought she'd fight them the way she always did, but instead one slipped over. He wiped it off her cheek. It meant more than words, that she'd finally let that wall down, no matter how reluctantly.

"I think I've been in love with you too," she whispered. "I'm not sure I'm going to be any good at that."

"Then let's agree to give each other a little bit of a learning curve, huh?"

She chuckled, but it was watery, then she leaned her

head on his shoulder. And they sat there, in his little farmhouse, holding on to each other in the quiet stillness. In the warmth of love, no matter how much they had to learn.

He had no doubt they'd do just fine.

Epilogue

For the first time in Selena's memory, she didn't particularly look forward to the traditional TCD end-of-mission dinner. As glad as she was the mission was over, and Peter and Axel were recovering, and Opaline hadn't lost her job, she was nervous.

Downright *sick* with nerves.

All she could think about was what Axel had said to her back in that cabin, that the entire team would *know*. Arriving together with him and Blanca was hardly going to help matters.

Not that she wanted to change anything. The whole *love* thing had been surprisingly easy to slip into when they were at the farm. It was *here*, surrounded by the people she worked with day in and out, respected and cared about, that she felt strung tight as a drum.

"What do you think they're going to do? Kick you out?"

She gave Axel a look, not pleased how easily he read her. Or at least, she told herself she wasn't pleased, but the more she thought about it—really let herself think about it and not push away the uncomfortable feelings—the more she realized it was a great comfort to have someone who understood her when she couldn't verbalize the things churning around inside her.

It was the thing she'd wanted from her family that they'd never been able to give, but now that she had it in Axel, it seemed to help her find the words with her family.

They walked into the conference room, shoulder to shoulder, to find just about everyone already in the room, helping themselves to the spread of food and drinks laid out, likely by Alana's assistant, Amanda.

Selena wasn't sure what she'd expected. Speculative looks. Teasing. *Something.* But everyone just called out a greeting or smiled.

"All hail the conquering heroes," Max said, lifting his cup.

"Team effort, I'm pretty sure," Axel returned, taking the plate Amanda offered him and handing it to Selena.

"Sure, but we were talking," Max said, gesturing to Carly and Aria. "If you guys hadn't wanted to split Leonard and Peter up, we'd all be in pieces on the forest floor."

Aria nodded. "If we'd kept together, made the circle, Bernard would have been able to blow us all up."

Selena exchanged a look with Axel. They'd gone over and over that moment themselves, but neither had thought...

But Selena supposed it was true. She'd had guilt there, about letting her personal feelings interfere with a case, but in this strange instance... Max was right. It had actually helped.

Selena let out a whoosh of breath. She'd been harboring guilt or worry or *something*. She'd thought it would take time to work through, but in the end... Everything she'd chosen had actually *helped*.

The team chatted, discussed details of the case and Peter's prognosis and potential trial outcomes. Leonard's ranting that cops had ruined his life, much like his brother's same anger, had earned him a trip to the psychiatric hospital. He'd be carefully monitored for a very long time. The mission was well and truly over.

Still, no one stared or commented on Axel and Selena coming together. No one even gave a second glance when Axel absently ran his hand over her hair. Even as Selena blushed furiously, *nothing* happened.

Alana came into the room, and the chatter quieted as Opaline came in behind her. Alana took the silence as an opportunity to speak.

"While Opaline will be serving a two-week suspension, she was imperative in finding the information that led us to understand Bernard's motives. Which gives me full faith that when she returns, she'll continue to be a fine asset to the team."

The team cheered, and Opaline dabbed at her wet eyes. But her colleagues shoved a plate at her and drinks and...

Everything was going to be okay. Really okay.

A little while later, when Selena was filling her cup in the corner, Carly came up next to her, leaning against the wall.

Selena braced herself. Finally someone was going to say something.

"It's good to see you happy, Selena." Carly patted her shoulder. "Really good." And then she walked off, petting Blanca on her way back to the table.

Selena took a deep breath and turned. Everyone else was eating, chatting. No one acted differently. And they weren't going to. It was simply…accepted.

Because they were a team. Because they were friends.

"Enjoy your win here, team." Alana tapped on the table. "But be ready for the next assignment."

They'd all be ready for the next one. And in the meantime, she'd have a life. With a sister, a brother. With friends.

And with Axel.

Family, friendship and love. All things that had been within her grasp before, but she'd been too scared to reach for.

She wasn't scared anymore.

She was ready.

* * * * *

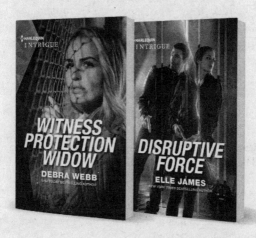

SPECIAL EXCERPT FROM

⒣ HARLEQUIN

INTRIGUE

*Thanks to a car accident, Melanie Blankenship has
returned to Kelby Creek with no memory of why she'd go
back to the place that turned against her. And when she's
reunited with Sheriff Sterling Costner, who vows to help
her uncover the truth, she's happy to have him by her side
for protection. And is more than surprised at the sparks
still flying between them after all these years…*

Keep reading for a sneak peek at
Accidental Amnesia,
part of The Saving Kelby Creek Series,
from Tyler Anne Snell.

Five years of memories didn't compare an ounce to the man
they'd been made about. Not when he seemingly materialized
out of midair, wrapped in a uniform that fit nicely, topped
with a cowboy hat his daddy had given him and carrying
some emotions behind clear blue eyes.

Eyes that, once they found Mel during her attempt to flee
the hospital, never strayed.

Not that she'd expected anything but full attention when
Sterling Costner found out she was back in town.

Though, silly ol' Mel had been hoping that she'd have more
time before she had this face-to-face.

Because, as much as she was hoping no one else would
catch wind of her arrival, she knew the gossip mill around
town was probably already aflame.

"I'm glad this wasn't destroyed," Mel said lamely once
she slid into the passenger seat, picking up her suitcase in the
process. She placed it on her lap.

She remembered leaving her apartment with it, but not
what she'd packed inside. At least now she could change out
of her hospital gown.

HIEXP0322

Sterling slid into his truck like a knife through butter.

The man could make anything look good.

"I didn't see your car, but Deputy Rossi said it looked like someone hit your back end," he said once the door was shut. "Whoever hit you probably got spooked and took off. We're looking for them, though, so don't worry."

Mel's stomach moved a little at that last part.

"Don't worry" in Sterling's voice used to be the soundtrack to her life. A comforting repetition that felt like it could fix everything.

She played with the zipper on her suitcase.

"I guess I'll deal with the technical stuff tomorrow. Not sure what my insurance is going to say about the whole situation. I suppose it depends on how many cases of amnesia they get."

Sterling shrugged. He was such a big man that even the most subtle movements drew attention.

"I'm sure you'll do fine with them," he said.

She decided talking about her past was as bad as talking about theirs, so she looked out the window and tried to pretend for a moment that nothing had changed.

That she hadn't married Rider Partridge.

That she hadn't waited so long to divorce him.

That she hadn't fallen in love with Sterling.

That she hadn't—

Mel sat up straighter.

She glanced at Sterling and found him already looking at her.

She smiled.

It wasn't returned.

Don't miss
Accidental Amnesia *by Tyler Anne Snell,*
available May 2022 wherever
Harlequin Intrigue books and ebooks are sold.

Harlequin.com

HIEXP0322

Love Harlequin romance?

DISCOVER.

Be the first to find out about promotions, news and exclusive content!

Facebook.com/HarlequinBooks

Twitter.com/HarlequinBooks

Instagram.com/HarlequinBooks

Pinterest.com/HarlequinBooks

YouTube.com/HarlequinBooks

ReaderService.com

EXPLORE.

Sign up for the Harlequin e-newsletter and download a free book from any series at **TryHarlequin.com**

CONNECT.

Join our Harlequin community to share your thoughts and connect with other romance readers! **Facebook.com/groups/HarlequinConnection**

HSOCIAL2021

HARLEQUIN

Heartfelt or thrilling, passionate or uplifting—Harlequin is more than just happily-ever-after.

With twelve different series to choose from and new books available every month, you are sure to find stories that will move you, uplift you, inspire and delight you.